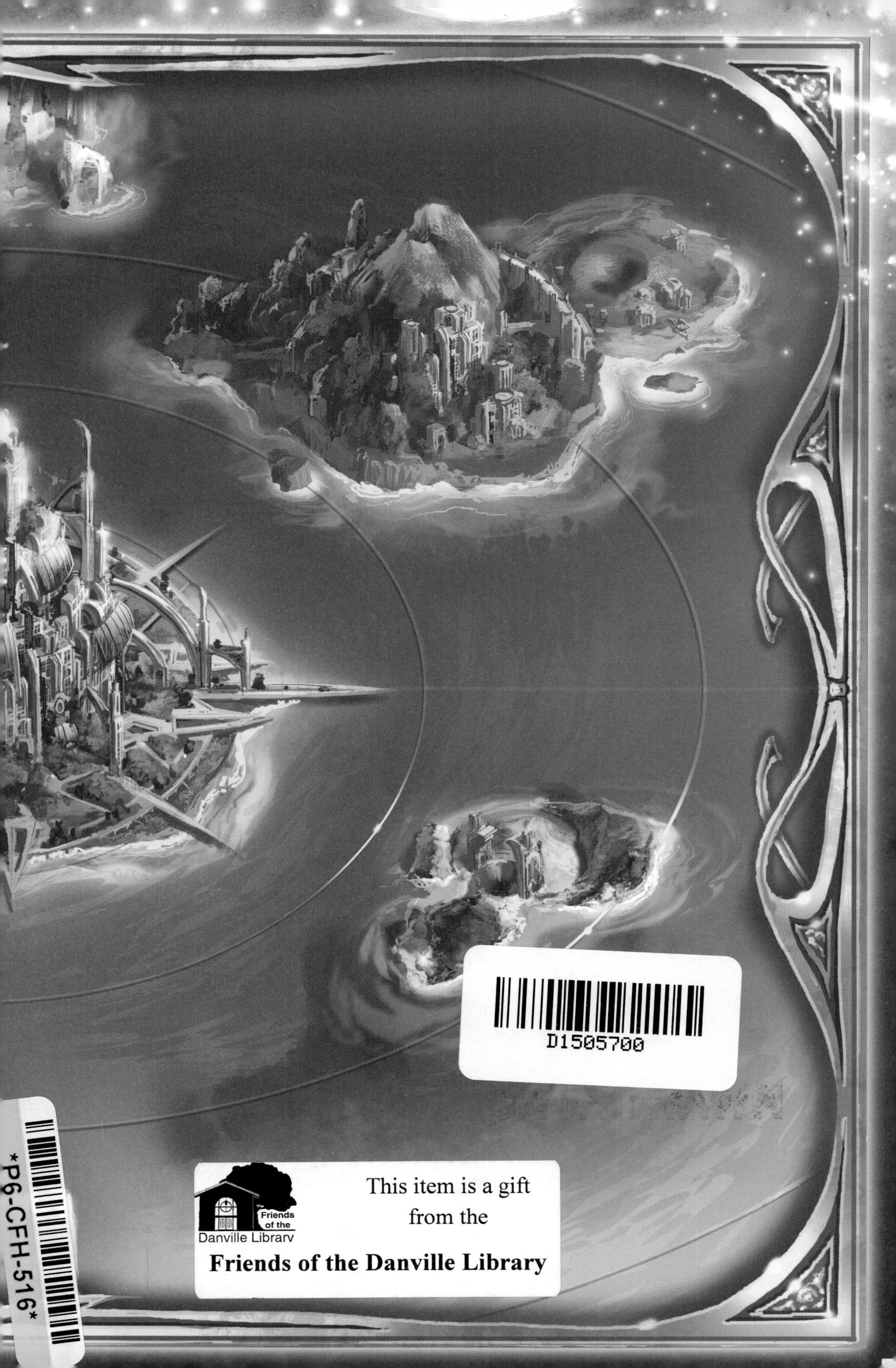

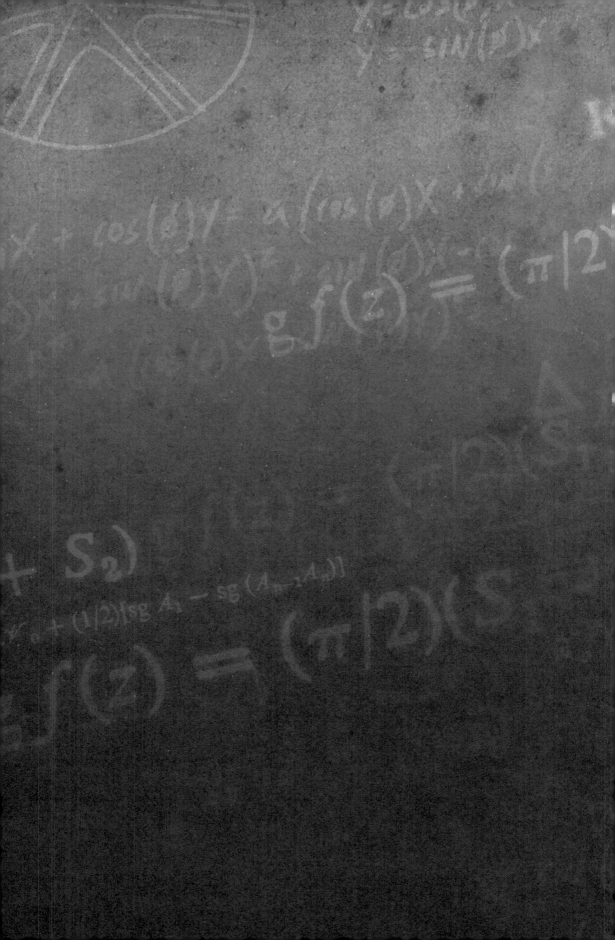

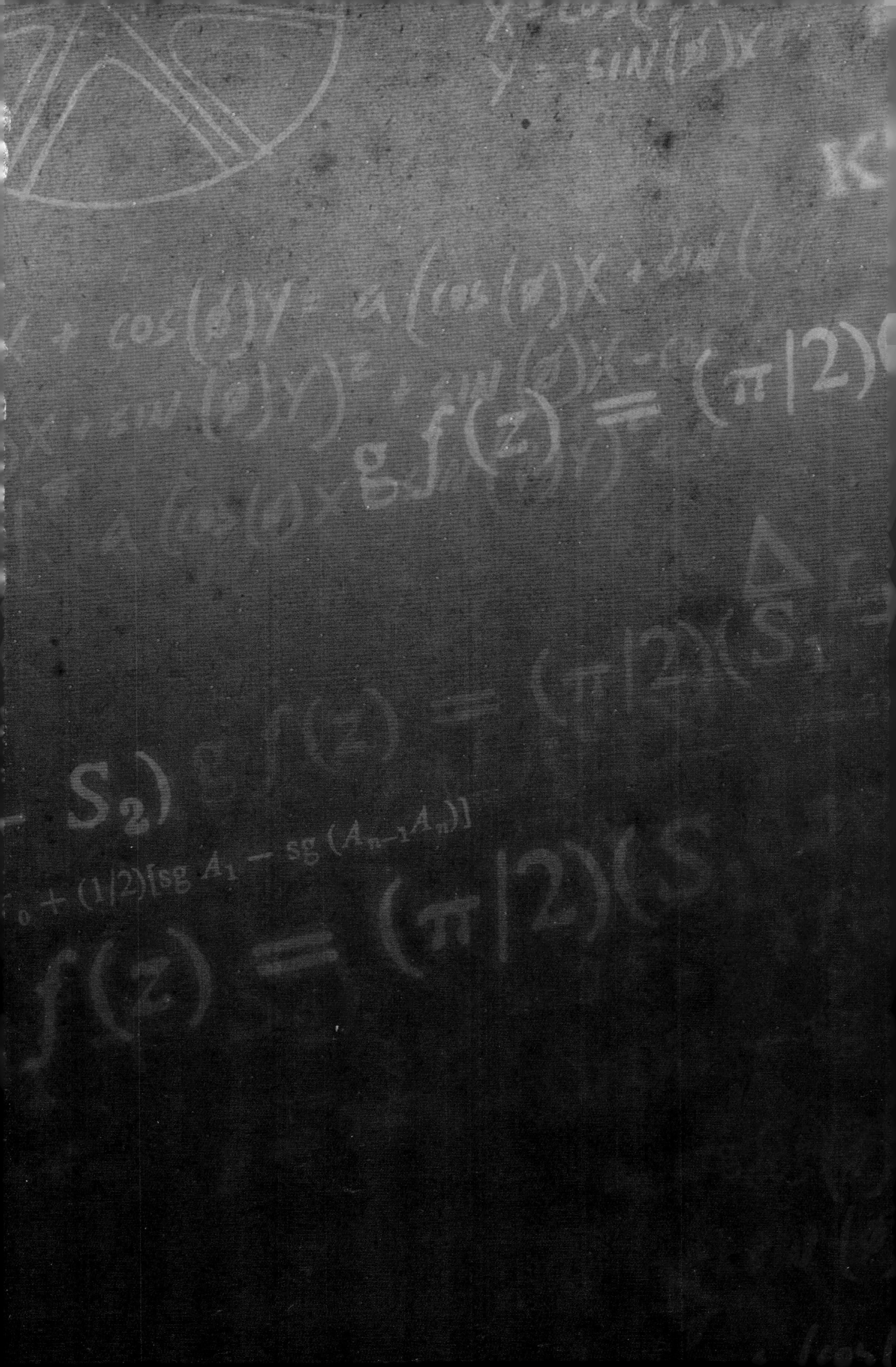
f(z) = (π|2)(S
S₂)
+ (1/2)[sg A₁ − sg (Aₙ₋₁Aₙ)]
f(z) = (π|2)(S

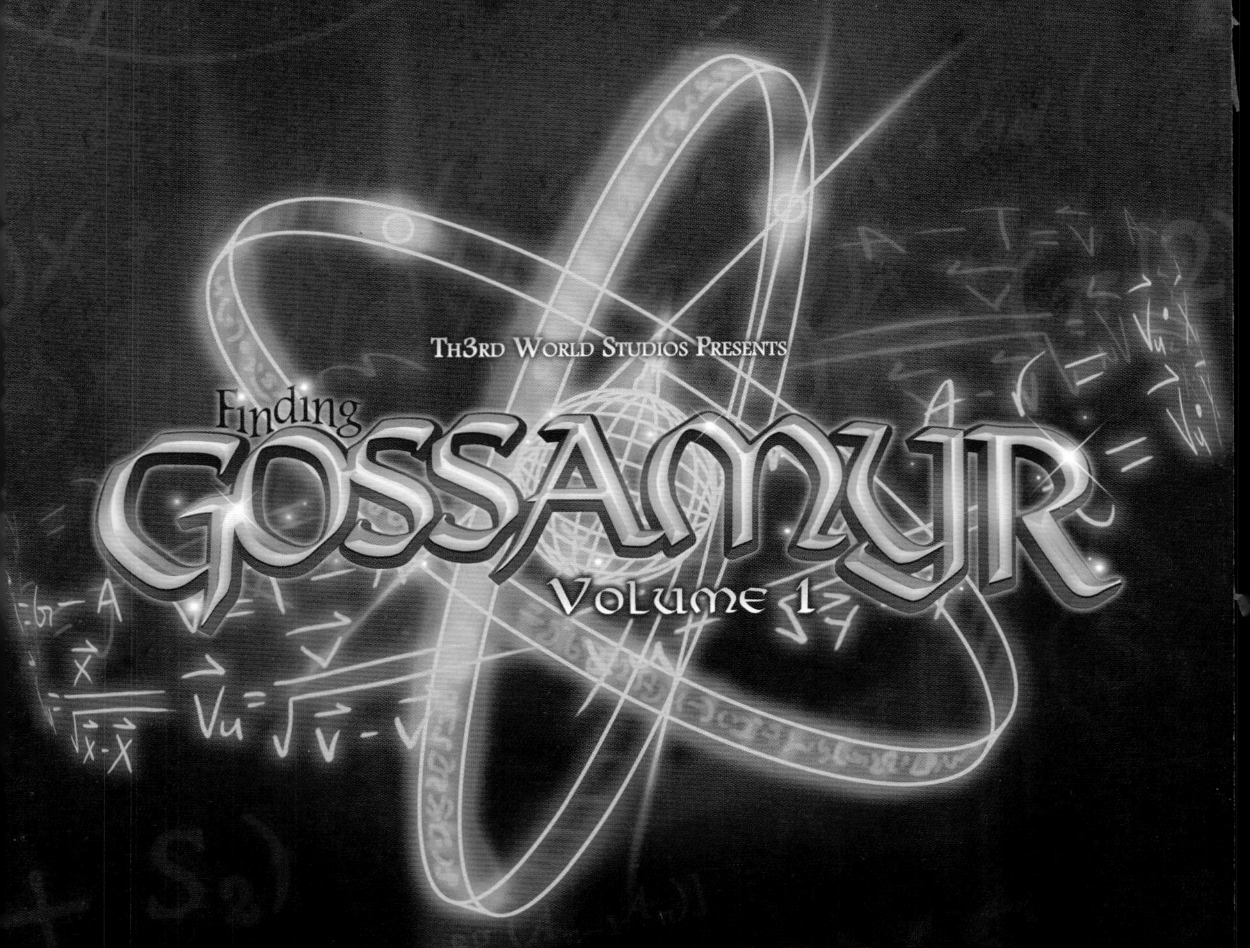

Th3rd World Studios Presents

Finding Gossamyr

Volume 1

Rodriguez & Ellerton

DeVito & Conkling

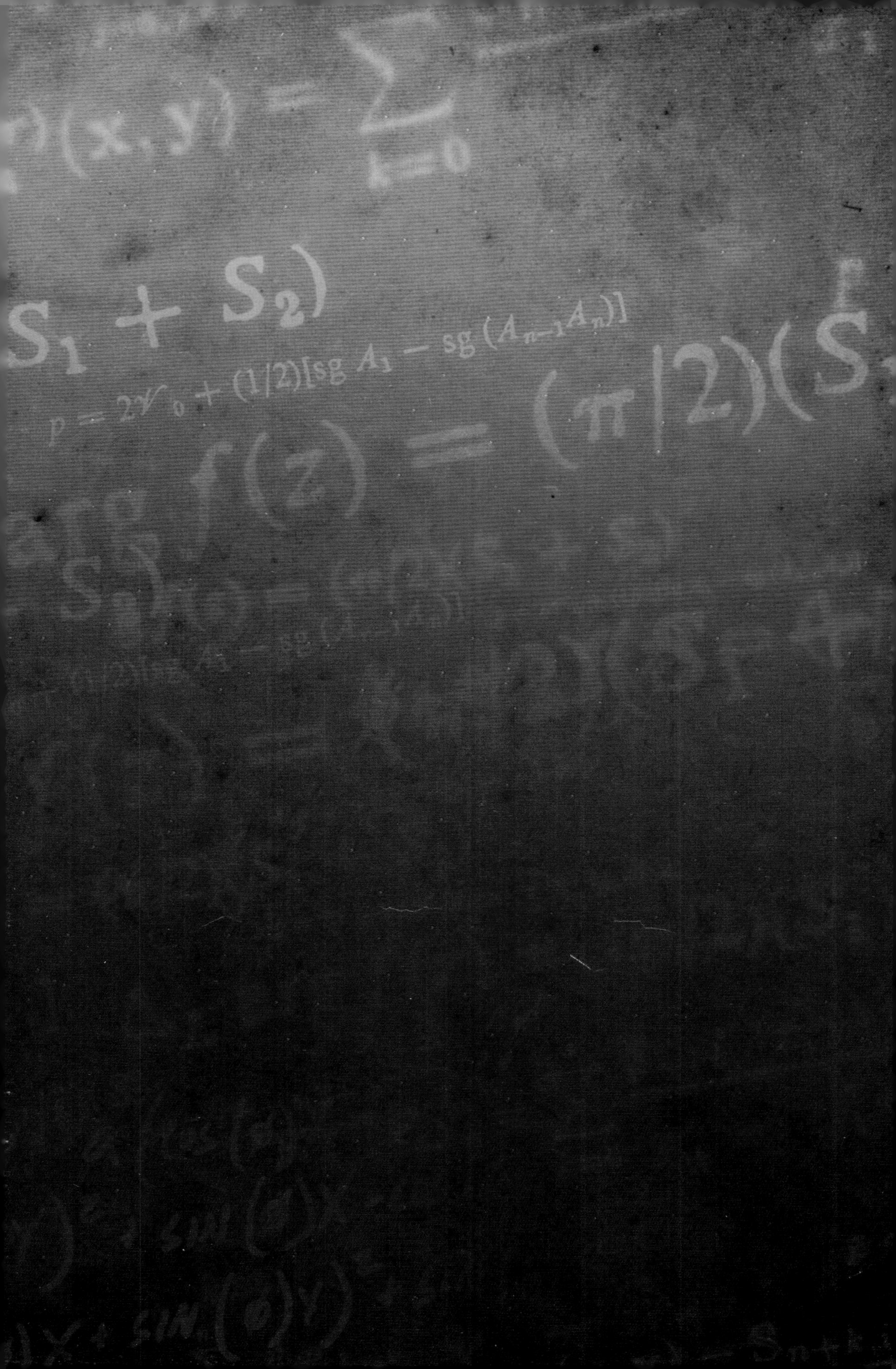

(x, y) = Σ
S1 + S2)
p = 2V0 + (1/2)[sg A1 − sg (An−1An)]
f(z) = (π/2)(S

WRITTEN BY
DAVID A. RODRIGUEZ
🐦 @davearodriguez

ILLUSTRATED BY
SARAH ELLERTON
🐦 @artsangel

DESIGN & LETTERS BY
MICHAEL DEVITO & JON CONKLING
🐦 @mdevito   🐦 @stoneconk

EDITED BY ANGELA NELSON

MATHEMATICS CONSULTANT ~ JOHN A. DAY

STORY EDITOR ~ JESI RODRIGUEZ

LEXICOGRAPHERS ~ ERIC CARTER AND SARAH-NICOLE RUDDY-CARTER

MAP ILLUSTRATION AND CARTOGRAPHY ~ STEVEN OLDS

Cover by: Sarah Ellerton

FIND US ON:

f facebook.com/th3rdworldstudios

t @th3rdworld

TH3RD WORLD STUDIOS PUBLISHERS
MICHAEL DEVITO & JON CONKLING

TH3RDWORLD studios

WWW.TH3RDWORLD.COM

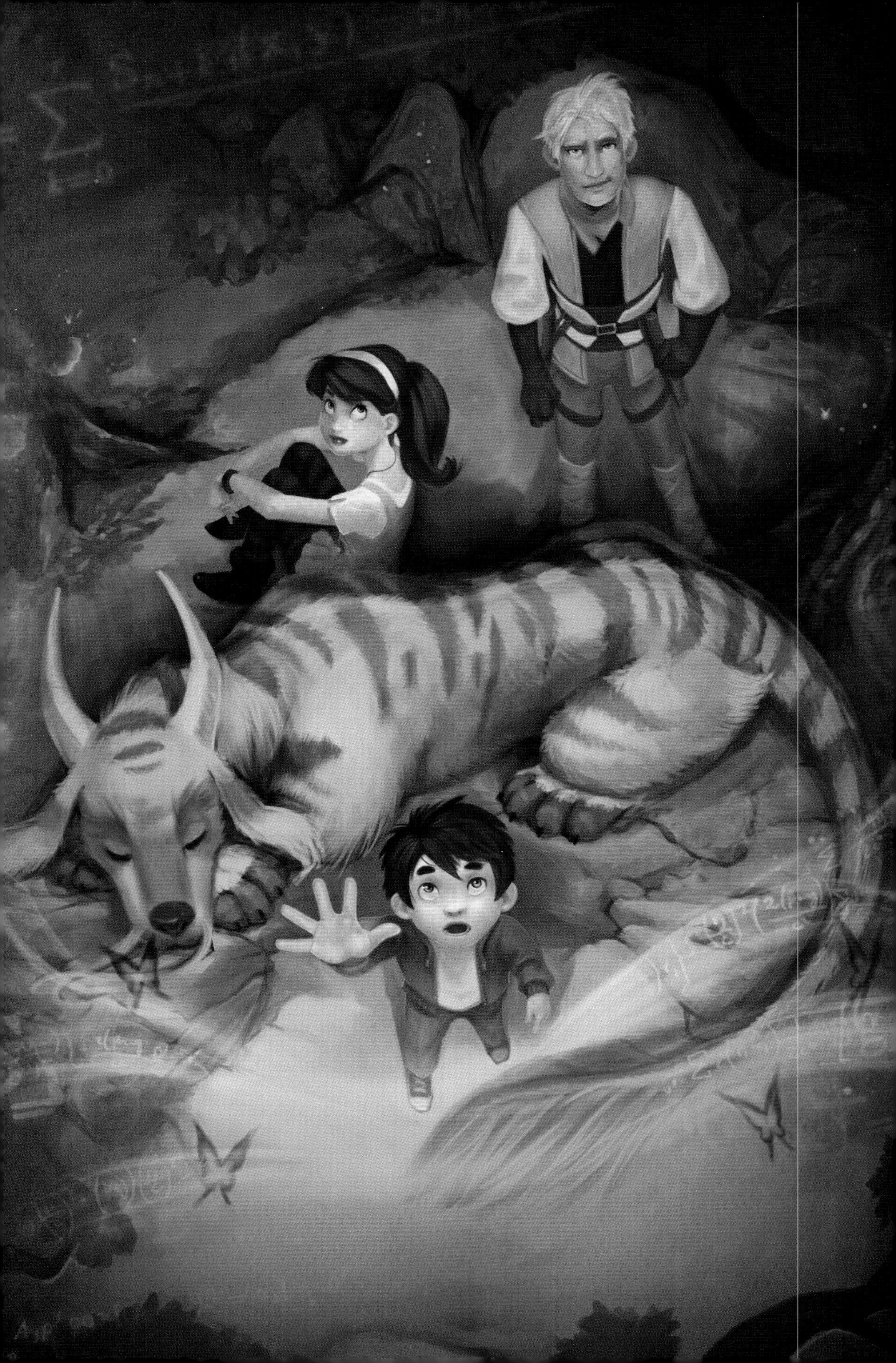

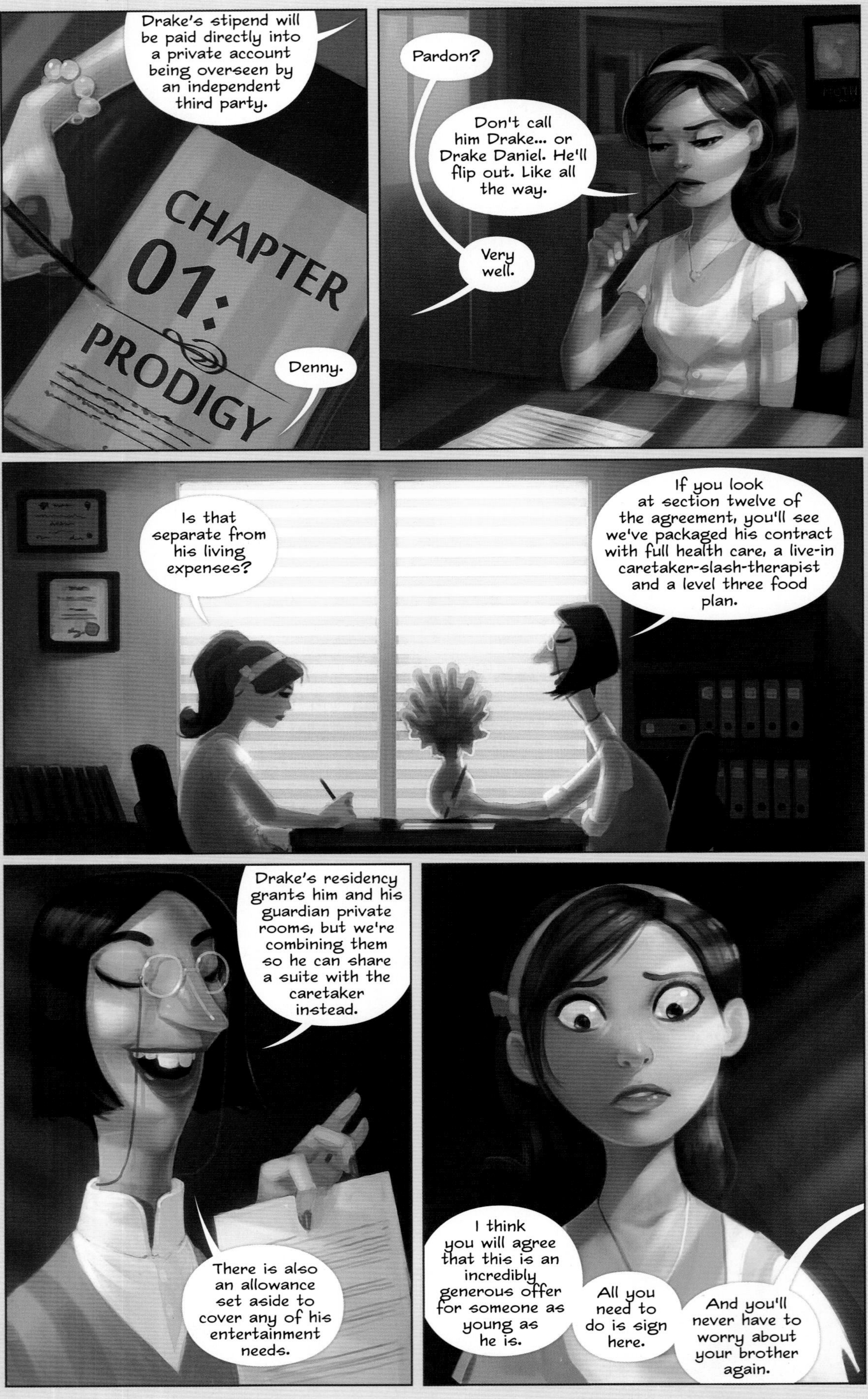
Drake's stipend will be paid directly into a private account being overseen by an independent third party.
CHAPTER 01: PRODIGY
Denny.
Pardon?
Don't call him Drake... or Drake Daniel. He'll flip out. Like all the way.
Very well.
Is that separate from his living expenses?
If you look at section twelve of the agreement, you'll see we've packaged his contract with full health care, a live-in caretaker-slash-therapist and a level three food plan.
Drake's residency grants him and his guardian private rooms, but we're combining them so he can share a suite with the caretaker instead.
There is also an allowance set aside to cover any of his entertainment needs.
I think you will agree that this is an incredibly generous offer for someone as young as he is.
All you need to do is sign here.
And you'll never have to worry about your brother again.

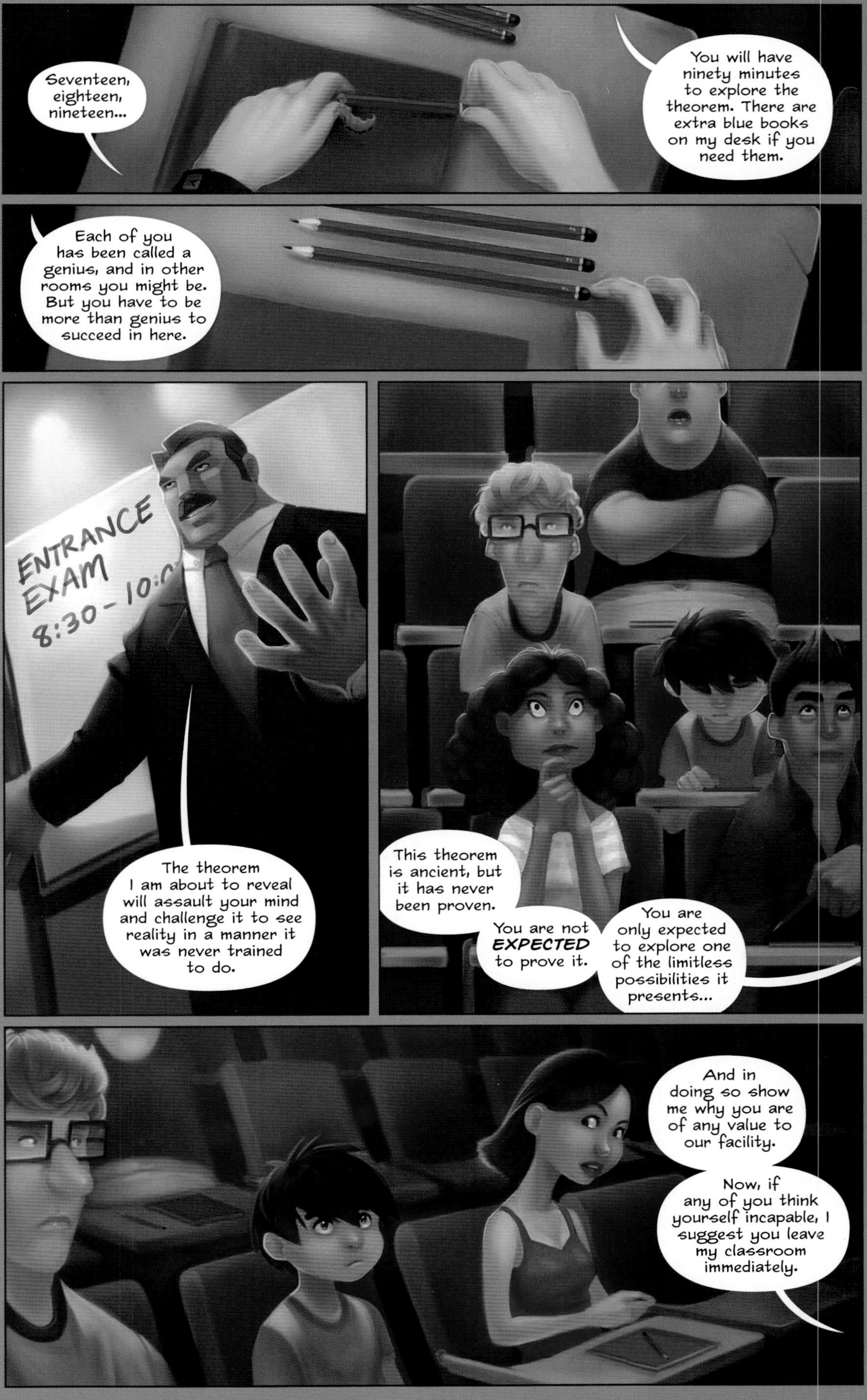
Seventeen, eighteen, nineteen...
You will have ninety minutes to explore the theorem. There are extra blue books on my desk if you need them.
Each of you has been called a genius, and in other rooms you might be. But you have to be more than genius to succeed in here.
ENTRANCE EXAM 8:30 - 10:0
The theorem I am about to reveal will assault your mind and challenge it to see reality in a manner it was never trained to do.
This theorem is ancient, but it has never been proven.
You are not **EXPECTED** to prove it.
You are only expected to explore one of the limitless possibilities it presents...
And in doing so show me why you are of any value to our facility.
Now, if any of you think yourself incapable, I suggest you leave my classroom immediately.

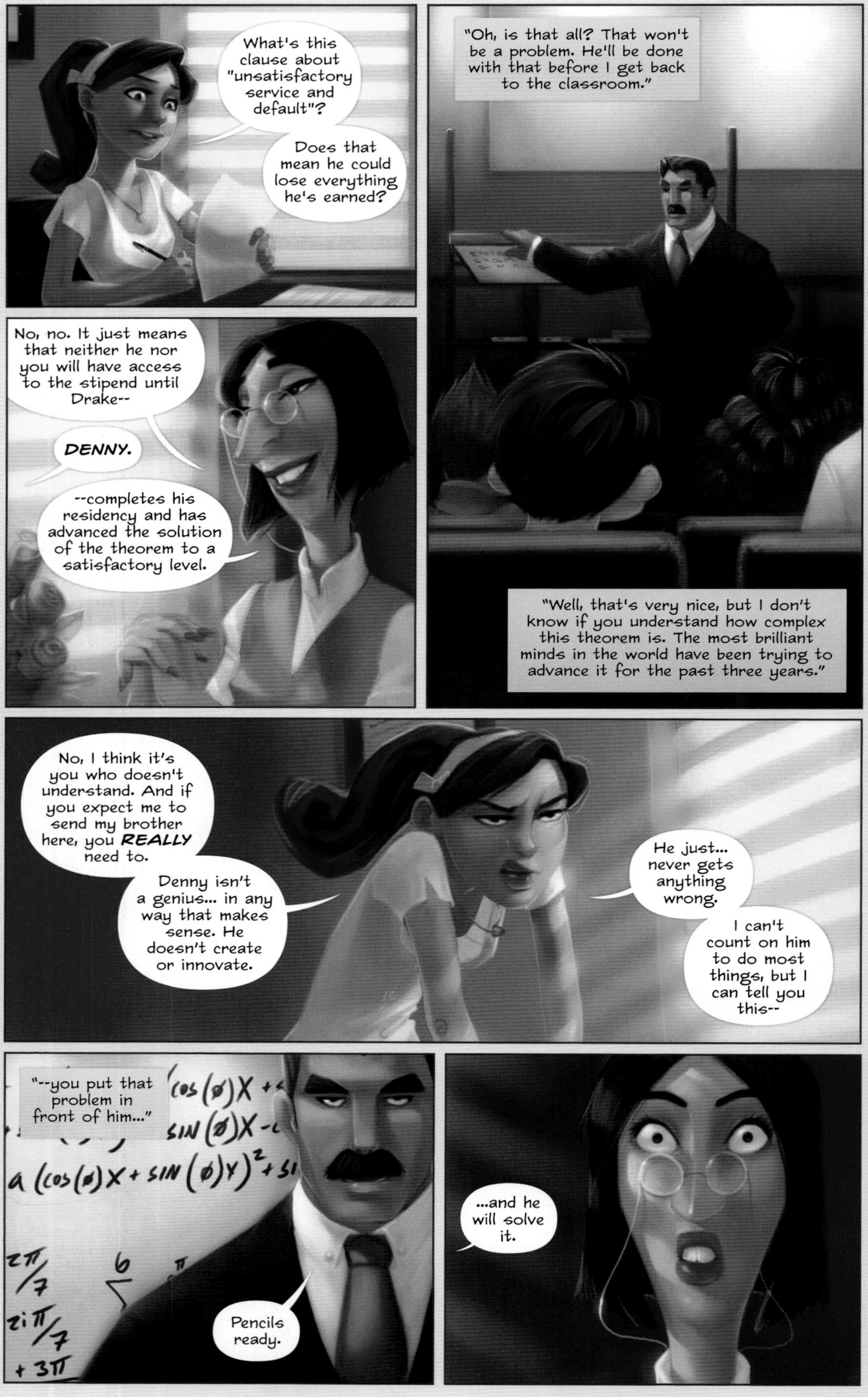
What's this clause about "unsatisfactory service and default"?
Does that mean he could lose everything he's earned?
No, no. It just means that neither he nor you will have access to the stipend until Drake--
DENNY.
--completes his residency and has advanced the solution of the theorem to a satisfactory level.
"Oh, is that all? That won't be a problem. He'll be done with that before I get back to the classroom."
"Well, that's very nice, but I don't know if you understand how complex this theorem is. The most brilliant minds in the world have been trying to advance it for the past three years."
No, I think it's you who doesn't understand. And if you expect me to send my brother here, you ***REALLY*** need to.
Denny isn't a genius... in any way that makes sense. He doesn't create or innovate.
He just... never gets anything wrong.
I can't count on him to do most things, but I can tell you this--
"--you put that problem in front of him..."
Pencils ready.
...and he will solve it.

"He won't be able not to."

Begin.

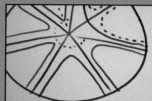

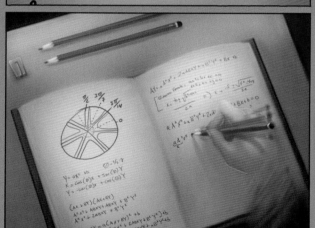

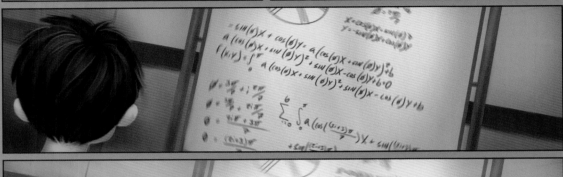
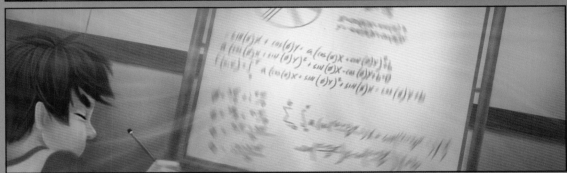
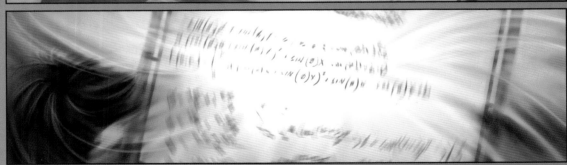

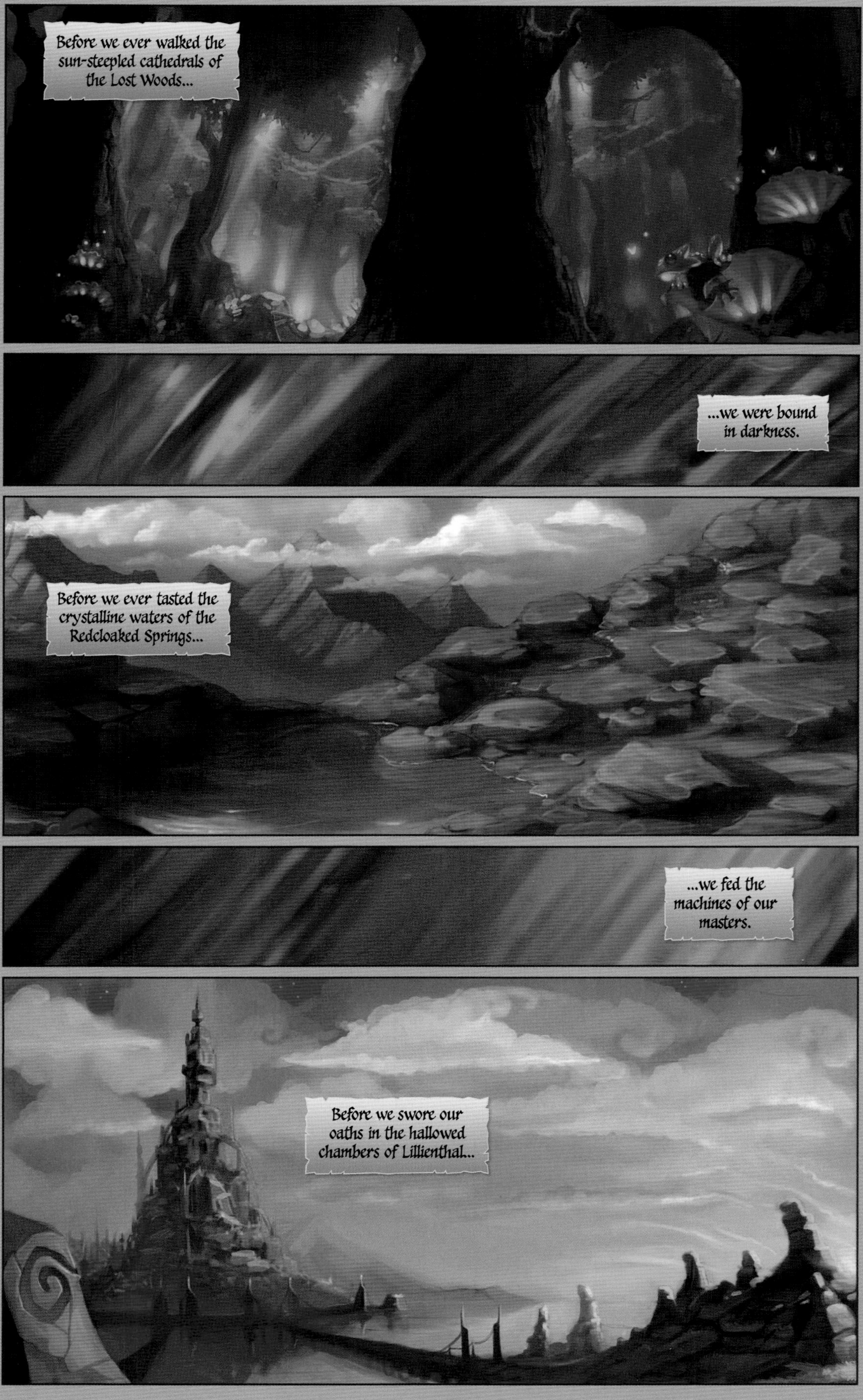
Before we ever walked the sun-steepled cathedrals of the Lost Woods...
...we were bound in darkness.
Before we ever tasted the crystalline waters of the Redcloaked Springs...
...we fed the machines of our masters.
Before we swore our oaths in the hallowed chambers of Lillienthal...

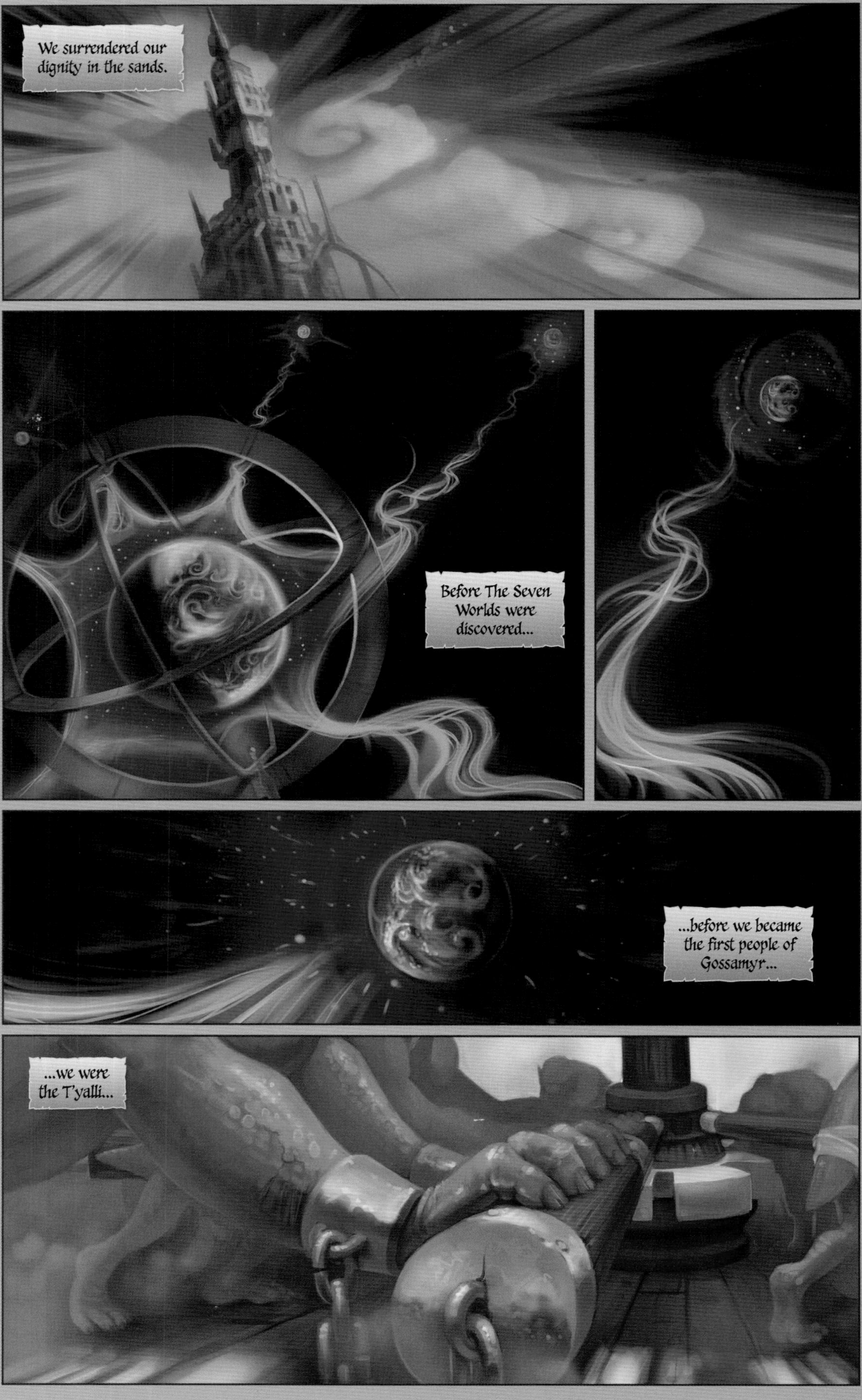
We surrendered our dignity in the sands.
Before The Seven Worlds were discovered...
...before we became the first people of Gossamyr...
...we were the T'yalli...

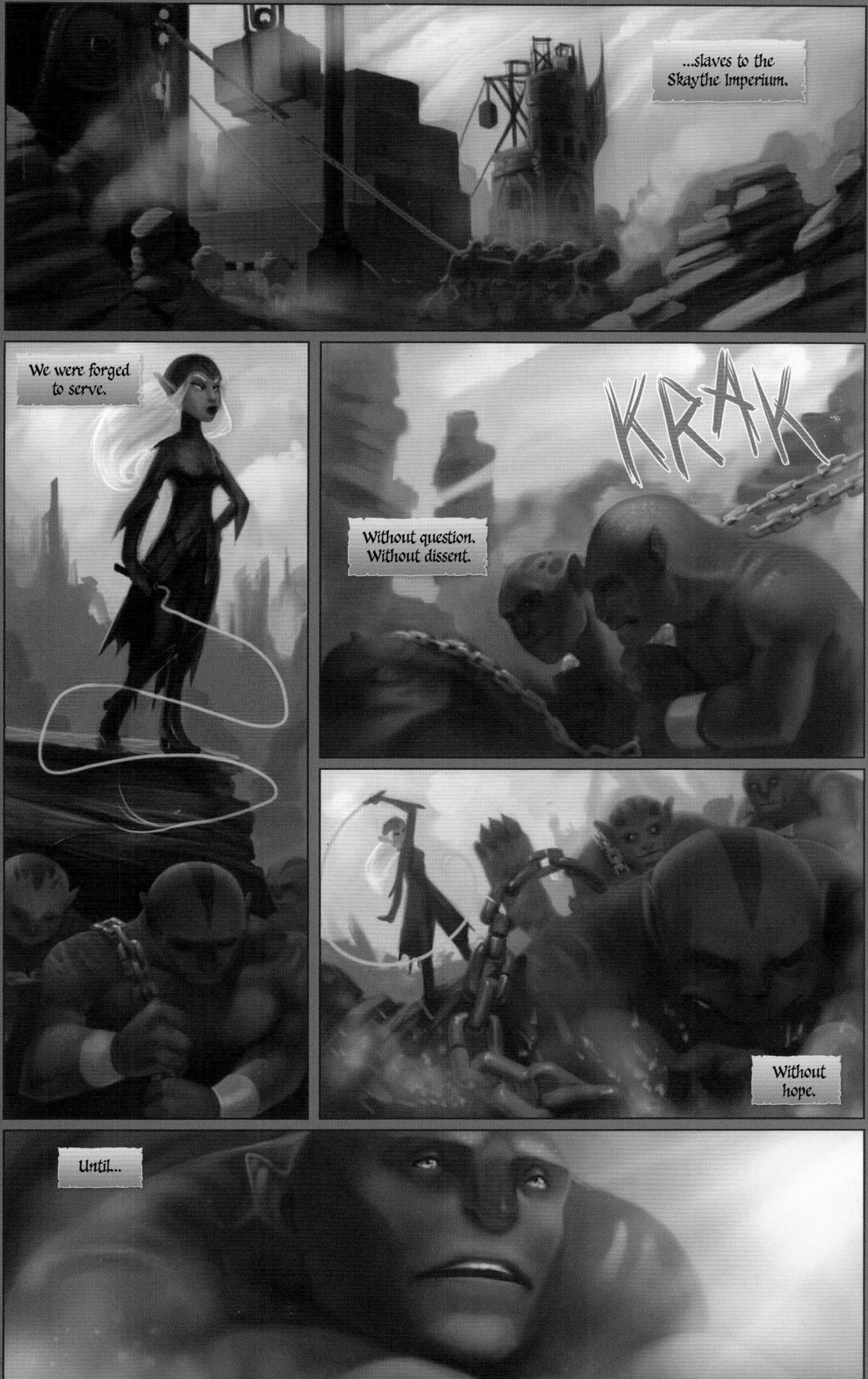
...slaves to the Skaythe Imperium.
We were forged to serve.
KRAK
Without question. Without dissent.
Without hope.
Until...

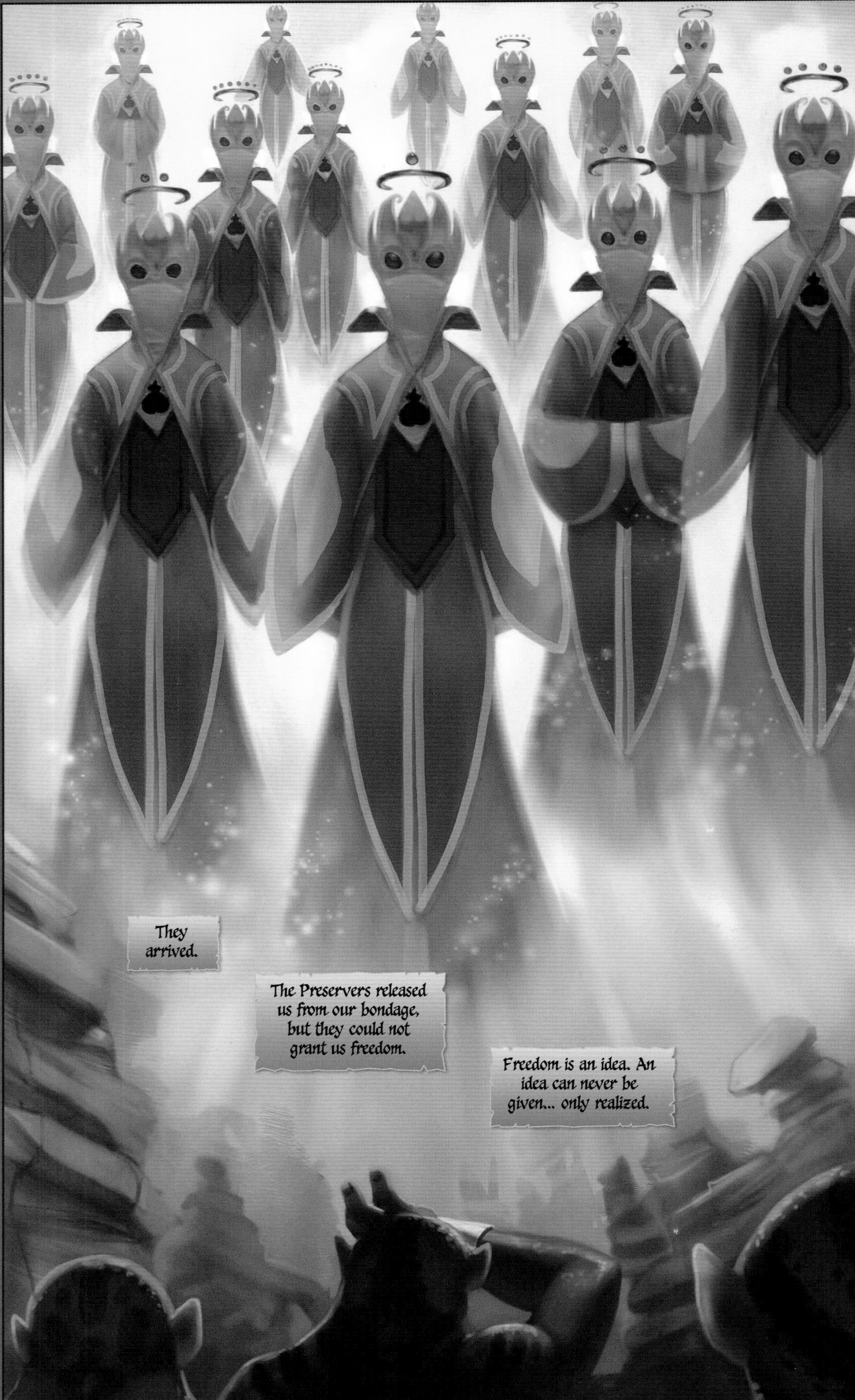
They arrived.
The Preservers released us from our bondage, but they could not grant us freedom.
Freedom is an idea. An idea can never be given... only realized.

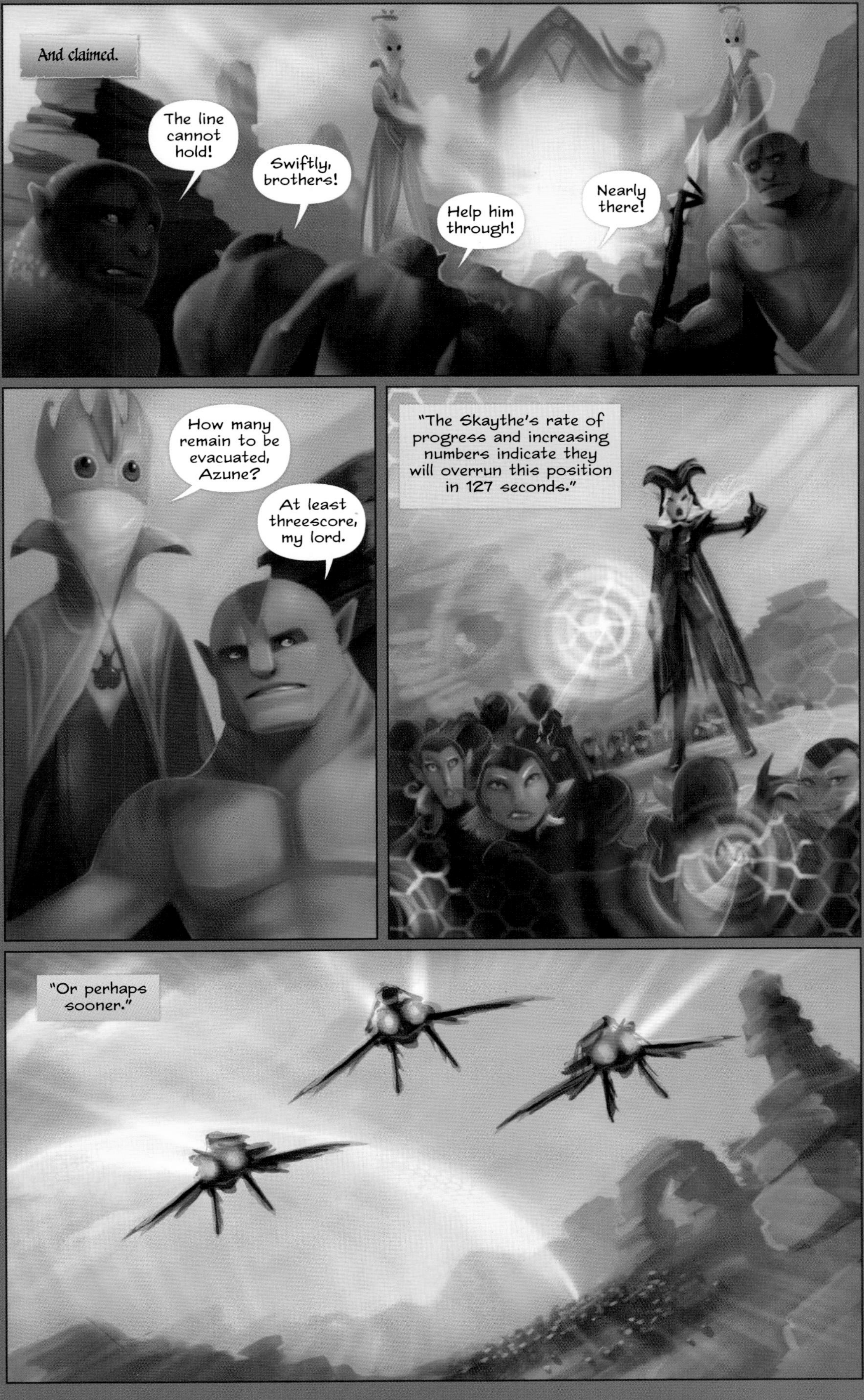
And claimed.
The line cannot hold!
Swiftly, brothers!
Help him through!
Nearly there!
How many remain to be evacuated, Azune?
At least threescore, my lord.
"The Skaythe's rate of progress and increasing numbers indicate they will overrun this position in 127 seconds."
"Or perhaps sooner."

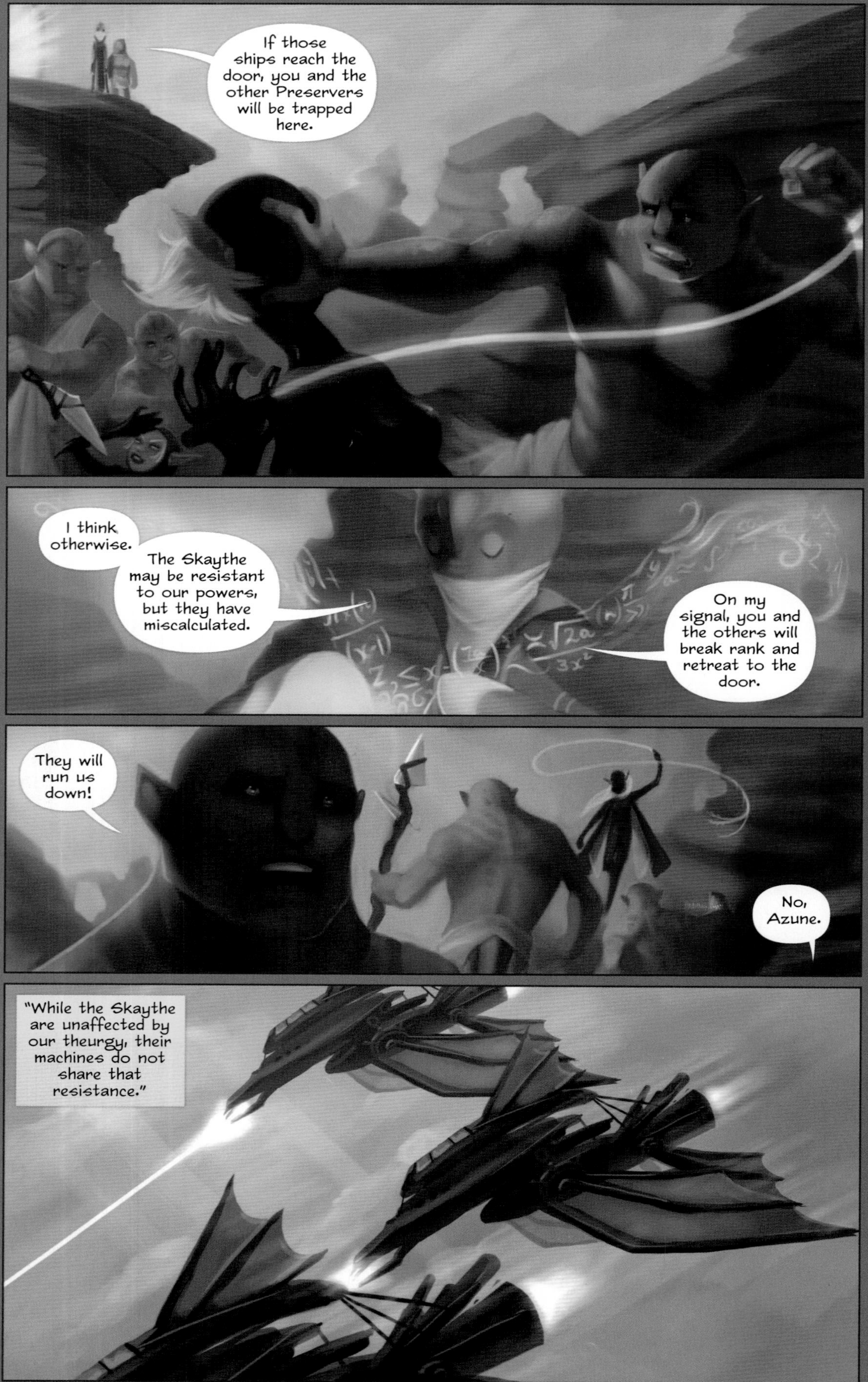
If those ships reach the door, you and the other Preservers will be trapped here.
I think otherwise.
The Skaythe may be resistant to our powers, but they have miscalculated.
On my signal, you and the others will break rank and retreat to the door.
They will run us down!
No, Azune.
"While the Skaythe are unaffected by our theurgy, their machines do not share that resistance."

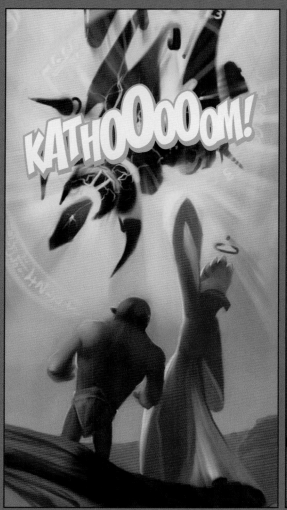

KATHOOOOOM!

That is the last of us, my lord. You must hurry.

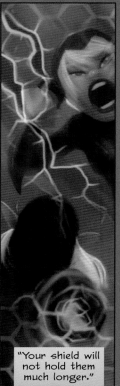

"Your shield will not hold them much longer."

It will suffice, Azune.

Now, Others, it is time to begin your work.

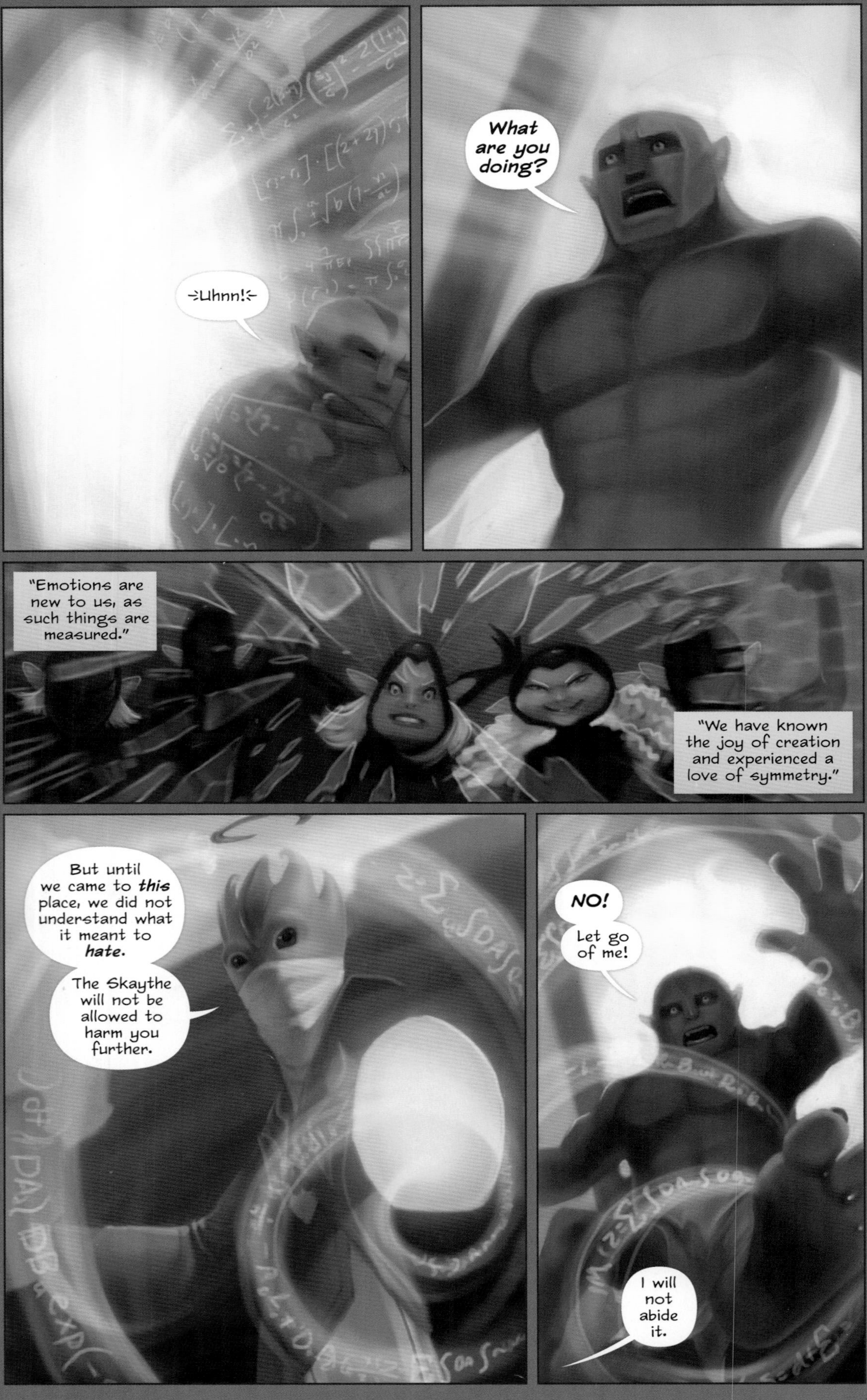

Uhhn!
What are you doing?
"Emotions are new to us, as such things are measured."
"We have known the joy of creation and experienced a love of symmetry."
But until we came to *this* place, we did not understand what it meant to *hate*.
The Skaythe will not be allowed to harm you further.
NO!
Let go of me!
I will not abide it.

"I must remain here to complete the theorem and seal the door."

If the Skaythe are ever allowed through, they will spread their evil across all worlds.

This outcome *must* be prevented.

It is a single life spent to preserve billions from harm.

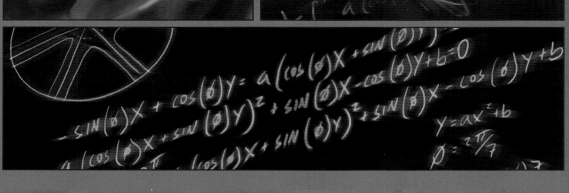

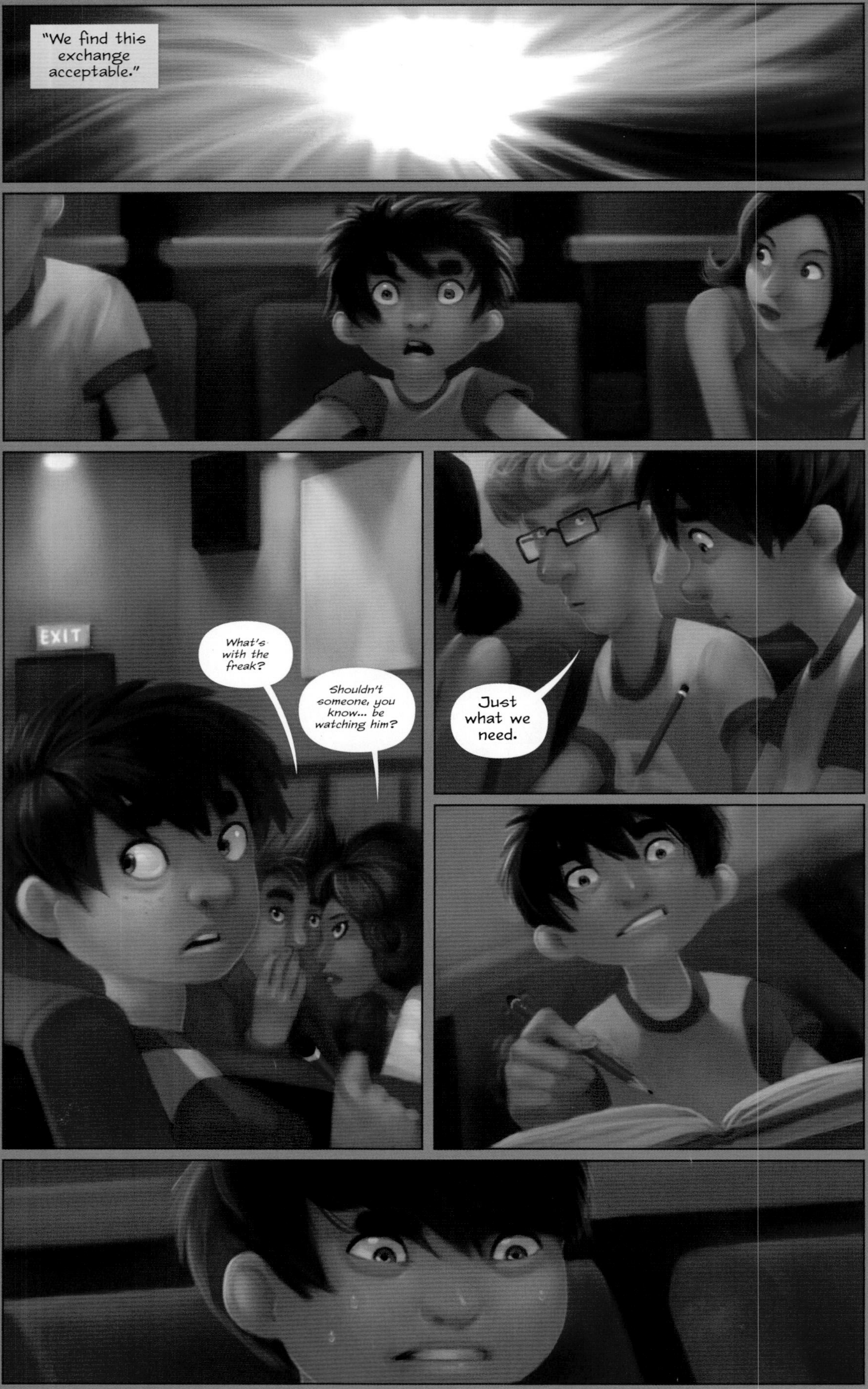
"We find this exchange acceptable."
What's with the freak?
Shouldn't someone, you know... be watching him?
EXIT
Just what we need.

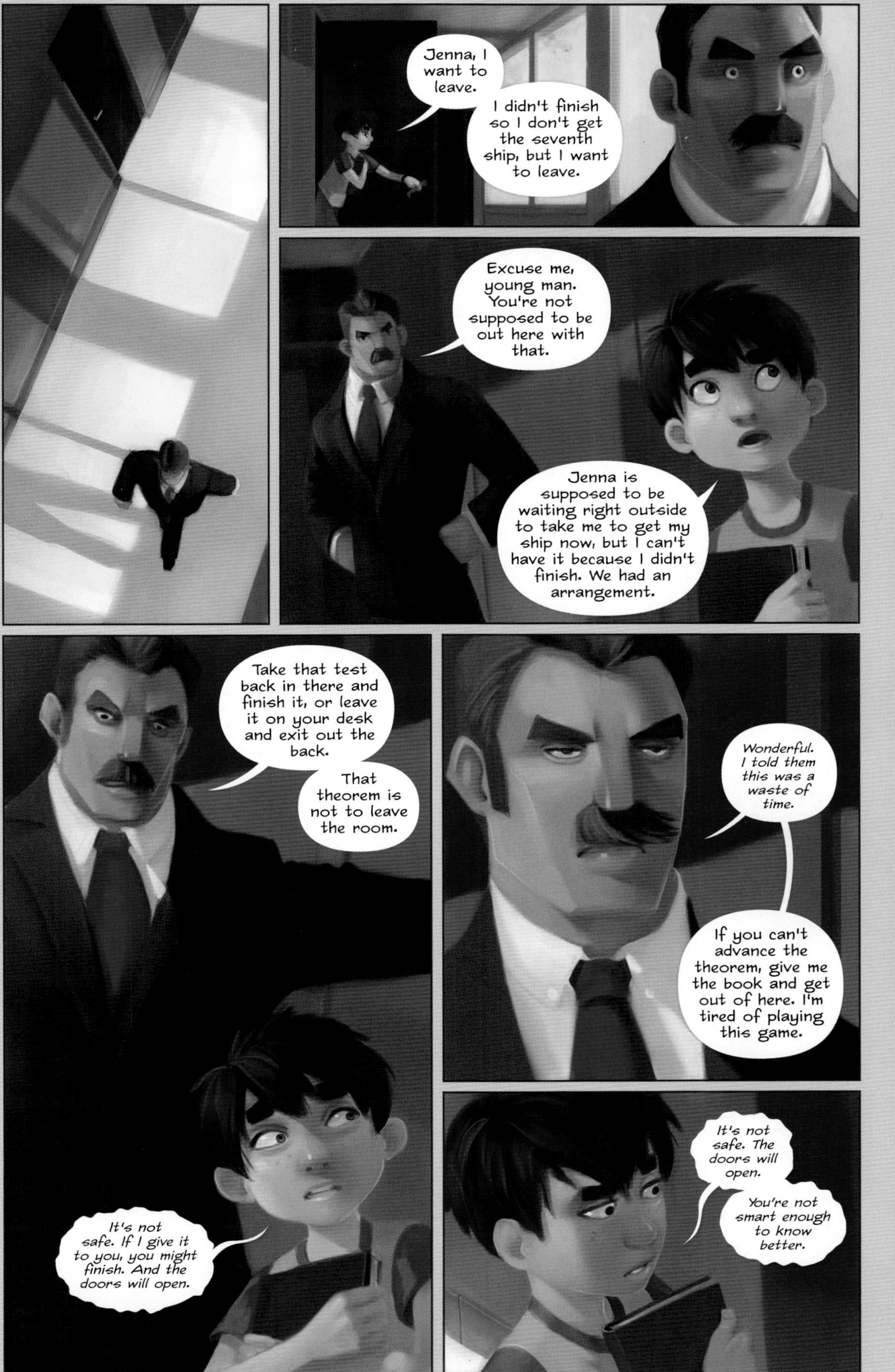
Jenna, I want to leave.
I didn't finish so I don't get the seventh ship, but I want to leave.
Excuse me, young man. You're not supposed to be out here with that.
Jenna is supposed to be waiting right outside to take me to get my ship now, but I can't have it because I didn't finish. We had an arrangement.
Take that test back in there and finish it, or leave it on your desk and exit out the back.
That theorem is not to leave the room.
It's not safe. If I give it to you, you might finish. And the doors will open.
Wonderful. I told them this was a waste of time.
If you can't advance the theorem, give me the book and get out of here. I'm tired of playing this game.
It's not safe. The doors will open.
You're not smart enough to know better.

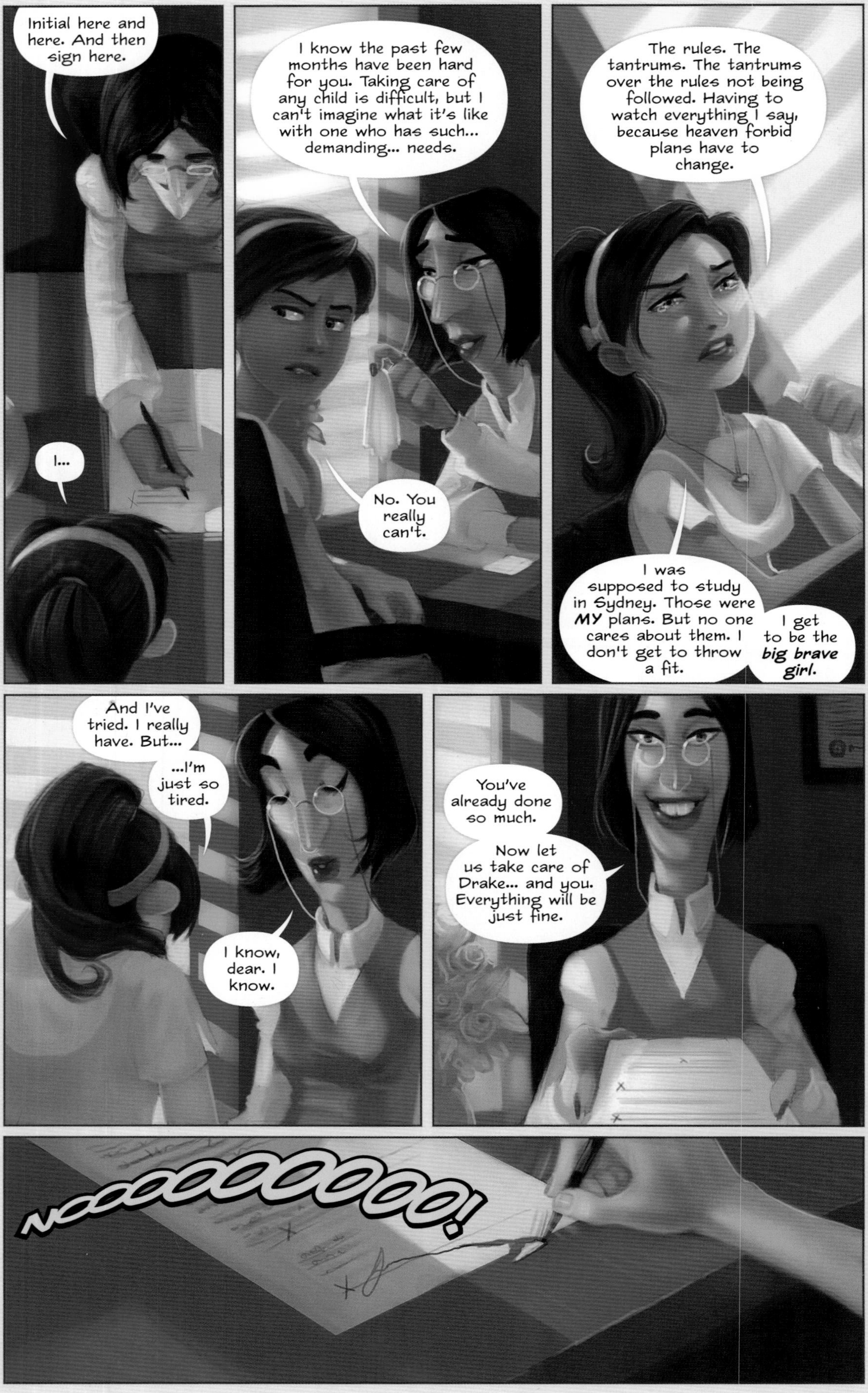
Initial here and here. And then sign here.
I...
I know the past few months have been hard for you. Taking care of any child is difficult, but I can't imagine what it's like with one who has such... demanding... needs.
No. You really can't.
The rules. The tantrums. The tantrums over the rules not being followed. Having to watch everything I say, because heaven forbid plans have to change.
I was supposed to study in Sydney. Those were **MY** plans. But no one cares about them. I don't get to throw a fit.
I get to be the ***big brave girl.***
And I've tried. I really have. But...
...I'm just so tired.
I know, dear. I know.
You've already done so much.
Now let us take care of Drake... and you. Everything will be just fine.
NOOOOOOOOOO!

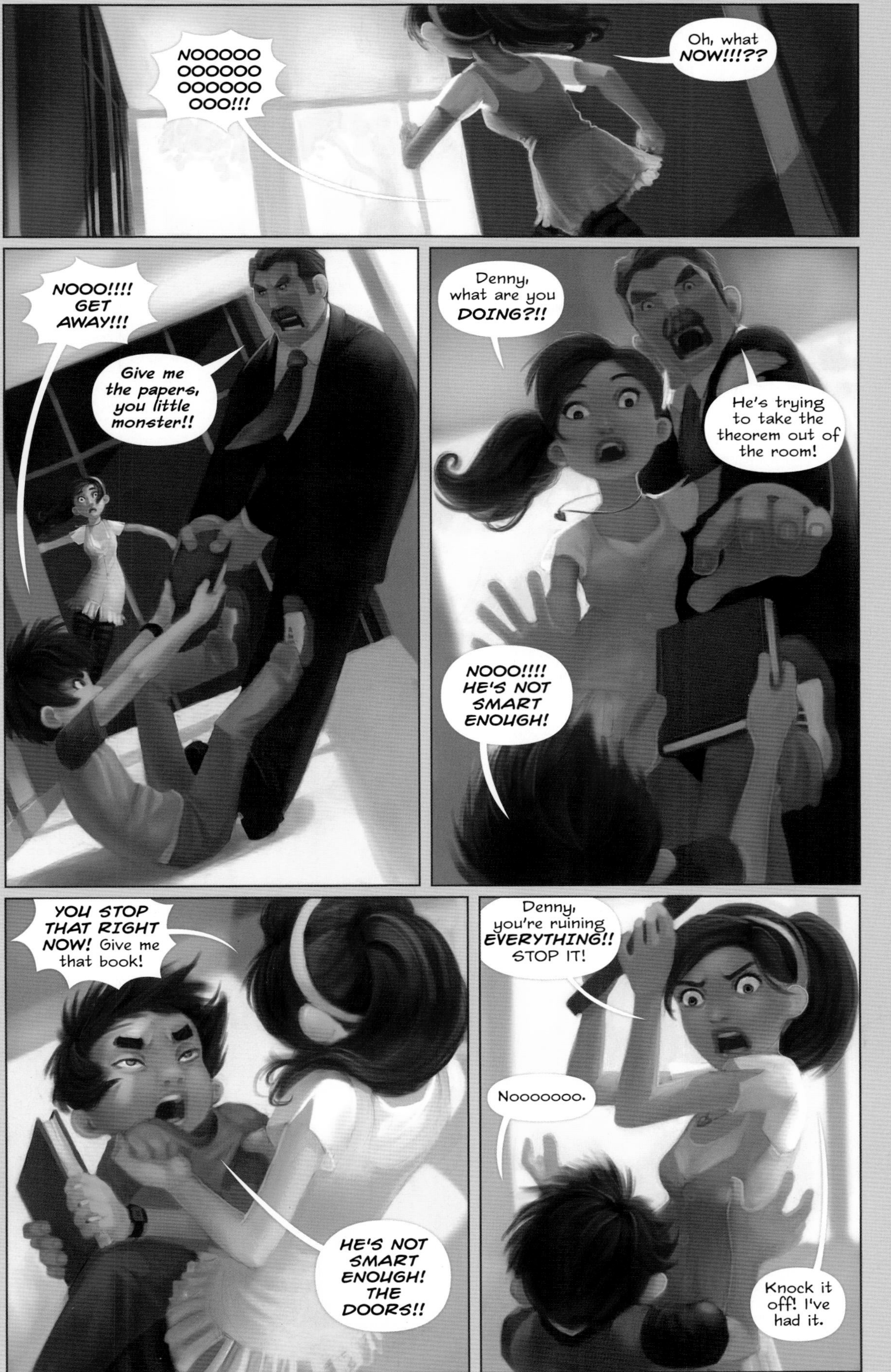
NOOOOO OOOOOO OOOOOO OOO!!!
Oh, what NOW!!!??
NOOO!!!! GET AWAY!!!
Give me the papers, you little monster!!
Denny, what are you DOING?!!
He's trying to take the theorem out of the room!
NOOO!!!! HE'S NOT SMART ENOUGH!
YOU STOP THAT RIGHT NOW! Give me that book!
HE'S NOT SMART ENOUGH! THE DOORS!!
Denny, you're ruining EVERYTHING!! STOP IT!
Nooooooo.
Knock it off! I've had it.

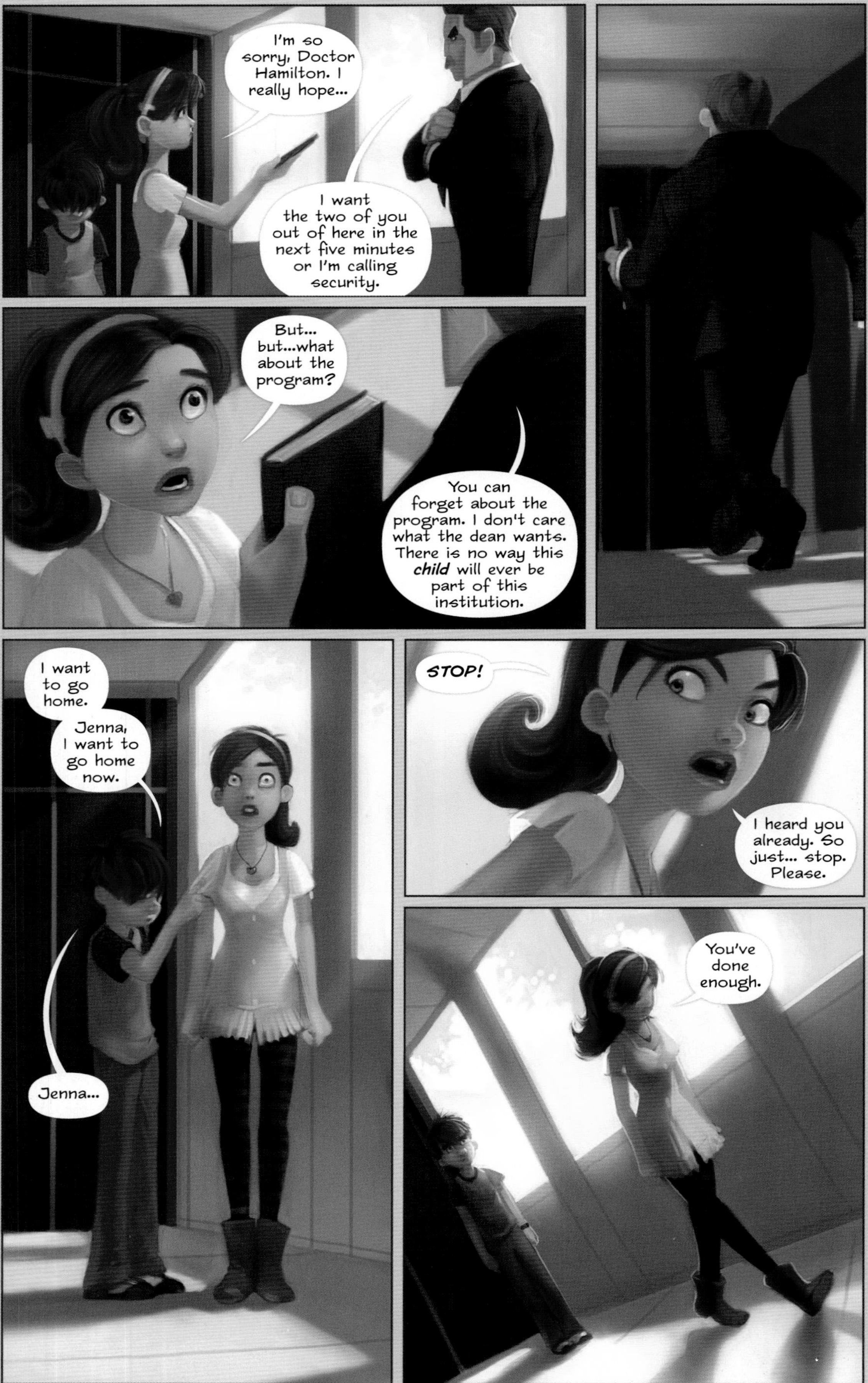
I'm so sorry, Doctor Hamilton. I really hope...
I want the two of you out of here in the next five minutes or I'm calling security.
But... but...what about the program?
You can forget about the program. I don't care what the dean wants. There is no way this **child** will ever be part of this institution.
I want to go home.
Jenna, I want to go home now.
Jenna...
STOP!
I heard you already. So just... stop. Please.
You've done enough.

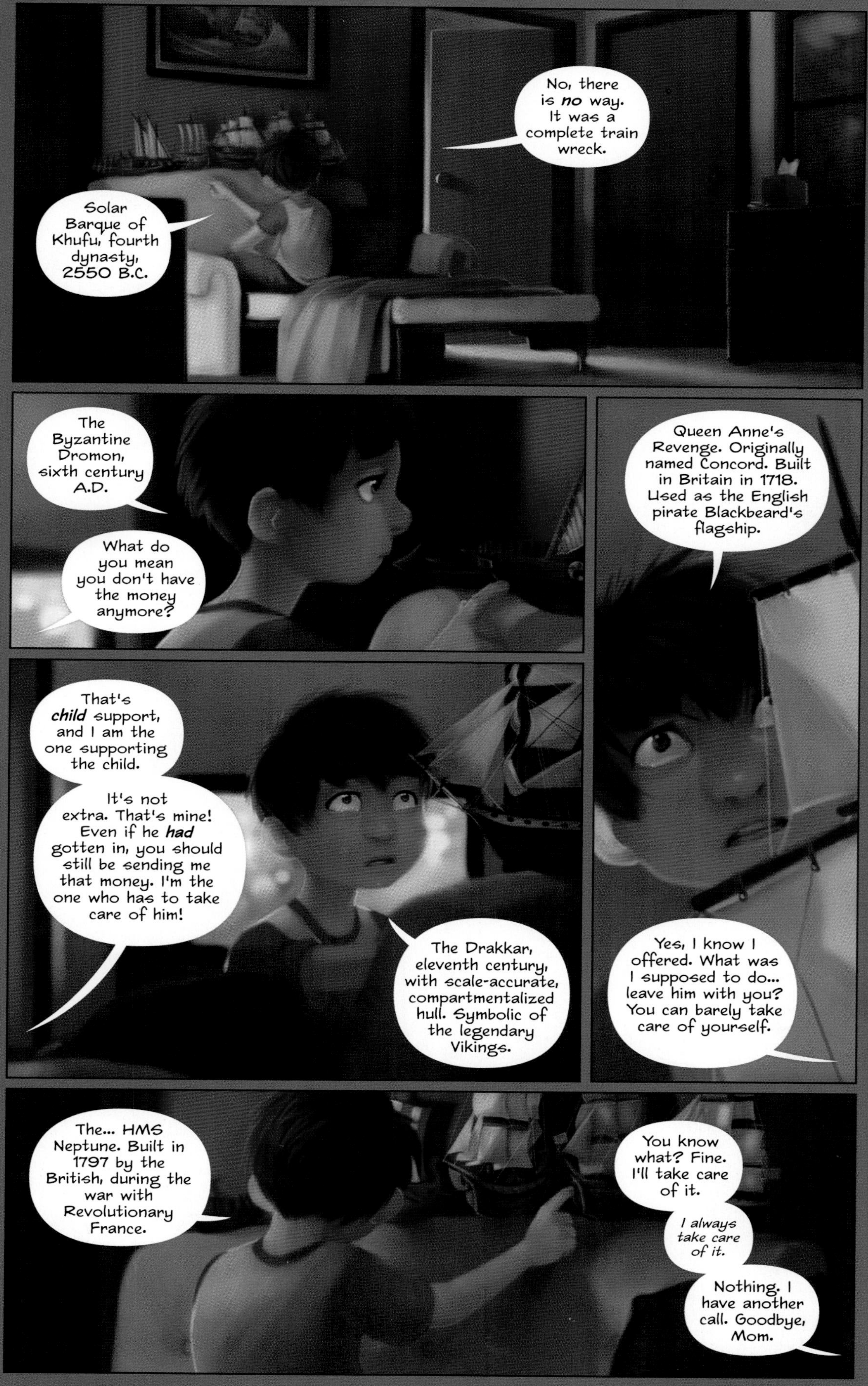
No, there is **no** way. It was a complete train wreck.
Solar Barque of Khufu, fourth dynasty, 2550 B.C.
The Byzantine Dromon, sixth century A.D.
What do you mean you don't have the money anymore?
That's ***child*** support, and I am the one supporting the child.
It's not extra. That's mine! Even if he ***had*** gotten in, you should still be sending me that money. I'm the one who has to take care of him!
The Drakkar, eleventh century, with scale-accurate, compartmentalized hull. Symbolic of the legendary Vikings.
Queen Anne's Revenge. Originally named Concord. Built in Britain in 1718. Used as the English pirate Blackbeard's flagship.
Yes, I know I offered. What was I supposed to do... leave him with you? You can barely take care of yourself.
The... HMS Neptune. Built in 1797 by the British, during the war with Revolutionary France.
You know what? Fine. I'll take care of it.
I always take care of it.
Nothing. I have another call. Goodbye, Mom.

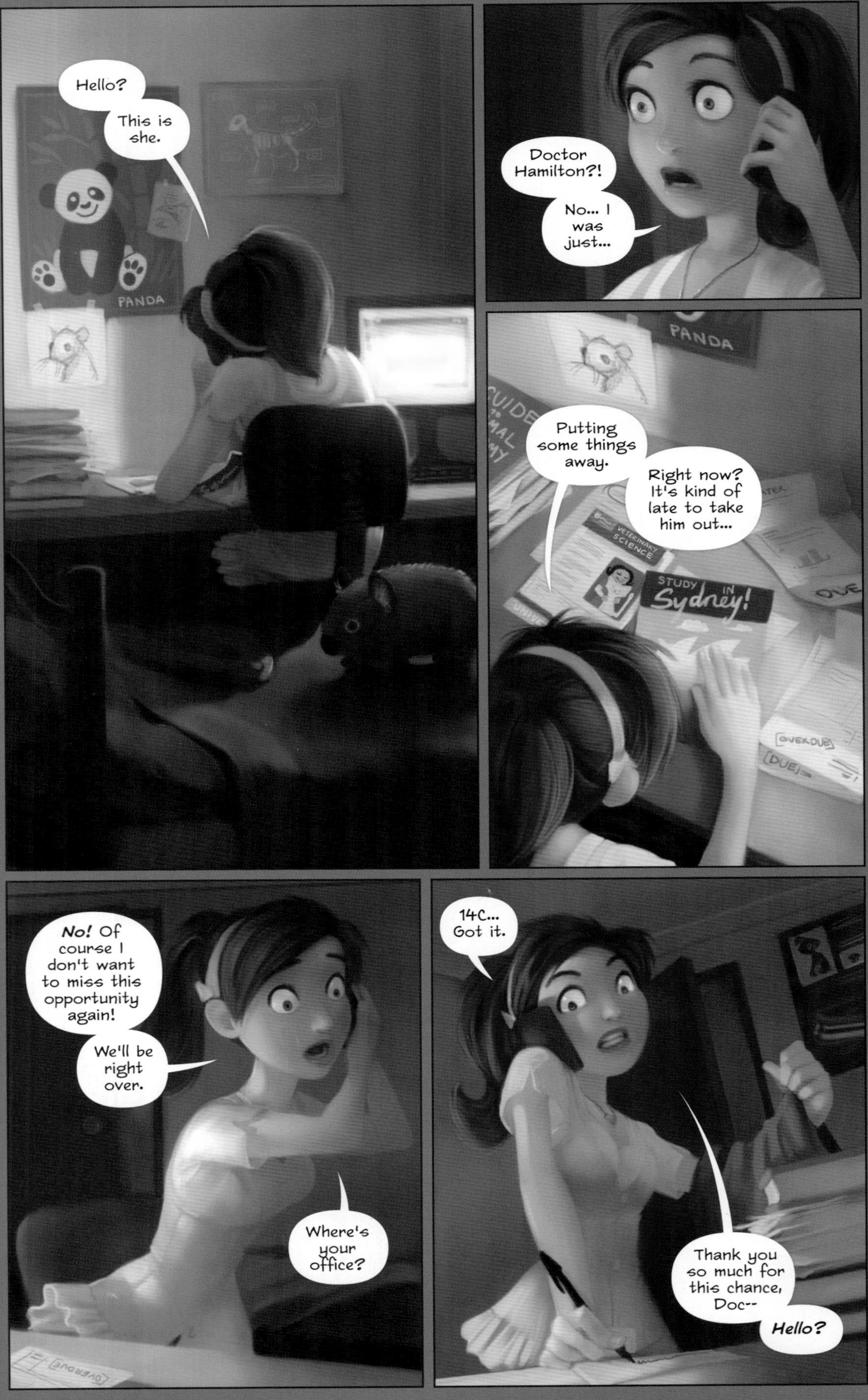
Hello?
This is she.
PANDA
Doctor Hamilton?!
No... I was just...
PANDA
VETERINARY SCIENCE
STUDY IN Sydney!
Putting some things away.
Right now? It's kind of late to take him out...
DUE
OVERDUE
DUE
No! Of course I don't want to miss this opportunity again!
We'll be right over.
Where's your office?
OVERDUE
14C... Got it.
Thank you so much for this chance, Doc--
Hello?

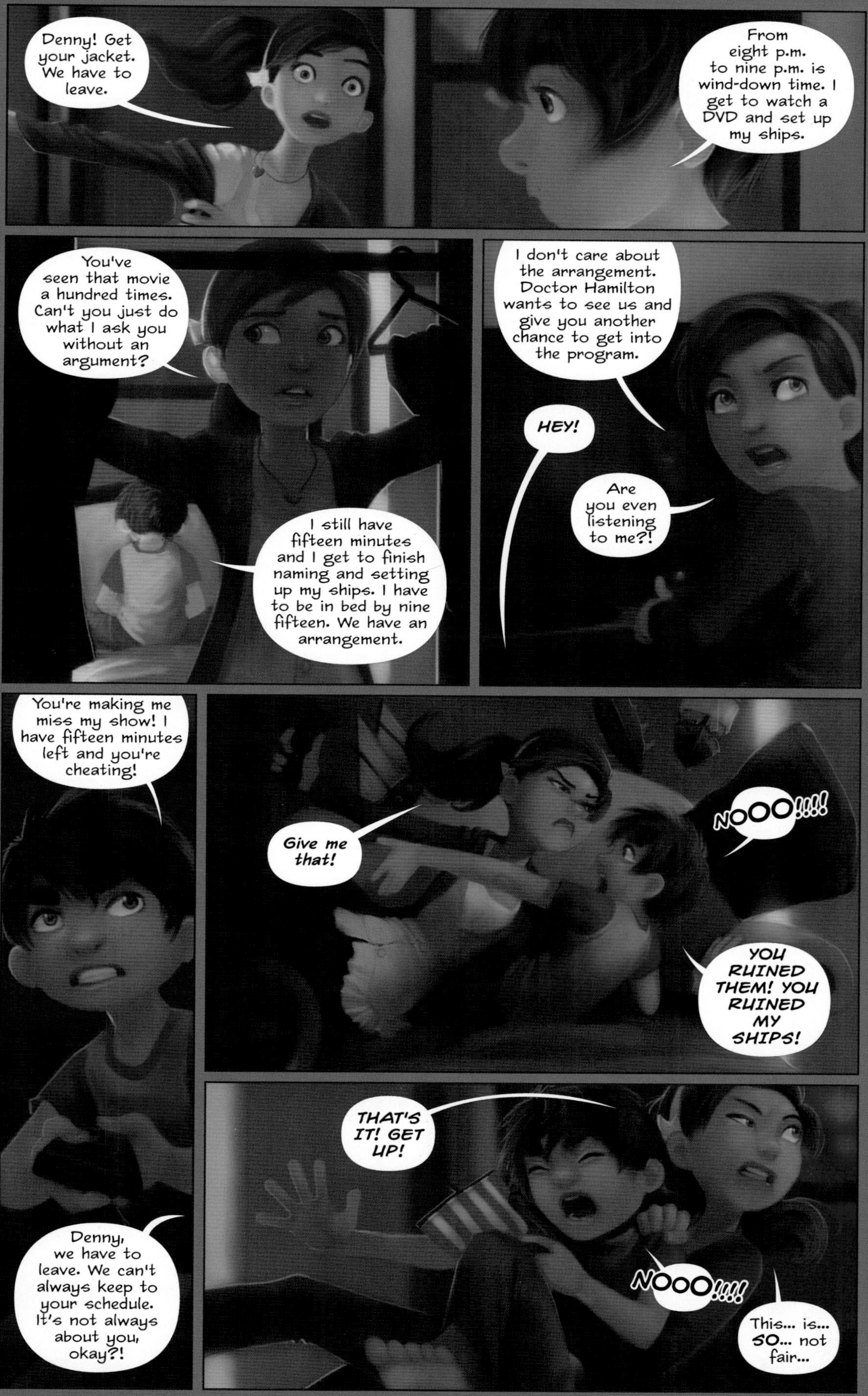
Denny! Get your jacket. We have to leave.
From eight p.m. to nine p.m. is wind-down time. I get to watch a DVD and set up my ships.
You've seen that movie a hundred times. Can't you just do what I ask you without an argument?
I still have fifteen minutes and I get to finish naming and setting up my ships. I have to be in bed by nine fifteen. We have an arrangement.
I don't care about the arrangement. Doctor Hamilton wants to see us and give you another chance to get into the program.
HEY!
Are you even listening to me?!
You're making me miss my show! I have fifteen minutes left and you're cheating!
Denny, we have to leave. We can't always keep to your schedule. It's not always about you, okay?!
Give me that!
NOOO!!!!
YOU RUINED THEM! YOU RUINED MY SHIPS!
THAT'S IT! GET UP!
NOOO!!!!
This... is... SO... not fair...

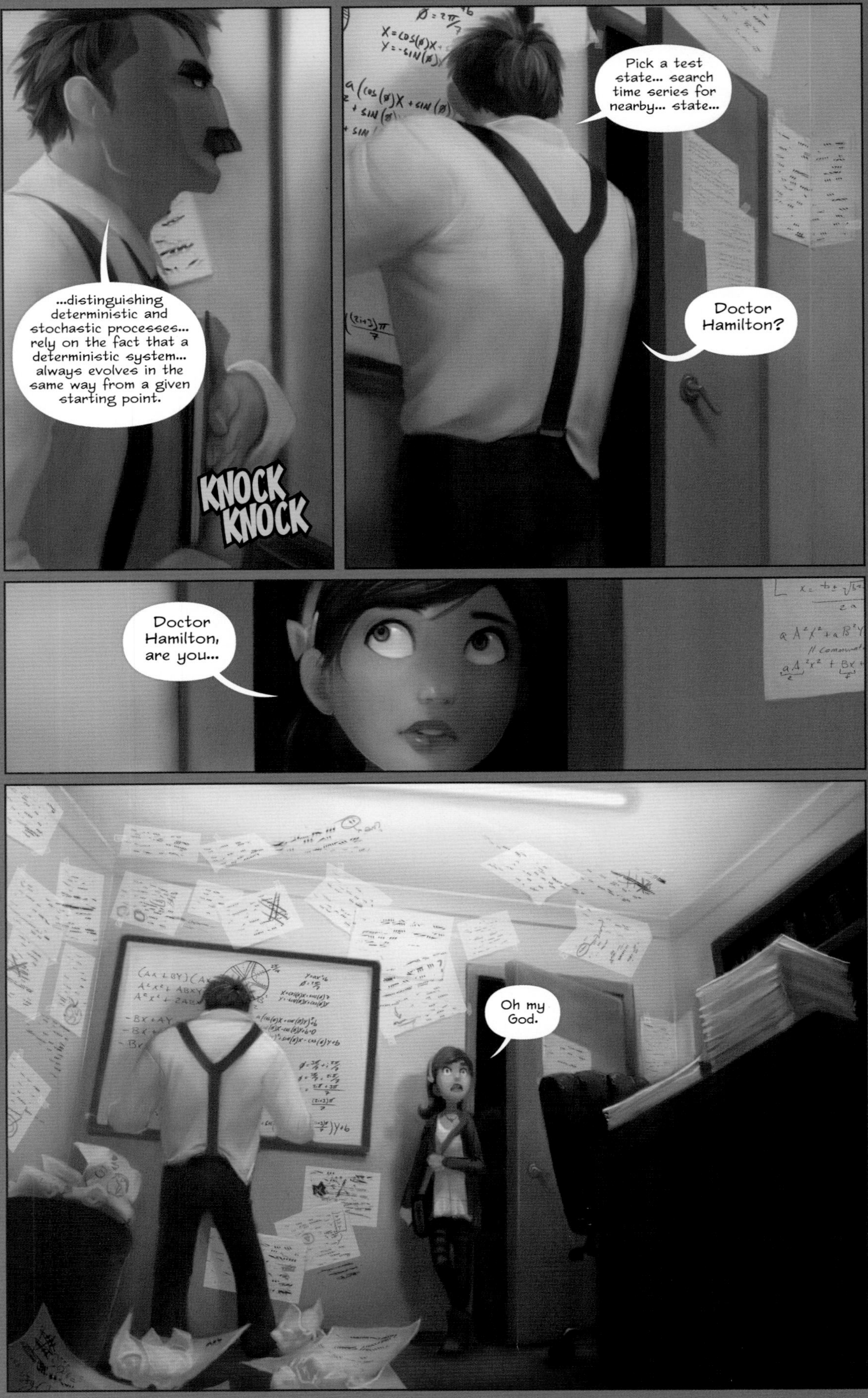
...distinguishing deterministic and stochastic processes... rely on the fact that a deterministic system... always evolves in the same way from a given starting point.
KNOCK KNOCK
Pick a test state... search time series for nearby... state...
Doctor Hamilton?
Doctor Hamilton, are you...
Oh my God.

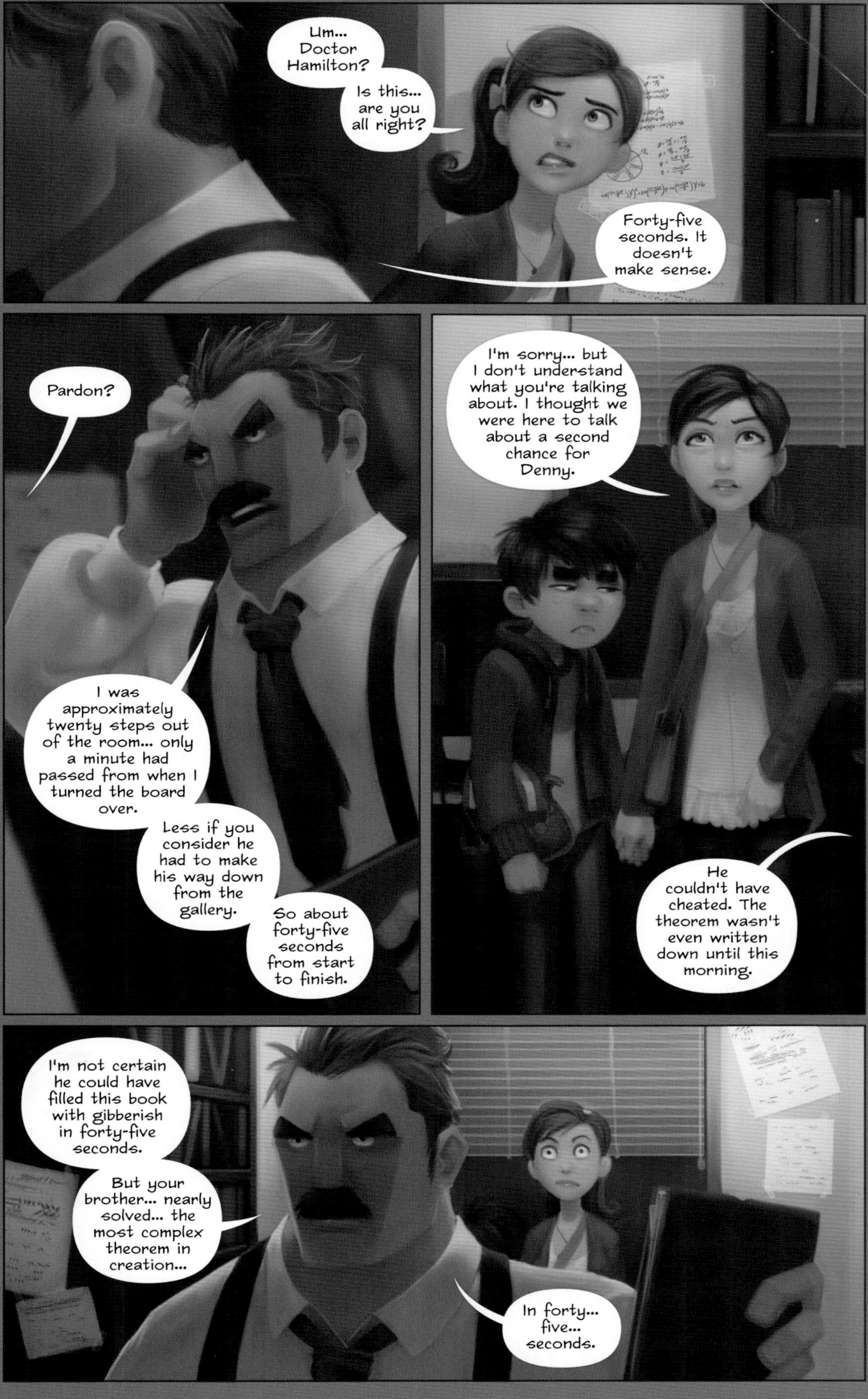
Um... Doctor Hamilton?
Is this... are you all right?
Forty-five seconds. It doesn't make sense.
Pardon?
I was approximately twenty steps out of the room... only a minute had passed from when I turned the board over.
Less if you consider he had to make his way down from the gallery.
So about forty-five seconds from start to finish.
I'm sorry... but I don't understand what you're talking about. I thought we were here to talk about a second chance for Denny.
He couldn't have cheated. The theorem wasn't even written down until this morning.
I'm not certain he could have filled this book with gibberish in forty-five seconds.
But your brother... nearly solved... the most complex theorem in creation...
In forty... five... seconds.

Isn't that... a good thing?

I say *nearly* because I have no doubt that he is capable. Even though I've copied every bit of his work... examined it from every angle for hours... I am *still* unable to complete it.

It appears your brother was right.

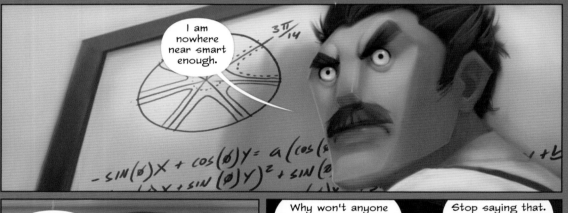

I am nowhere near smart enough.

$3\pi/14$

$-\sin(\emptyset)x + \cos(\emptyset)y = a\,(\cos(s$

$(\Delta x + \sin(\emptyset)y)^2 + \sin(\emptyset)$

Denny? Do you know the answer to this?

Yes.

Will you solve it for Doctor Hamilton?

Why won't anyone listen to me?! It's not supposed to open. No one knows any better.

Stop saying that. He's giving you a chance to fix your mistake.

I didn't make a mistake! I don't make mistakes.

Ever.

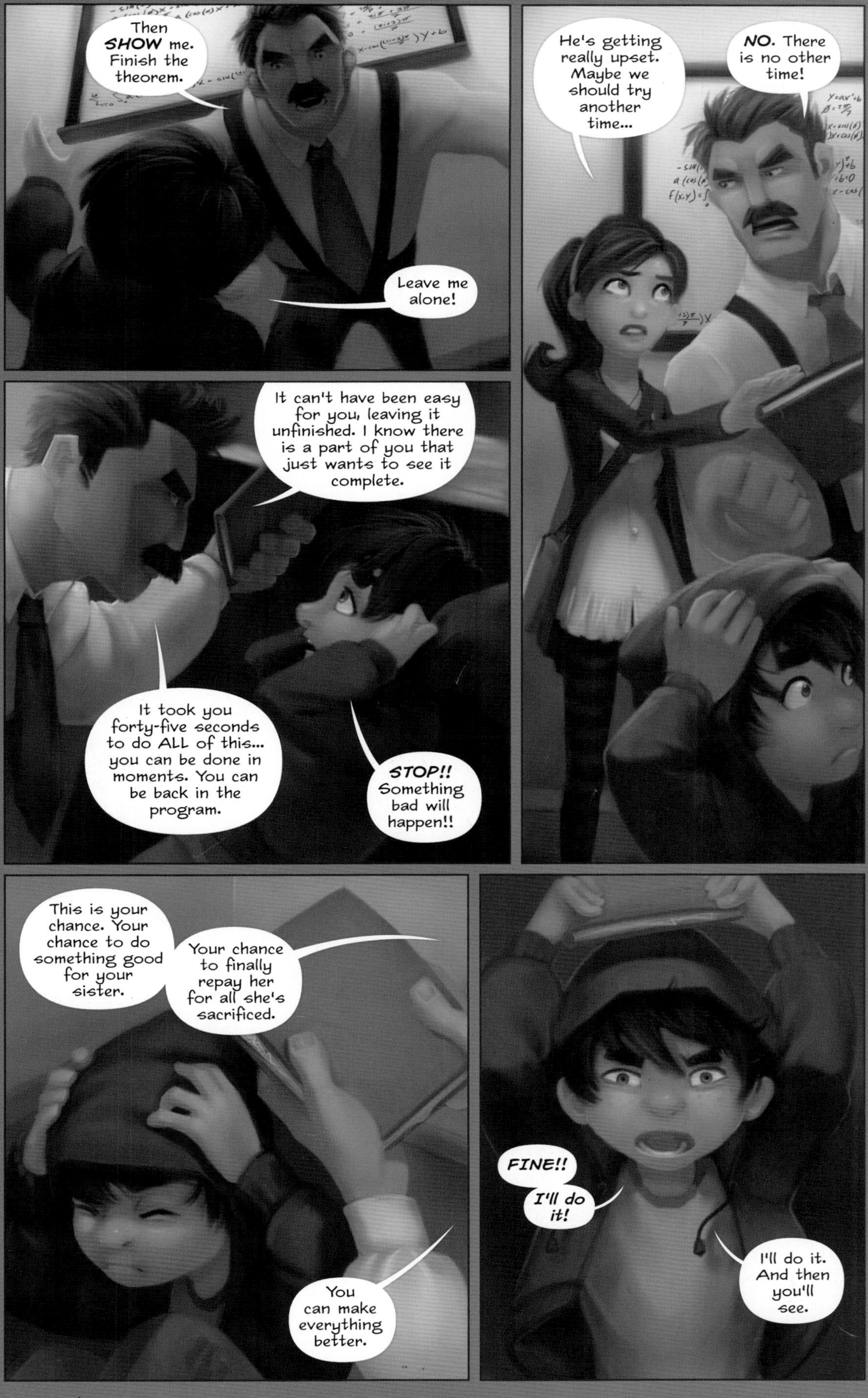

Then **SHOW** me. Finish the theorem.
Leave me alone!
It can't have been easy for you, leaving it unfinished. I know there is a part of you that just wants to see it complete.
It took you forty-five seconds to do ALL of this... you can be done in moments. You can be back in the program.
STOP!! Something bad will happen!!
He's getting really upset. Maybe we should try another time...
NO. There is no other time!
This is your chance. Your chance to do something good for your sister.
Your chance to finally repay her for all she's sacrificed.
You can make everything better.
FINE!!
I'll do it!
I'll do it. And then you'll see.

Can't you just fill in the end?

No. **THIS** is an answer... not a problem.

You have to know the problem before you can solve it. Don't be dumb.

That's impossible.

He's going to hurt himself!

Stop! He's almost there...

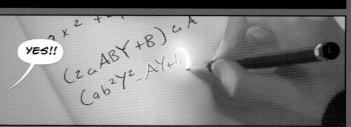

YES!!

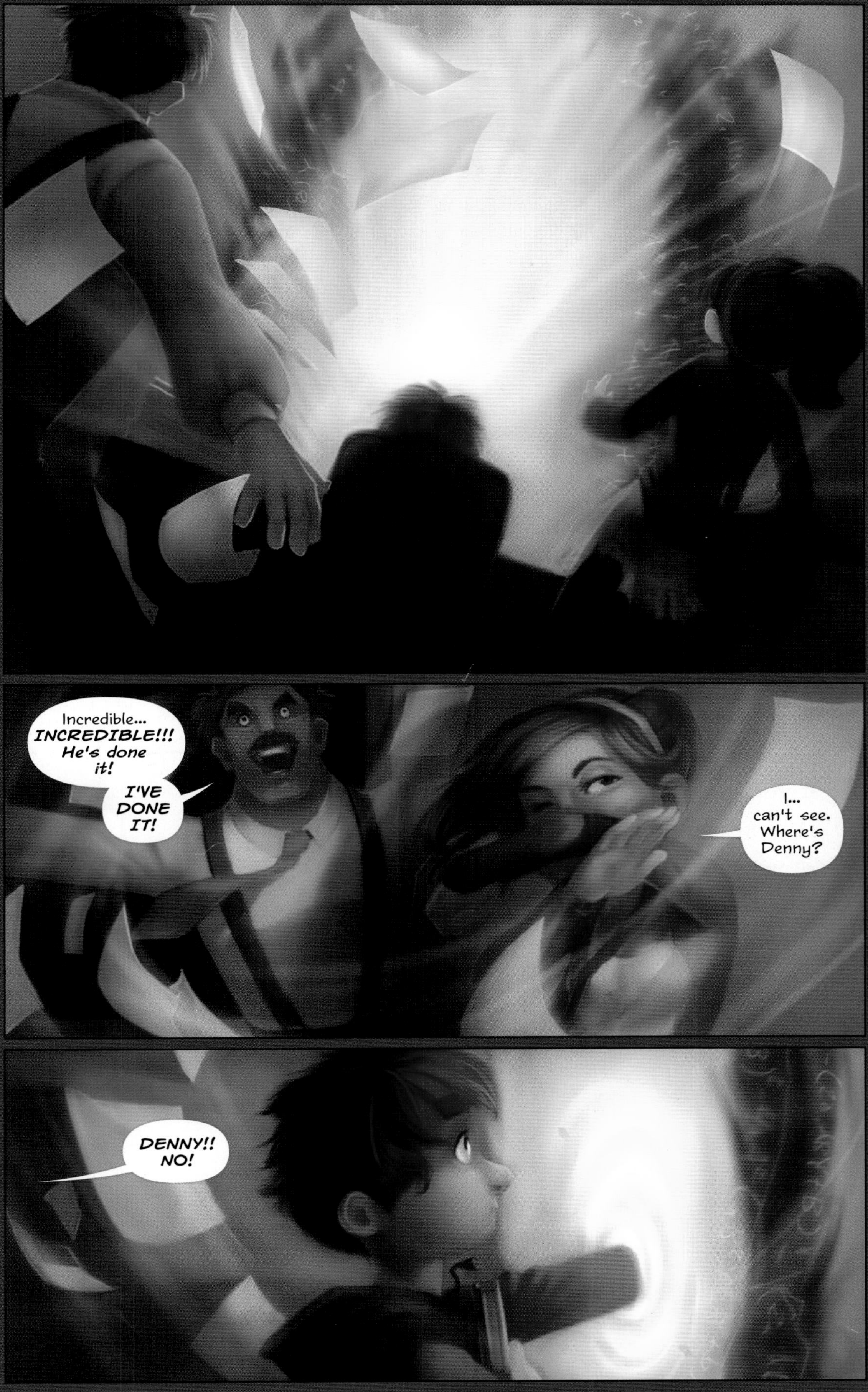
Incredible... INCREDIBLE!!! He's done it!
I'VE DONE IT!
I... can't see. Where's Denny?
DENNY!! NO!

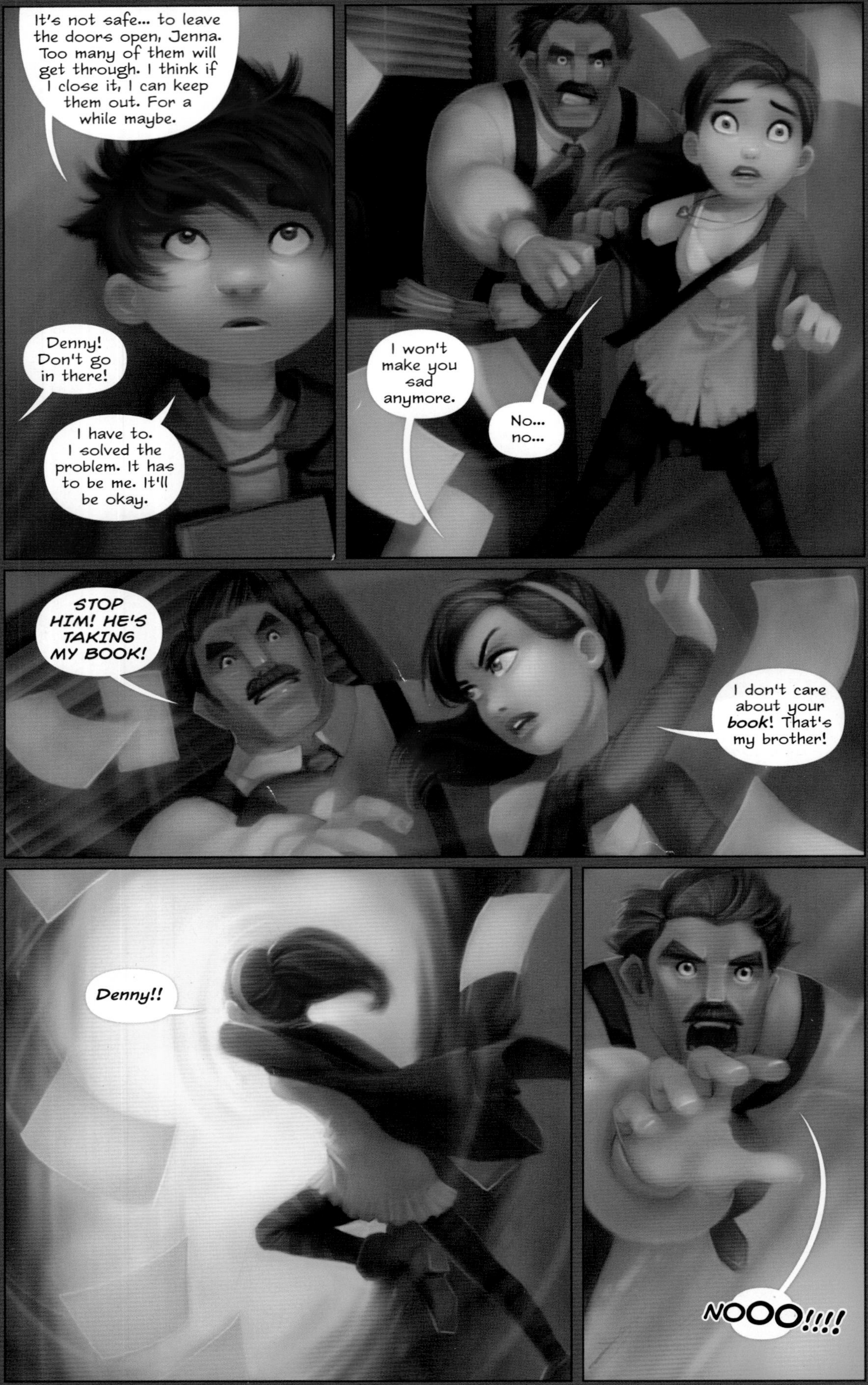
It's not safe... to leave the doors open, Jenna. Too many of them will get through. I think if I close it, I can keep them out. For a while maybe.
Denny! Don't go in there!
I have to. I solved the problem. It has to be me. It'll be okay.
I won't make you sad anymore.
No... no...
STOP HIM! HE'S TAKING MY BOOK!
I don't care about your *book*! That's my brother!
Denny!!
NOOO!!!!

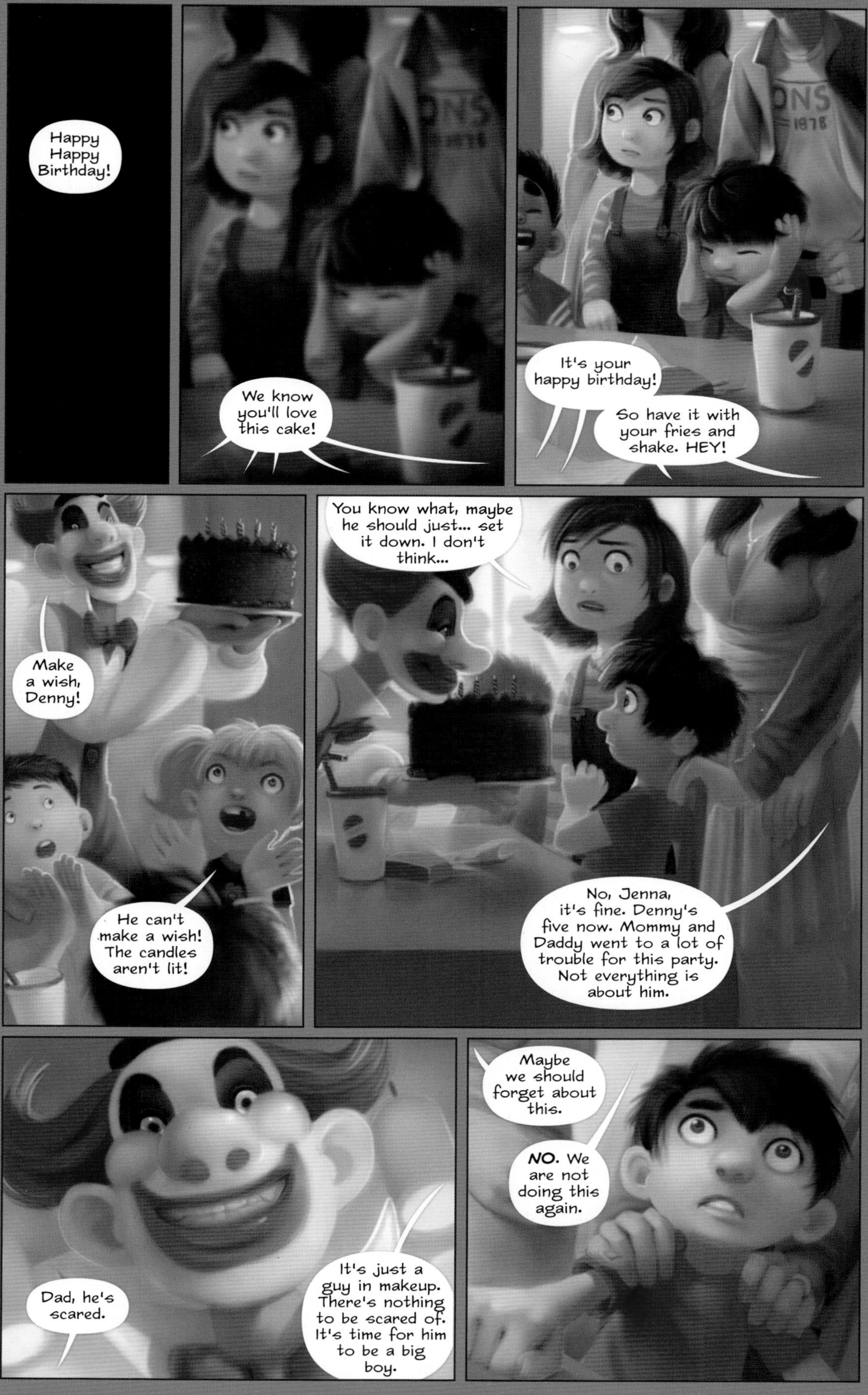
Happy Happy Birthday!
We know you'll love this cake!
It's your happy birthday!
So have it with your fries and shake. HEY!
Make a wish, Denny!
He can't make a wish! The candles aren't lit!
You know what, maybe he should just... set it down. I don't think...
No, Jenna, it's fine. Denny's five now. Mommy and Daddy went to a lot of trouble for this party. Not everything is about him.
Dad, he's scared.
It's just a guy in makeup. There's nothing to be scared of. It's time for him to be a big boy.
Maybe we should forget about this.
NO. We are not doing this again.

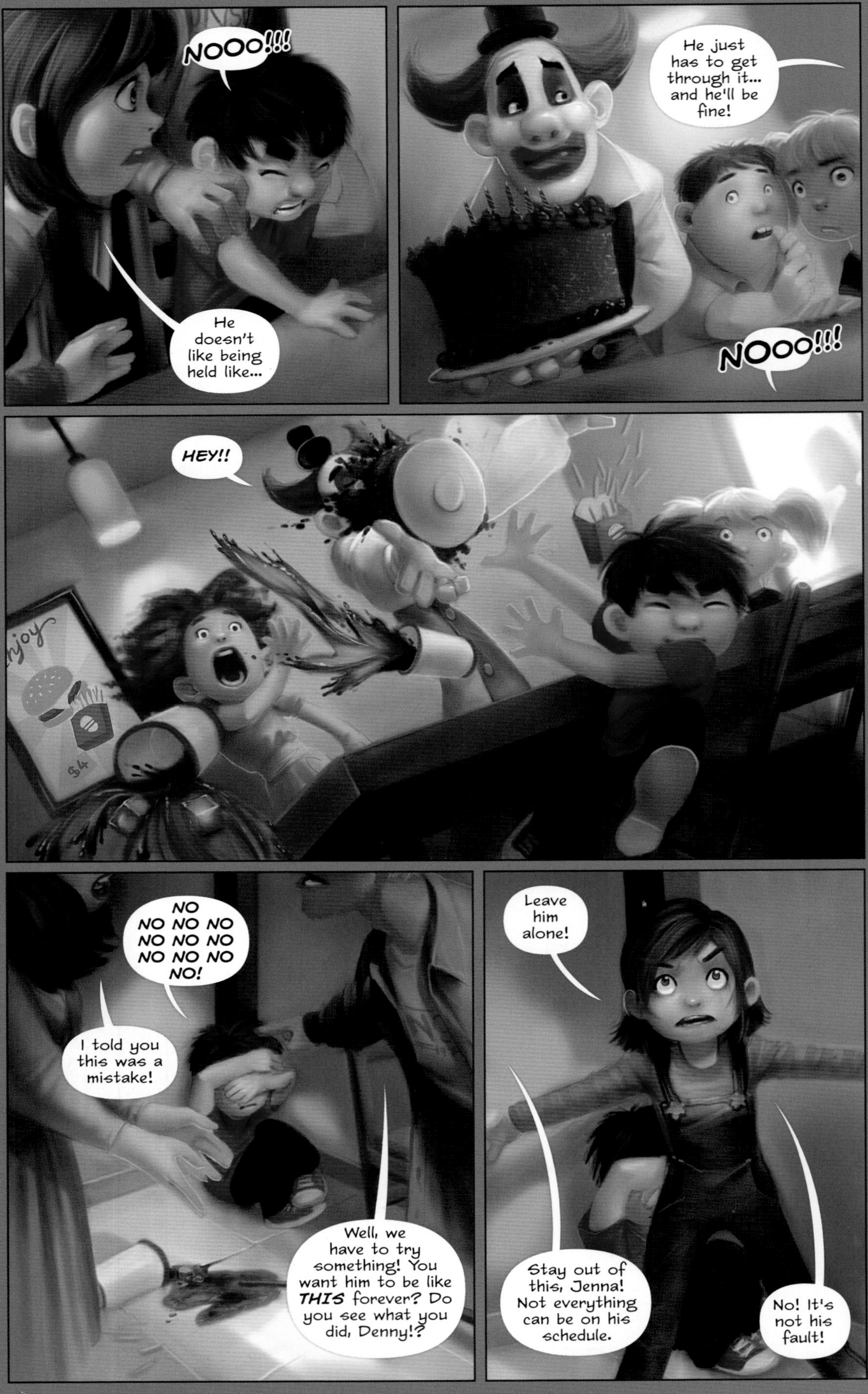

NOOO!!!
He doesn't like being held like...
He just has to get through it... and he'll be fine!
NOOO!!!
HEY!!
NO NO NO NO NO NO NO NO NO NO NO!
I told you this was a mistake!
Well, we have to try something! You want him to be like *THIS* forever? Do you see what you did, Denny!?
Leave him alone!
Stay out of this, Jenna! Not everything can be on his schedule.
No! It's not his fault!

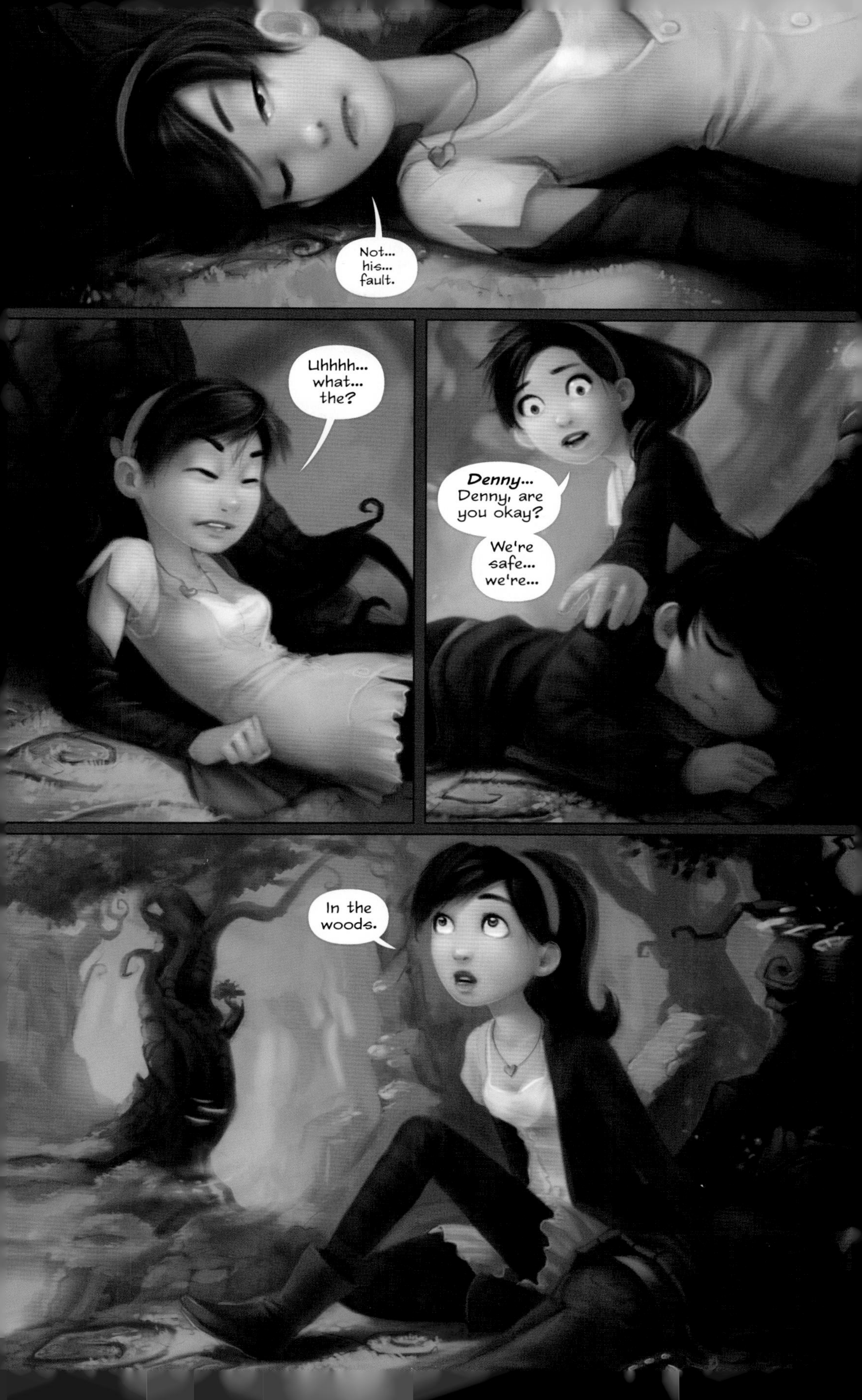
Not... his... fault.
Uhhhh... what... the?
Denny... Denny, are you okay?
We're safe... we're...
In the woods.

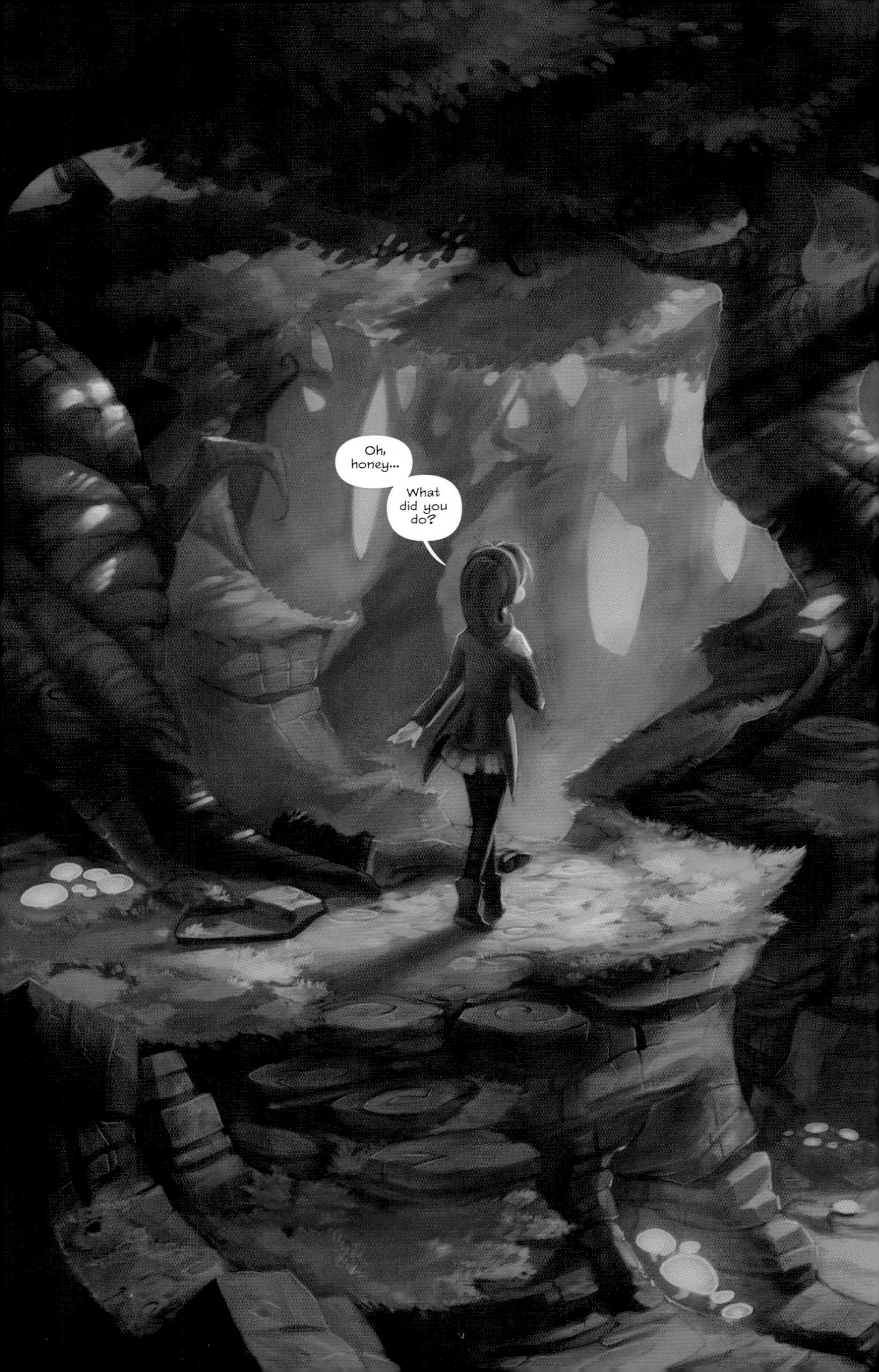
Oh, honey...
What did you do?

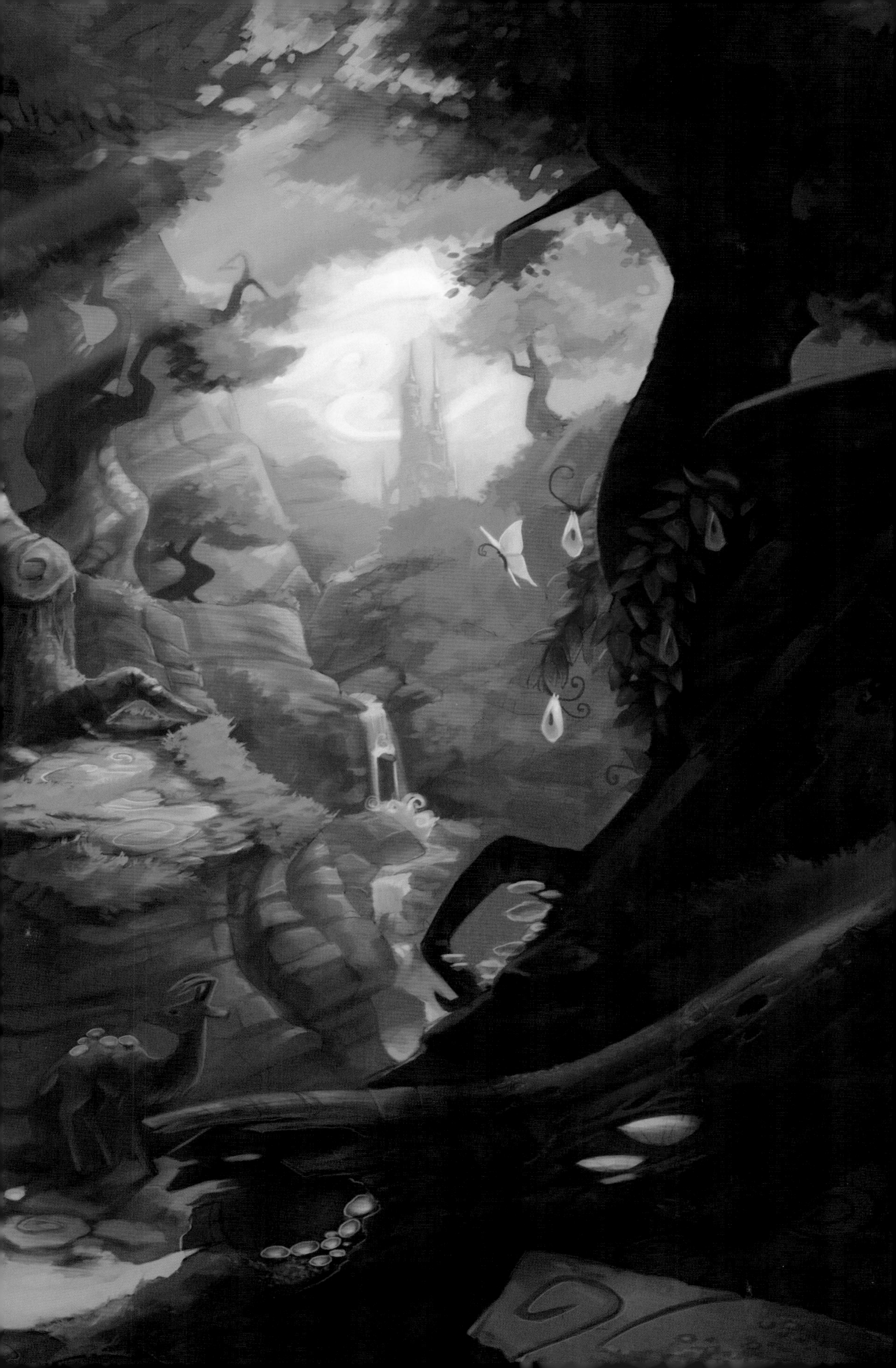

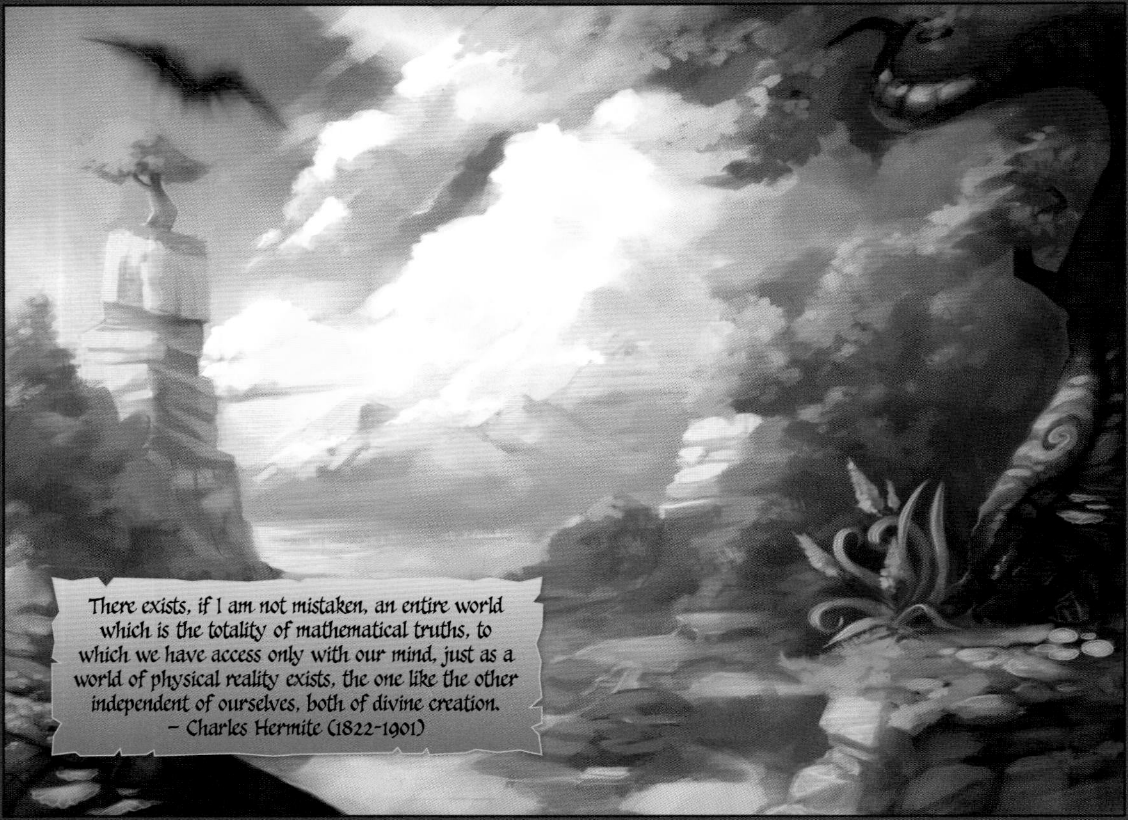
There exists, if I am not mistaken, an entire world which is the totality of mathematical truths, to which we have access only with our mind, just as a world of physical reality exists, the one like the other independent of ourselves, both of divine creation.
– Charles Hermite (1822-1901)

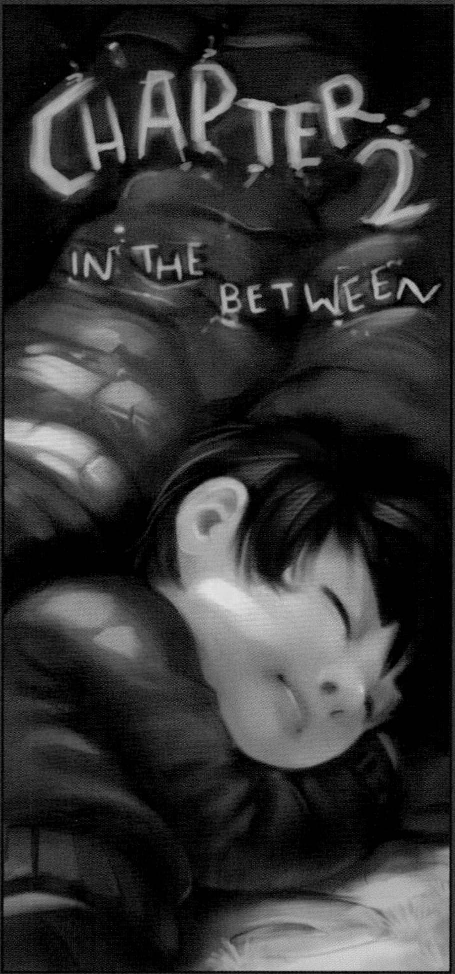
CHAPTER 2
IN THE BETWEEN

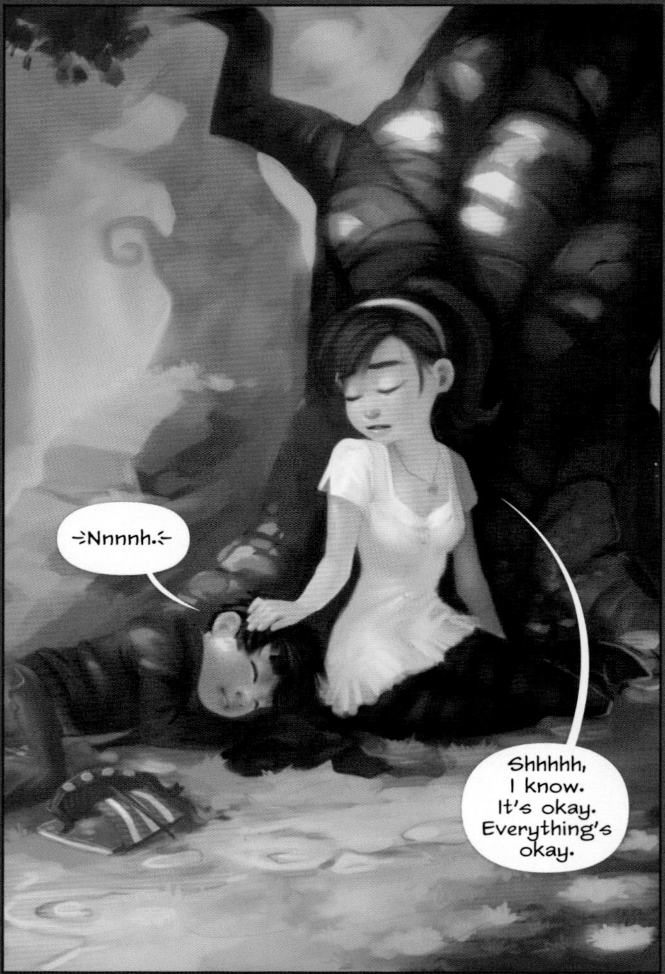
Nnnnh.
Shhhhh, I know. It's okay. Everything's okay.

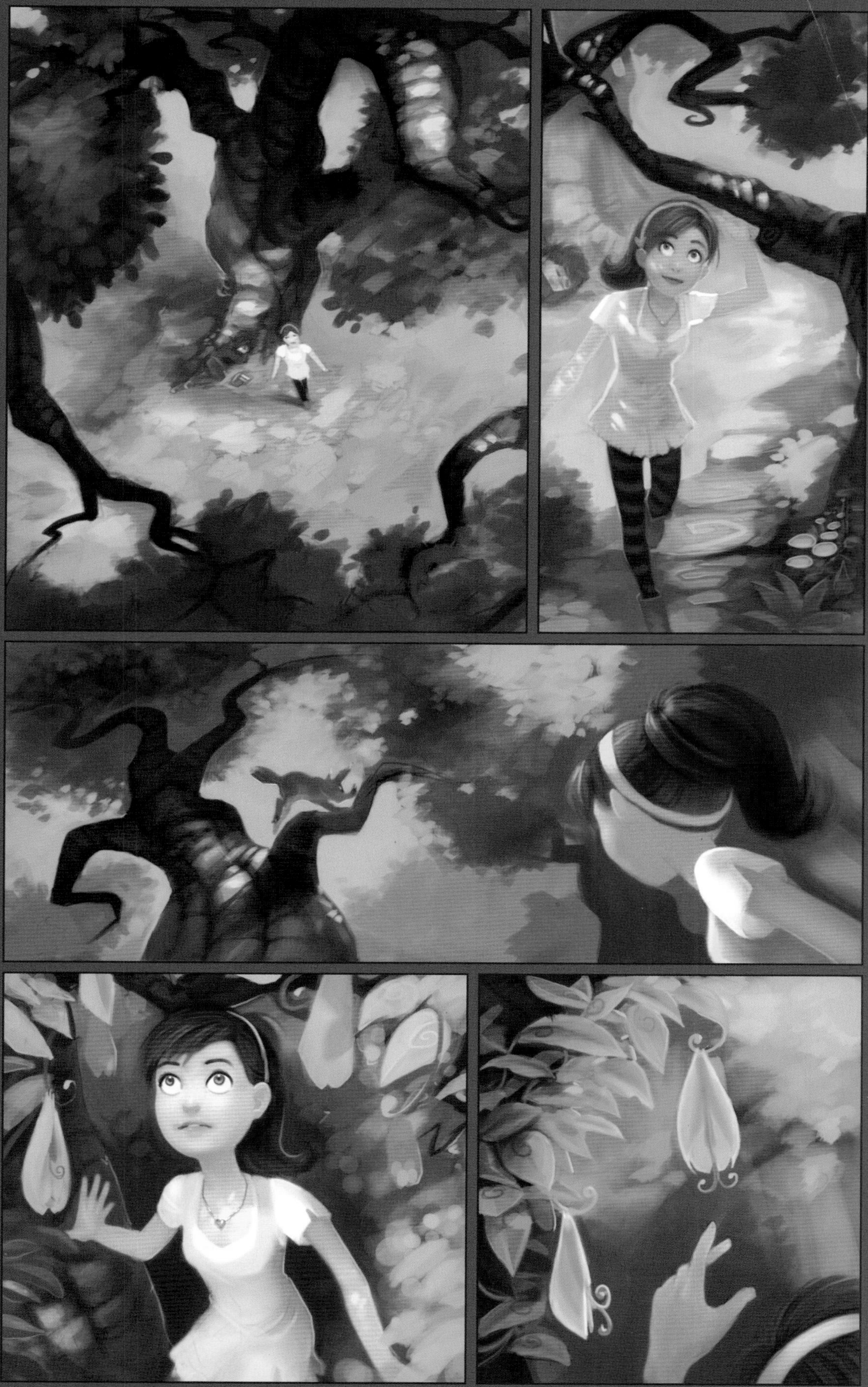

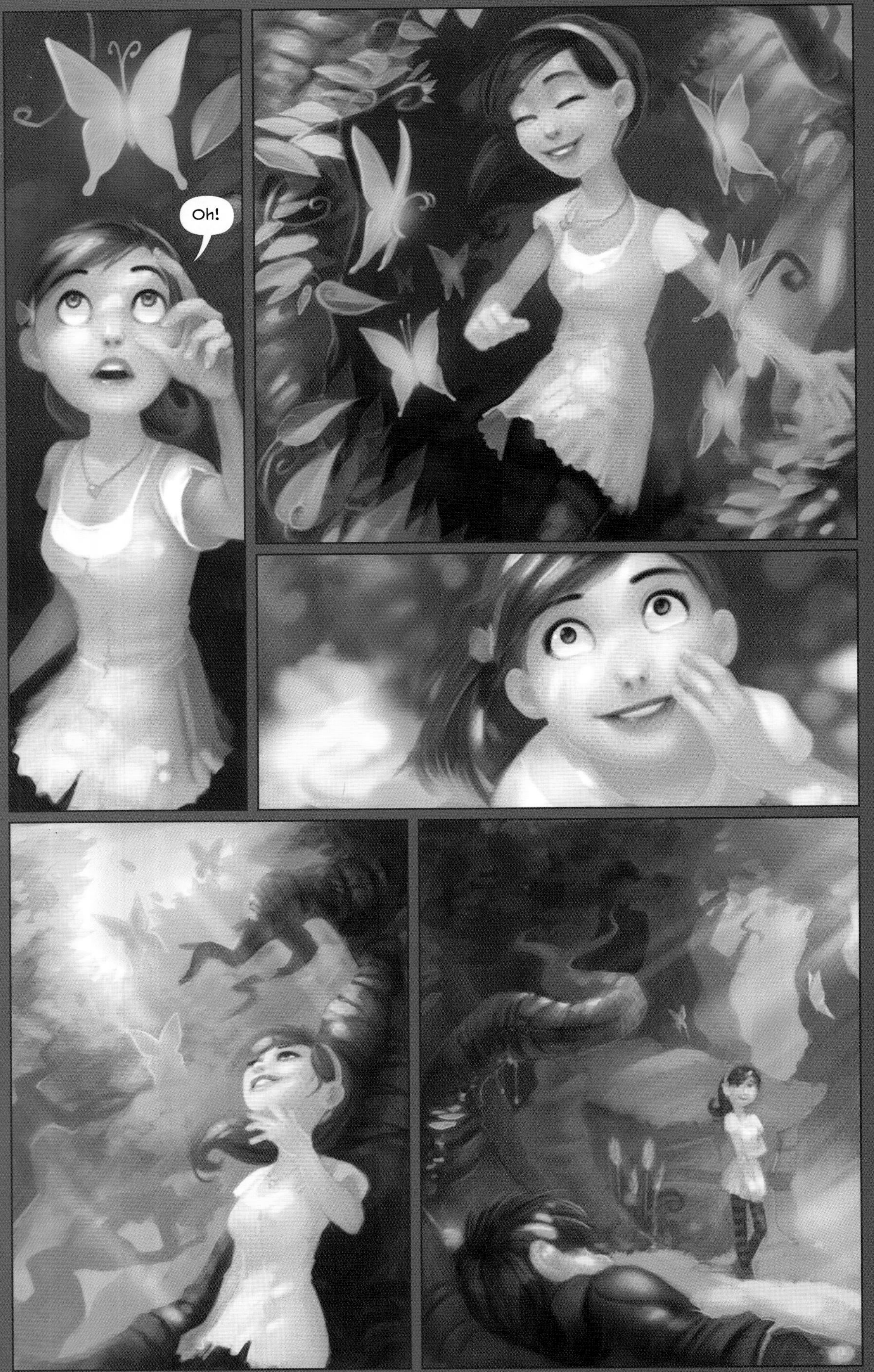
Oh!

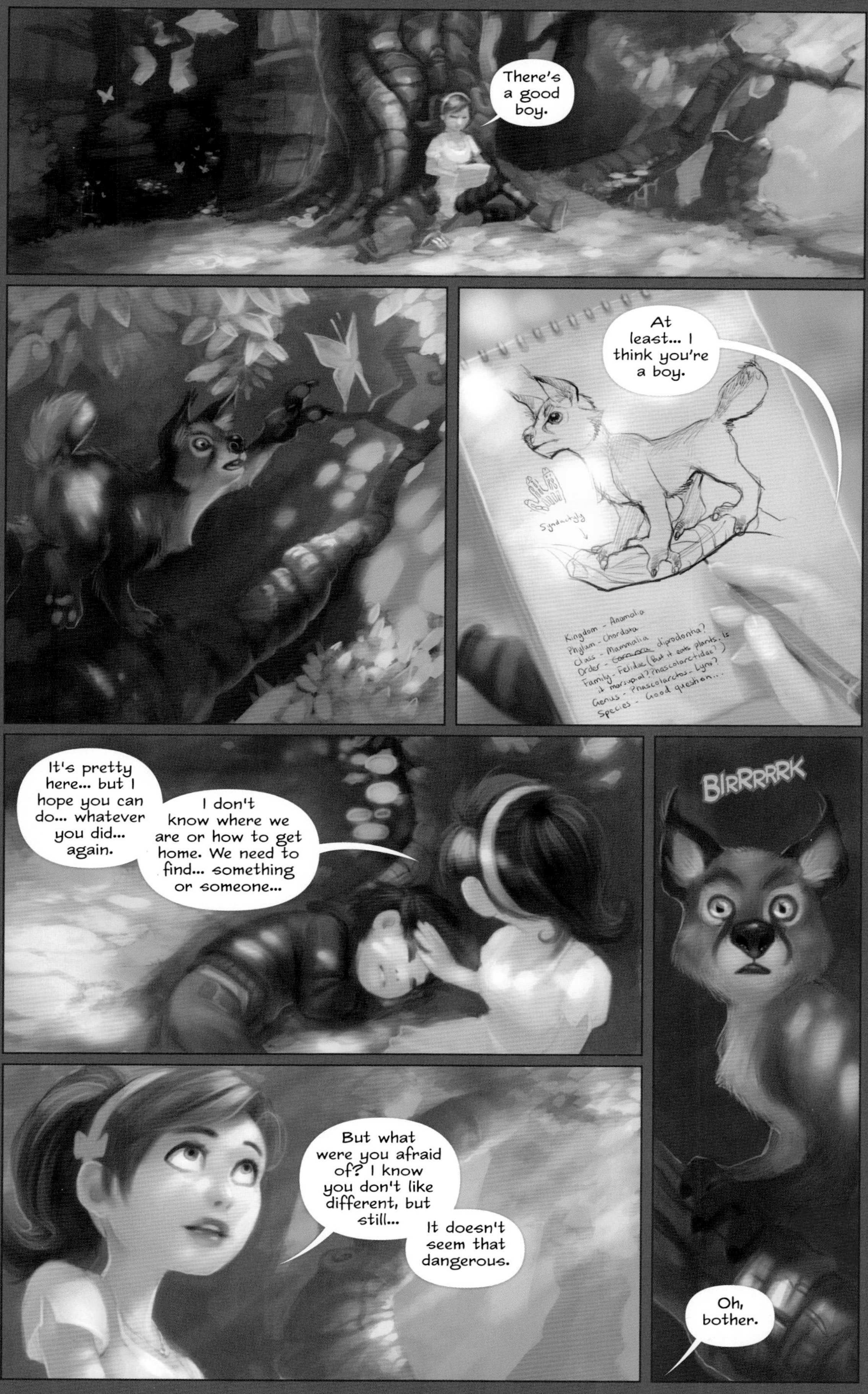
There's a good boy.
At least... I think you're a boy.
Syndactyly
Kingdom - Anamalia
Phylum - Chordata
Class - Mammalia
Order - Carnivora diprodontia?
Family - Felidae (But it eats plants. Is it marsupial?) Phascolarctidae?)
Genus - Phascolarctos - Lynx?
Species - Good question...
It's pretty here... but I hope you can do... whatever you did... again.
I don't know where we are or how to get home. We need to find... something or someone...
But what were you afraid of? I know you don't like different, but still...
It doesn't seem that dangerous.
BIRRRRRK
Oh, bother.

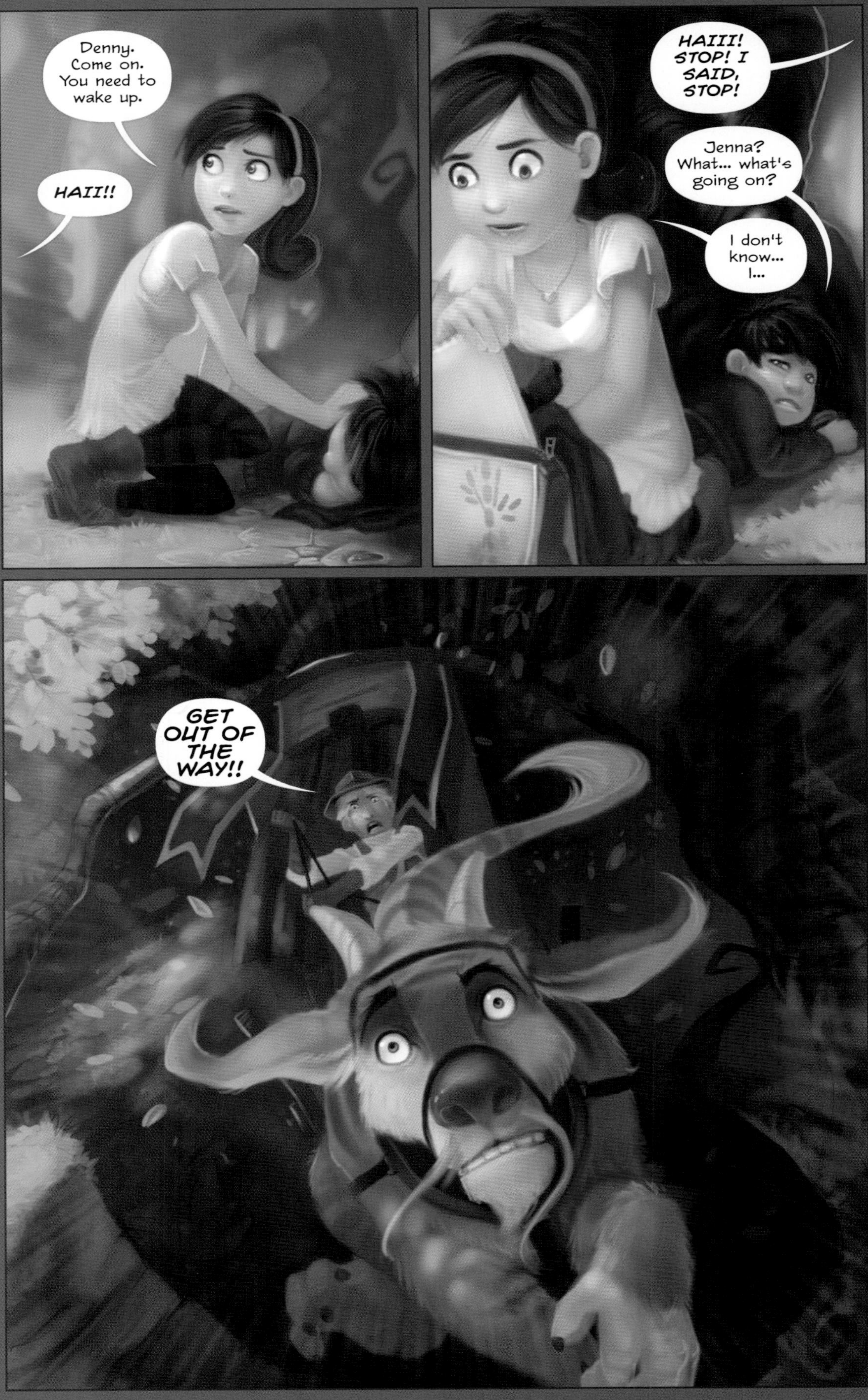
Denny. Come on. You need to wake up.
HAII!!
HAIII! STOP! I SAID, STOP!
Jenna? What... what's going on?
I don't know... I...
GET OUT OF THE WAY!!

Run, Denny!

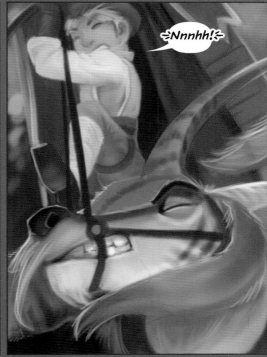

≈Nnnhh!≈

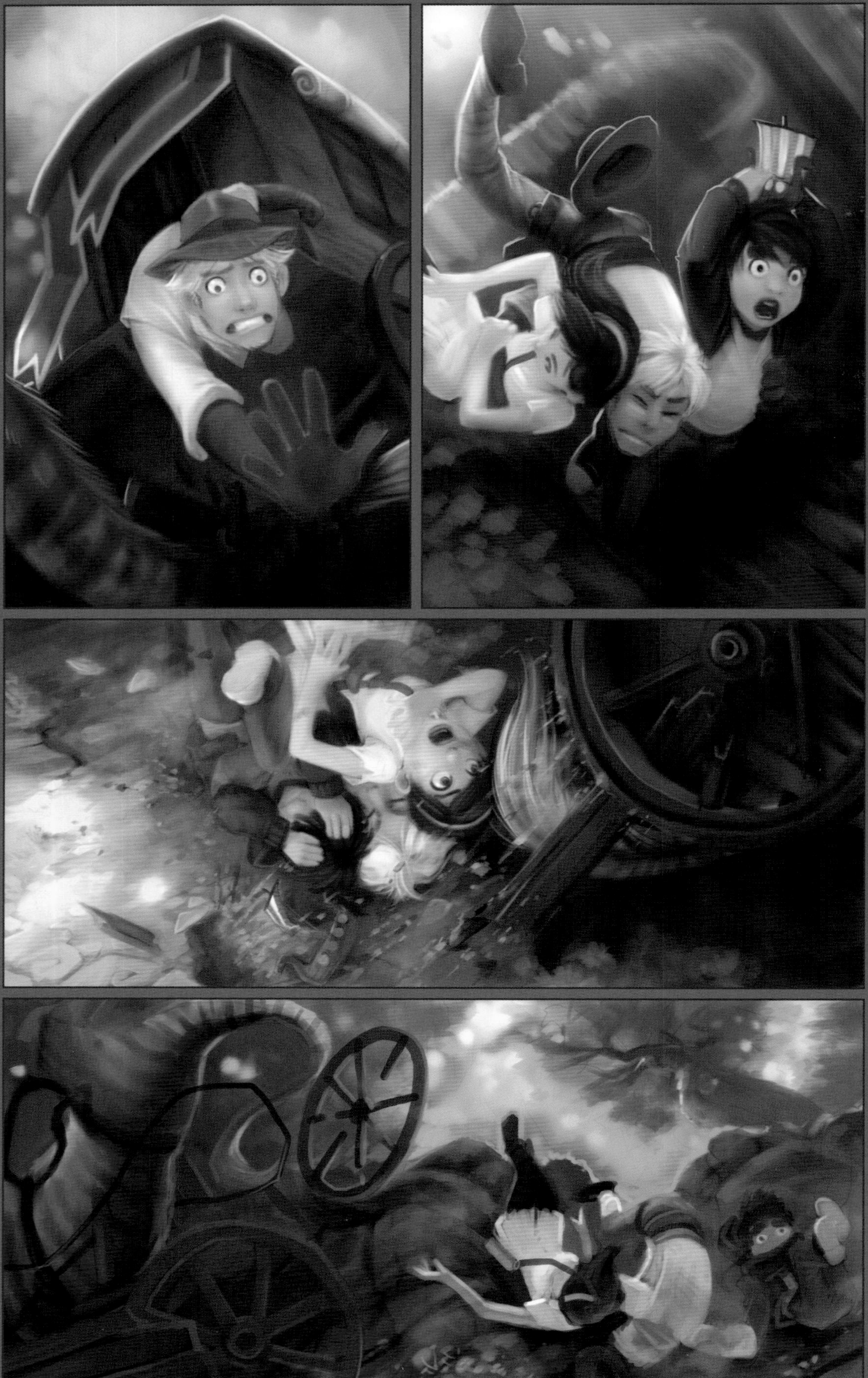

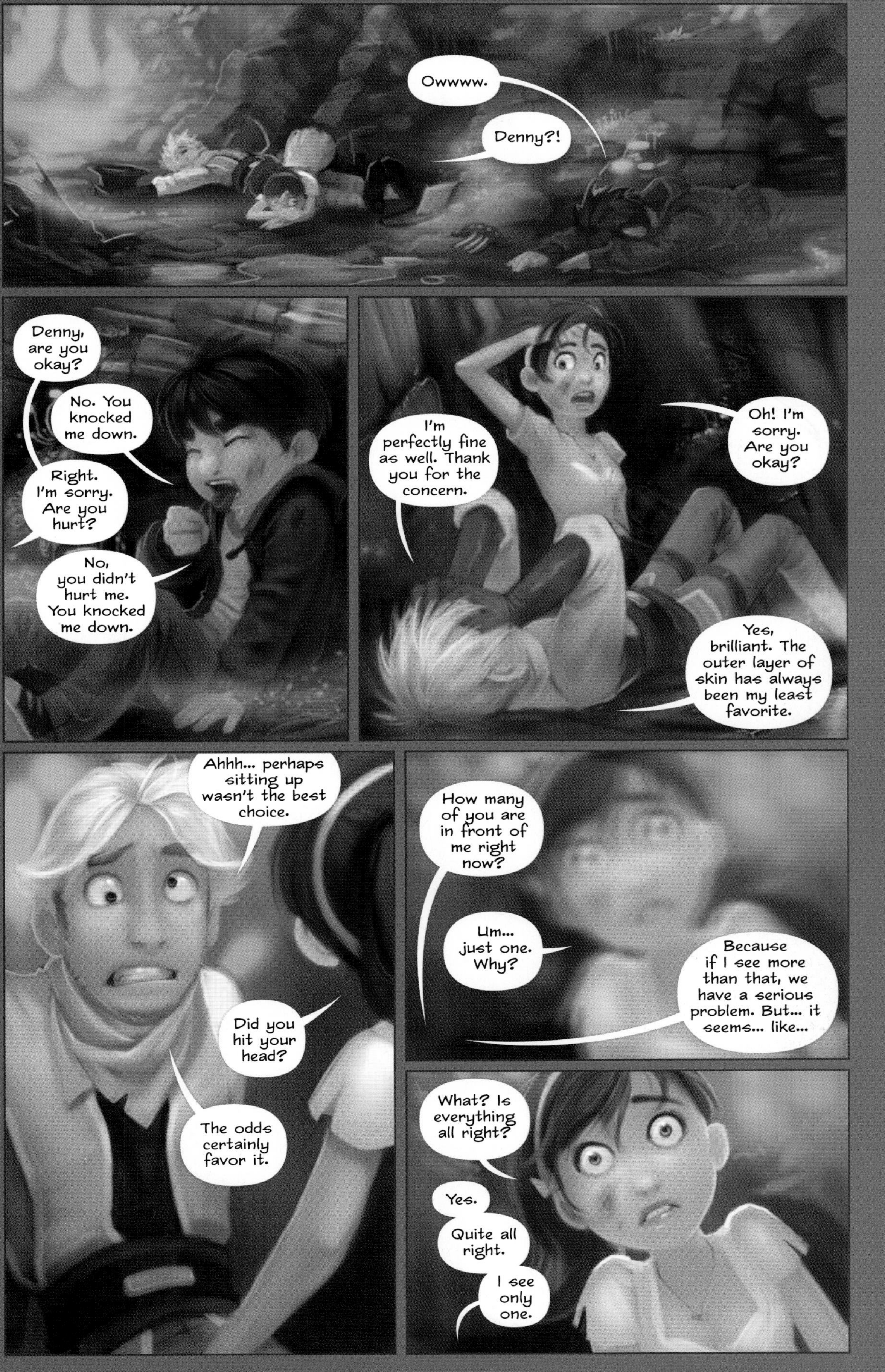
Owwww.
Denny?!
Denny, are you okay?
No. You knocked me down.
Right. I'm sorry. Are you hurt?
No, you didn't hurt me. You knocked me down.
I'm perfectly fine as well. Thank you for the concern.
Oh! I'm sorry. Are you okay?
Yes, brilliant. The outer layer of skin has always been my least favorite.
Ahhh... perhaps sitting up wasn't the best choice.
Did you hit your head?
The odds certainly favor it.
How many of you are in front of me right now?
Um... just one. Why?
Because if I see more than that, we have a serious problem. But... it seems... like...
What? Is everything all right?
Yes.
Quite all right.
I see only one.

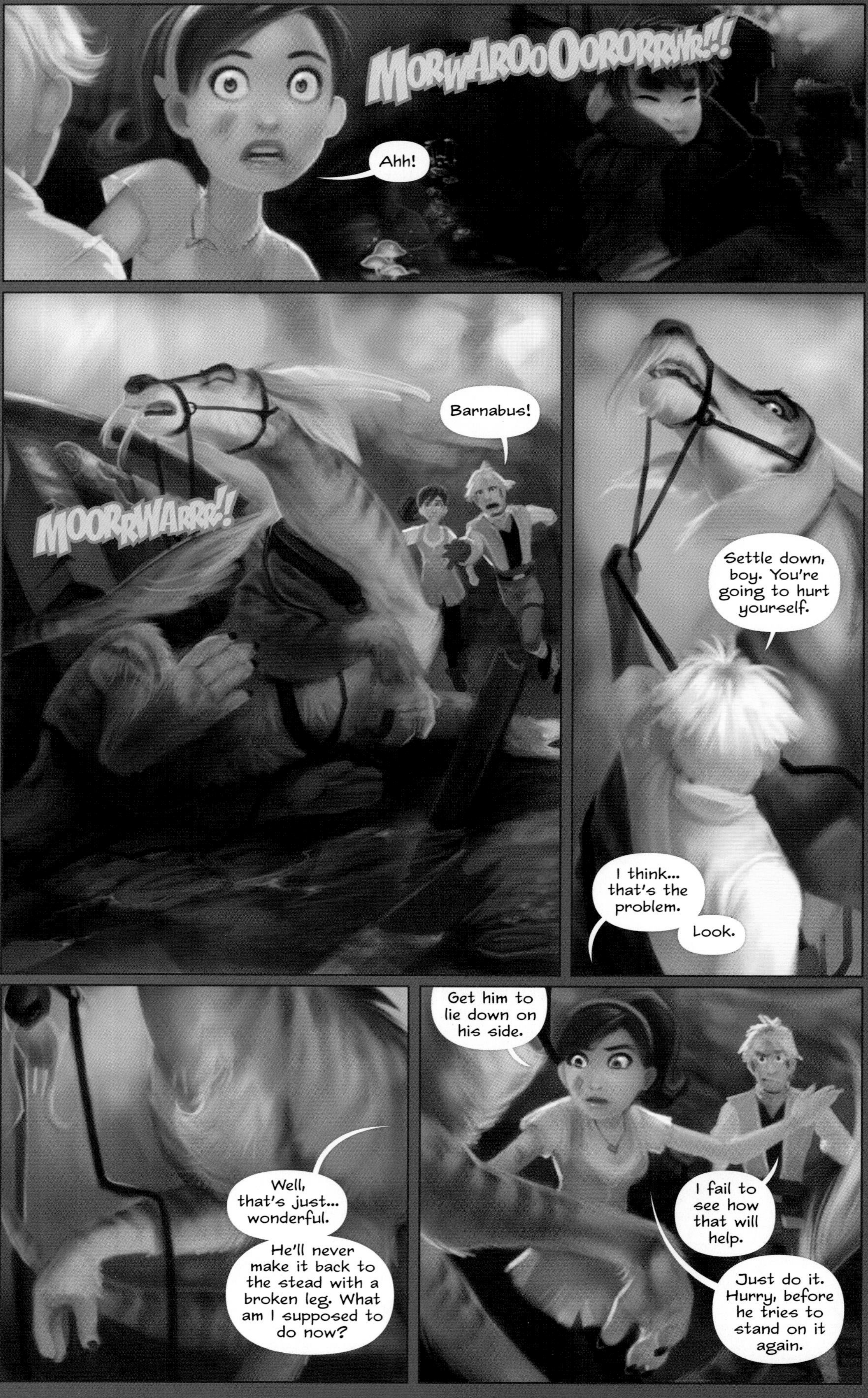
MORWAROoOORORRRWR!!
Ahh!
Barnabus!
MOORRWARRR!!
Settle down, boy. You're going to hurt yourself.
I think... that's the problem.
Look.
Well, that's just... wonderful.
He'll never make it back to the stead with a broken leg. What am I supposed to do now?
Get him to lie down on his side.
I fail to see how that will help.
Just do it. Hurry, before he tries to stand on it again.

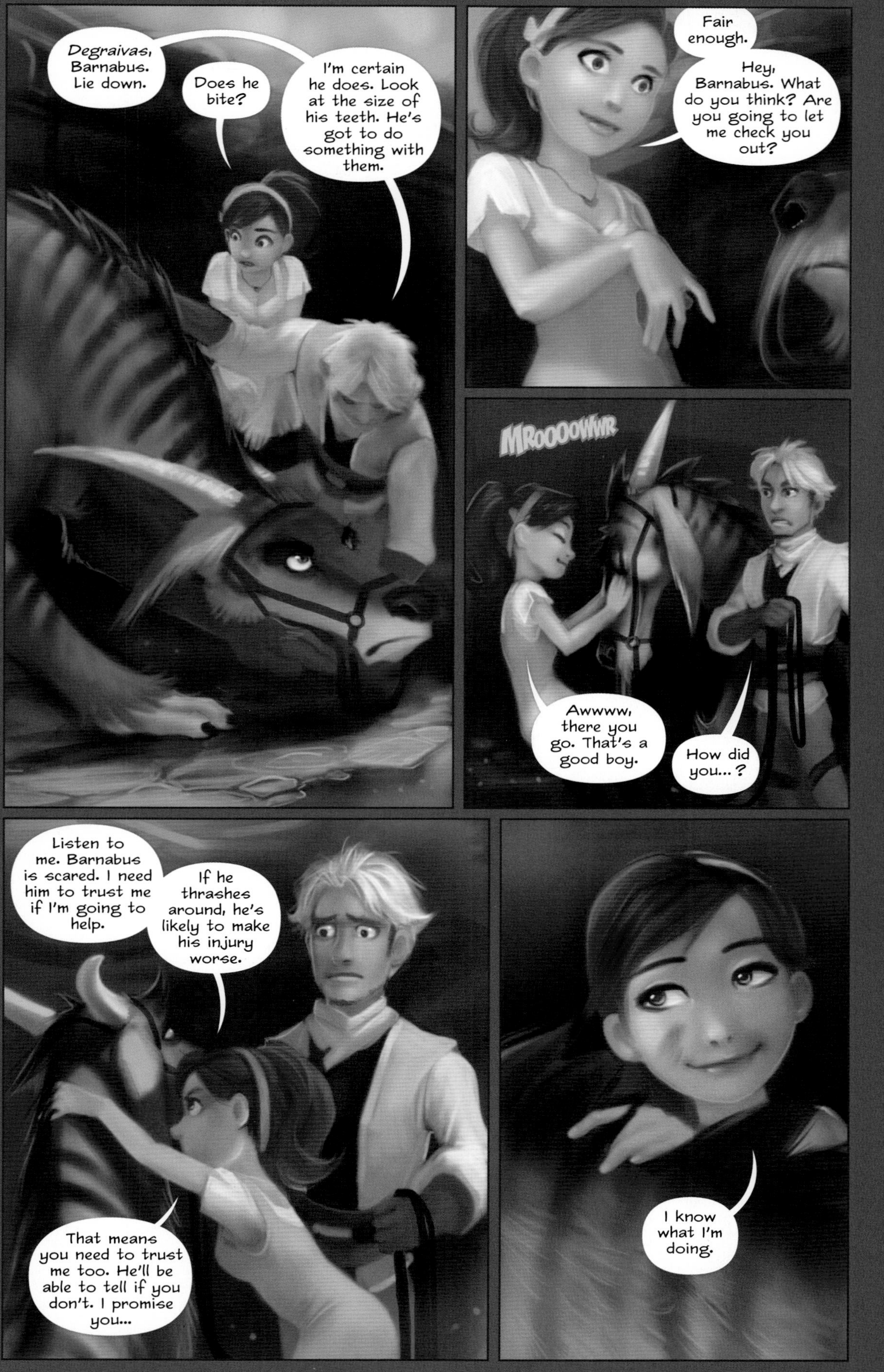
Degraivas, Barnabus. Lie down.
Does he bite?
I'm certain he does. Look at the size of his teeth. He's got to do something with them.
Fair enough.
Hey, Barnabus. What do you think? Are you going to let me check you out?
MROOOOWWR
Awwww, there you go. That's a good boy.
How did you...?
Listen to me. Barnabus is scared. I need him to trust me if I'm going to help.
If he thrashes around, he's likely to make his injury worse.
That means you need to trust me too. He'll be able to tell if you don't. I promise you...
I know what I'm doing.

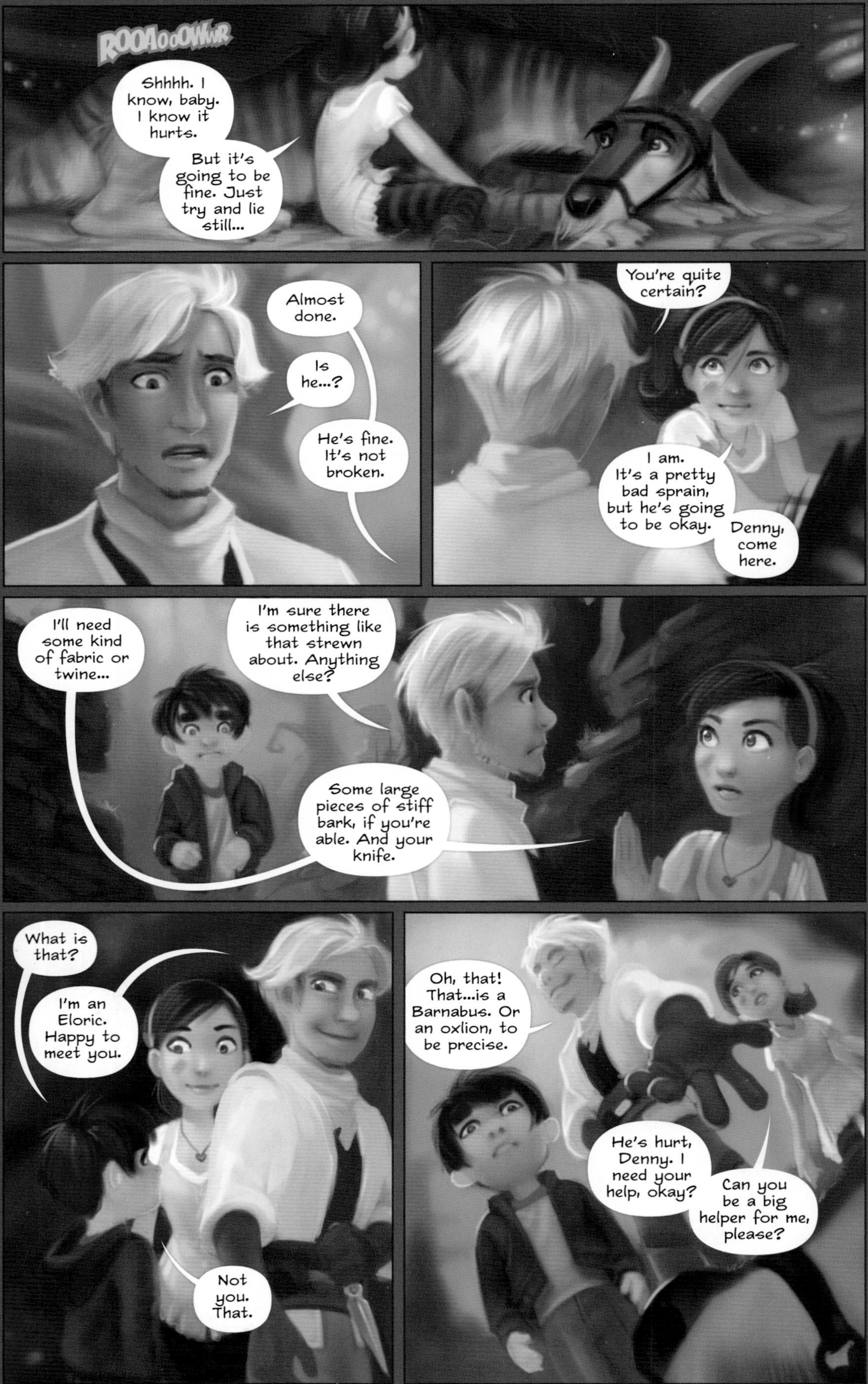
ROOAoOOWwR
Shhhh. I know, baby. I know it hurts.
But it's going to be fine. Just try and lie still...
Almost done.
Is he...?
He's fine. It's not broken.
You're quite certain?
I am. It's a pretty bad sprain, but he's going to be okay.
Denny, come here.
I'll need some kind of fabric or twine...
I'm sure there is something like that strewn about. Anything else?
Some large pieces of stiff bark, if you're able. And your knife.
What is that?
I'm an Eloric. Happy to meet you.
Not you. That.
Oh, that! That...is a Barnabus. Or an oxlion, to be precise.
He's hurt, Denny. I need your help, okay?
Can you be a big helper for me, please?

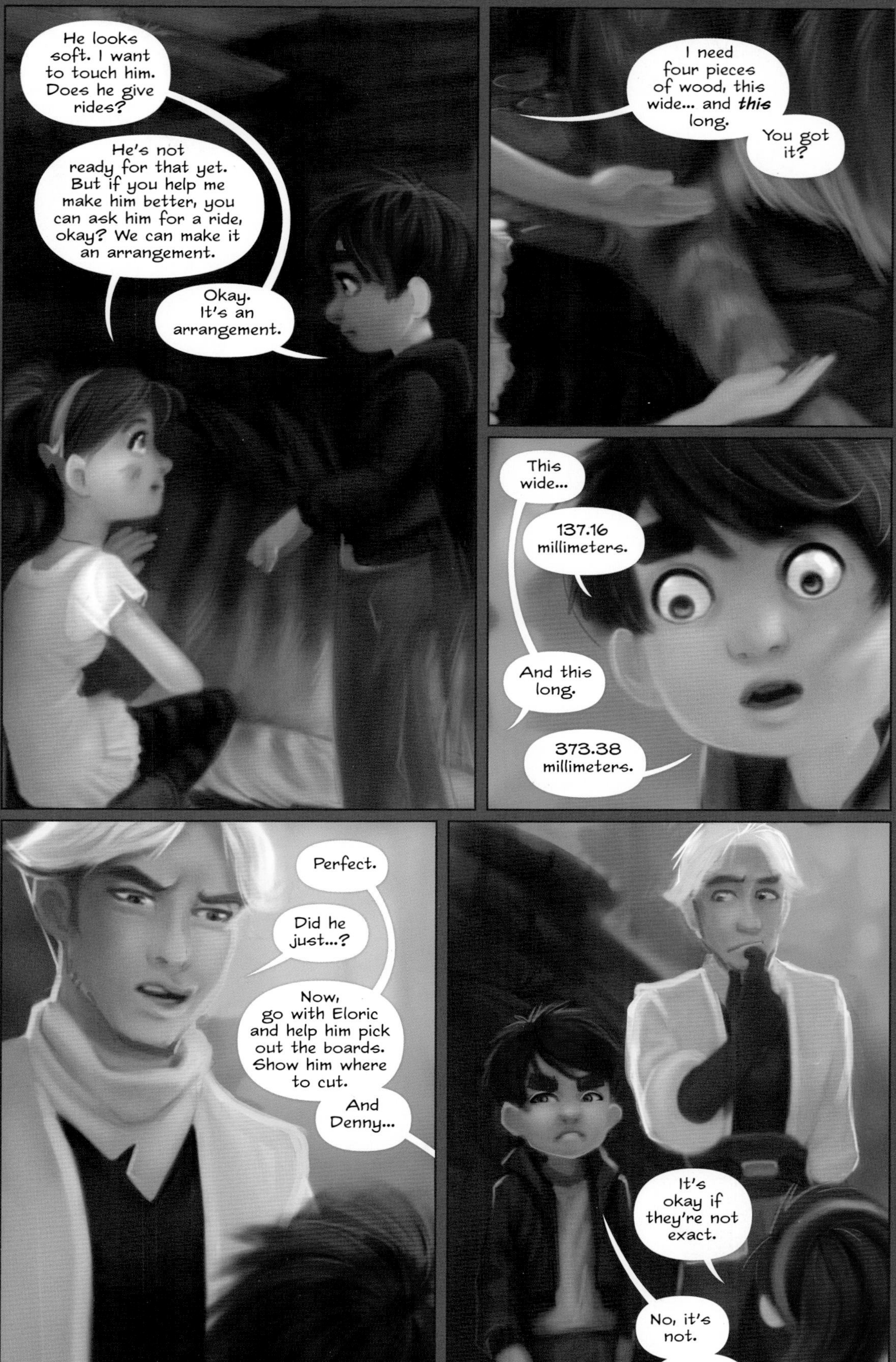
He looks soft. I want to touch him. Does he give rides?
He's not ready for that yet. But if you help me make him better, you can ask him for a ride, okay? We can make it an arrangement.
Okay. It's an arrangement.
I need four pieces of wood, this wide... and *this* long.
You got it?
This wide...
137.16 millimeters.
And this long.
373.38 millimeters.
Perfect.
Did he just...?
Now, go with Eloric and help him pick out the boards. Show him where to cut.
And Denny...
It's okay if they're not exact.
No, it's not.
Come on, Eloric.

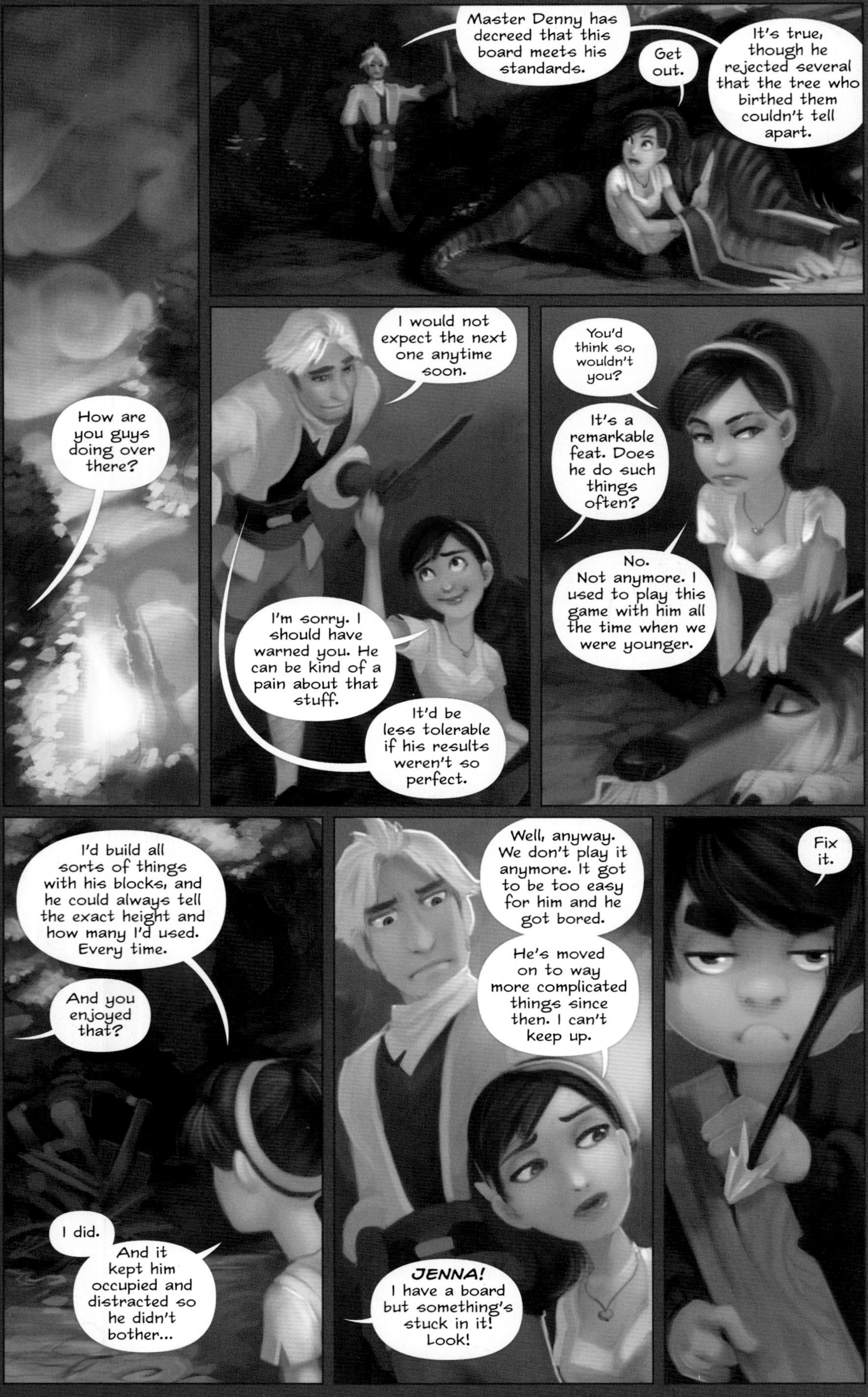
How are you guys doing over there?
Master Denny has decreed that this board meets his standards.
Get out.
It's true, though he rejected several that the tree who birthed them couldn't tell apart.
I would not expect the next one anytime soon.
I'm sorry. I should have warned you. He can be kind of a pain about that stuff.
It'd be less tolerable if his results weren't so perfect.
You'd think so, wouldn't you?
It's a remarkable feat. Does he do such things often?
No. Not anymore. I used to play this game with him all the time when we were younger.
I'd build all sorts of things with his blocks, and he could always tell the exact height and how many I'd used. Every time.
And you enjoyed that?
I did.
And it kept him occupied and distracted so he didn't bother...
Well, anyway. We don't play it anymore. It got to be too easy for him and he got bored.
He's moved on to way more complicated things since then. I can't keep up.
JENNA! I have a board but something's stuck in it! Look!
Fix it.

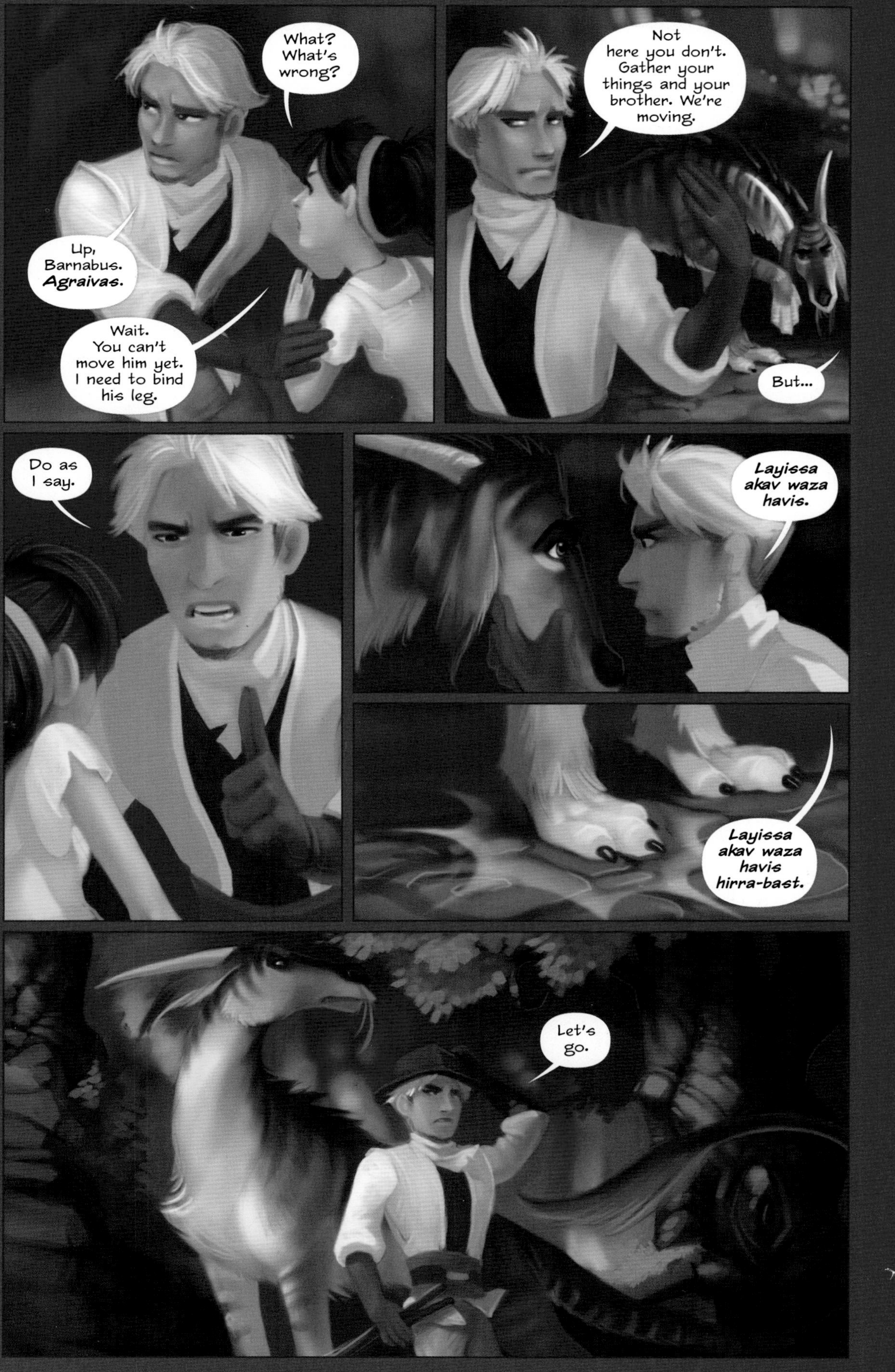
What? What's wrong?
Up, Barnabus. **Agraivas.**
Wait. You can't move him yet. I need to bind his leg.
Not here you don't. Gather your things and your brother. We're moving.
But...
Do as I say.
Layissa akav waza havis.
Layissa akav waza havis hirra-bast.
Let's go.

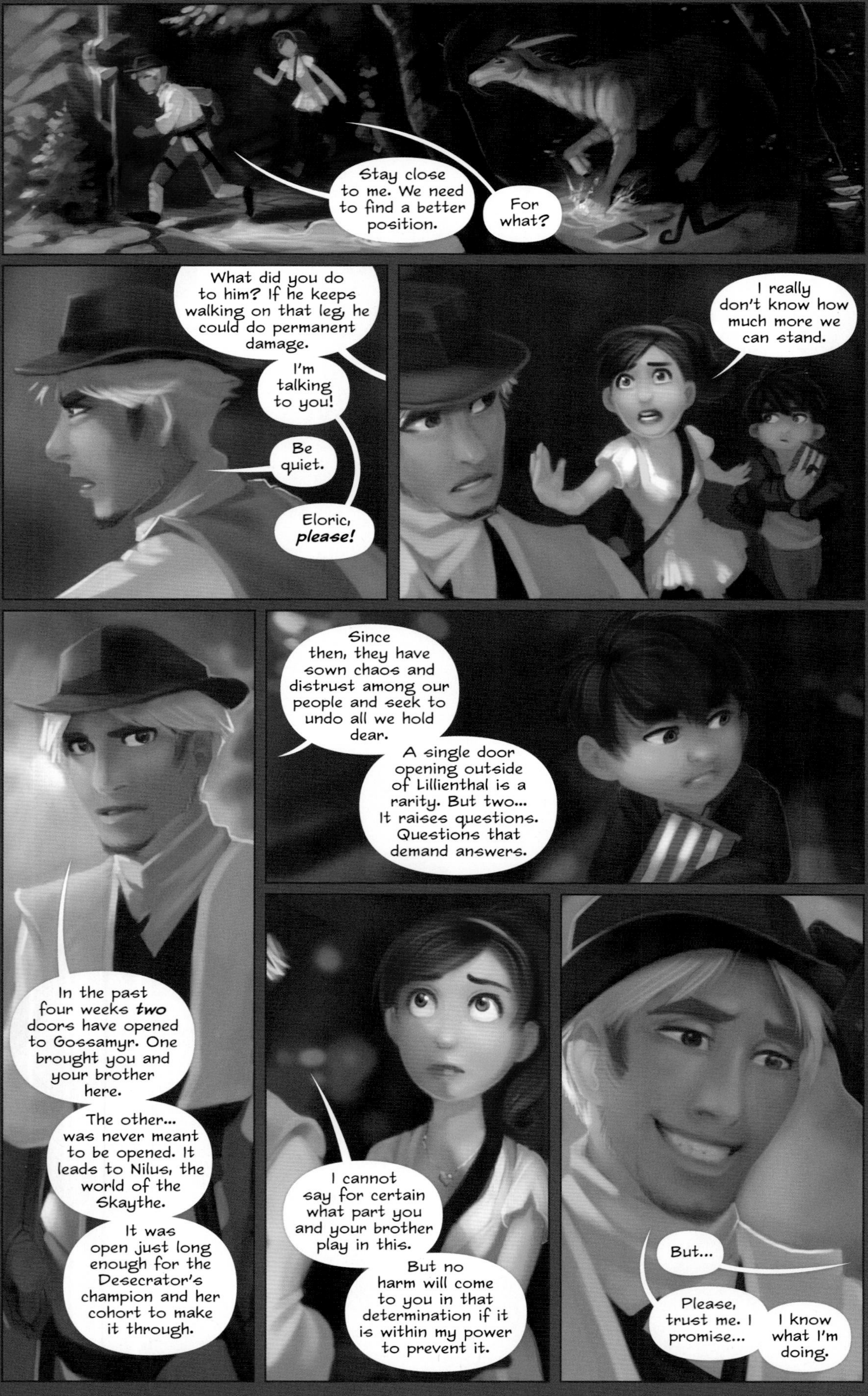
Stay close to me. We need to find a better position.
For what?
What did you do to him? If he keeps walking on that leg, he could do permanent damage.
I'm talking to you!
Be quiet.
Eloric, ***please!***
I really don't know how much more we can stand.
In the past four weeks ***two*** doors have opened to Gossamyr. One brought you and your brother here.
The other... was never meant to be opened. It leads to Nilus, the world of the Skaythe.
It was open just long enough for the Desecrator's champion and her cohort to make it through.
Since then, they have sown chaos and distrust among our people and seek to undo all we hold dear.
A single door opening outside of Lillienthal is a rarity. But two... It raises questions. Questions that demand answers.
I cannot say for certain what part you and your brother play in this.
But no harm will come to you in that determination if it is within my power to prevent it.
But...
Please, trust me. I promise...
I know what I'm doing.

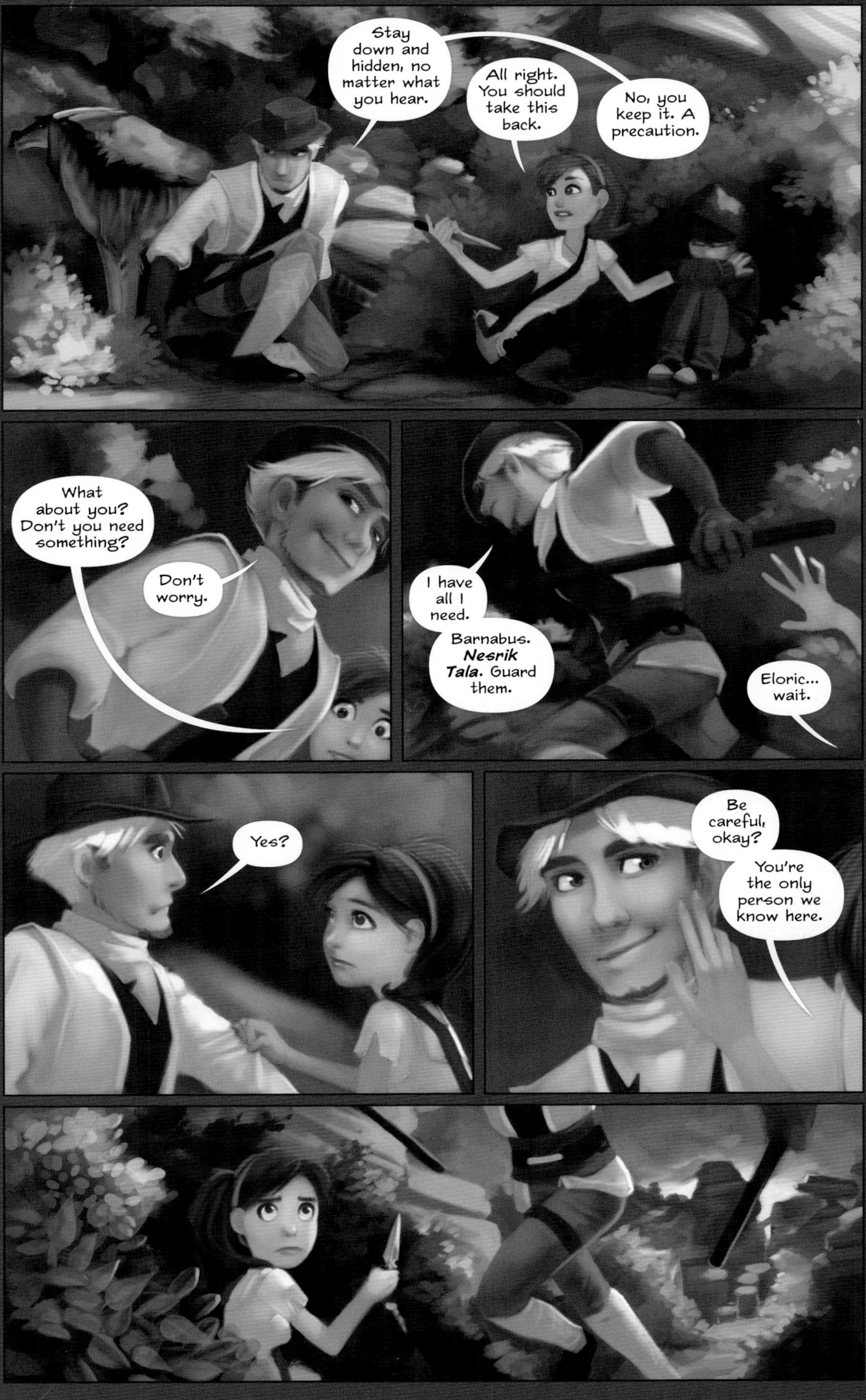
Stay down and hidden, no matter what you hear.
All right. You should take this back.
No, you keep it. A precaution.
What about you? Don't you need something?
Don't worry.
I have all I need.
Barnabus. ***Nesrik Tala***. Guard them.
Eloric... wait.
Yes?
Be careful, okay?
You're the only person we know here.

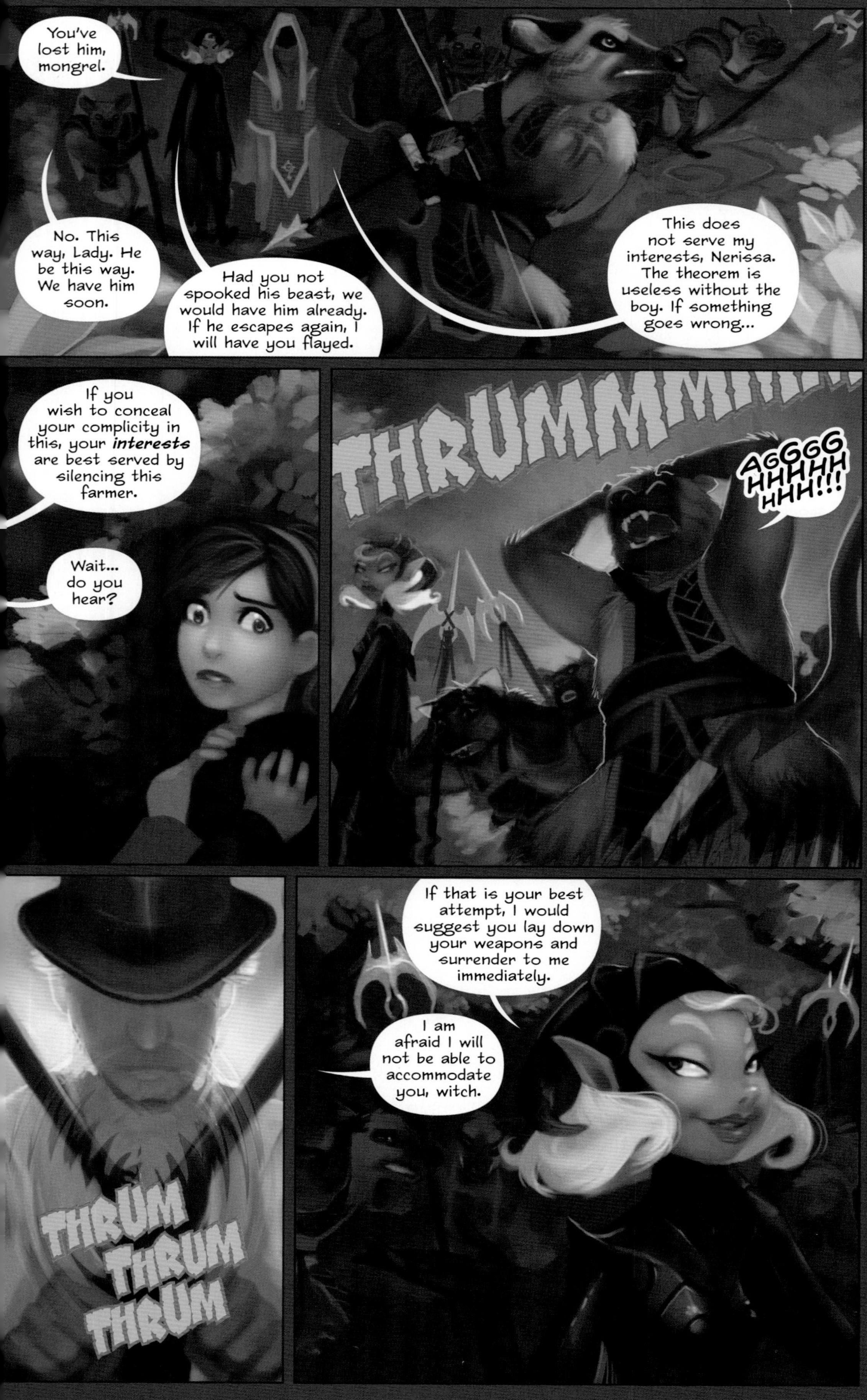
You've lost him, mongrel.
No. This way, Lady. He be this way. We have him soon.
Had you not spooked his beast, we would have him already. If he escapes again, I will have you flayed.
This does not serve my interests, Nerissa. The theorem is useless without the boy. If something goes wrong...
If you wish to conceal your complicity in this, your *interests* are best served by silencing this farmer.
Wait... do you hear?
THRUMMMM
AGGGG HHHHH HHH!!!
THRUM THRUM THRUM
If that is your best attempt, I would suggest you lay down your weapons and surrender to me immediately.
I am afraid I will not be able to accommodate you, witch.

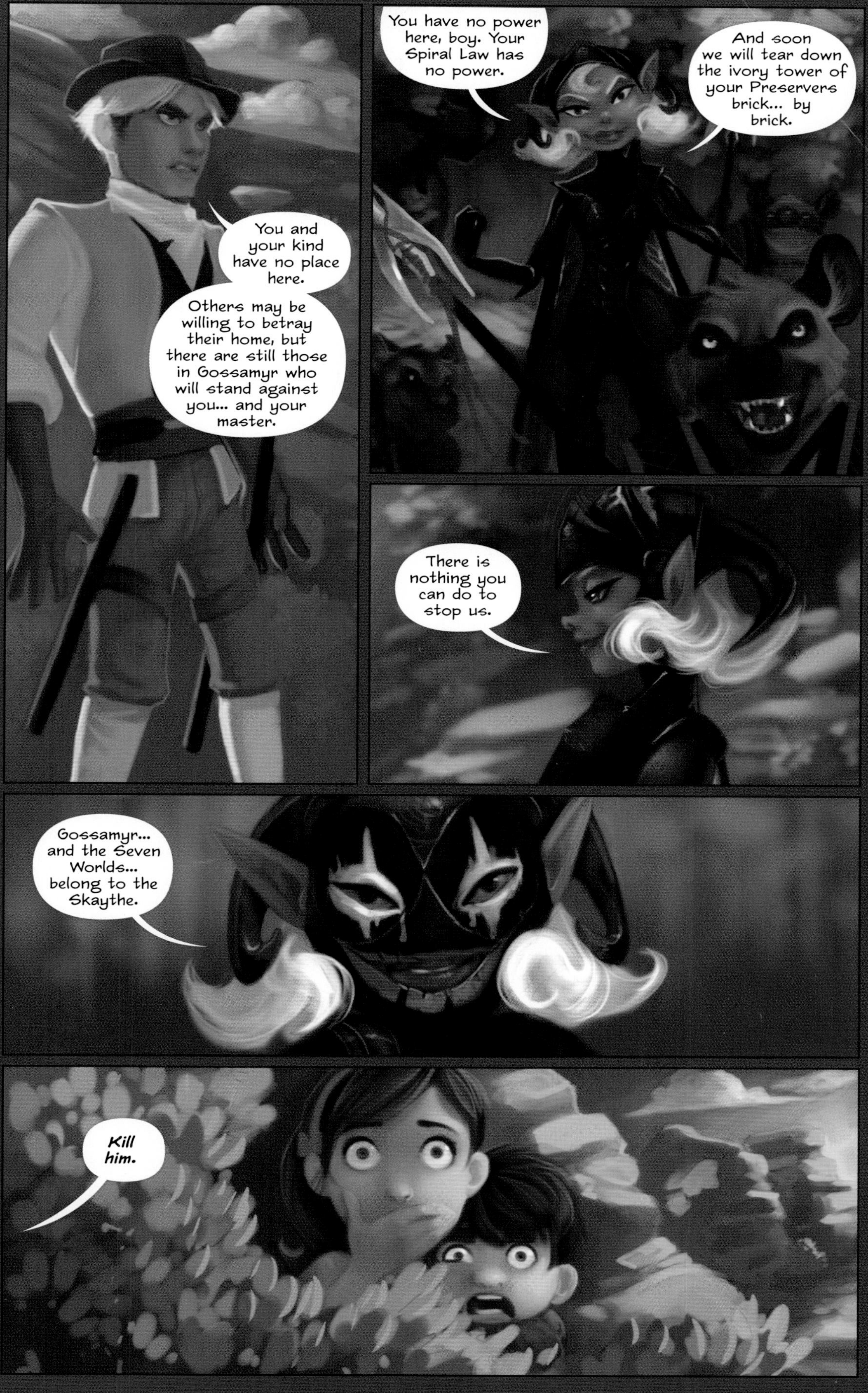
You and your kind have no place here.
Others may be willing to betray their home, but there are still those in Gossamyr who will stand against you... and your master.
You have no power here, boy. Your Spiral Law has no power.
And soon we will tear down the ivory tower of your Preservers brick... by brick.
There is nothing you can do to stop us.
Gossamyr... and the Seven Worlds... belong to the Skaythe.
Kill him.

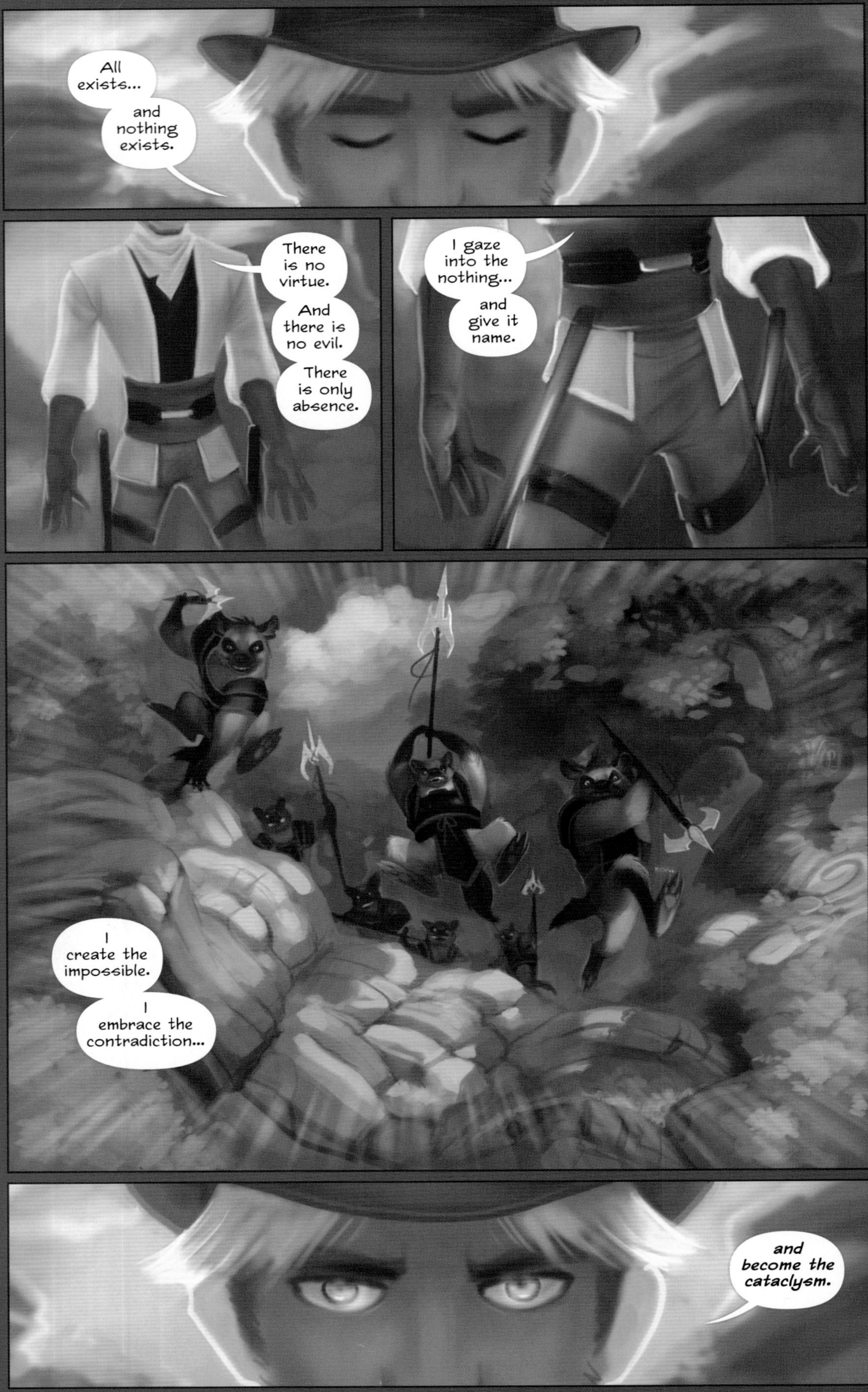
All exists...
and nothing exists.
There is no virtue.
And there is no evil.
There is only absence.
I gaze into the nothing...
and give it name.
I create the impossible.
I embrace the contradiction...
and become the cataclysm.

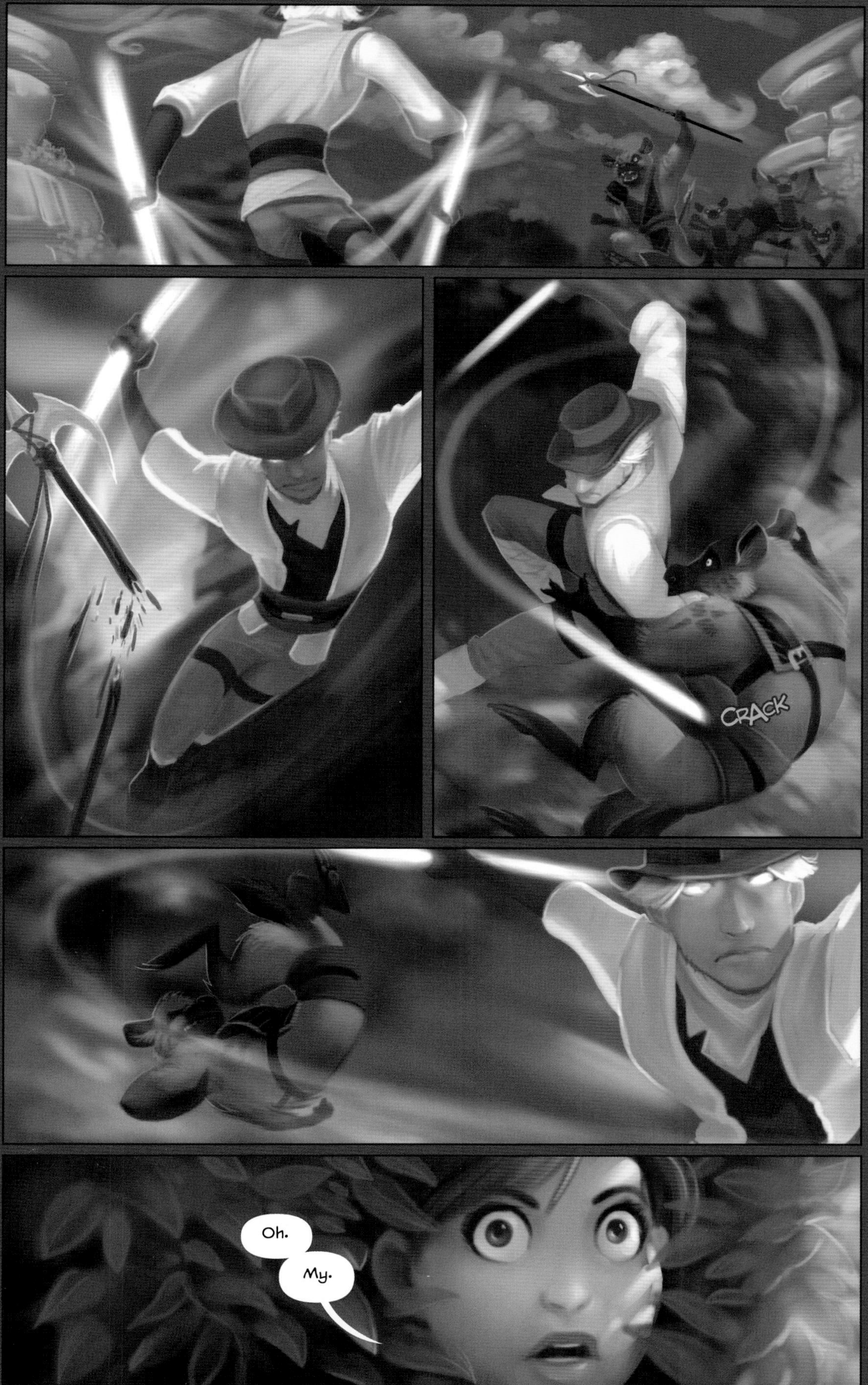
CRACK
Oh.
My.

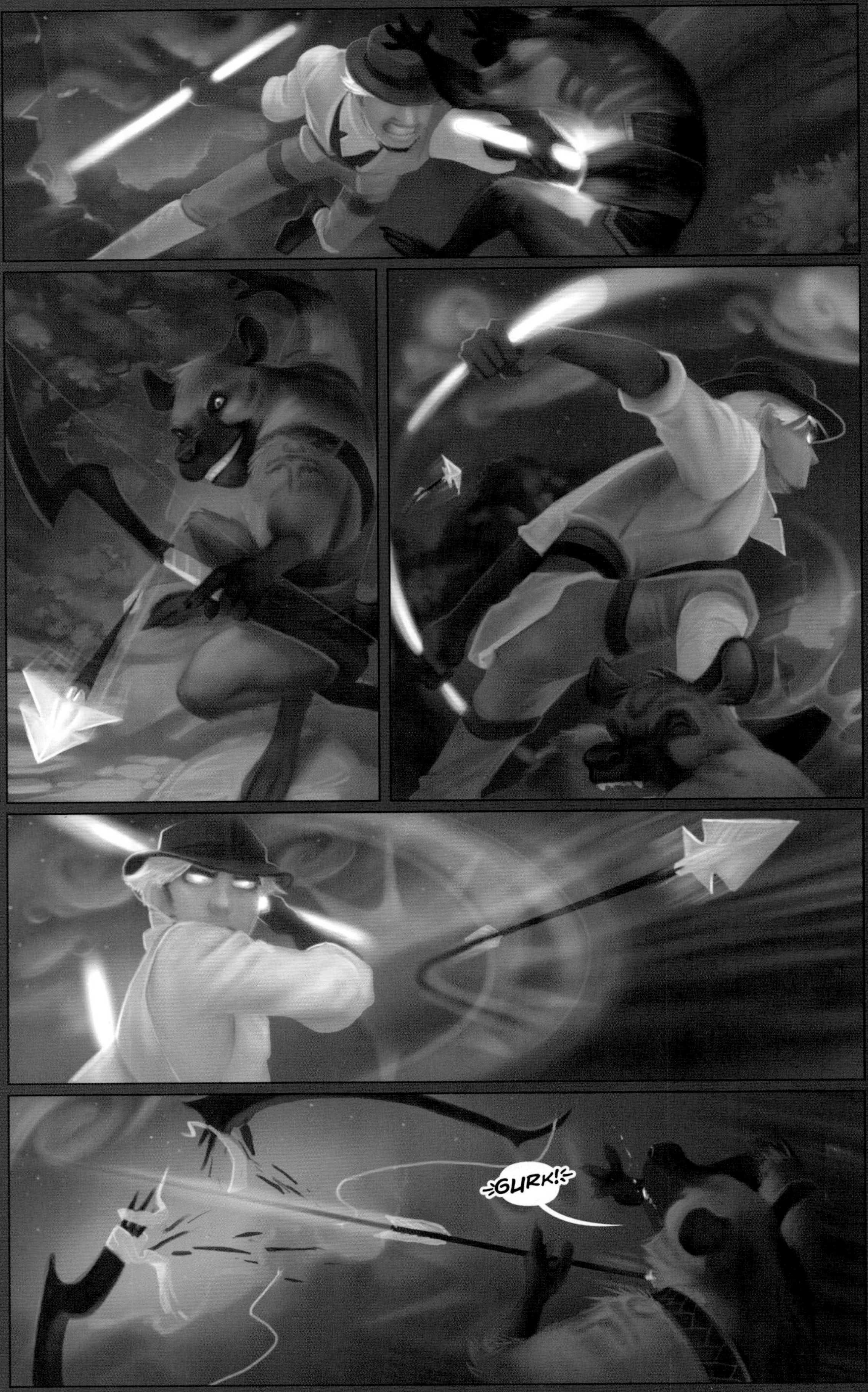
GURK!

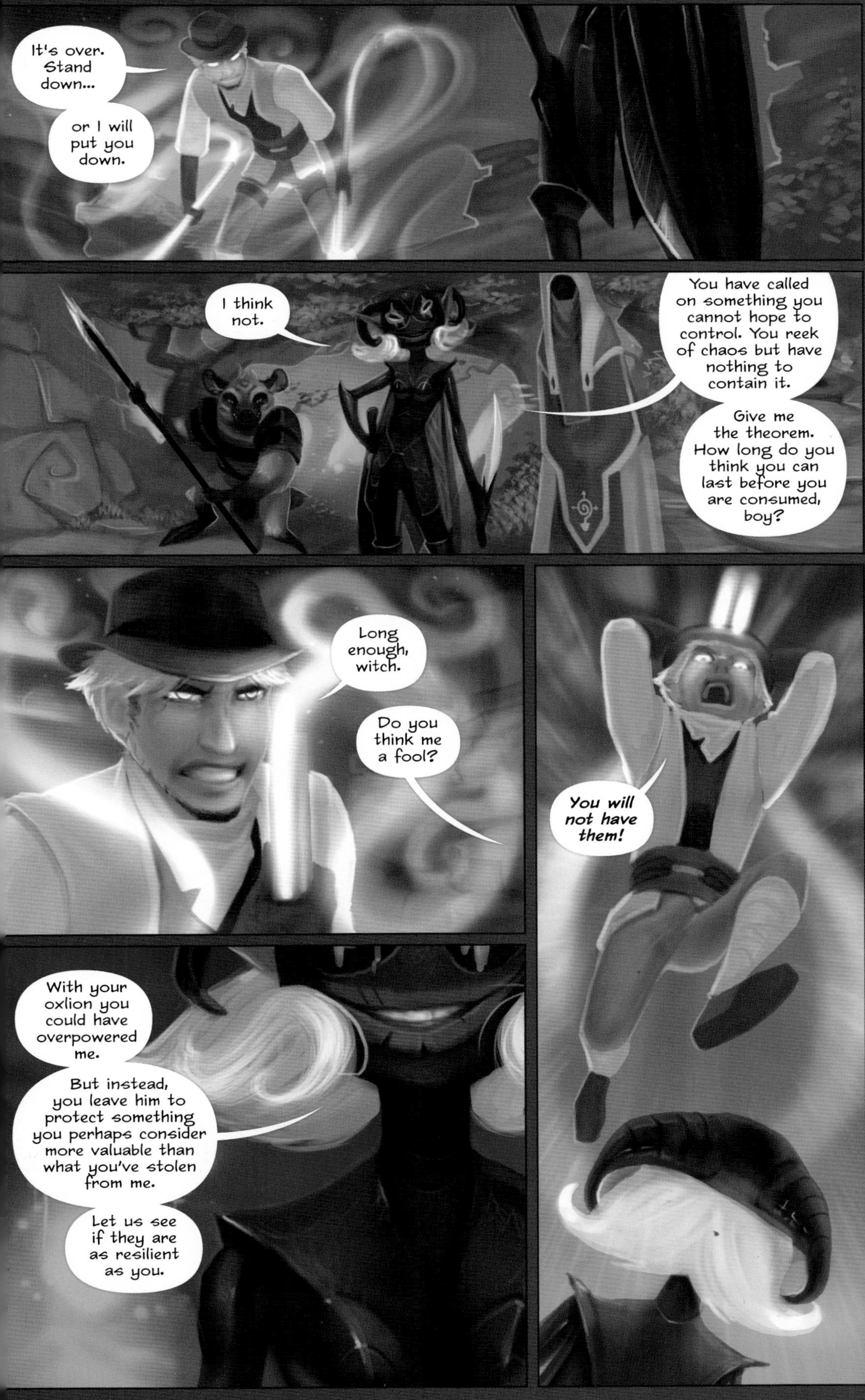
It's over. Stand down...
or I will put you down.
I think not.
You have called on something you cannot hope to control. You reek of chaos but have nothing to contain it.
Give me the theorem. How long do you think you can last before you are consumed, boy?
Long enough, witch.
Do you think me a fool?
With your oxlion you could have overpowered me.
But instead, you leave him to protect something you perhaps consider more valuable than what you've stolen from me.
Let us see if they are as resilient as you.
You will not have them!

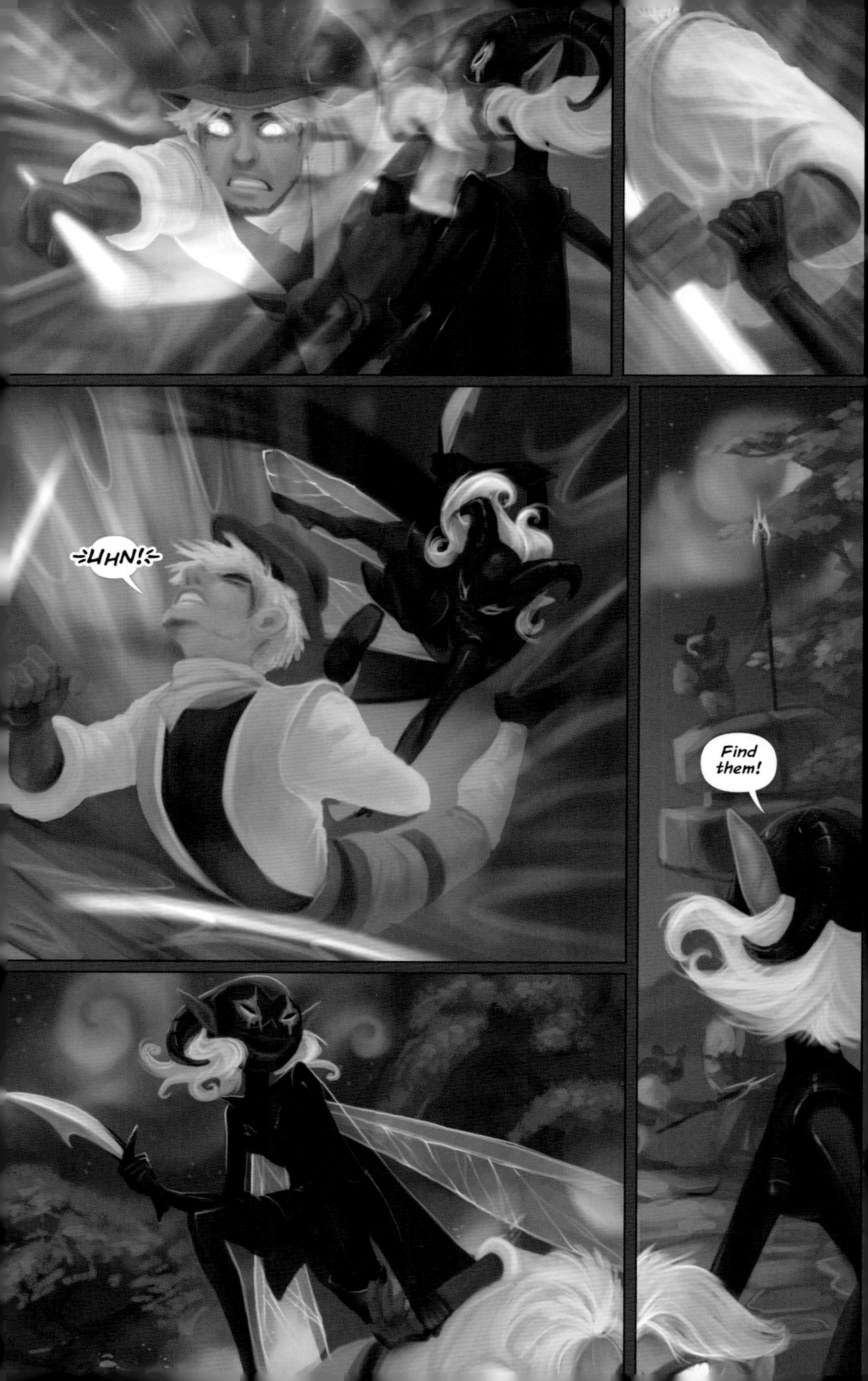
UHN!
Find them!

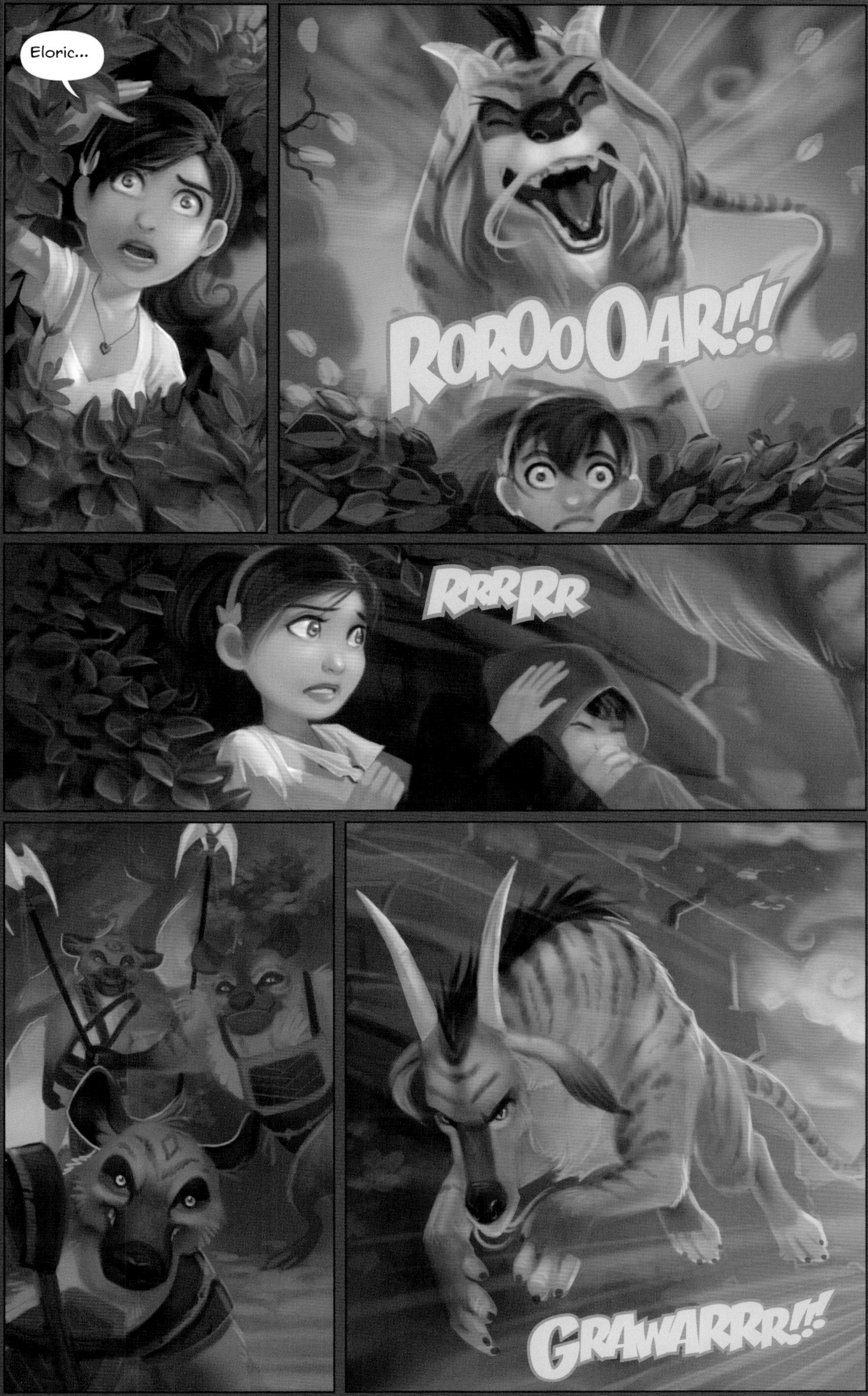
Eloric...
ROROOOAR!!!
RRRRR
GRAWARRR!!!

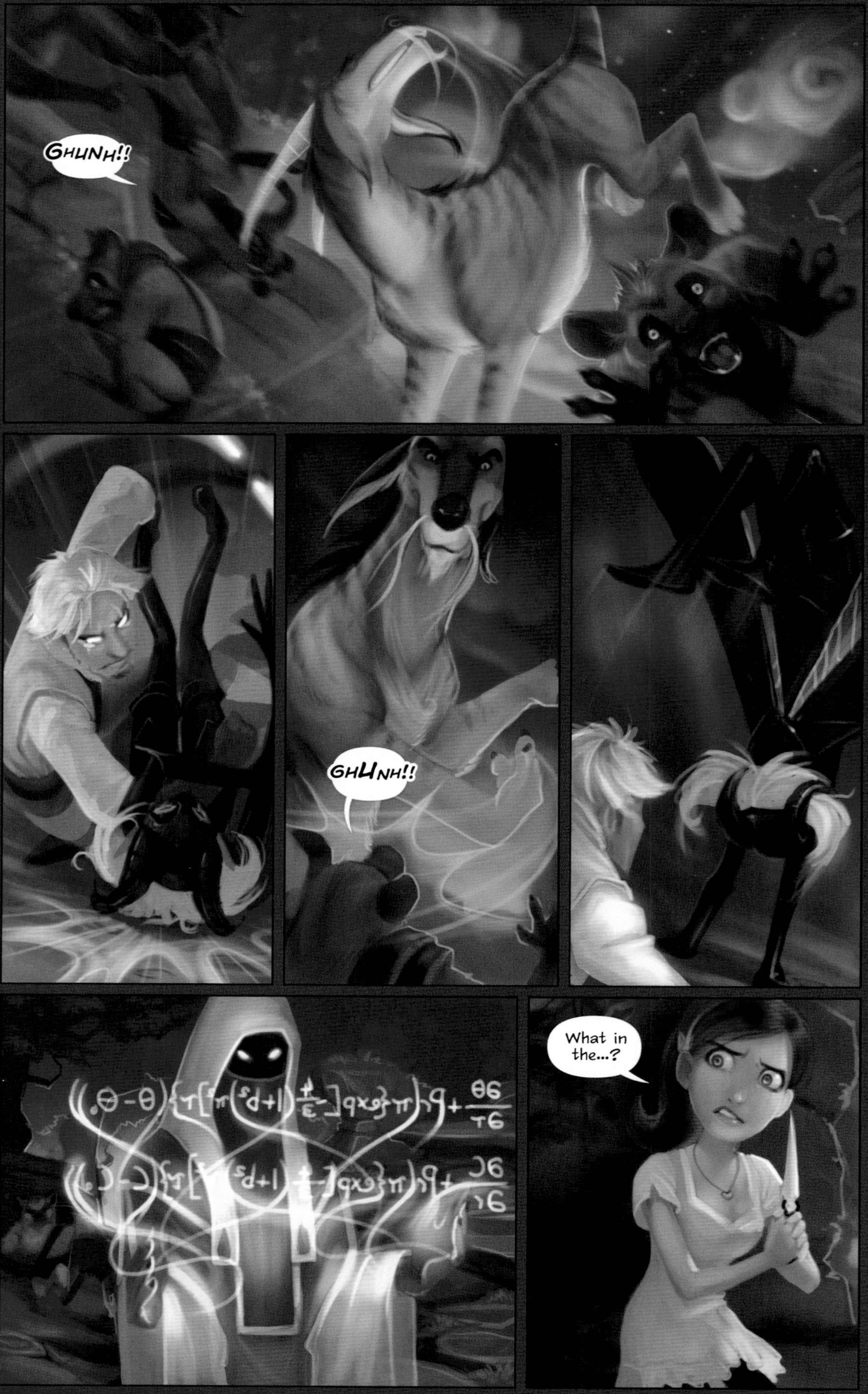
GHUNH!!
GHUNH!!
What in the...?

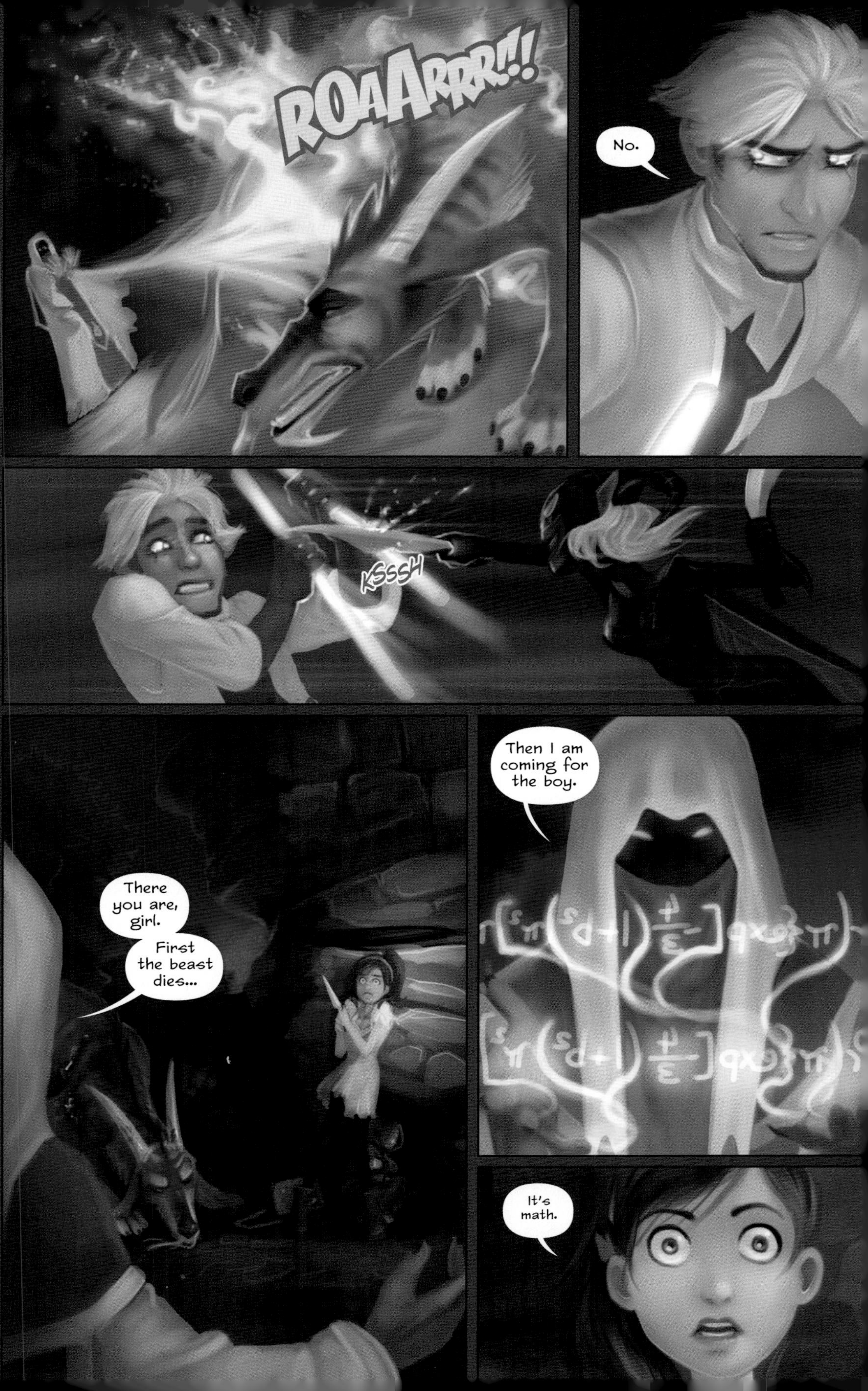
ROAARRR!!
No.
KSSSH
There you are, girl.
First the beast dies...
Then I am coming for the boy.
It's math.

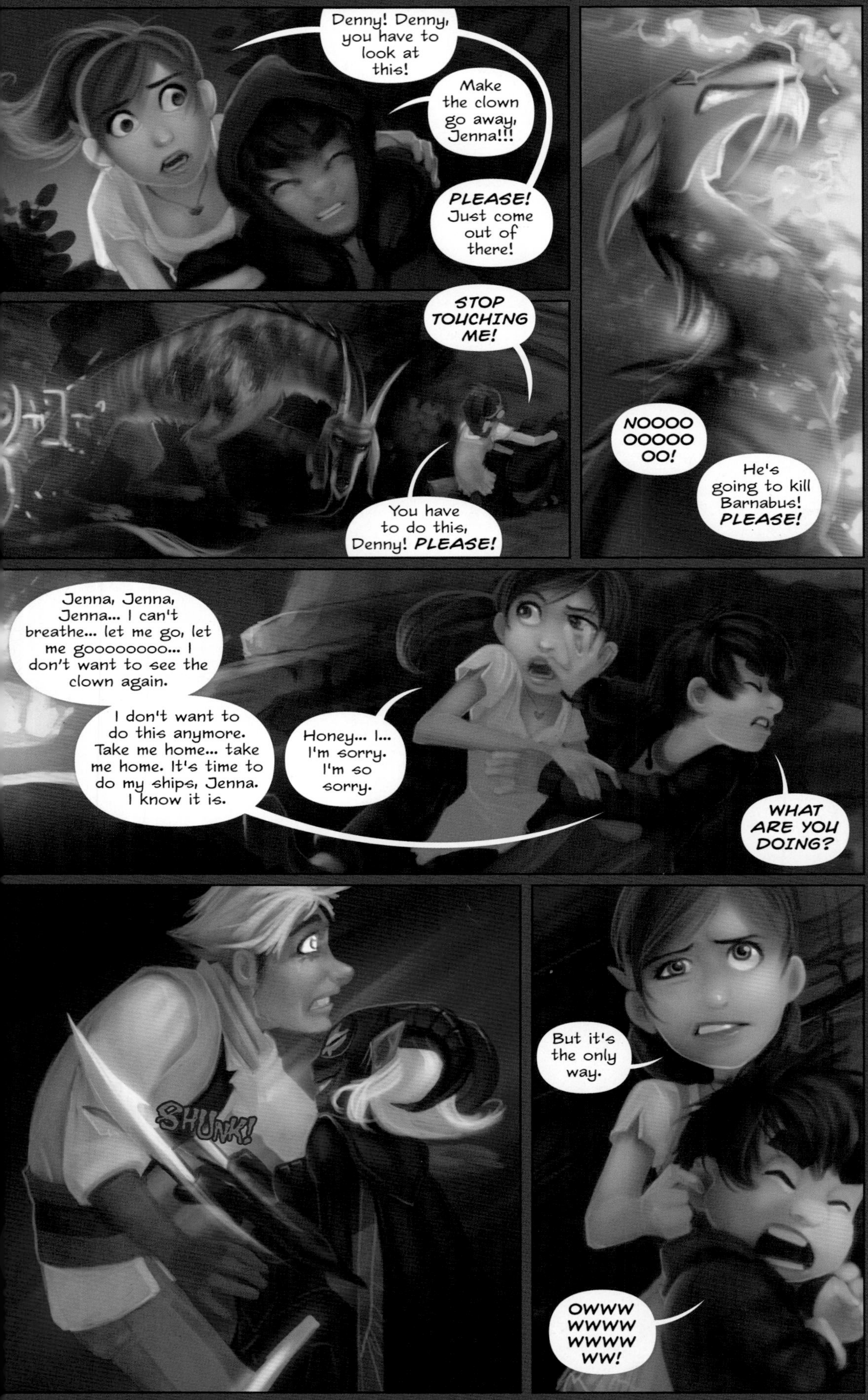
Denny! Denny, you have to look at this!
Make the clown go away, Jenna!!!
PLEASE! Just come out of there!
STOP TOUCHING ME!
You have to do this, Denny! PLEASE!
NOOOOOOOOOOO!
He's going to kill Barnabus! PLEASE!
Jenna, Jenna, Jenna... I can't breathe... let me go, let me goooooooo... I don't want to see the clown again.
I don't want to do this anymore. Take me home... take me home. It's time to do my ships, Jenna. I know it is.
Honey... I... I'm sorry. I'm so sorry.
WHAT ARE YOU DOING?
SHUNK!
But it's the only way.
OWWWWWWWWWWWWWW!

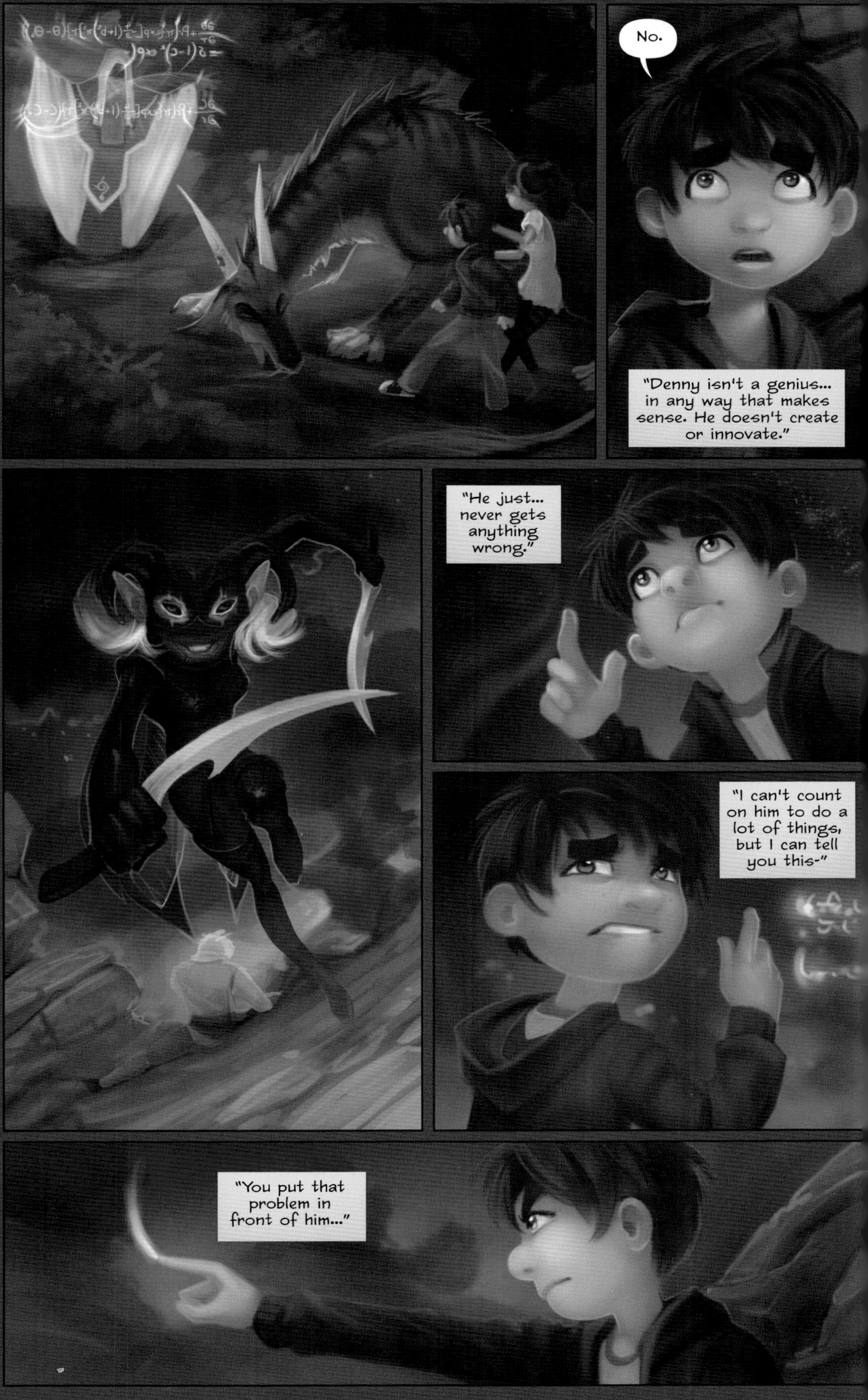
No.
"Denny isn't a genius... in any way that makes sense. He doesn't create or innovate."
"He just... never gets anything wrong."
"I can't count on him to do a lot of things, but I can tell you this-"
"You put that problem in front of him..."

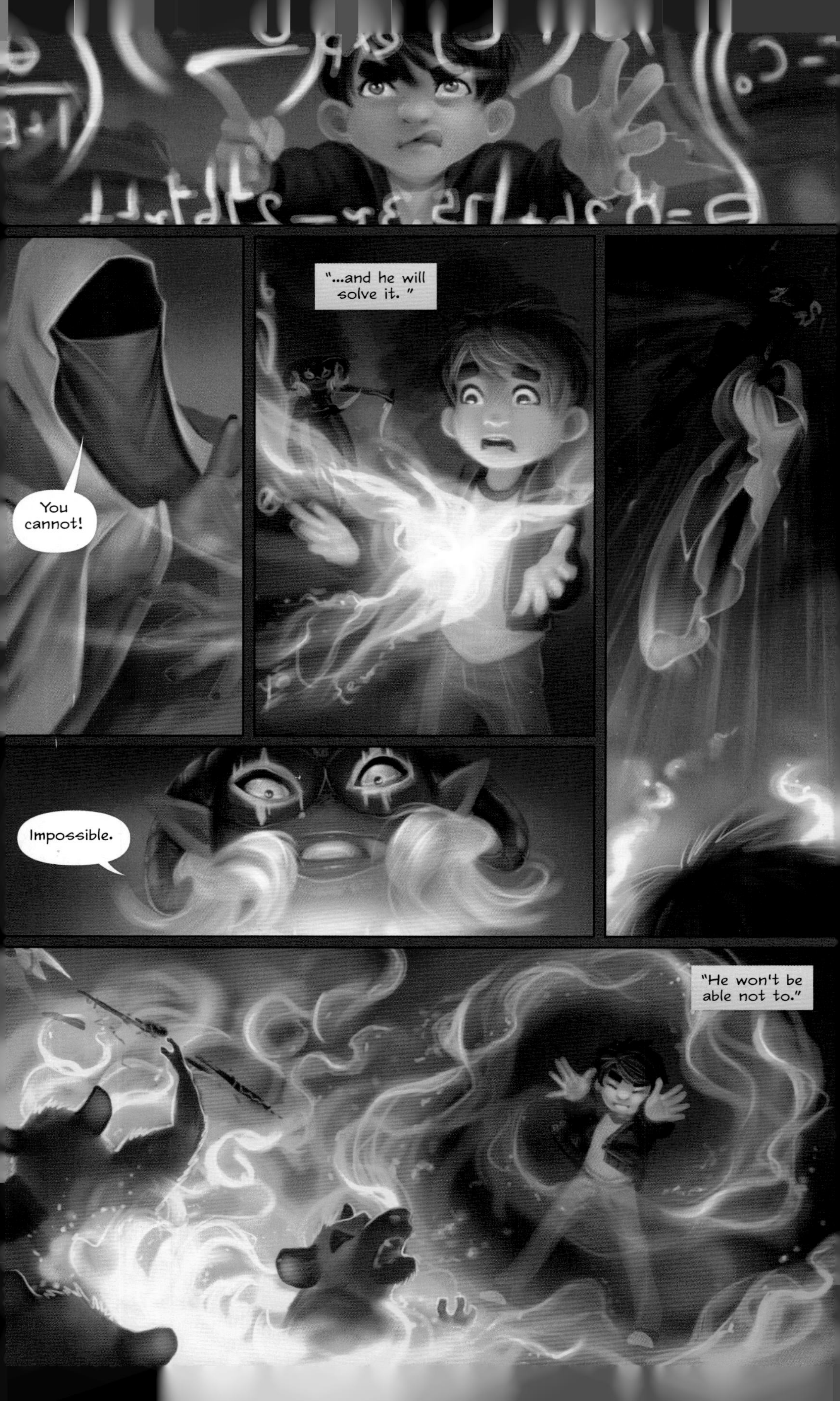
You cannot!
"...and he will solve it."
Impossible.
"He won't be able not to."

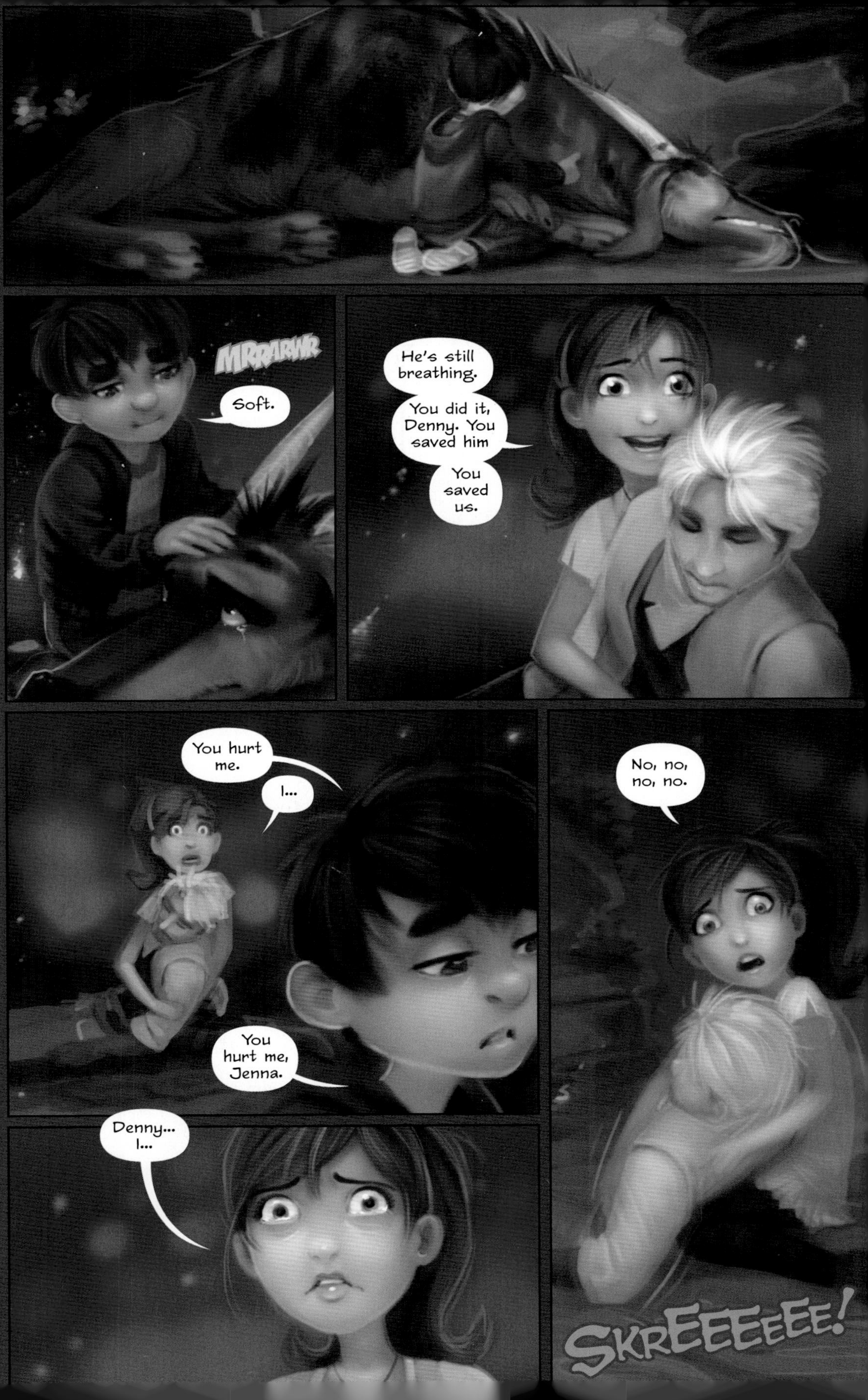

MRRARWR
Soft.
He's still breathing.
You did it, Denny. You saved him
You saved us.
You hurt me.
I...
You hurt me, Jenna.
No, no, no, no.
Denny... I...
SKREEEEEEE!

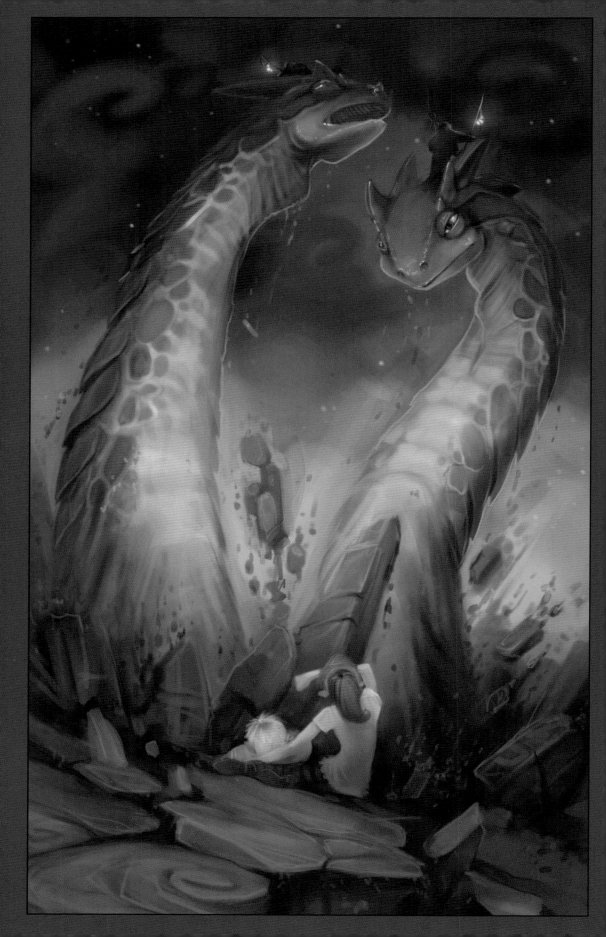

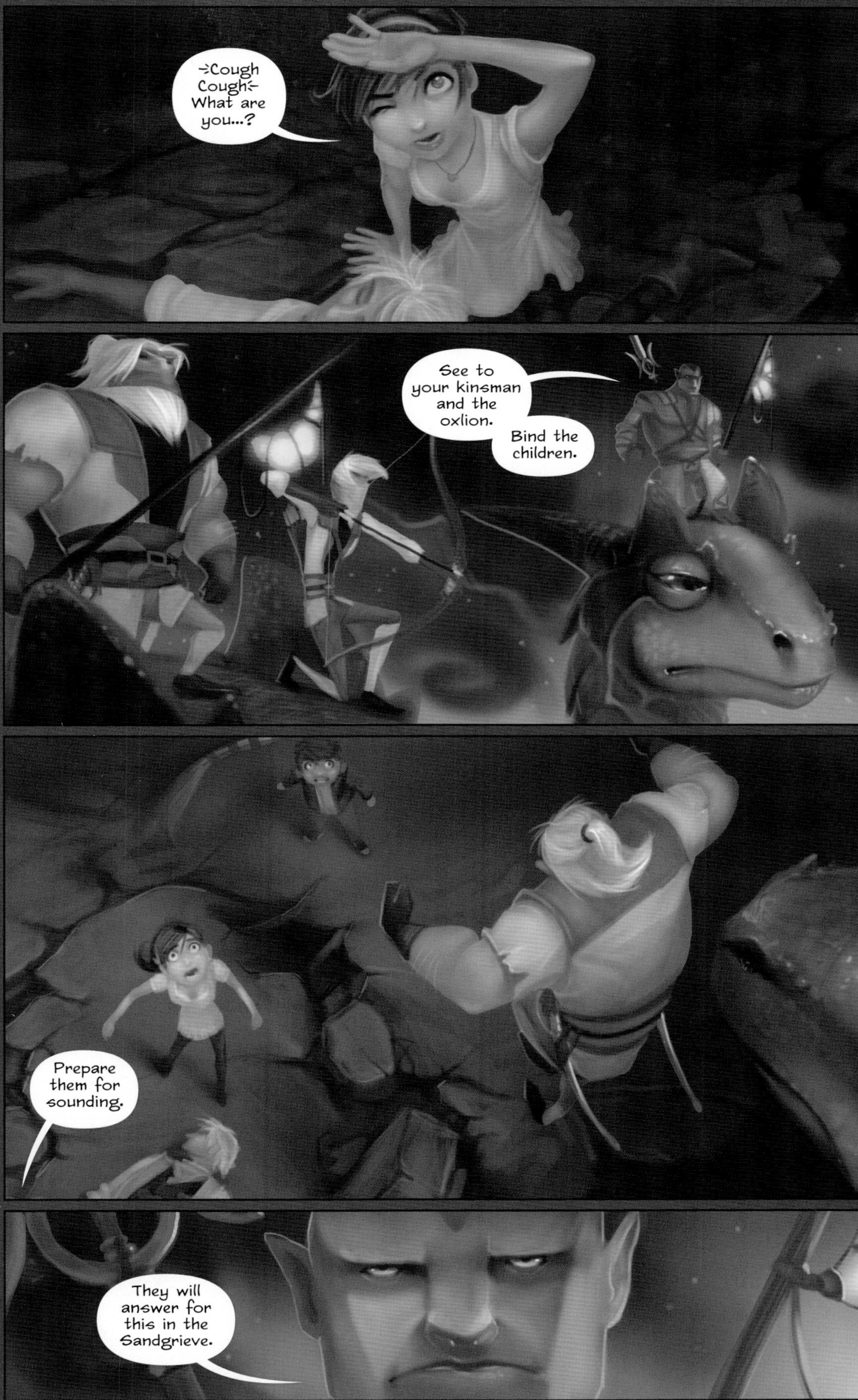

=Cough Cough= What are you...?
See to your kinsman and the oxlion.
Bind the children.
Prepare them for sounding.
They will answer for this in the Sandgrieve.

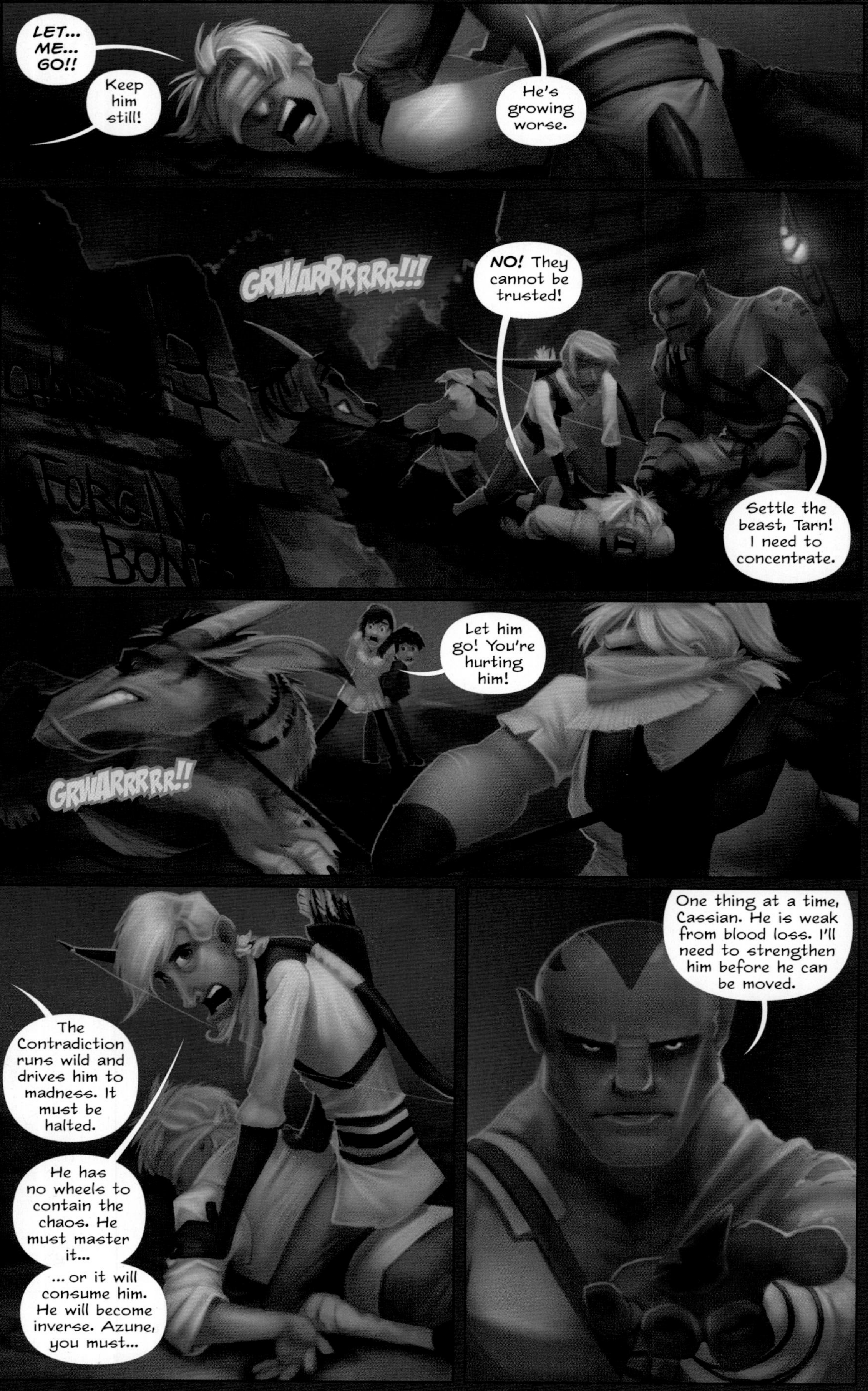
LET... ME... GO!!
Keep him still!
He's growing worse.
GRWARRRRRR!!!
NO! They cannot be trusted!
Settle the beast, Tarn! I need to concentrate.
Let him go! You're hurting him!
GRWARRRRR!!
The Contradiction runs wild and drives him to madness. It must be halted.
He has no wheels to contain the chaos. He must master it...
...or it will consume him. He will become inverse. Azune, you must...
One thing at a time, Cassian. He is weak from blood loss. I'll need to strengthen him before he can be moved.

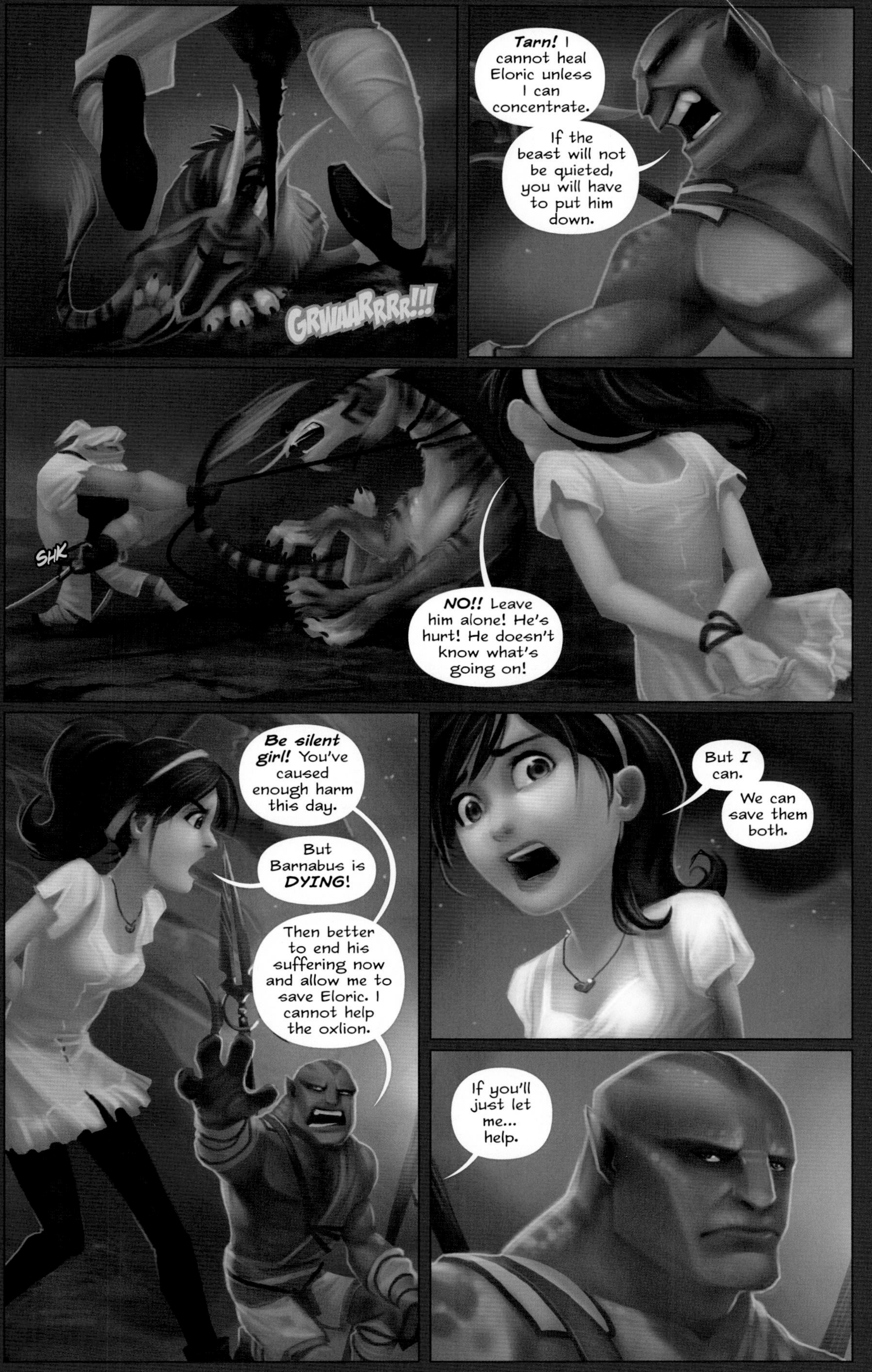
GRWAARRRR!!!
Tarn! I cannot heal Eloric unless I can concentrate.
If the beast will not be quieted, you will have to put him down.
SHK
NO!! Leave him alone! He's hurt! He doesn't know what's going on!
Be silent girl! You've caused enough harm this day.
But Barnabus is DYING!
Then better to end his suffering now and allow me to save Eloric. I cannot help the oxlion.
But I can.
We can save them both.
If you'll just let me... help.

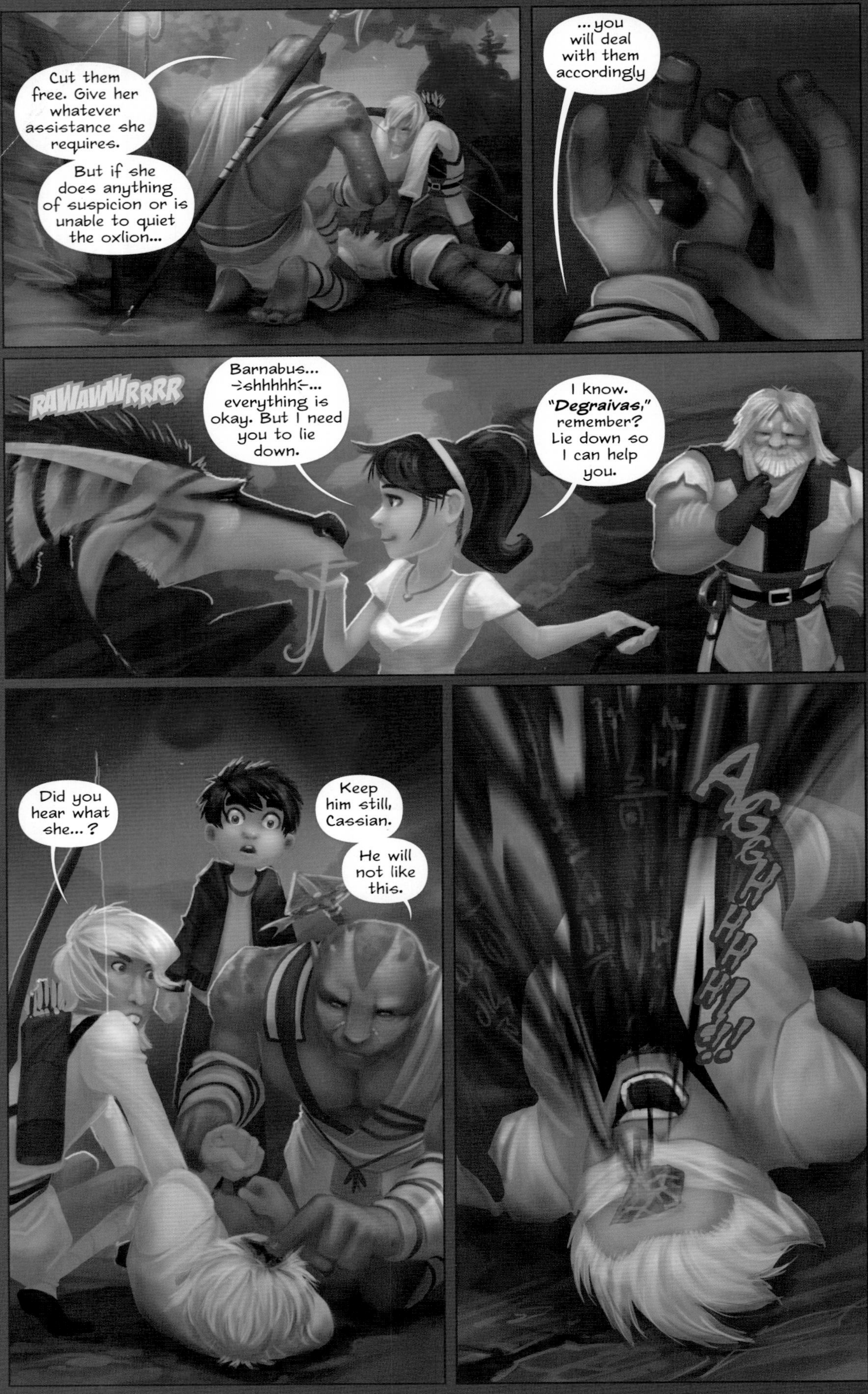
Cut them free. Give her whatever assistance she requires.
But if she does anything of suspicion or is unable to quiet the oxlion...
...you will deal with them accordingly
RAWAWWRRRR
Barnabus... ~shhhhh~... everything is okay. But I need you to lie down.
I know. "Degraivas," remember? Lie down so I can help you.
Did you hear what she...?
Keep him still, Cassian.
He will not like this.
AGGHHHHH!!!

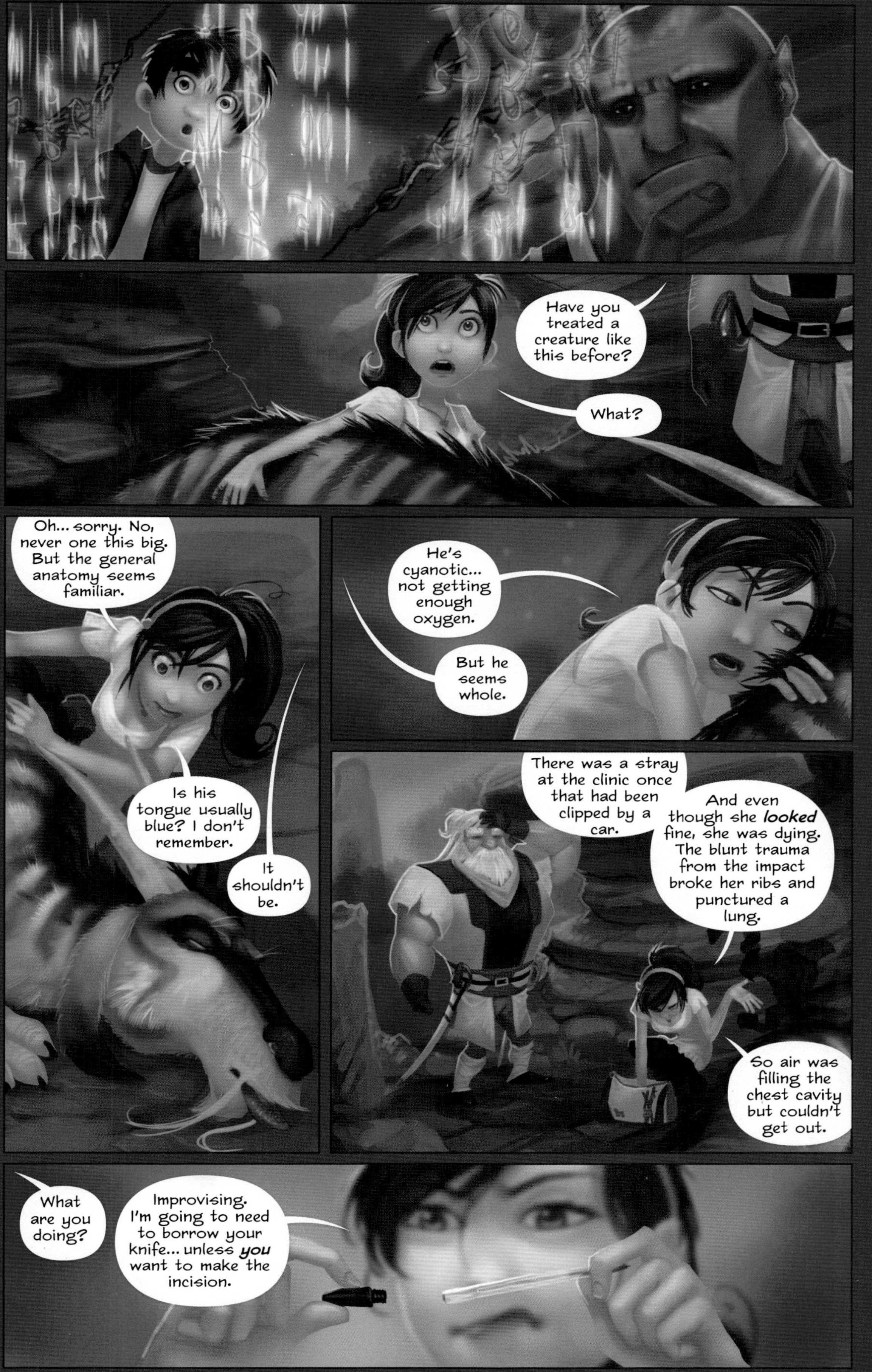
Have you treated a creature like this before?
What?
Oh... sorry. No, never one this big. But the general anatomy seems familiar.
Is his tongue usually blue? I don't remember.
It shouldn't be.
He's cyanotic... not getting enough oxygen.
But he seems whole.
There was a stray at the clinic once that had been clipped by a car.
And even though she *looked* fine, she was dying. The blunt trauma from the impact broke her ribs and punctured a lung.
So air was filling the chest cavity but couldn't get out.
What are you doing?
Improvising. I'm going to need to borrow your knife... unless ***you*** want to make the incision.

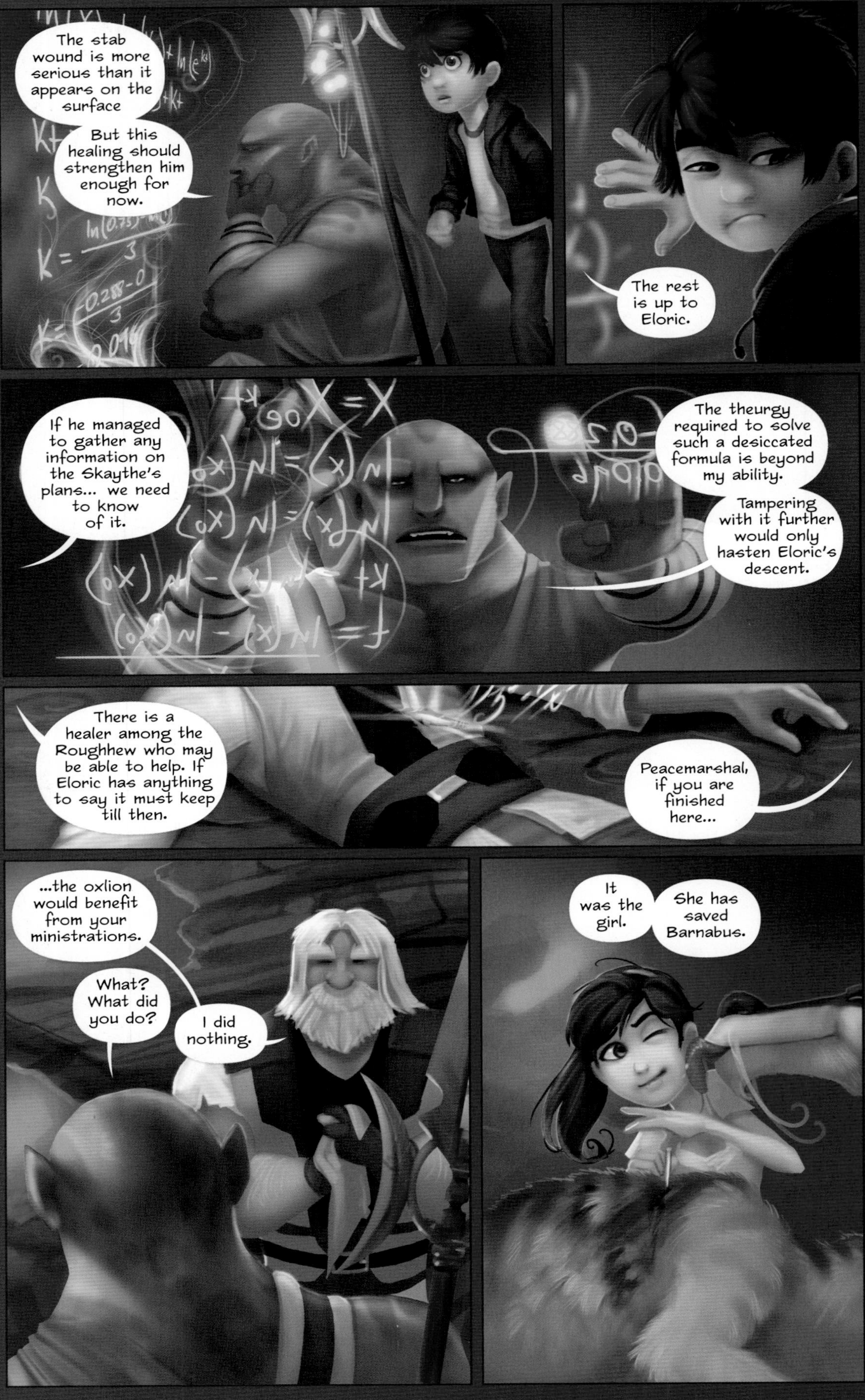
The stab wound is more serious than it appears on the surface
But this healing should strengthen him enough for now.
The rest is up to Eloric.
If he managed to gather any information on the Skaythe's plans... we need to know of it.
The theurgy required to solve such a desiccated formula is beyond my ability.
Tampering with it further would only hasten Eloric's descent.
There is a healer among the Roughhew who may be able to help. If Eloric has anything to say it must keep till then.
Peacemarshal, if you are finished here...
...the oxlion would benefit from your ministrations.
What? What did you do?
I did nothing.
It was the girl.
She has saved Barnabus.

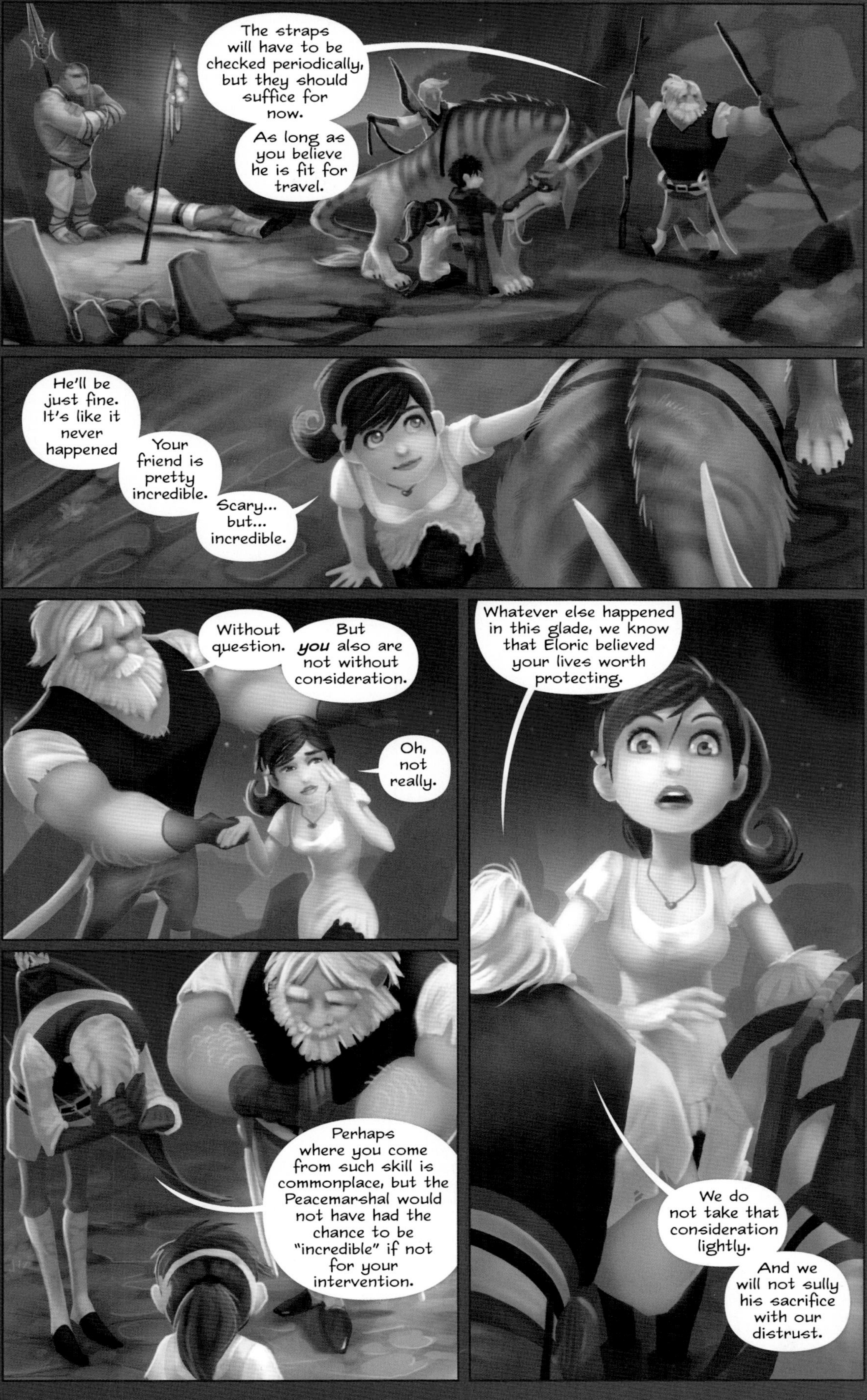

The straps will have to be checked periodically, but they should suffice for now.
As long as you believe he is fit for travel.
He'll be just fine. It's like it never happened
Your friend is pretty incredible.
Scary... but... incredible.
Without question.
But *you* also are not without consideration.
Oh, not really.
Perhaps where you come from such skill is commonplace, but the Peacemarshal would not have had the chance to be "incredible" if not for your intervention.
Whatever else happened in this glade, we know that Eloric believed your lives worth protecting.
We do not take that consideration lightly.
And we will not sully his sacrifice with our distrust.

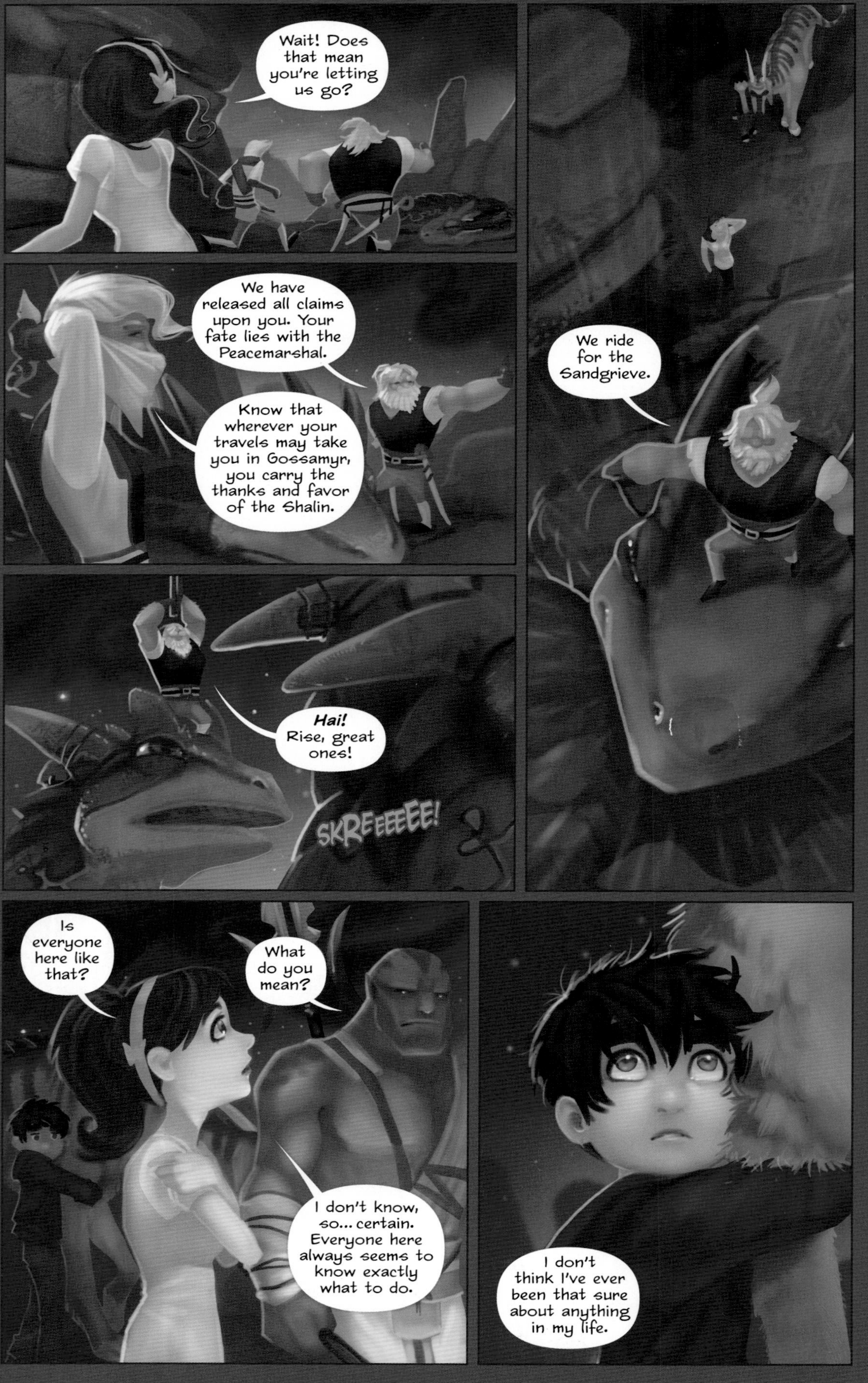

Wait! Does that mean you're letting us go?
We have released all claims upon you. Your fate lies with the Peacemarshal.
Know that wherever your travels may take you in Gossamyr, you carry the thanks and favor of the Shalin.
Hai! Rise, great ones!
SKREEEEEE!
We ride for the Sandgrieve.
Is everyone here like that?
What do you mean?
I don't know, so... certain. Everyone here always seems to know exactly what to do.
I don't think I've ever been that sure about anything in my life.

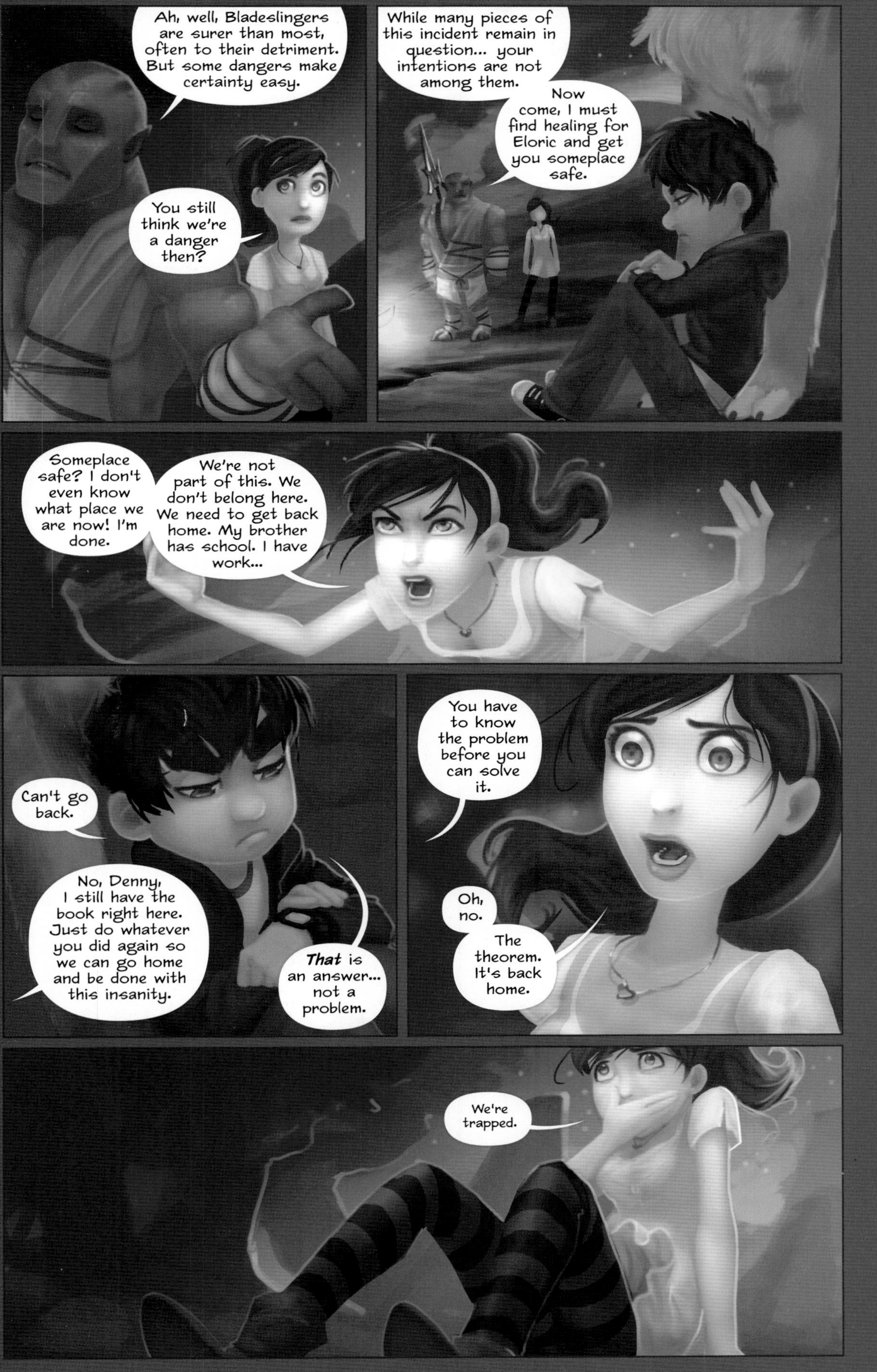
Ah, well, Bladeslingers are surer than most, often to their detriment. But some dangers make certainty easy.
You still think we're a danger then?
While many pieces of this incident remain in question... your intentions are not among them.
Now come, I must find healing for Eloric and get you someplace safe.
Someplace safe? I don't even know what place we are now! I'm done.
We're not part of this. We don't belong here. We need to get back home. My brother has school. I have work...
Can't go back.
No, Denny, I still have the book right here. Just do whatever you did again so we can go home and be done with this insanity.
That is an answer... not a problem.
You have to know the problem before you can solve it.
Oh, no.
The theorem. It's back home.
We're trapped.

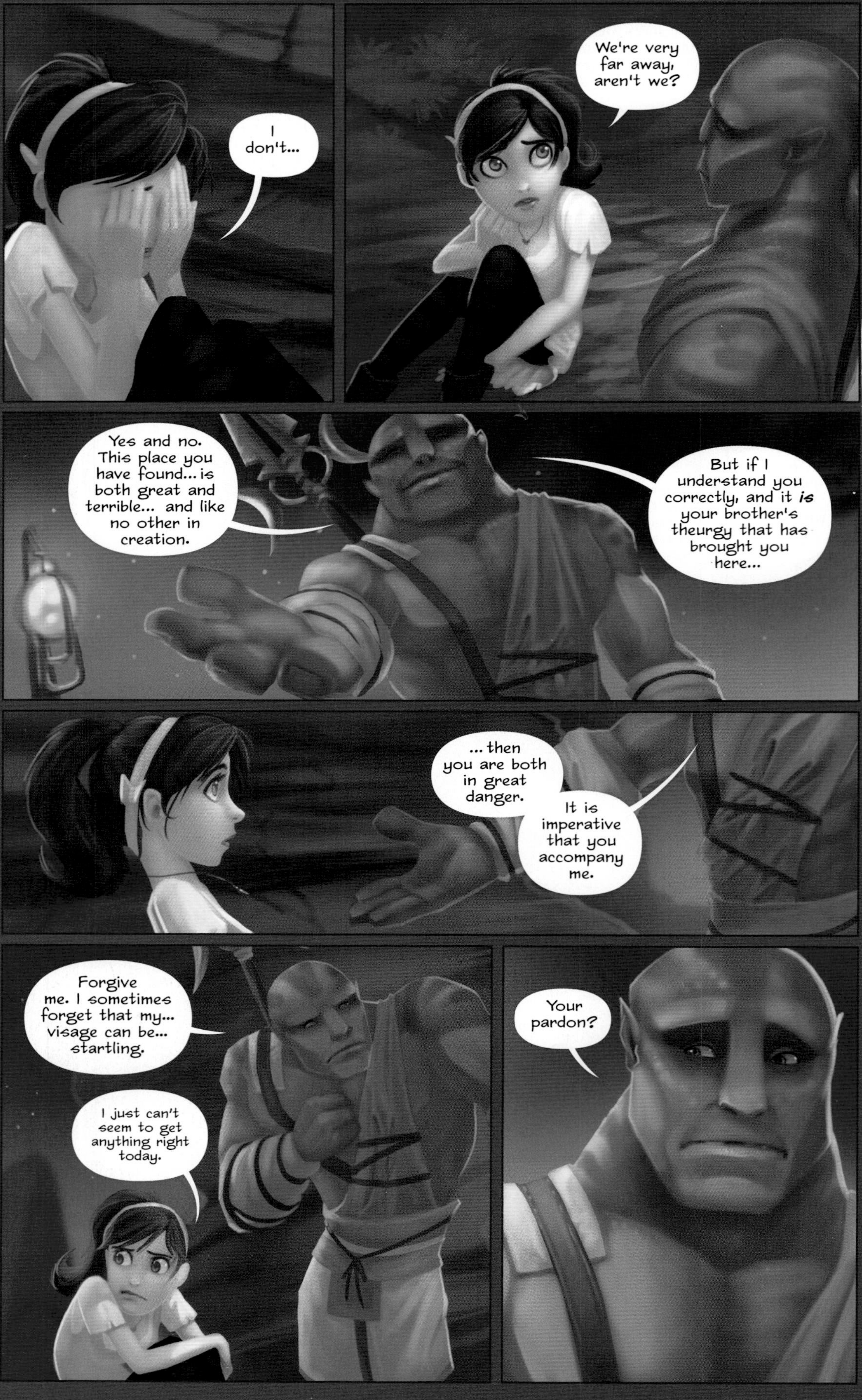
I don't...
We're very far away, aren't we?
Yes and no. This place you have found... is both great and terrible... and like no other in creation.
But if I understand you correctly, and it *is* your brother's theurgy that has brought you here...
...then you are both in great danger.
It is imperative that you accompany me.
Forgive me. I sometimes forget that my... visage can be... startling.
I just can't seem to get anything right today.
Your pardon?

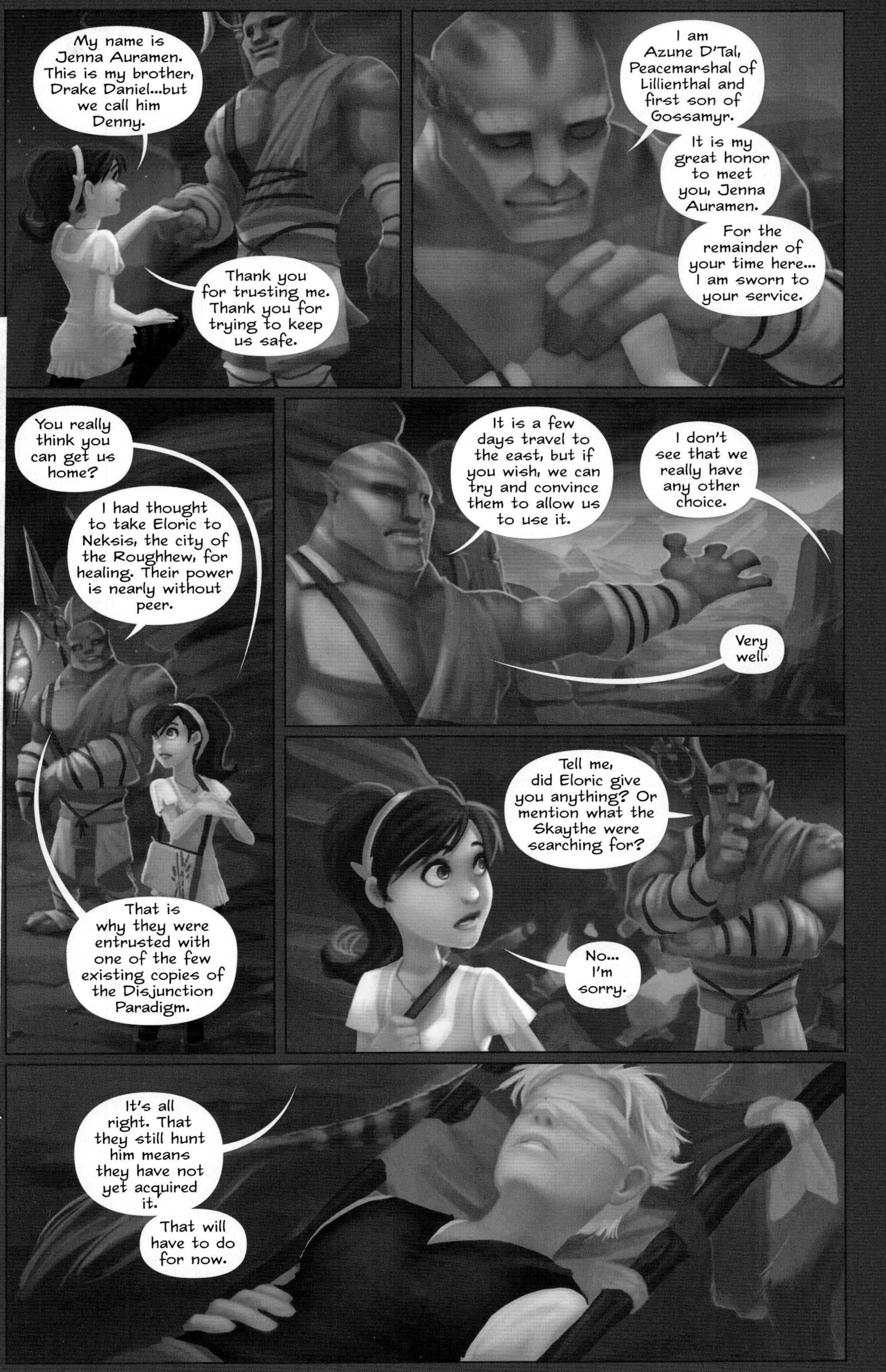
My name is Jenna Auramen. This is my brother, Drake Daniel...but we call him Denny.
Thank you for trusting me. Thank you for trying to keep us safe.
I am Azune D'Tal, Peacemarshal of Lillienthal and first son of Gossamyr.
It is my great honor to meet you, Jenna Auramen.
For the remainder of your time here... I am sworn to your service.
You really think you can get us home?
I had thought to take Eloric to Neksis, the city of the Roughhew, for healing. Their power is nearly without peer.
That is why they were entrusted with one of the few existing copies of the Disjunction Paradigm.
It is a few days travel to the east, but if you wish, we can try and convince them to allow us to use it.
I don't see that we really have any other choice.
Very well.
Tell me, did Eloric give you anything? Or mention what the Skaythe were searching for?
No... I'm sorry.
It's all right. That they still hunt him means they have not yet acquired it.
That will have to do for now.

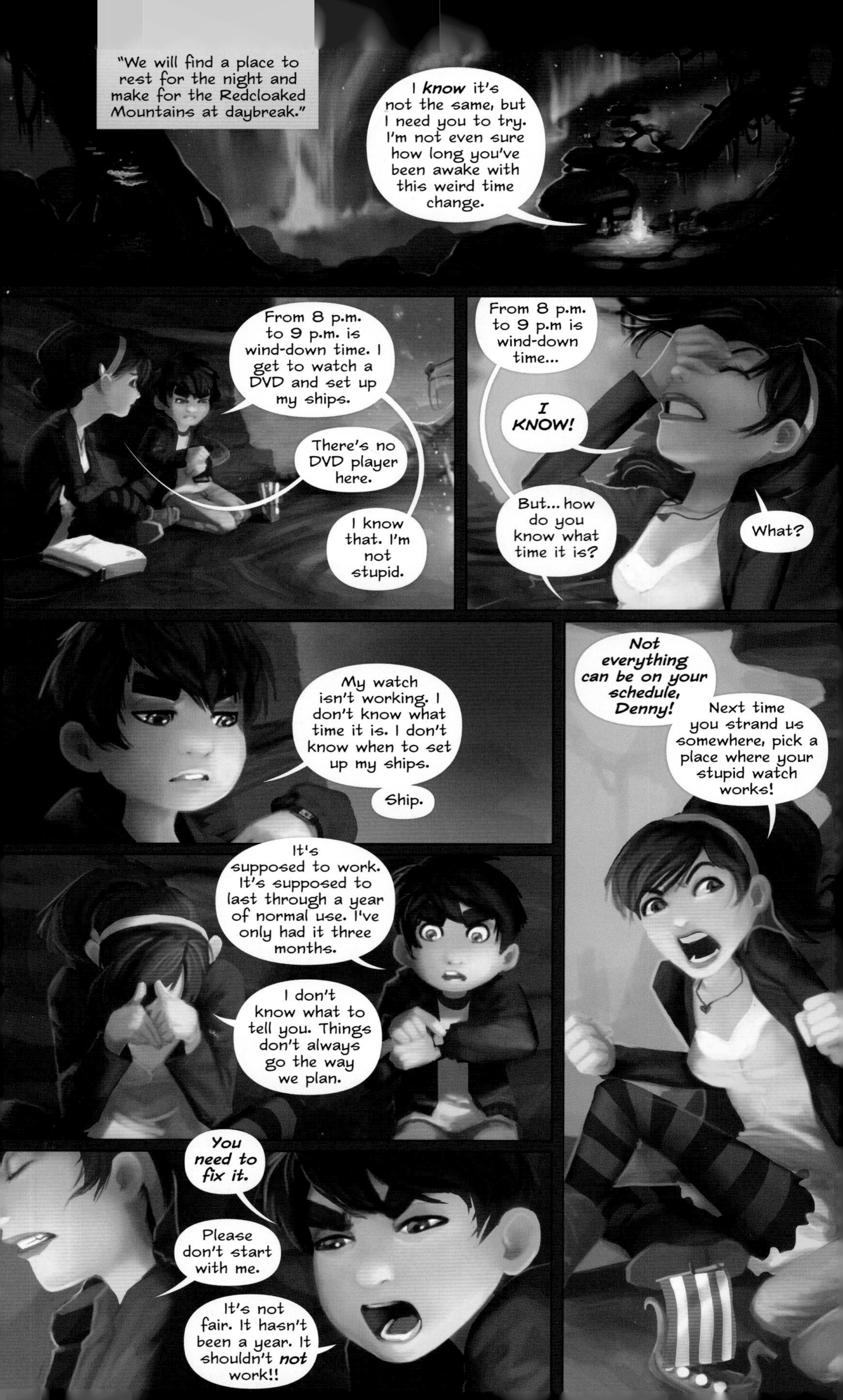

"We will find a place to rest for the night and make for the Redcloaked Mountains at daybreak."
I *know* it's not the same, but I need you to try. I'm not even sure how long you've been awake with this weird time change.
From 8 p.m. to 9 p.m. is wind-down time. I get to watch a DVD and set up my ships.
There's no DVD player here.
I know that. I'm not stupid.
From 8 p.m. to 9 p.m is wind-down time...
I KNOW!
But... how do you know what time it is?
What?
My watch isn't working. I don't know what time it is. I don't know when to set up my ships.
Ship.
It's supposed to work. It's supposed to last through a year of normal use. I've only had it three months.
I don't know what to tell you. Things don't always go the way we plan.
You need to fix it.
Please don't start with me.
It's not fair. It hasn't been a year. It shouldn't *not* work!!
Not everything can be on your schedule, Denny!
Next time you strand us somewhere, pick a place where your stupid watch works!

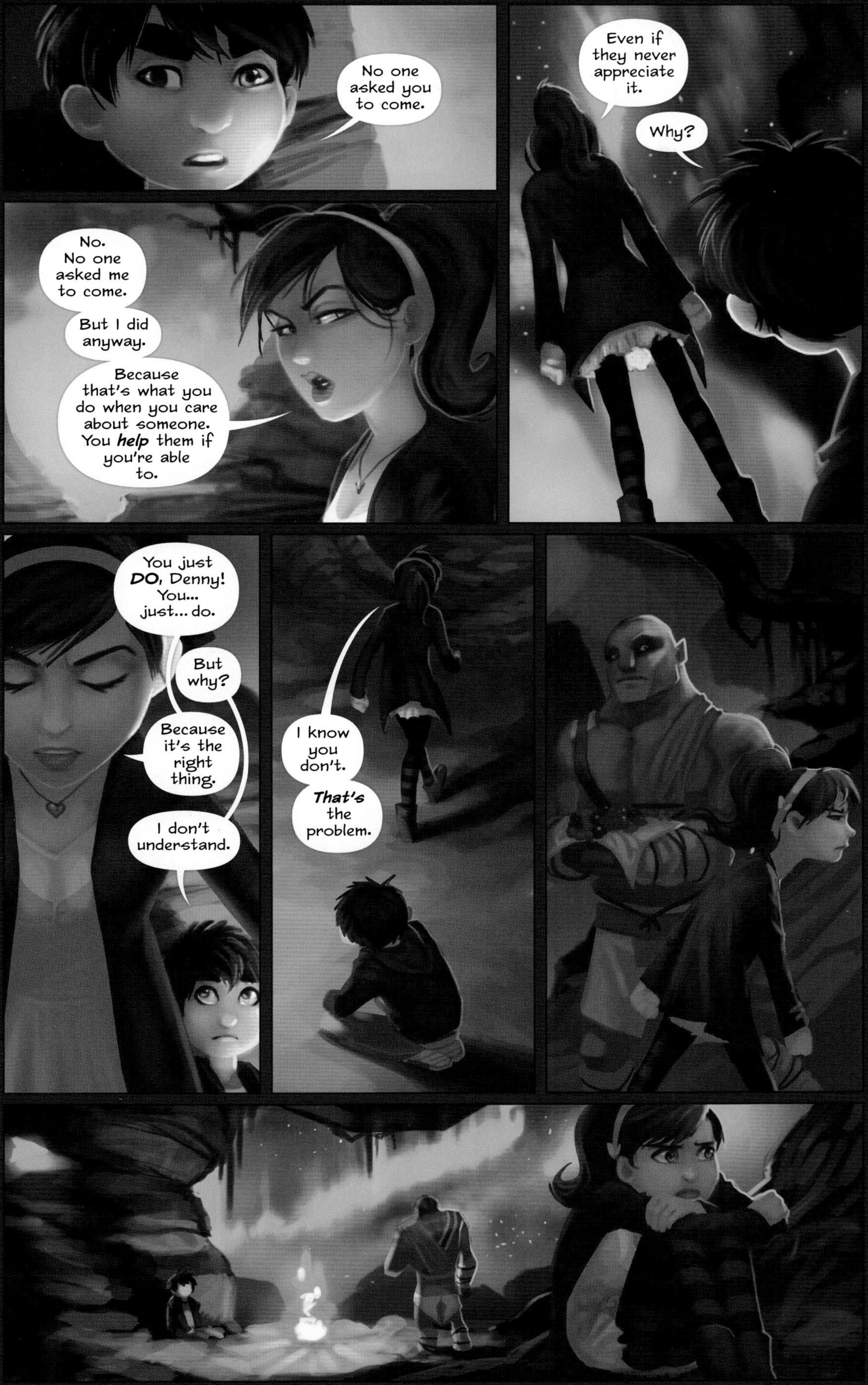

No one asked you to come.
No. No one asked me to come.
But I did anyway.
Because that's what you do when you care about someone. You *help* them if you're able to.
Even if they never appreciate it.
Why?
You just *DO*, Denny! You... just... do.
But why?
Because it's the right thing.
I don't understand.
I know you don't.
That's the problem.

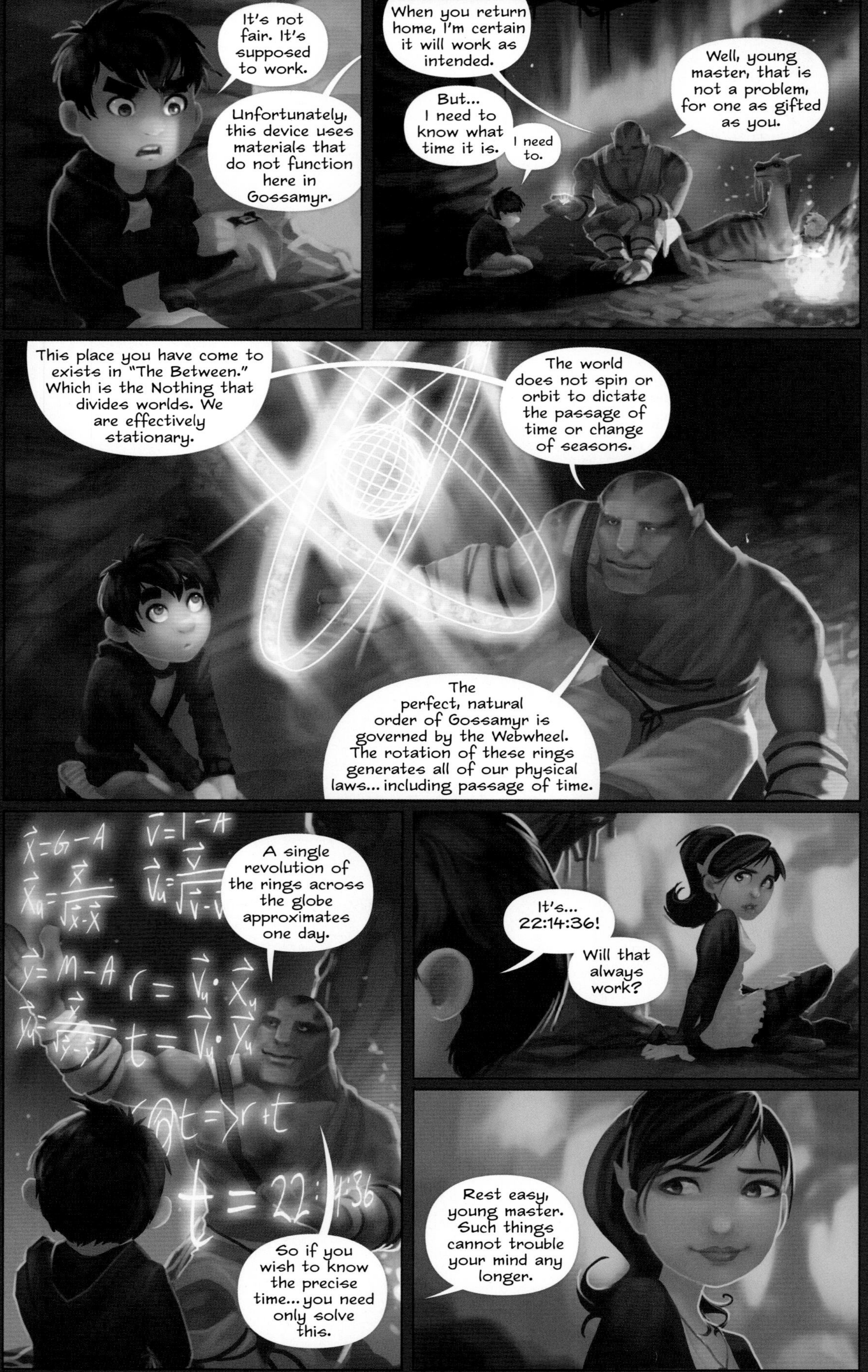
It's not fair. It's supposed to work.
Unfortunately, this device uses materials that do not function here in Gossamyr.
When you return home, I'm certain it will work as intended.
But... I need to know what time it is.
I need to.
Well, young master, that is not a problem, for one as gifted as you.
This place you have come to exists in "The Between." Which is the Nothing that divides worlds. We are effectively stationary.
The world does not spin or orbit to dictate the passage of time or change of seasons.
The perfect, natural order of Gossamyr is governed by the Webwheel. The rotation of these rings generates all of our physical laws... including passage of time.
A single revolution of the rings across the globe approximates one day.
So if you wish to know the precise time... you need only solve this.
It's... 22:14:36!
Will that always work?
Rest easy, young master. Such things cannot trouble your mind any longer.

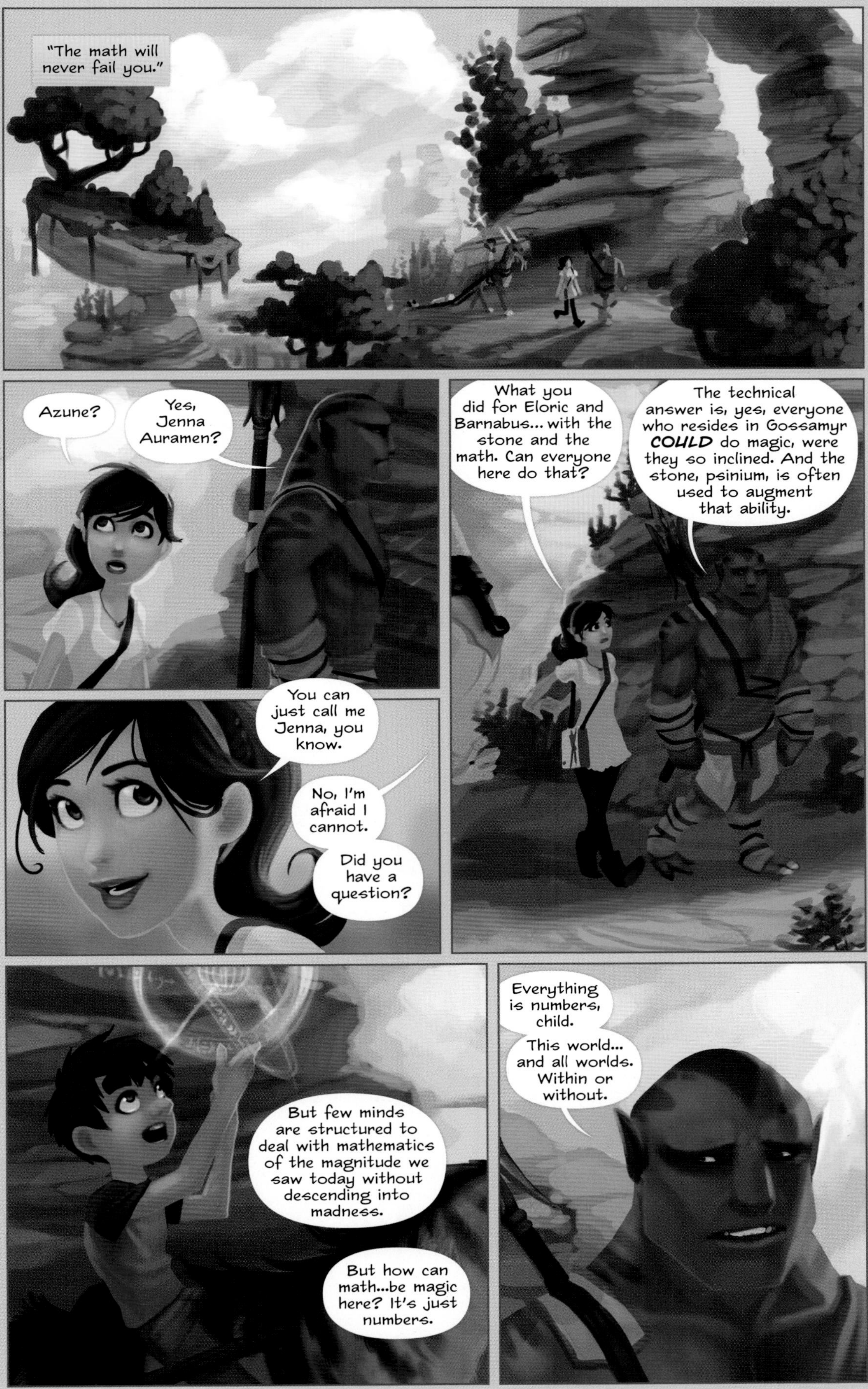
"The math will never fail you."
Azune?
Yes, Jenna Auramen?
You can just call me Jenna, you know.
No, I'm afraid I cannot.
Did you have a question?
What you did for Eloric and Barnabus... with the stone and the math. Can everyone here do that?
The technical answer is, yes, everyone who resides in Gossamyr COULD do magic, were they so inclined. And the stone, psinium, is often used to augment that ability.
But few minds are structured to deal with mathematics of the magnitude we saw today without descending into madness.
But how can math...be magic here? It's just numbers.
Everything is numbers, child.
This world... and all worlds. Within or without.

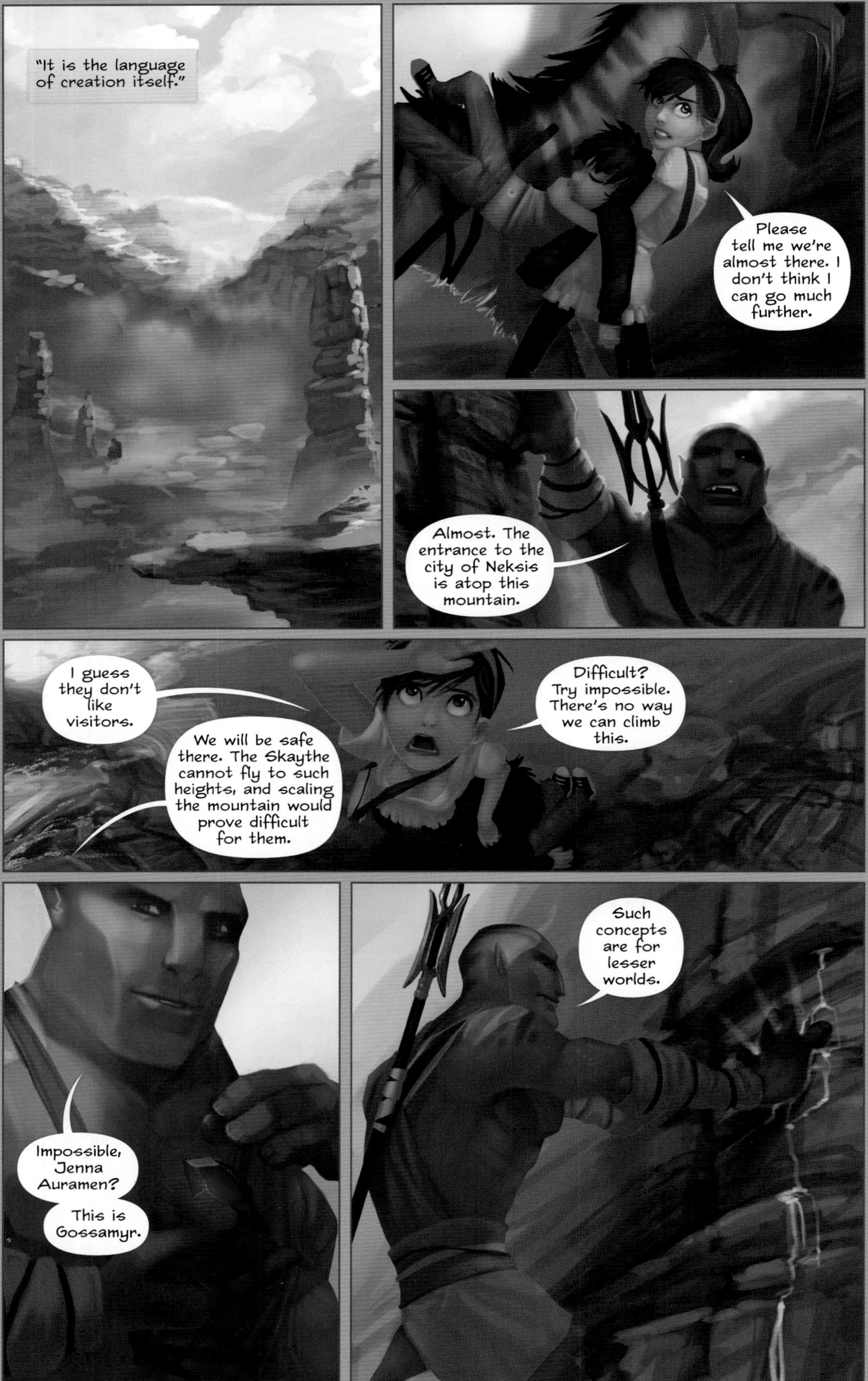
"It is the language of creation itself."
Please tell me we're almost there. I don't think I can go much further.
Almost. The entrance to the city of Neksis is atop this mountain.
I guess they don't like visitors.
We will be safe there. The Skaythe cannot fly to such heights, and scaling the mountain would prove difficult for them.
Difficult? Try impossible. There's no way we can climb this.
Impossible, Jenna Auramen?
This is Gossamyr.
Such concepts are for lesser worlds.

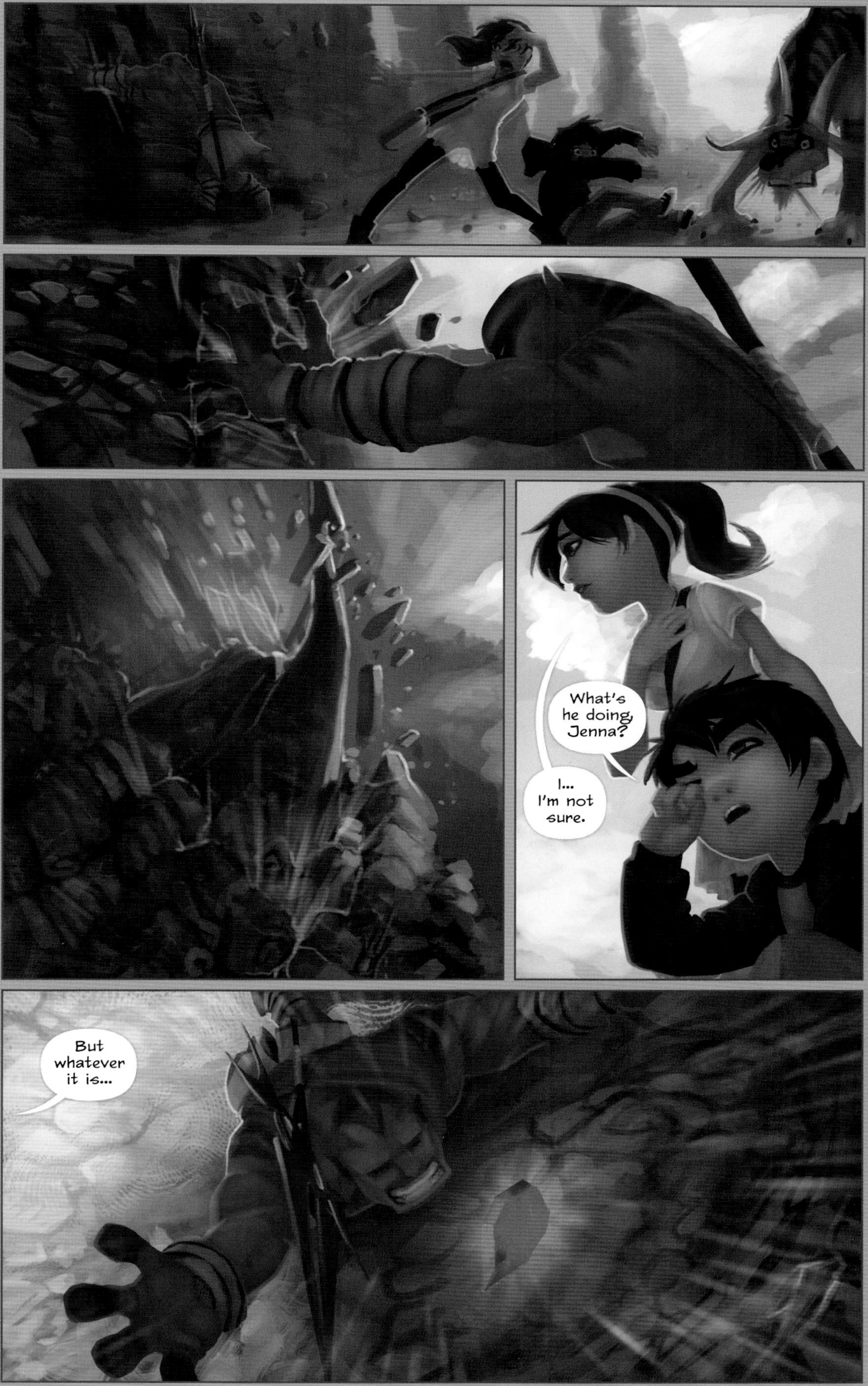
What's he doing, Jenna?
I... I'm not sure.
But whatever it is...

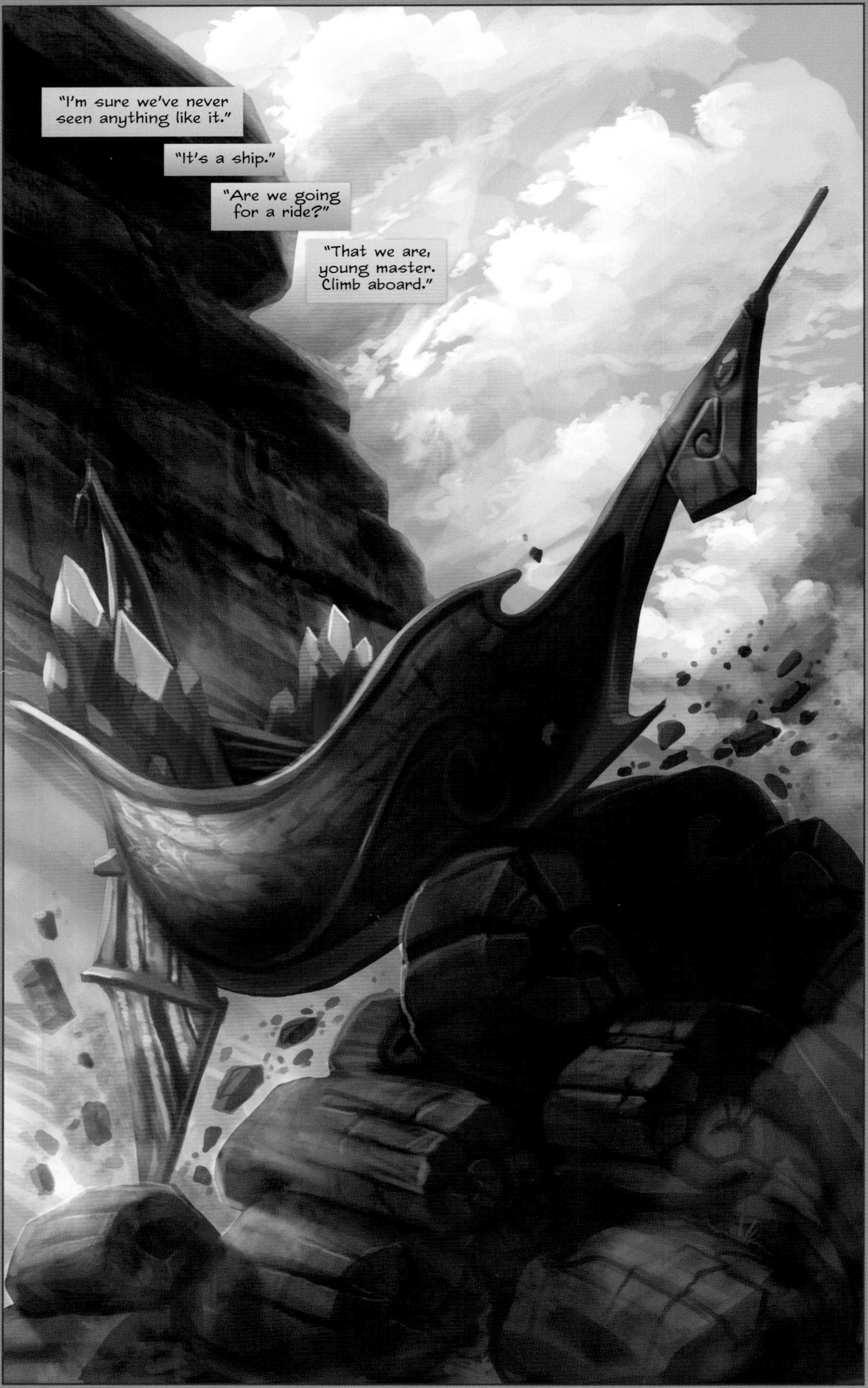
"I'm sure we've never seen anything like it."
"It's a ship."
"Are we going for a ride?"
"That we are, young master. Climb aboard."

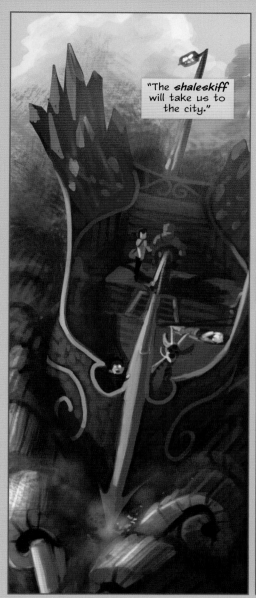

"The *shaleskiff* will take us to the city."

I've got Eloric's pallet tied down. He should be pretty secure for the rest of the trip.

Very good. And your brother?

He...

KKKRRRK

AHHH!!!

Are you all right?

I... think so.

It feels like we're dragging something. I'll try and break us free.

Take the helm.

Hold tight. It's likely to lurch forward.

I don't know how to pilot one of these!

Don't worry, it will just be...

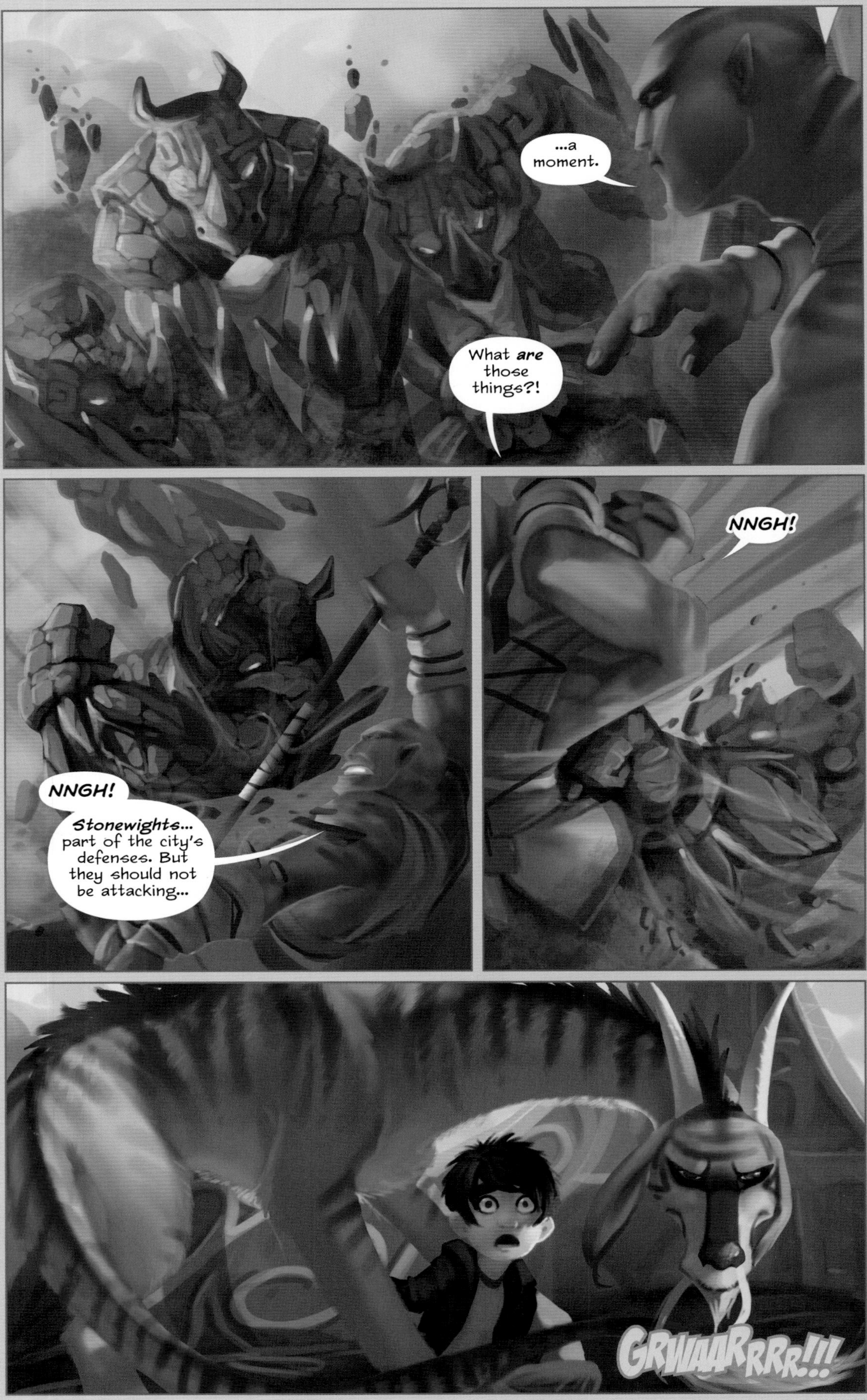
...a moment.
What are those things?!
NNGH!
Stonewights... part of the city's defenses. But they should not be attacking...
NNGH!
GRWAARRRR!!!

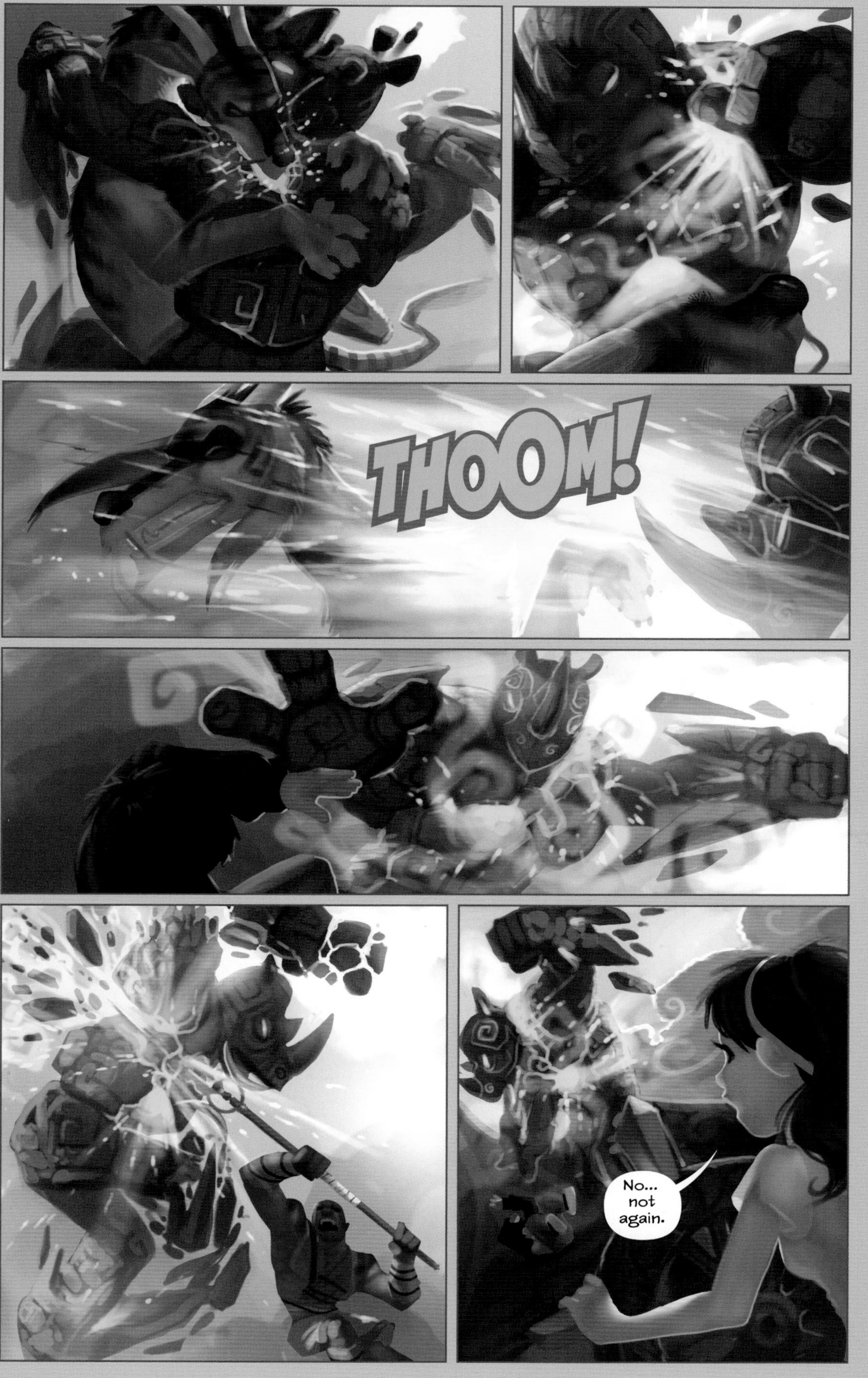
THOOM!
No... not again.

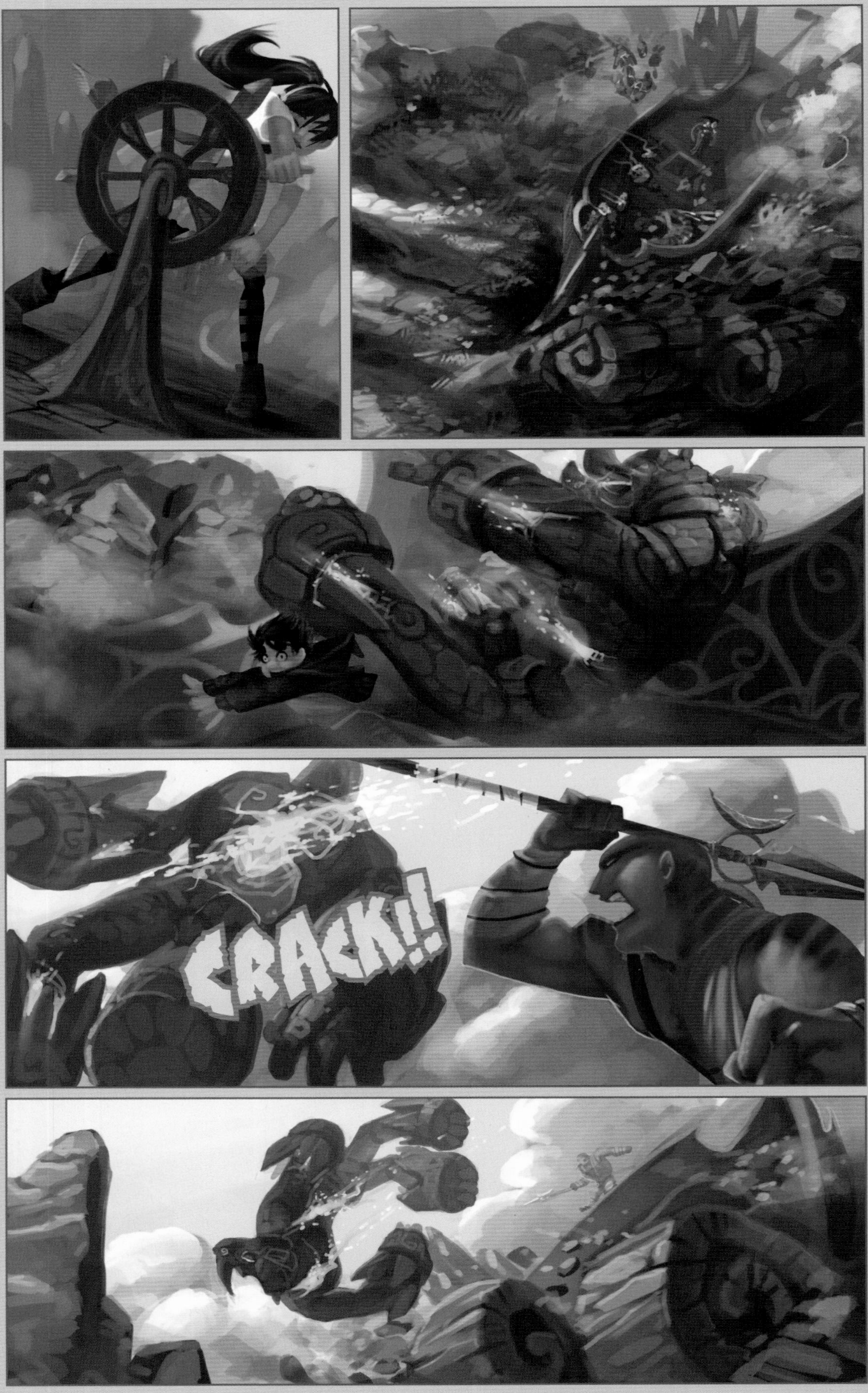
CRACK!!

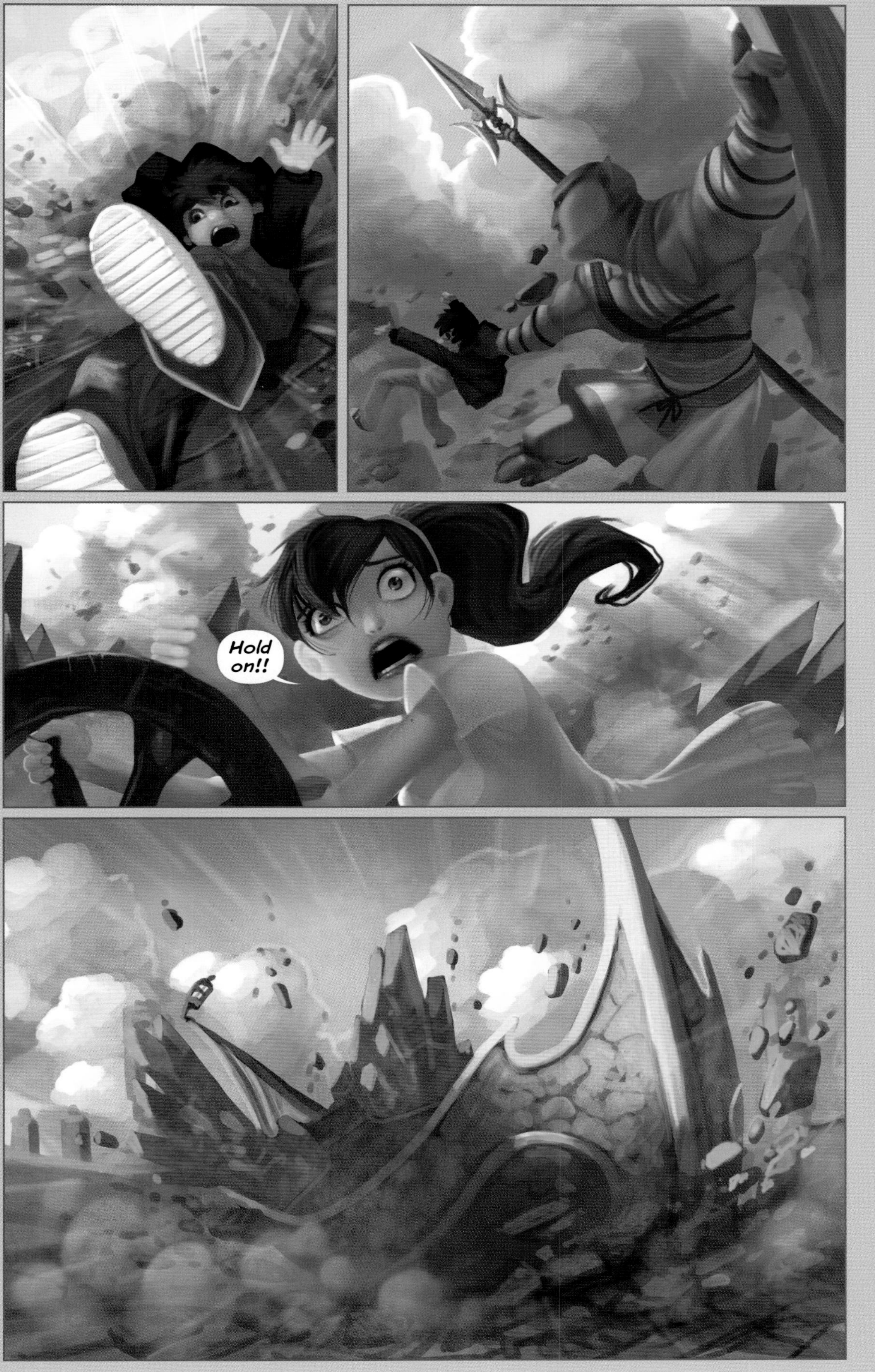
Hold on!!

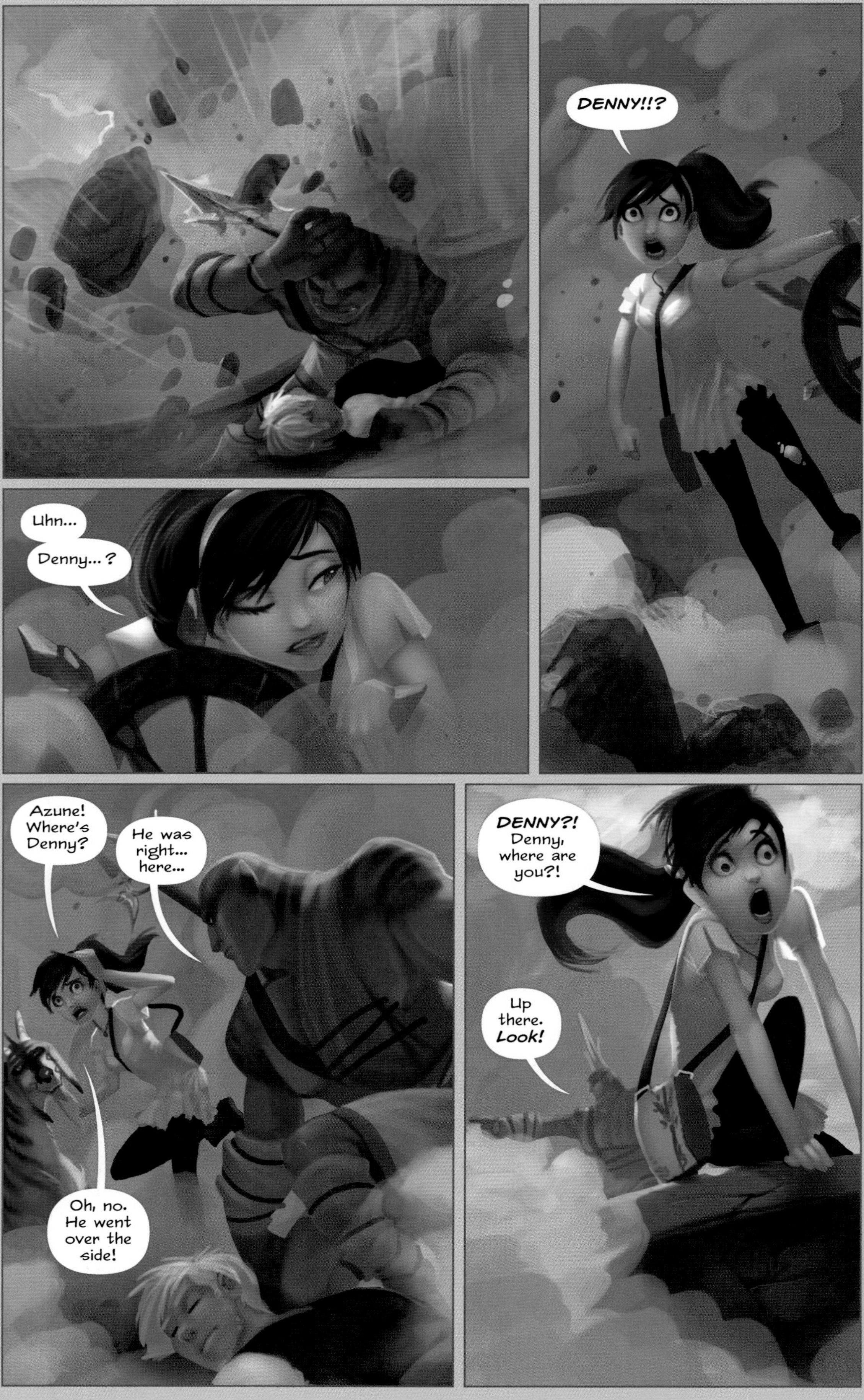
Uhn...
Denny...?
DENNY!!?
Azune! Where's Denny?
He was right... here...
Oh, no. He went over the side!
DENNY?! Denny, where are you?!
Up there. Look!

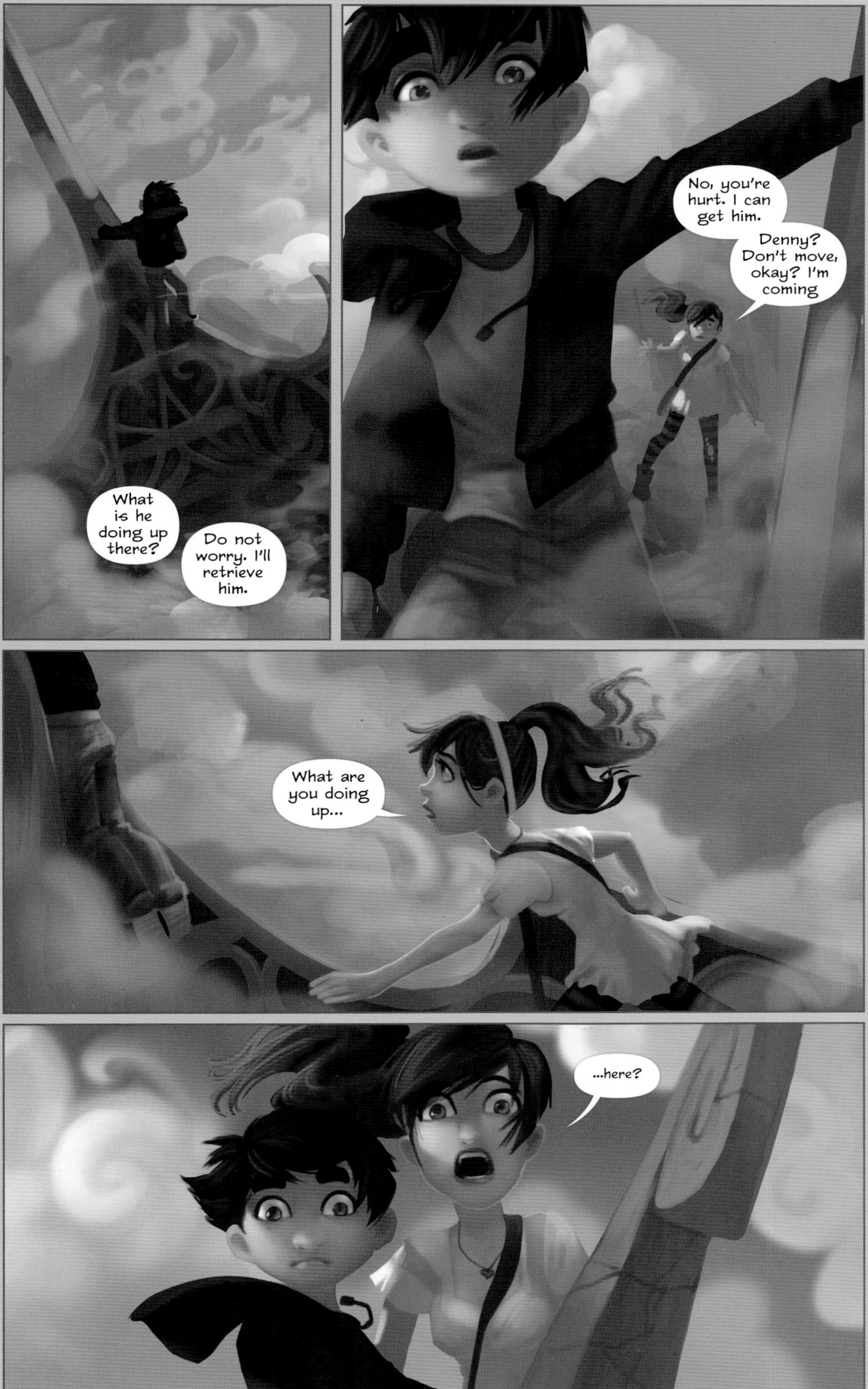
What is he doing up there?
Do not worry. I'll retrieve him.
No, you're hurt. I can get him.
Denny? Don't move, okay? I'm coming
What are you doing up...
...here?

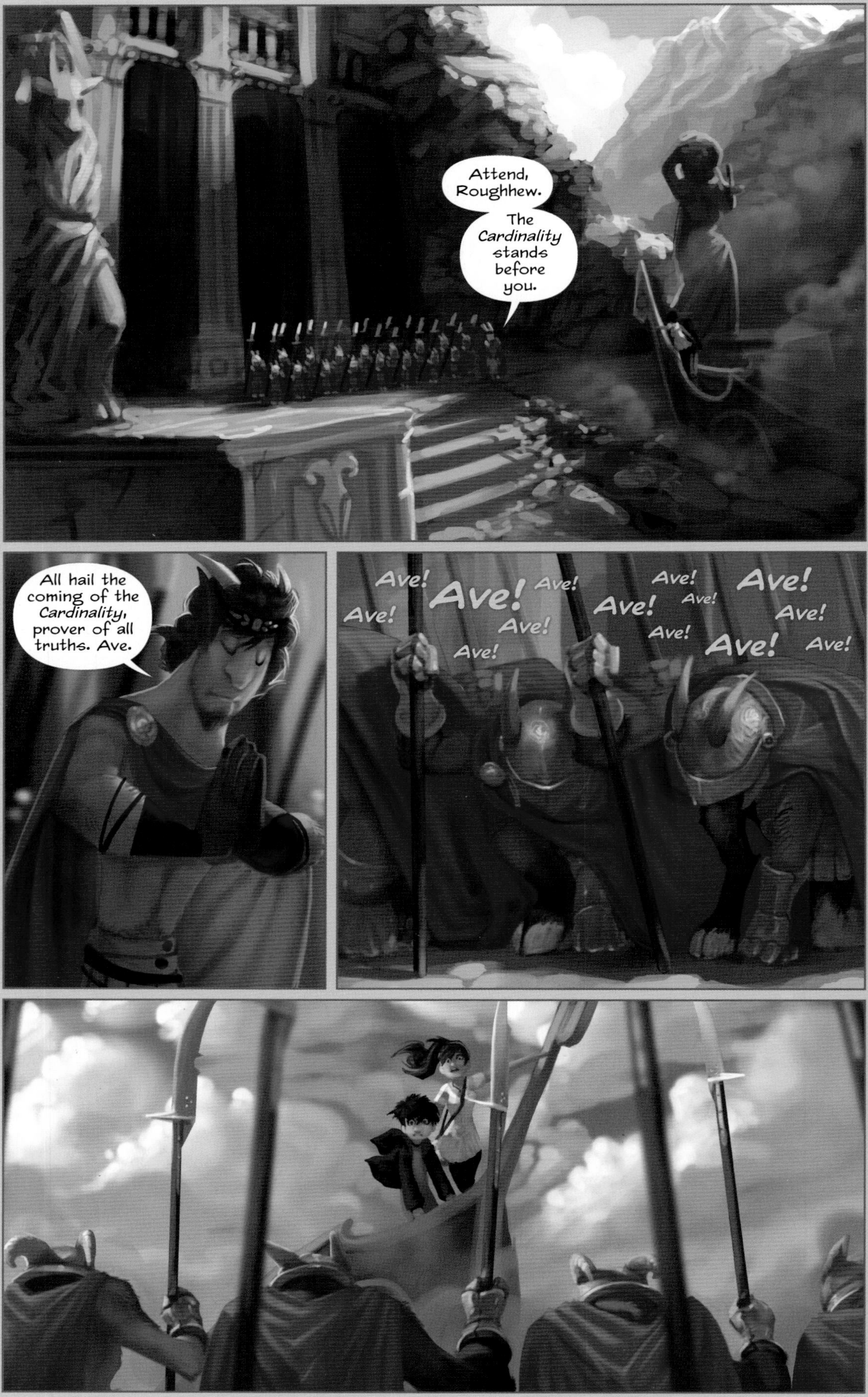
Attend, Roughhew.
The *Cardinality* stands before you.
All hail the coming of the *Cardinality*, prover of all truths. Ave.
Ave!
Ave!
Ave!
Ave!
Ave!
Ave!
Ave!
Ave!
Ave!
Ave!
Ave!
Ave!
Ave!
Ave!

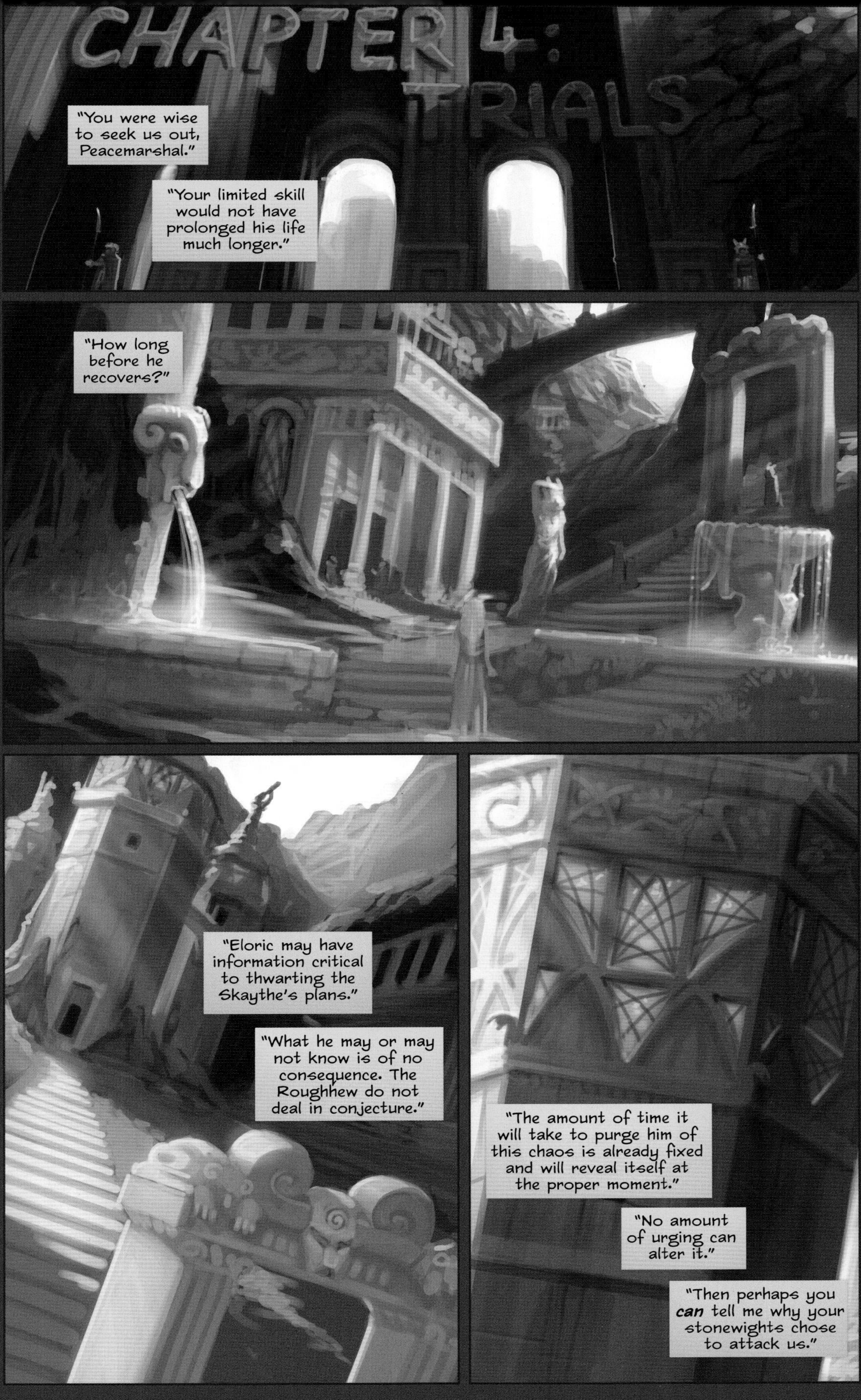
CHAPTER 4: TRIALS
"You were wise to seek us out, Peacemarshal."
"Your limited skill would not have prolonged his life much longer."
"How long before he recovers?"
"Eloric may have information critical to thwarting the Skaythe's plans."
"What he may or may not know is of no consequence. The Roughhew do not deal in conjecture."
"The amount of time it will take to purge him of this chaos is already fixed and will reveal itself at the proper moment."
"No amount of urging can alter it."
"Then perhaps you ***can*** tell me why your stonewights chose to attack us."

I can only assume you made an error during your summoning of the shaleskiff. They would have remained sleeping otherwise.

You accuse me of incompetence?

No, Peacemarshal. I am acknowledging your limitations.

You are not equal to the tasks before you.

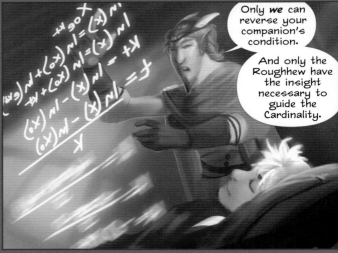

Only *we* can reverse your companion's condition.

And only the Roughhew have the insight necessary to guide the Cardinality.

Now wait just a second! Who do you think you are?

We came looking for help for Eloric, not Denny. All we need is the theorem.

Whether it was a matter of intention or happenstance is irrelevant, child.

For our assistance you now have.

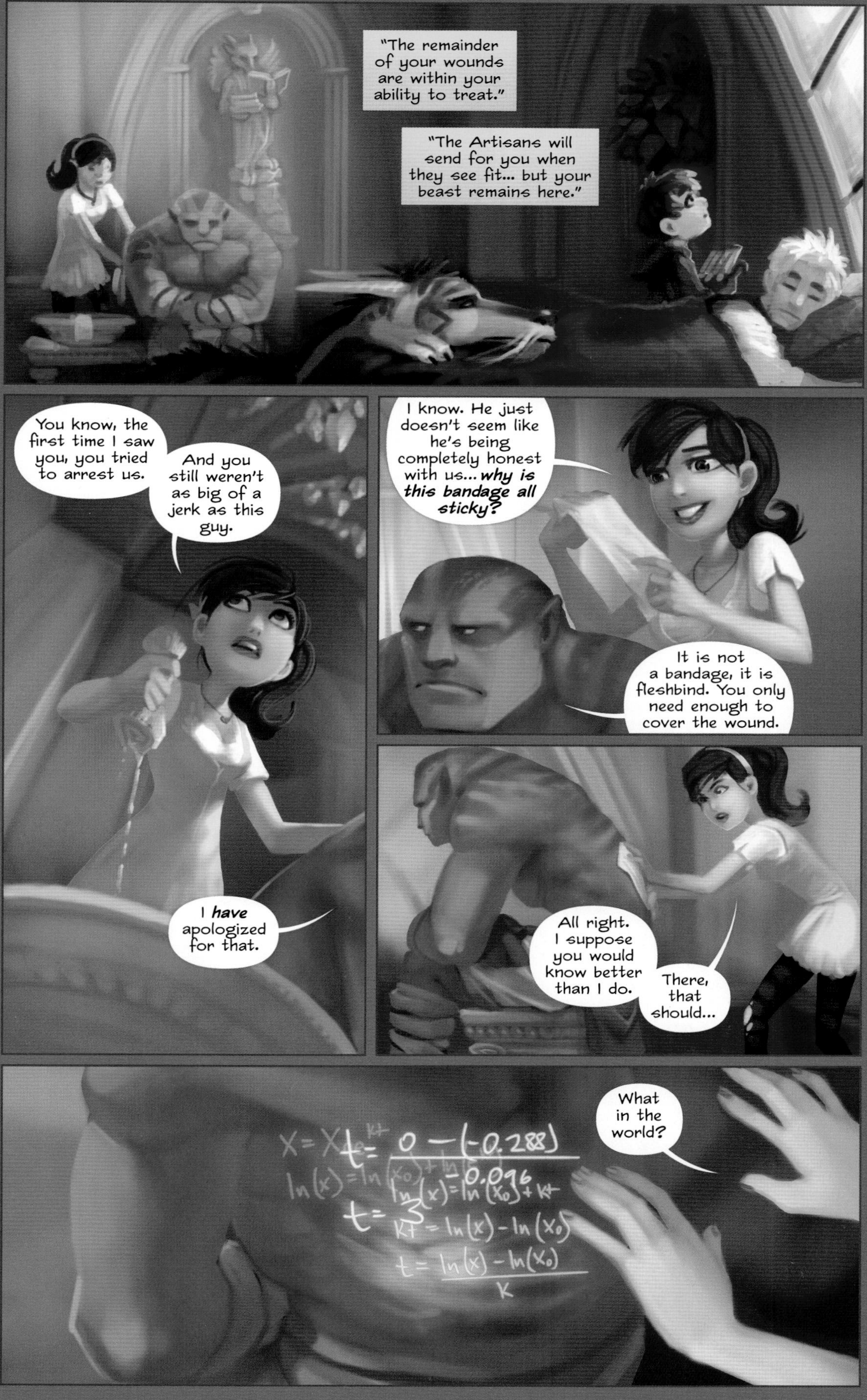
"The remainder of your wounds are within your ability to treat."
"The Artisans will send for you when they see fit... but your beast remains here."
You know, the first time I saw you, you tried to arrest us.
And you still weren't as big of a jerk as this guy.
I *have* apologized for that.
I know. He just doesn't seem like he's being completely honest with us... ***why is this bandage all sticky?***
It is not a bandage, it is fleshbind. You only need enough to cover the wound.
All right. I suppose you would know better than I do.
There, that should...
ln(x) = ln(x0) + kt
t = 3
kt = ln(x) - ln(x0)
t = ln(x) - ln(x0) / k
What in the world?

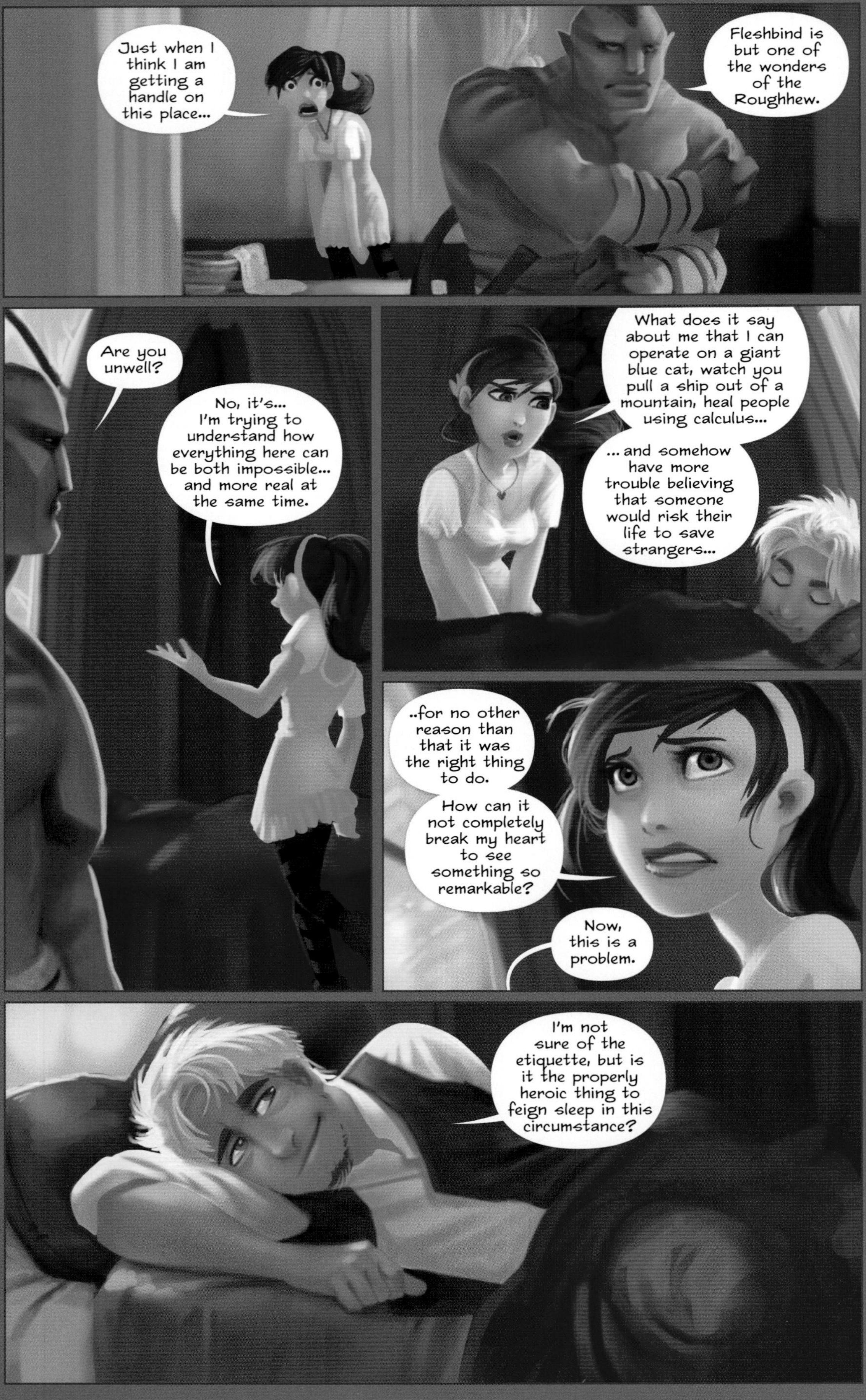
Just when I think I am getting a handle on this place...
Fleshbind is but one of the wonders of the Roughhew.
Are you unwell?
No, it's... I'm trying to understand how everything here can be both impossible... and more real at the same time.
What does it say about me that I can operate on a giant blue cat, watch you pull a ship out of a mountain, heal people using calculus...
... and somehow have more trouble believing that someone would risk their life to save strangers...
..for no other reason than that it was the right thing to do.
How can it not completely break my heart to see something so remarkable?
Now, this is a problem.
I'm not sure of the etiquette, but is it the properly heroic thing to feign sleep in this circumstance?

I don't think anyone said the word "hero."

It was clearly implied.

I'm glad your near-death experience hasn't affected your ego.

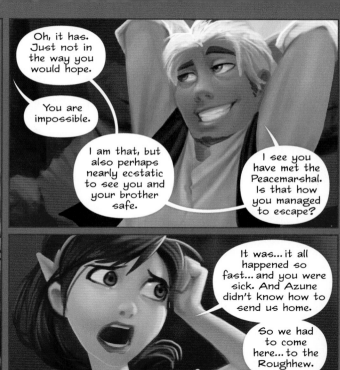

Oh, it has. Just not in the way you would hope.

You are impossible.

I am that, but also perhaps nearly ecstatic to see you and your brother safe.

I see you have met the Peacemarshal. Is that how you managed to escape?

It was...it all happened so fast...and you were sick. And Azune didn't know how to send us home.

So we had to come here...to the Roughhew.

You brought me to the *Roughhew*?!

I...

No. I brought you here. You would have died otherwise.

Oh, Azune...we are lost. It is all lost.

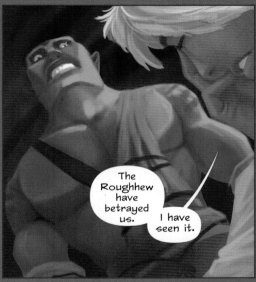

The Roughhew have betrayed us.

I have seen it.

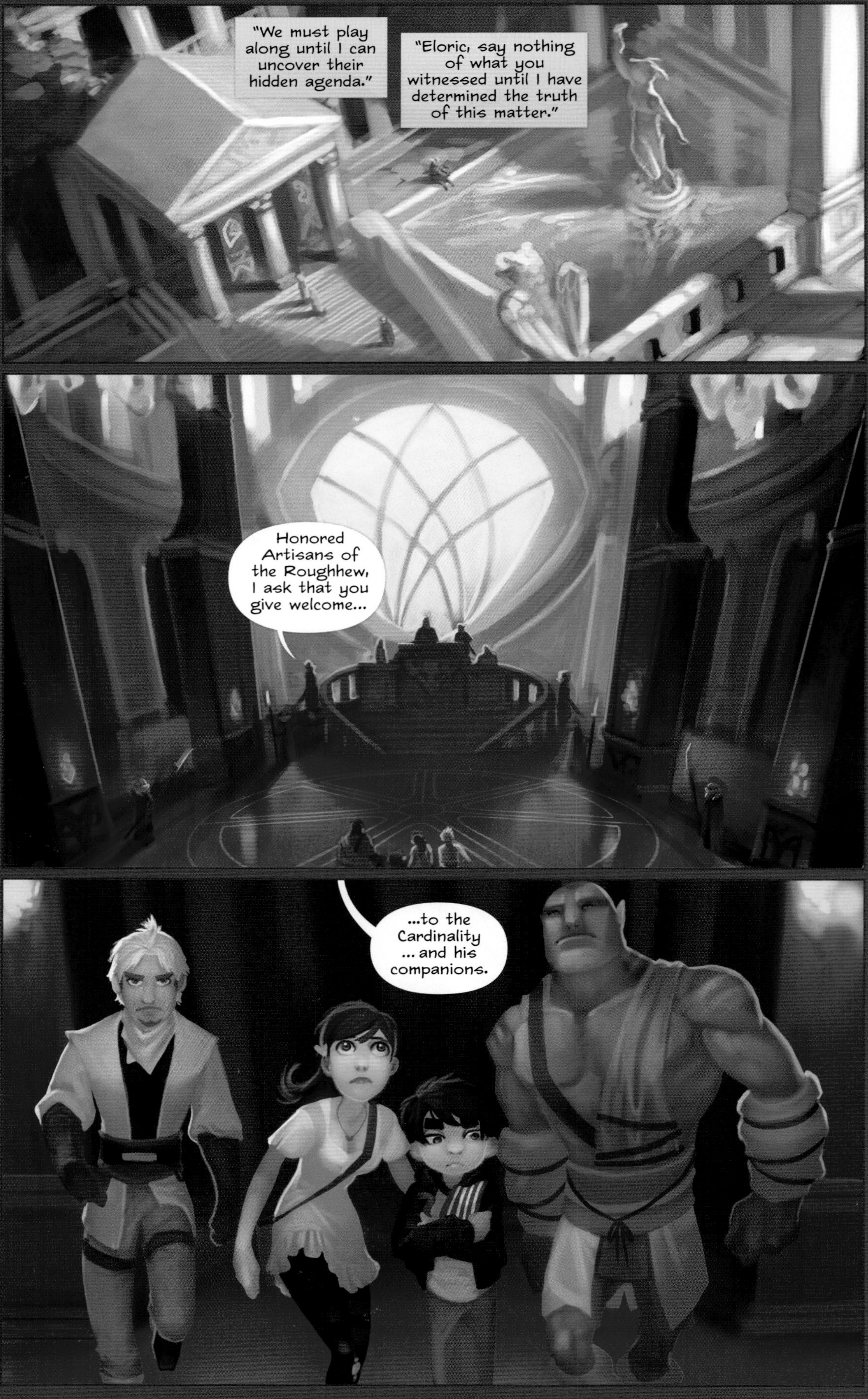
"We must play along until I can uncover their hidden agenda."
"Eloric, say nothing of what you witnessed until I have determined the truth of this matter."
Honored Artisans of the Roughhew, I ask that you give welcome...
...to the Cardinality ...and his companions.

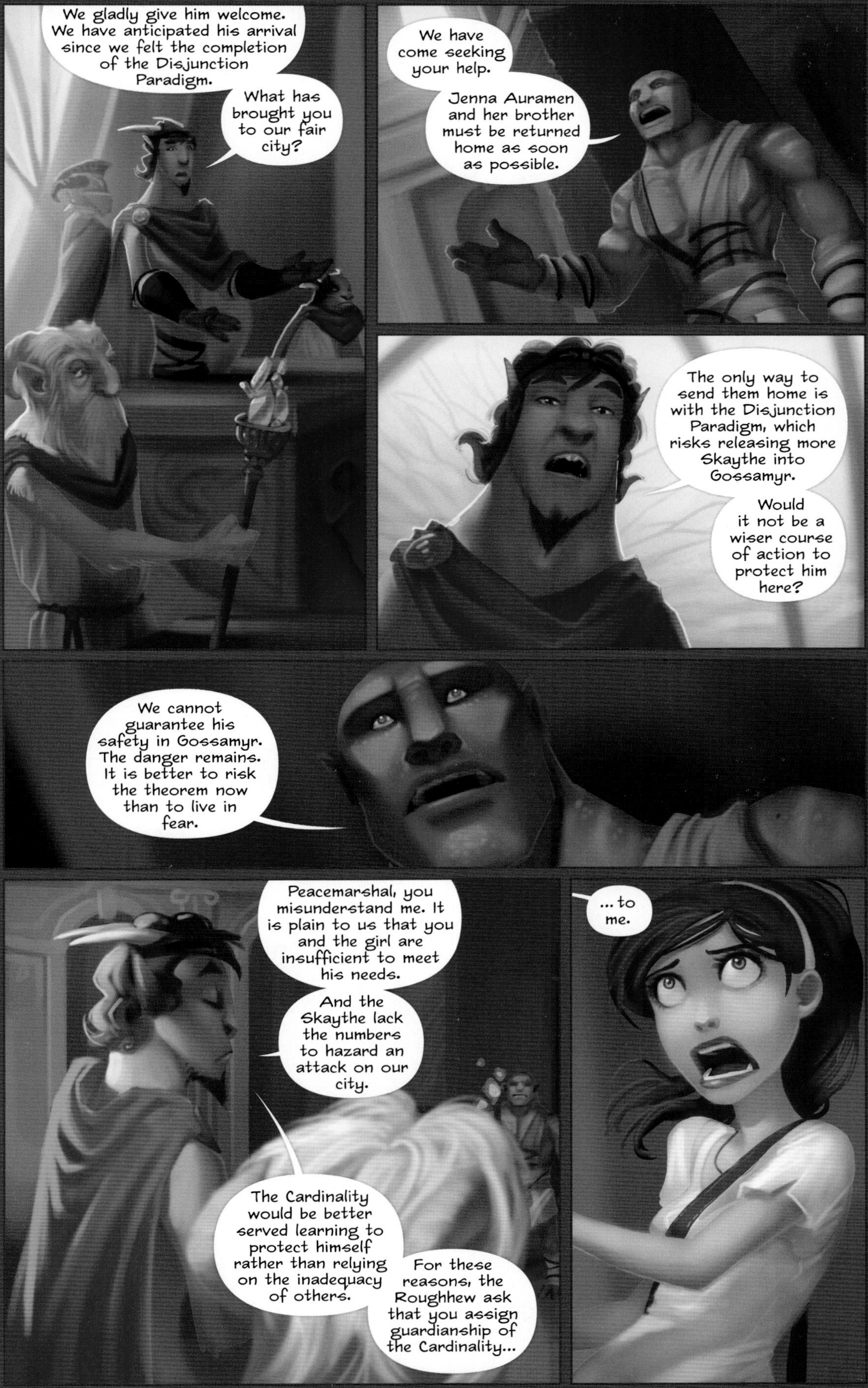
We gladly give him welcome. We have anticipated his arrival since we felt the completion of the Disjunction Paradigm.
What has brought you to our fair city?
We have come seeking your help.
Jenna Auramen and her brother must be returned home as soon as possible.
The only way to send them home is with the Disjunction Paradigm, which risks releasing more Skaythe into Gossamyr.
Would it not be a wiser course of action to protect him here?
We cannot guarantee his safety in Gossamyr. The danger remains. It is better to risk the theorem now than to live in fear.
Peacemarshal, you misunderstand me. It is plain to us that you and the girl are insufficient to meet his needs.
And the Skaythe lack the numbers to hazard an attack on our city.
The Cardinality would be better served learning to protect himself rather than relying on the inadequacy of others.
For these reasons, the Roughhew ask that you assign guardianship of the Cardinality...
...to me.

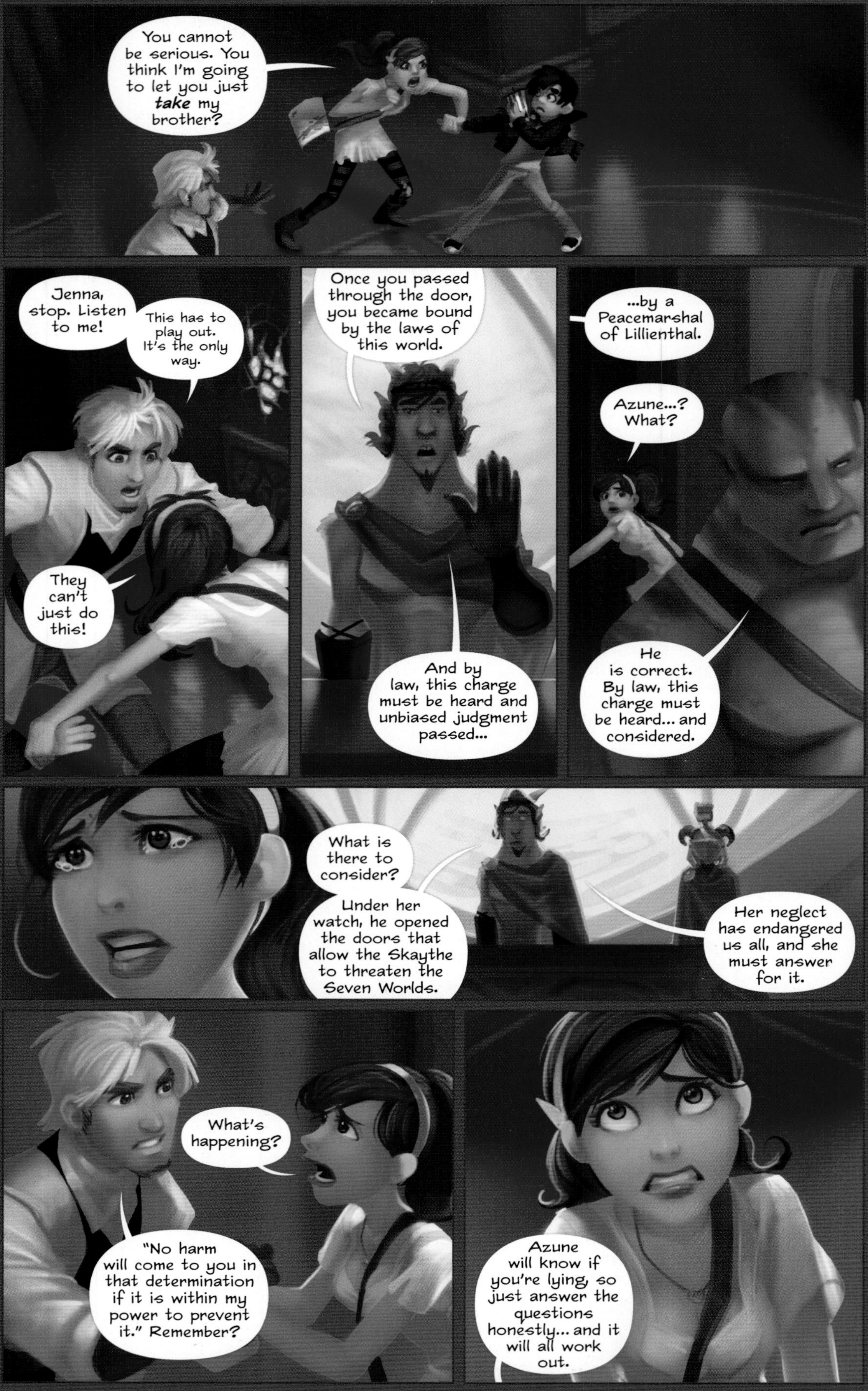
You cannot be serious. You think I'm going to let you just *take* my brother?
Jenna, stop. Listen to me!
This has to play out. It's the only way.
They can't just do this!
Once you passed through the door, you became bound by the laws of this world.
And by law, this charge must be heard and unbiased judgment passed...
...by a Peacemarshal of Lillienthal.
Azune...? What?
He is correct. By law, this charge must be heard... and considered.
What is there to consider?
Under her watch, he opened the doors that allow the Skaythe to threaten the Seven Worlds.
Her neglect has endangered us all, and she must answer for it.
What's happening?
"No harm will come to you in that determination if it is within my power to prevent it." Remember?
Azune will know if you're lying, so just answer the questions honestly... and it will all work out.

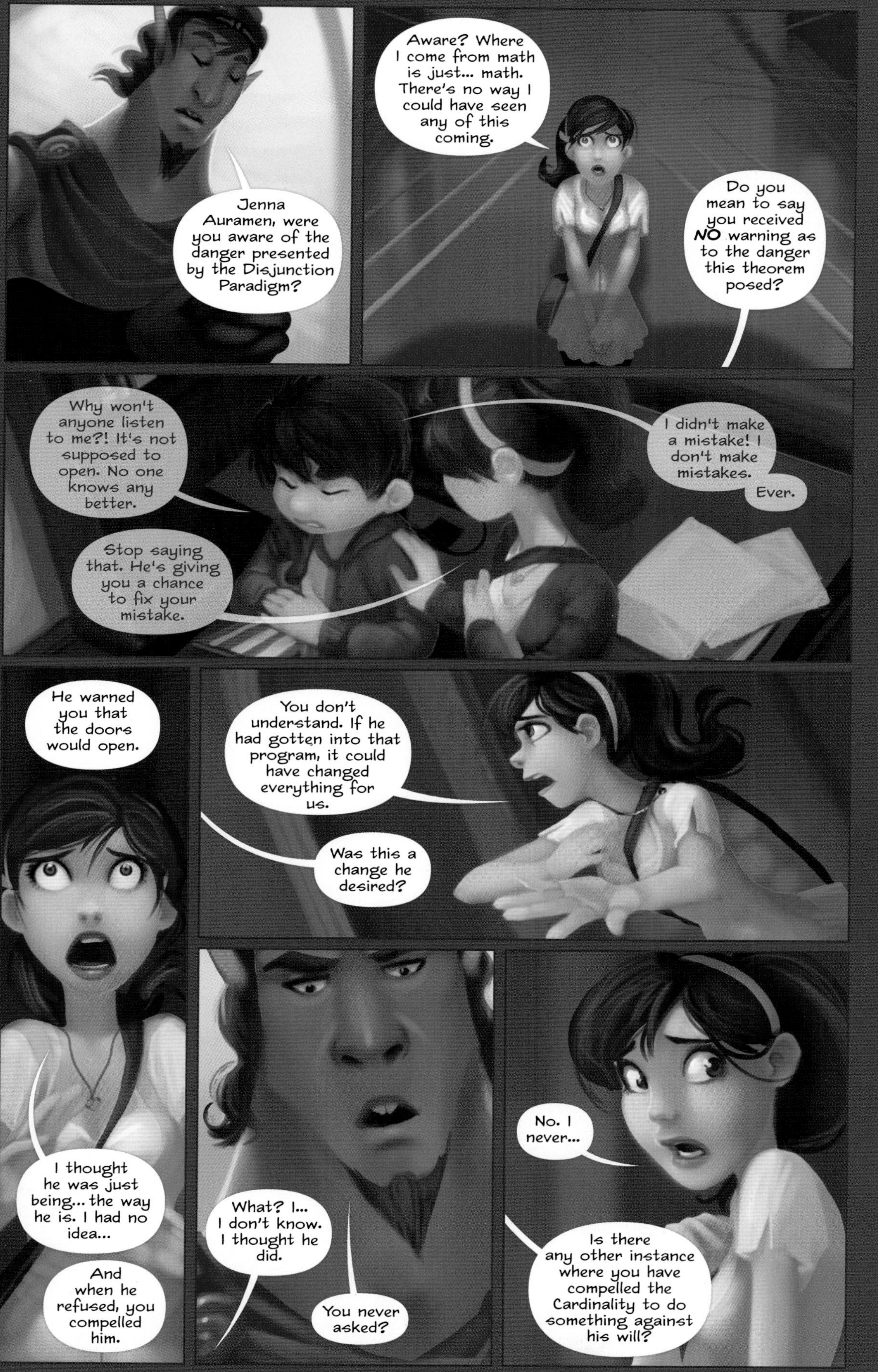
Jenna Auramen, were you aware of the danger presented by the Disjunction Paradigm?
Aware? Where I come from math is just... math. There's no way I could have seen any of this coming.
Do you mean to say you received NO warning as to the danger this theorem posed?
Why won't anyone listen to me?! It's not supposed to open. No one knows any better.
I didn't make a mistake! I don't make mistakes.
Ever.
Stop saying that. He's giving you a chance to fix your mistake.
He warned you that the doors would open.
You don't understand. If he had gotten into that program, it could have changed everything for us.
Was this a change he desired?
I thought he was just being... the way he is. I had no idea...
And when he refused, you compelled him.
What? I... I don't know. I thought he did.
You never asked?
No. I never...
Is there any other instance where you have compelled the Cardinality to do something against his will?

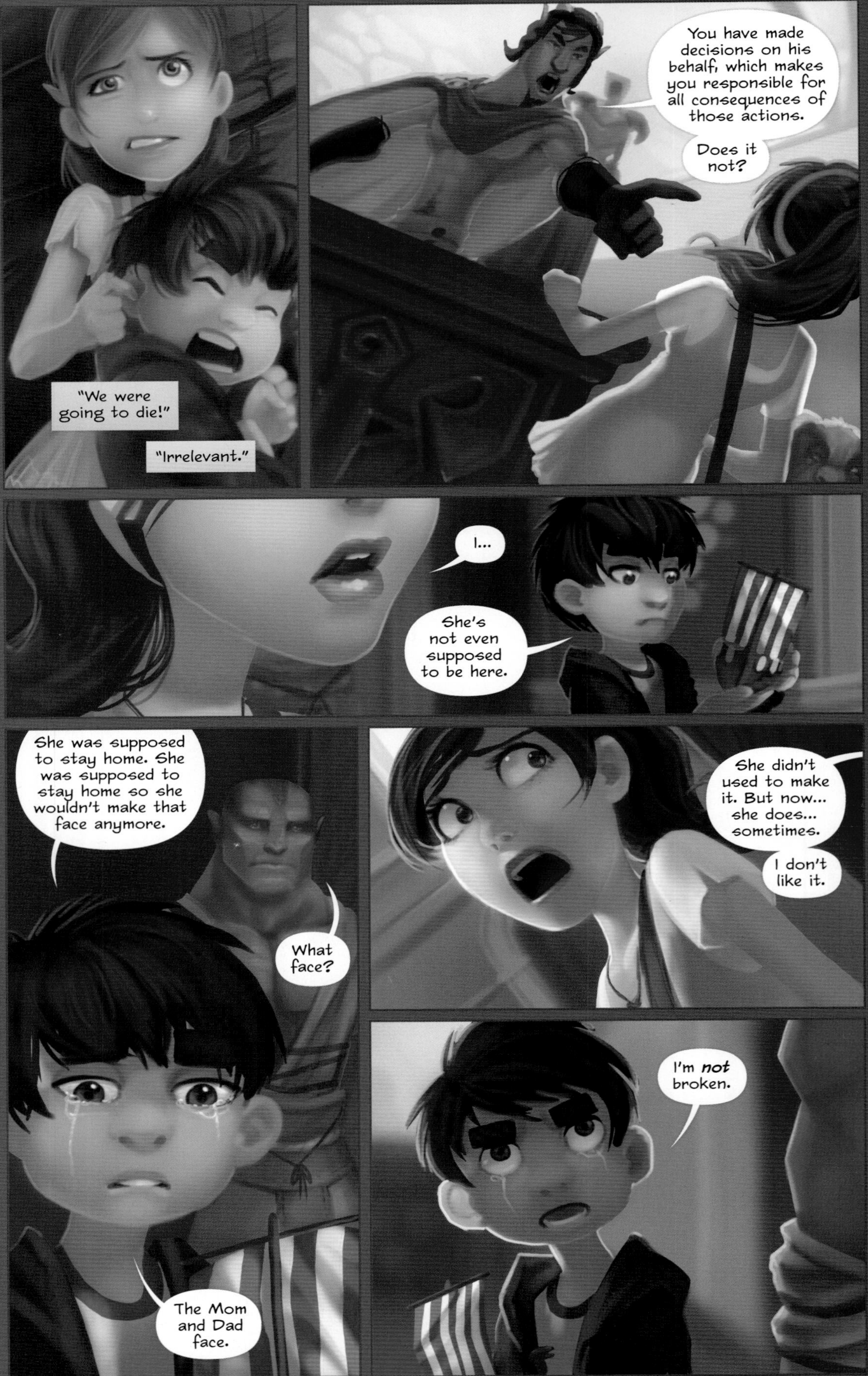

"We were going to die!"
"Irrelevant."
You have made decisions on his behalf, which makes you responsible for all consequences of those actions.
Does it not?
I...
She's not even supposed to be here.
She was supposed to stay home. She was supposed to stay home so she wouldn't make that face anymore.
What face?
The Mom and Dad face.
She didn't used to make it. But now... she does... sometimes.
I don't like it.
I'm *not* broken.

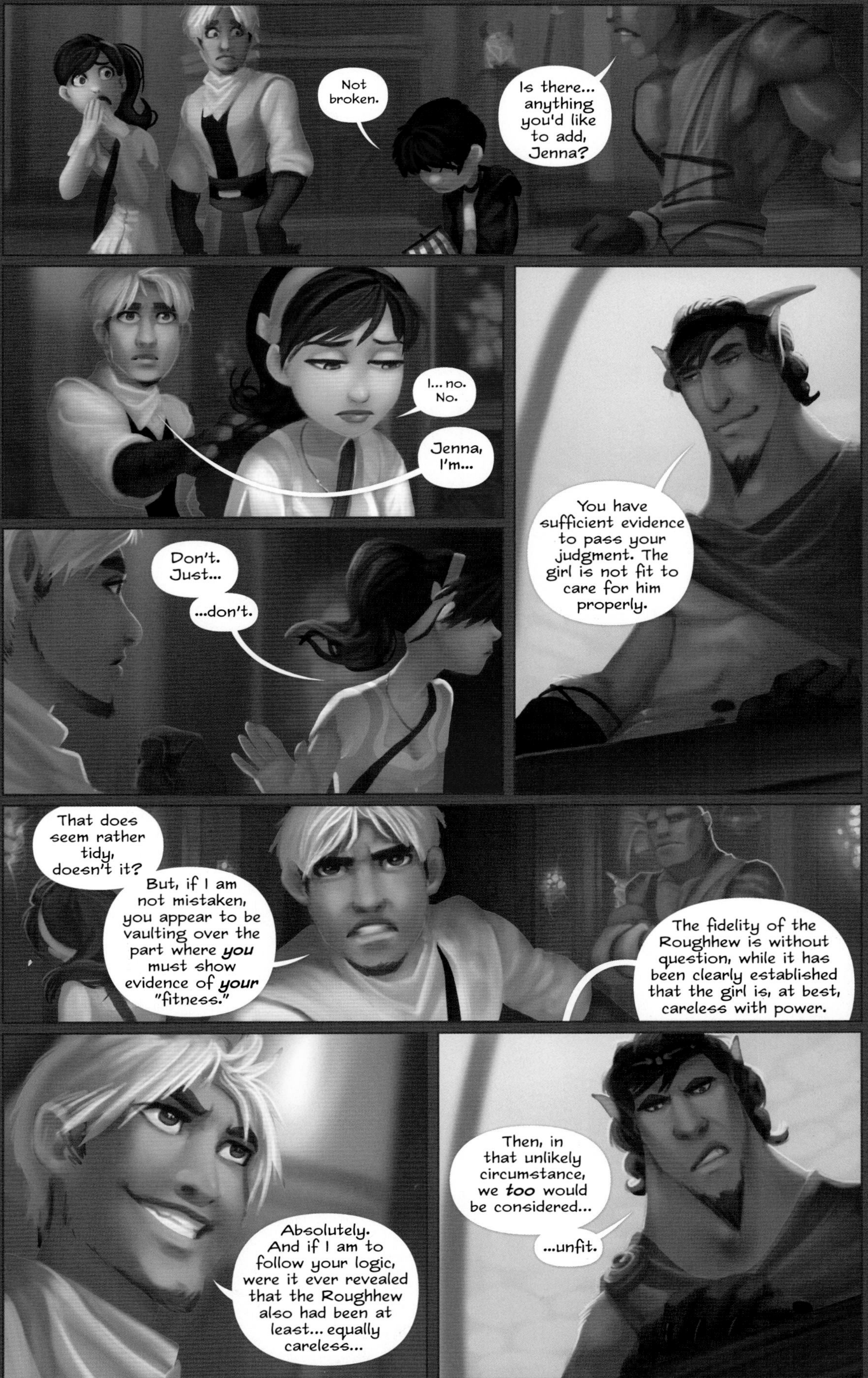
Not broken.
Is there... anything you'd like to add, Jenna?
I... no. No.
Jenna, I'm...
You have sufficient evidence to pass your judgment. The girl is not fit to care for him properly.
Don't. Just...
...don't.
That does seem rather tidy, doesn't it?
But, if I am not mistaken, you appear to be vaulting over the part where *you* must show evidence of *your* "fitness."
The fidelity of the Roughhew is without question, while it has been clearly established that the girl is, at best, careless with power.
Absolutely. And if I am to follow your logic, were it ever revealed that the Roughhew also had been at least... equally careless...
Then, in that unlikely circumstance, we *too* would be considered...
...unfit.

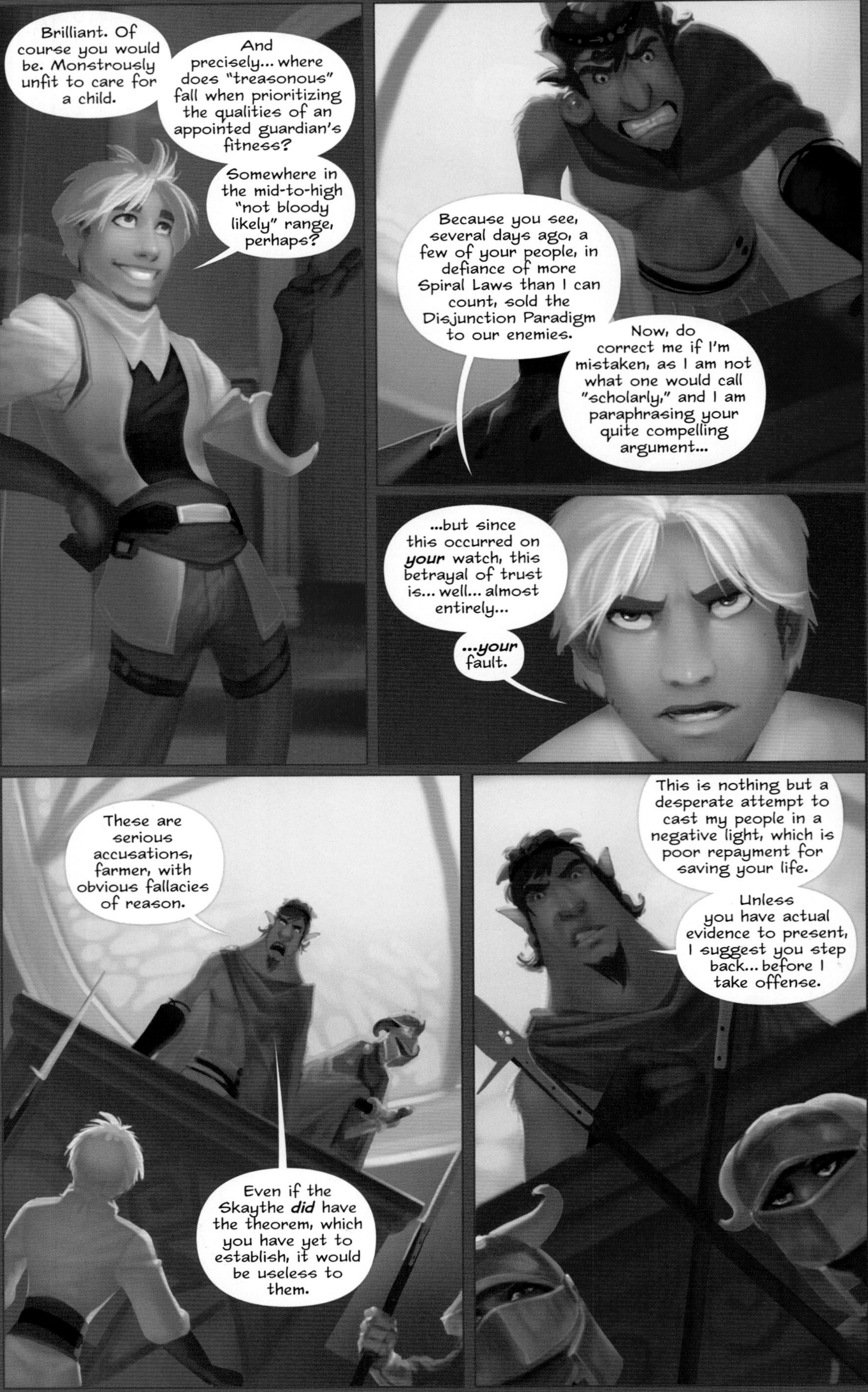
Brilliant. Of course you would be. Monstrously unfit to care for a child.
And precisely... where does "treasonous" fall when prioritizing the qualities of an appointed guardian's fitness?
Somewhere in the mid-to-high "not bloody likely" range, perhaps?
Because you see, several days ago, a few of your people, in defiance of more Spiral Laws than I can count, sold the Disjunction Paradigm to our enemies.
Now, do correct me if I'm mistaken, as I am not what one would call "scholarly," and I am paraphrasing your quite compelling argument...
...but since this occurred on ***your*** watch, this betrayal of trust is... well... almost entirely...
...your fault.
These are serious accusations, farmer, with obvious fallacies of reason.
Even if the Skaythe ***did*** have the theorem, which you have yet to establish, it would be useless to them.
This is nothing but a desperate attempt to cast my people in a negative light, which is poor repayment for saving your life.
Unless you have actual evidence to present, I suggest you step back... before I take offense.

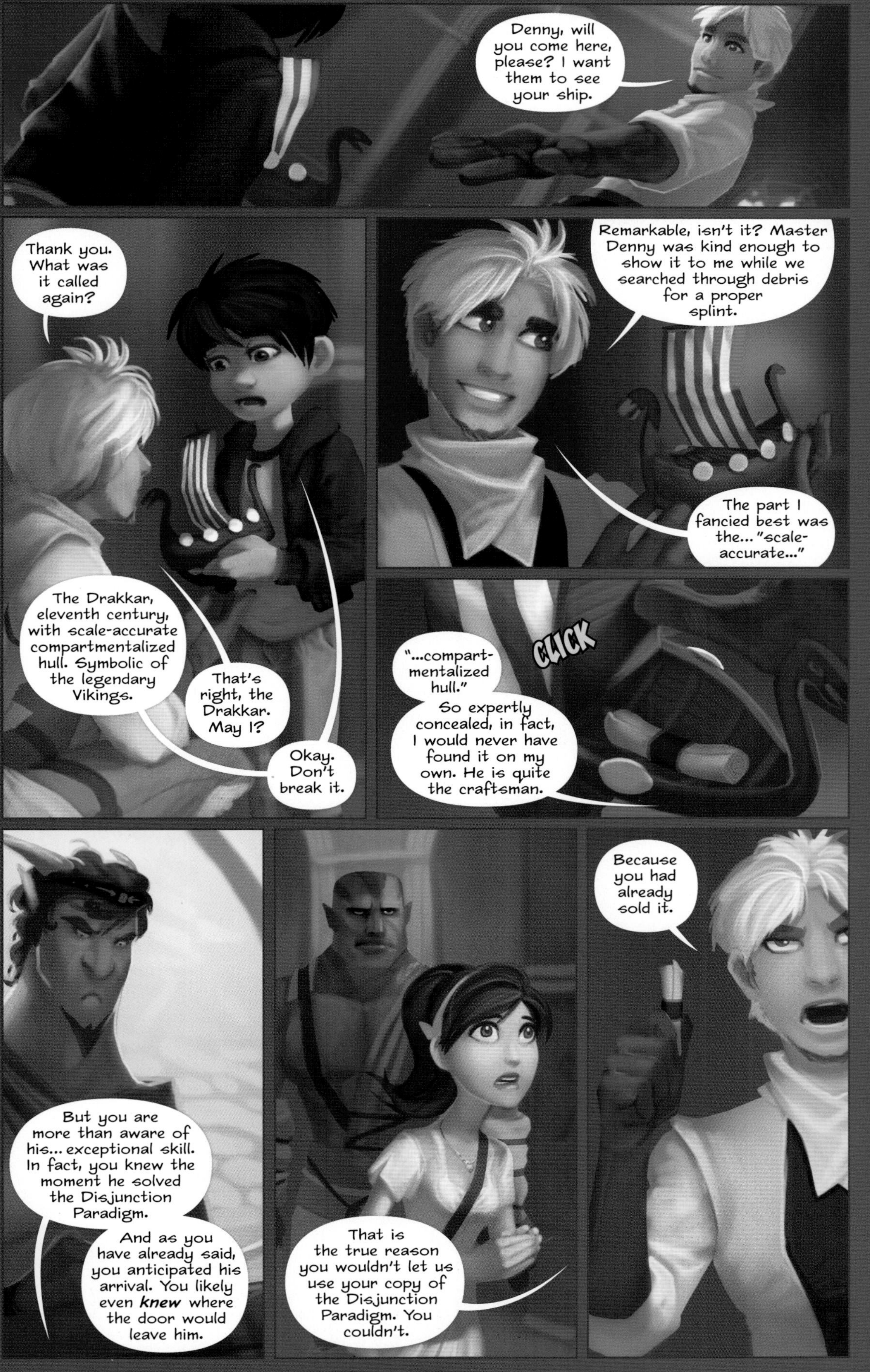
Denny, will you come here, please? I want them to see your ship.
Thank you. What was it called again?
The Drakkar, eleventh century, with scale-accurate compartmentalized hull. Symbolic of the legendary Vikings.
That's right, the Drakkar. May I?
Okay. Don't break it.
Remarkable, isn't it? Master Denny was kind enough to show it to me while we searched through debris for a proper splint.
The part I fancied best was the... "scale-accurate..."
CLICK
"...compartmentalized hull."
So expertly concealed, in fact, I would never have found it on my own. He is quite the craftsman.
But you are more than aware of his... exceptional skill. In fact, you knew the moment he solved the Disjunction Paradigm.
And as you have already said, you anticipated his arrival. You likely even ***knew*** where the door would leave him.
That is the true reason you wouldn't let us use your copy of the Disjunction Paradigm. You couldn't.
Because you had already sold it.

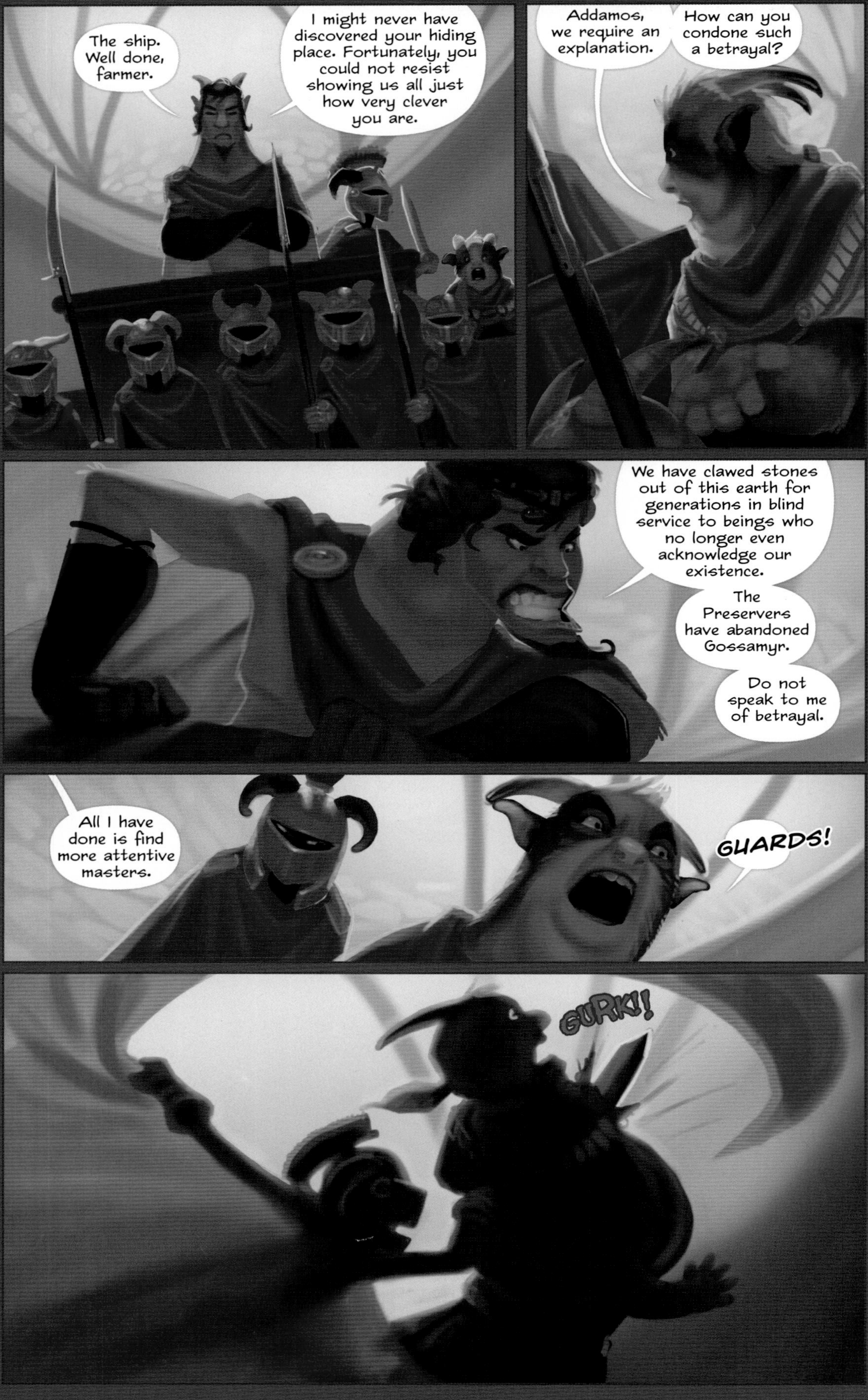
The ship. Well done, farmer.
I might never have discovered your hiding place. Fortunately, you could not resist showing us all just how very clever you are.
Addamos, we require an explanation.
How can you condone such a betrayal?
We have clawed stones out of this earth for generations in blind service to beings who no longer even acknowledge our existence.
The Preservers have abandoned Gossamyr.
Do not speak to me of betrayal.
All I have done is find more attentive masters.
GUARDS!
GURK!

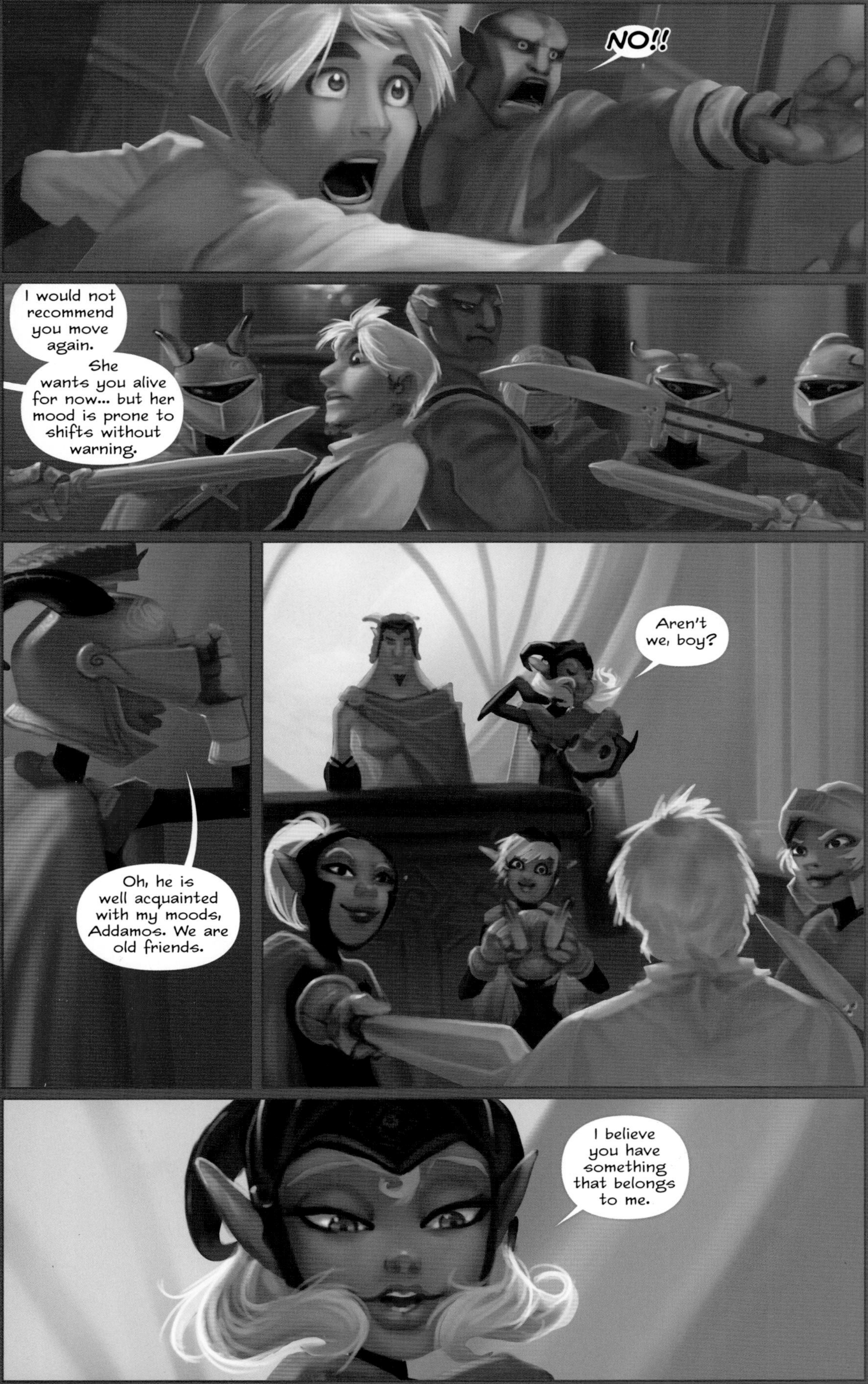
NO!!
I would not recommend you move again.
She wants you alive for now... but her mood is prone to shifts without warning.
Oh, he is well acquainted with my moods, Addamos. We are old friends.
Aren't we, boy?
I believe you have something that belongs to me.

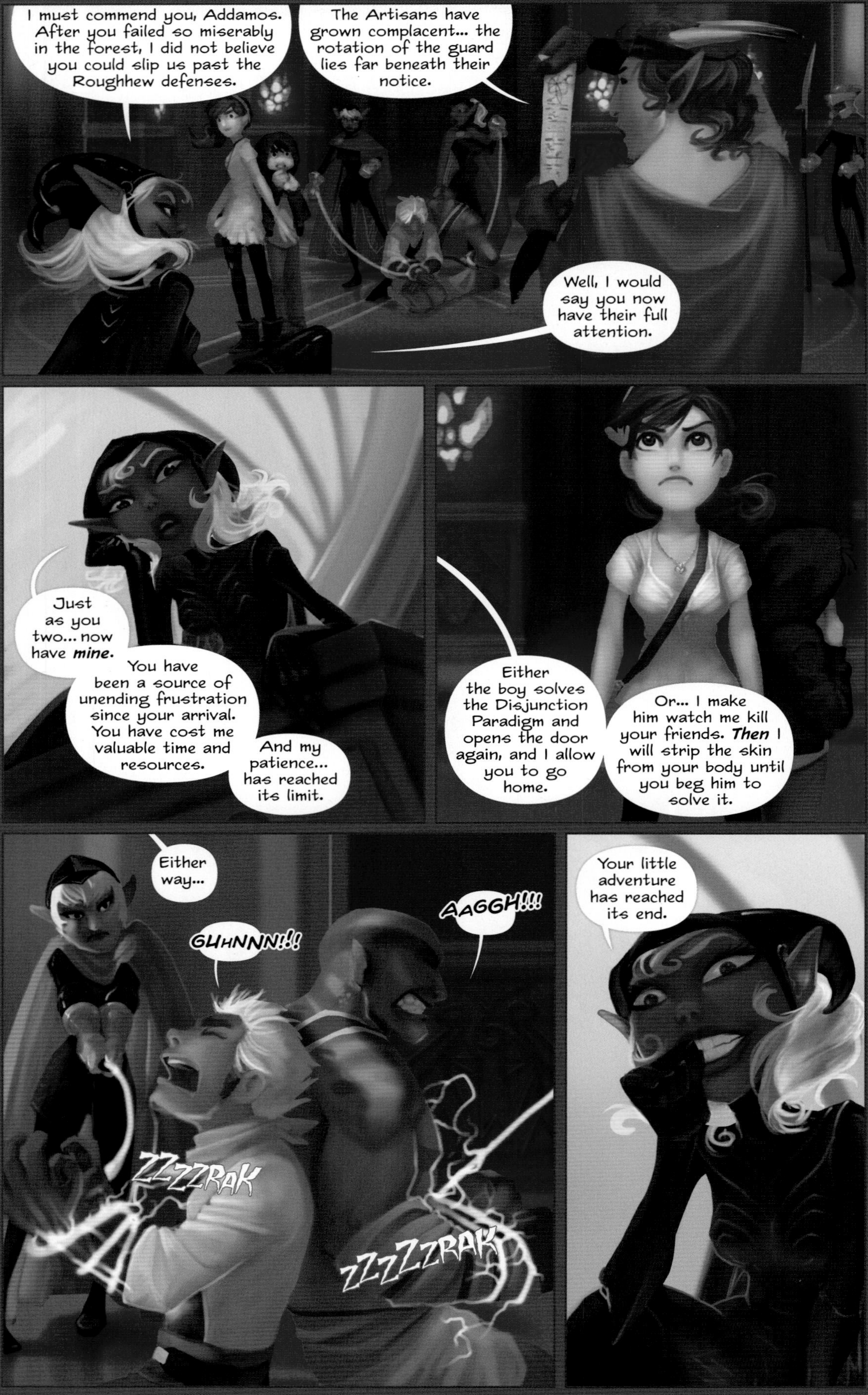
I must commend you, Addamos. After you failed so miserably in the forest, I did not believe you could slip us past the Roughhew defenses.
The Artisans have grown complacent... the rotation of the guard lies far beneath their notice.
Well, I would say you now have their full attention.
Just as you two... now have *mine*.
You have been a source of unending frustration since your arrival. You have cost me valuable time and resources.
And my patience... has reached its limit.
Either the boy solves the Disjunction Paradigm and opens the door again, and I allow you to go home.
Or... I make him watch me kill your friends. *Then* I will strip the skin from your body until you beg him to solve it.
Either way...
GUHNNN!!!
AAGGH!!!
ZZZZZRAK
ZZZZZRAK
Your little adventure has reached its end.

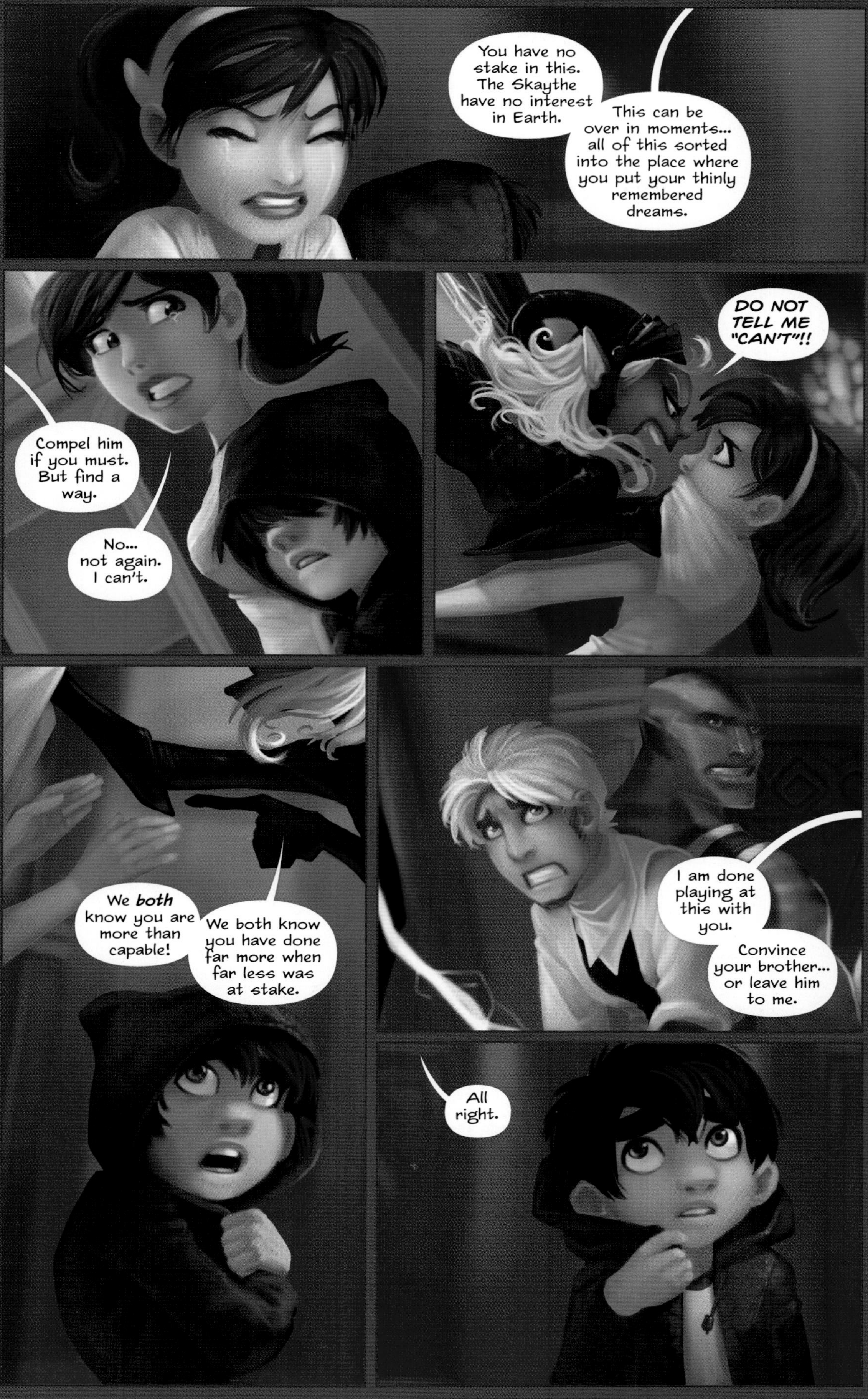
You have no stake in this. The Skaythe have no interest in Earth.
This can be over in moments... all of this sorted into the place where you put your thinly remembered dreams.
Compel him if you must. But find a way.
No... not again. I can't.
DO NOT TELL ME "CAN'T"!!
We *both* know you are more than capable!
We both know you have done far more when far less was at stake.
I am done playing at this with you.
Convince your brother... or leave him to me.
All right.

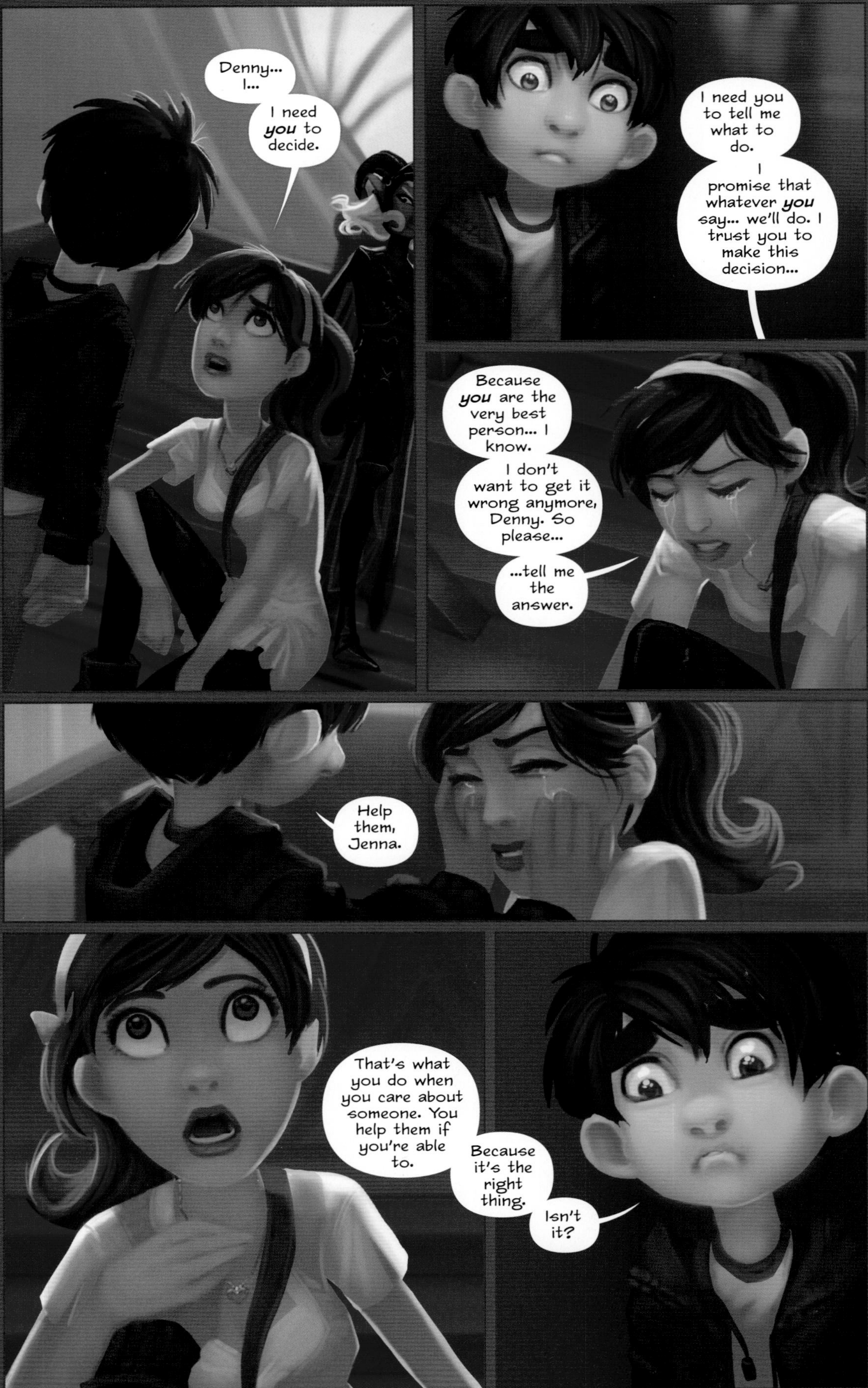
Denny... I...
I need *you* to decide.
I need you to tell me what to do.
I promise that whatever *you* say... we'll do. I trust you to make this decision...
Because *you* are the very best person... I know.
I don't want to get it wrong anymore, Denny. So please...
...tell me the answer.
Help them, Jenna.
That's what you do when you care about someone. You help them if you're able to.
Because it's the right thing.
Isn't it?

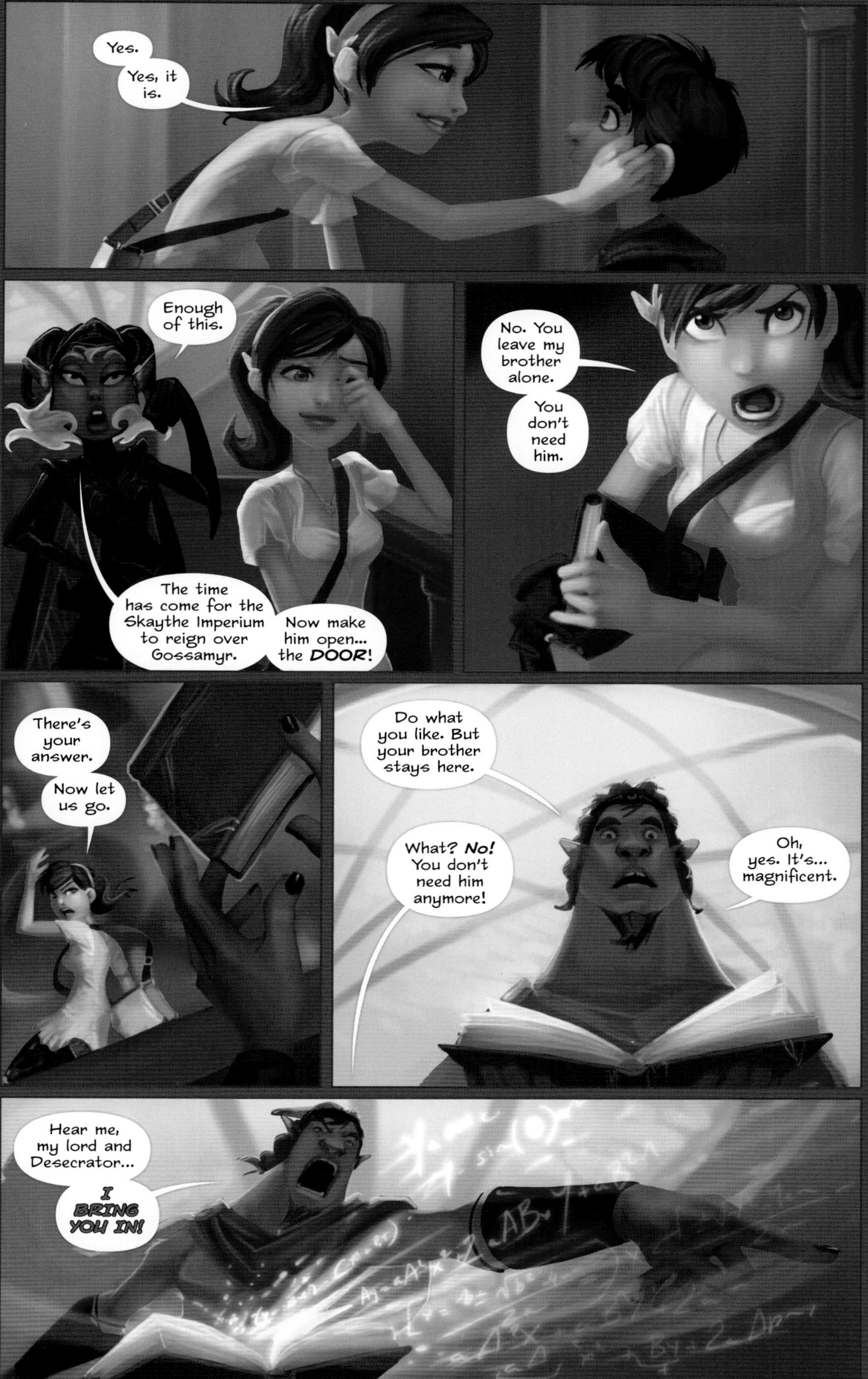
Yes.
Yes, it is.
Enough of this.
The time has come for the Skaythe Imperium to reign over Gossamyr.
Now make him open... the DOOR!
No. You leave my brother alone.
You don't need him.
There's your answer.
Now let us go.
Do what you like. But your brother stays here.
What? No! You don't need him anymore!
Oh, yes. It's... magnificent.
Hear me, my lord and Desecrator...
I BRING YOU IN!

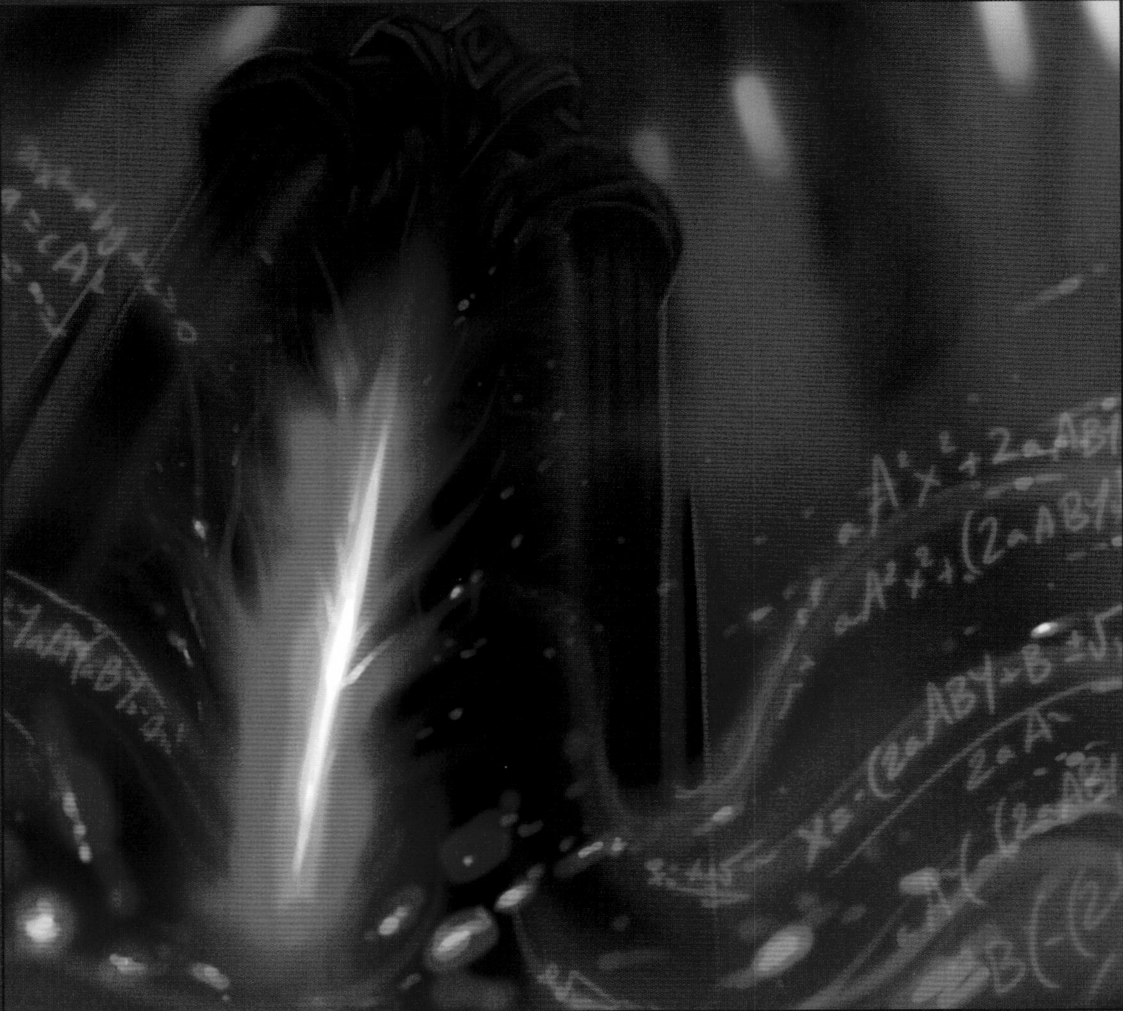

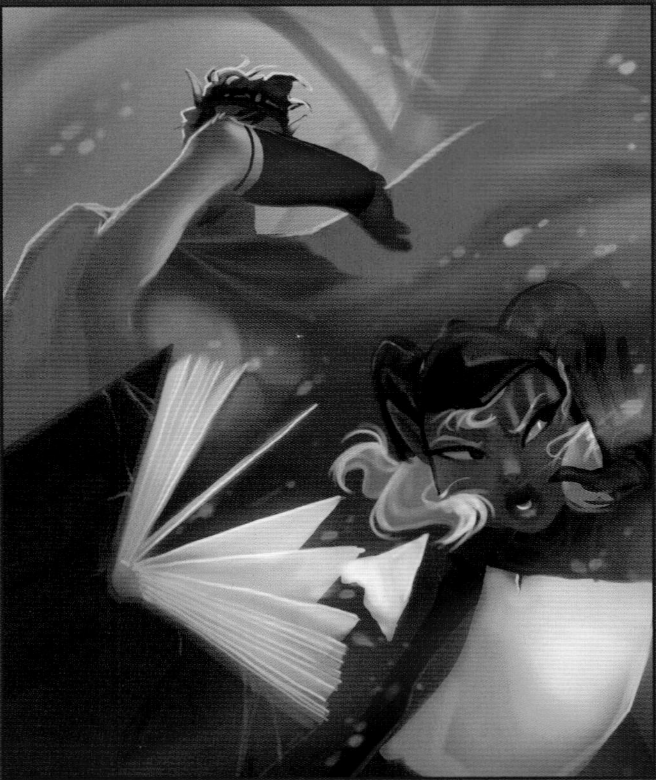

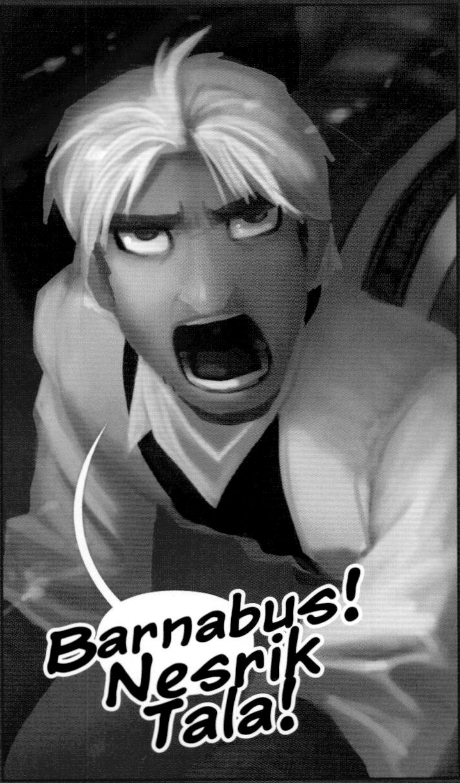
Barnabus! Nesrik Tala!

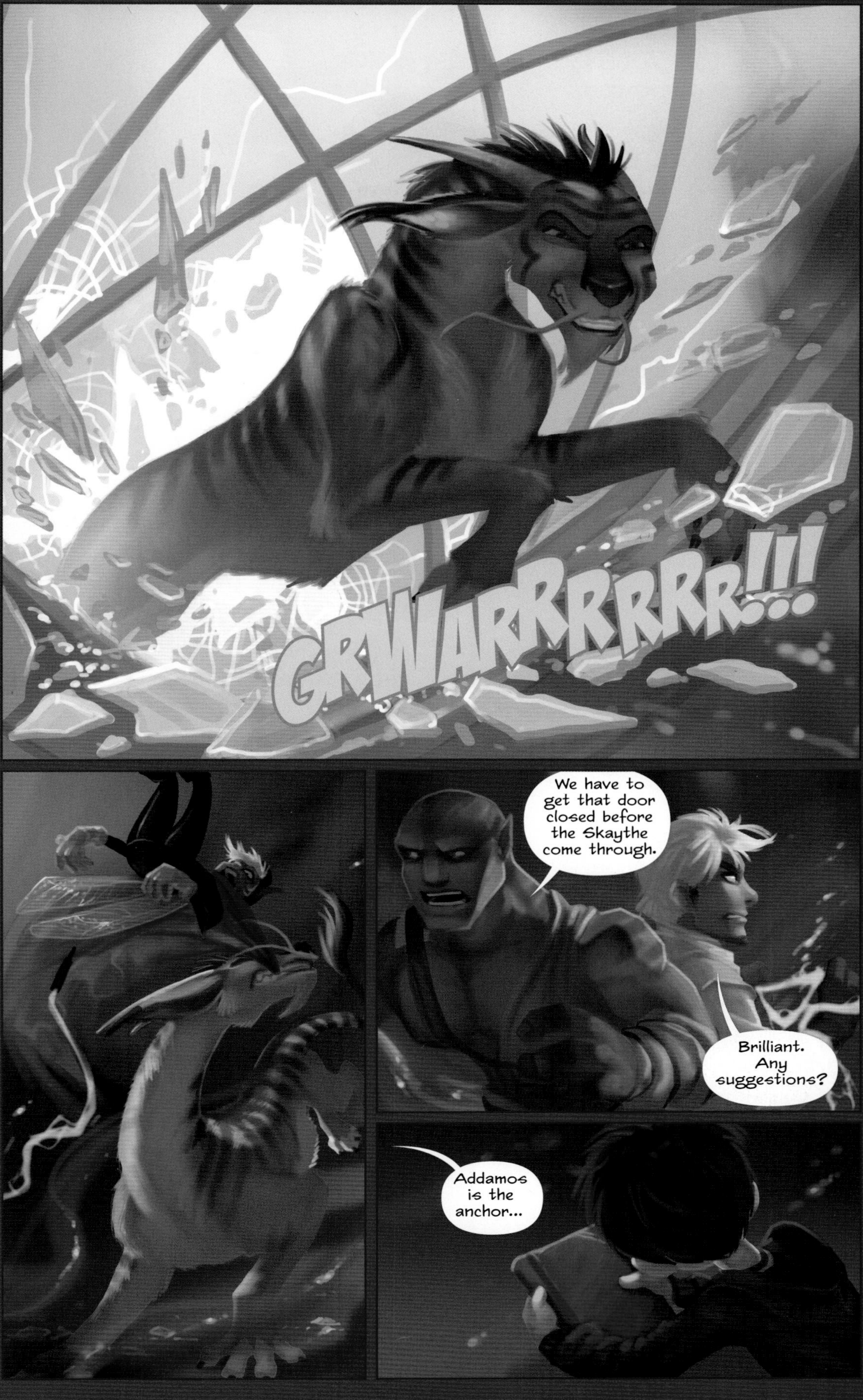
GRWARRRRRR!!!
We have to get that door closed before the Skaythe come through.
Brilliant. Any suggestions?
Addamos is the anchor...

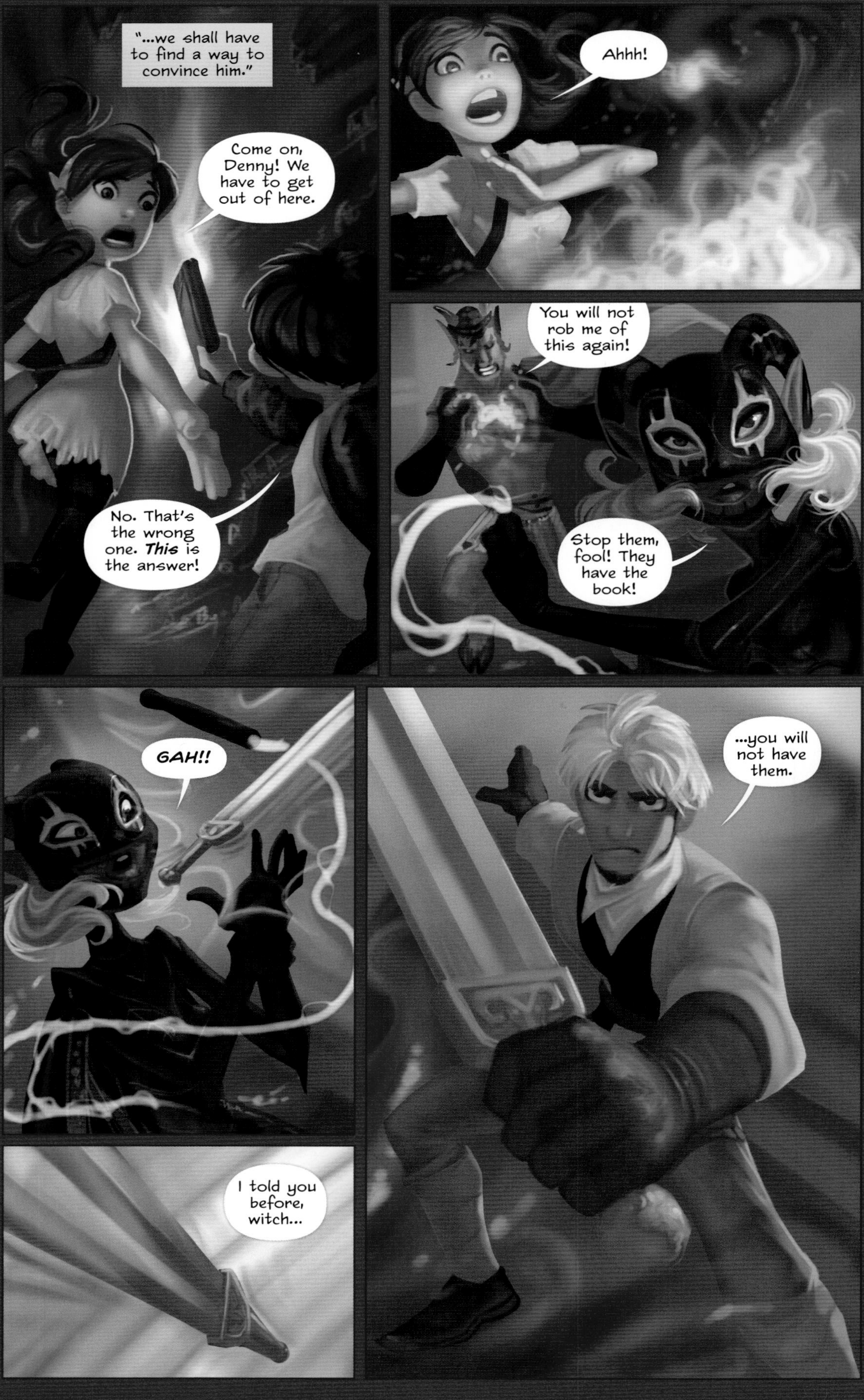
"...we shall have to find a way to convince him."
Come on, Denny! We have to get out of here.
No. That's the wrong one. ***This*** is the answer!
Ahhh!
You will not rob me of this again!
Stop them, fool! They have the book!
GAH!!
I told you before, witch...
...you will not have them.

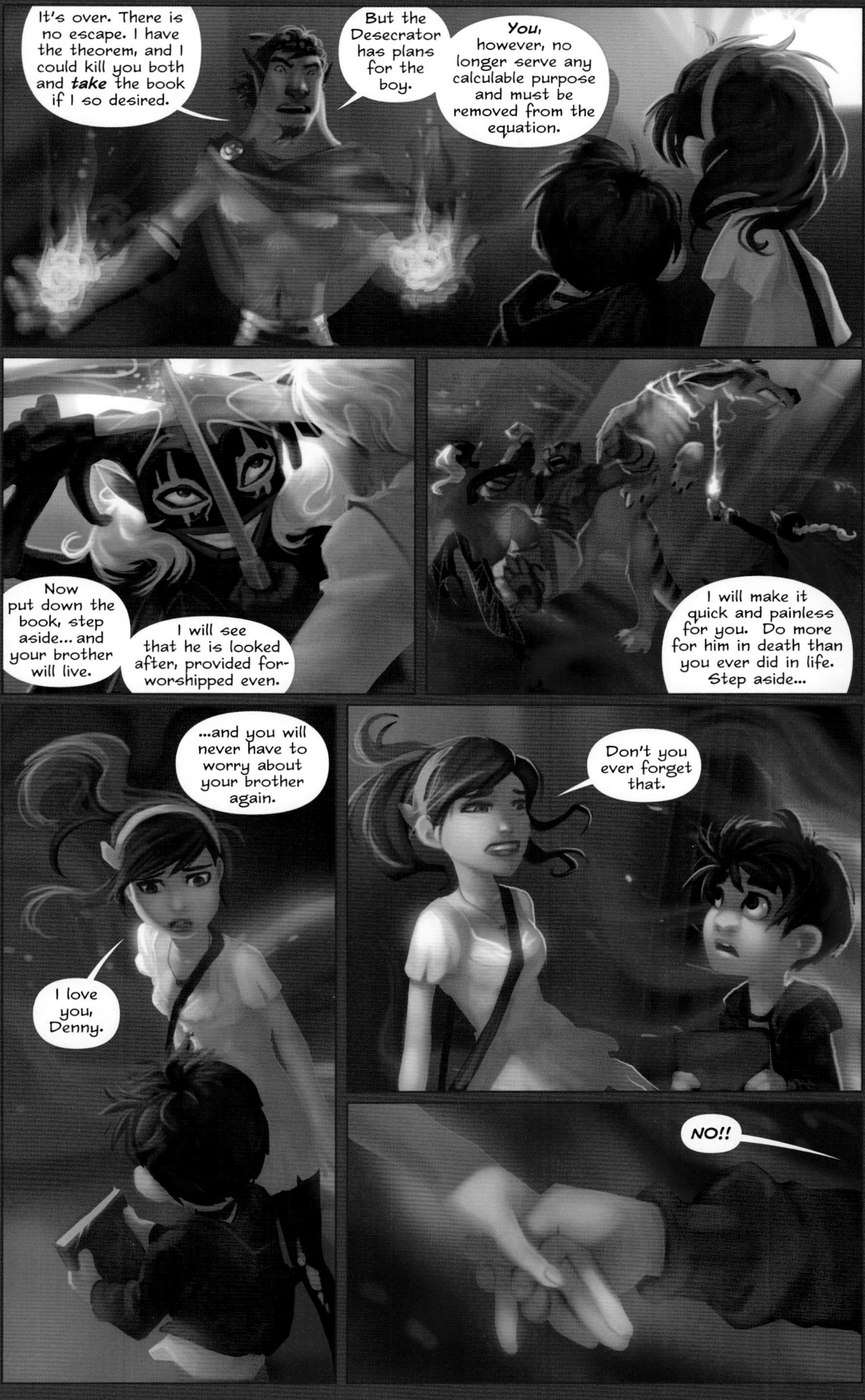

It's over. There is no escape. I have the theorem, and I could kill you both and *take* the book if I so desired.
But the Desecrator has plans for the boy.
You, however, no longer serve any calculable purpose and must be removed from the equation.
Now put down the book, step aside... and your brother will live.
I will see that he is looked after, provided for- worshipped even.
I will make it quick and painless for you. Do more for him in death than you ever did in life. Step aside...
...and you will never have to worry about your brother again.
I love you, Denny.
Don't you ever forget that.
NO!!

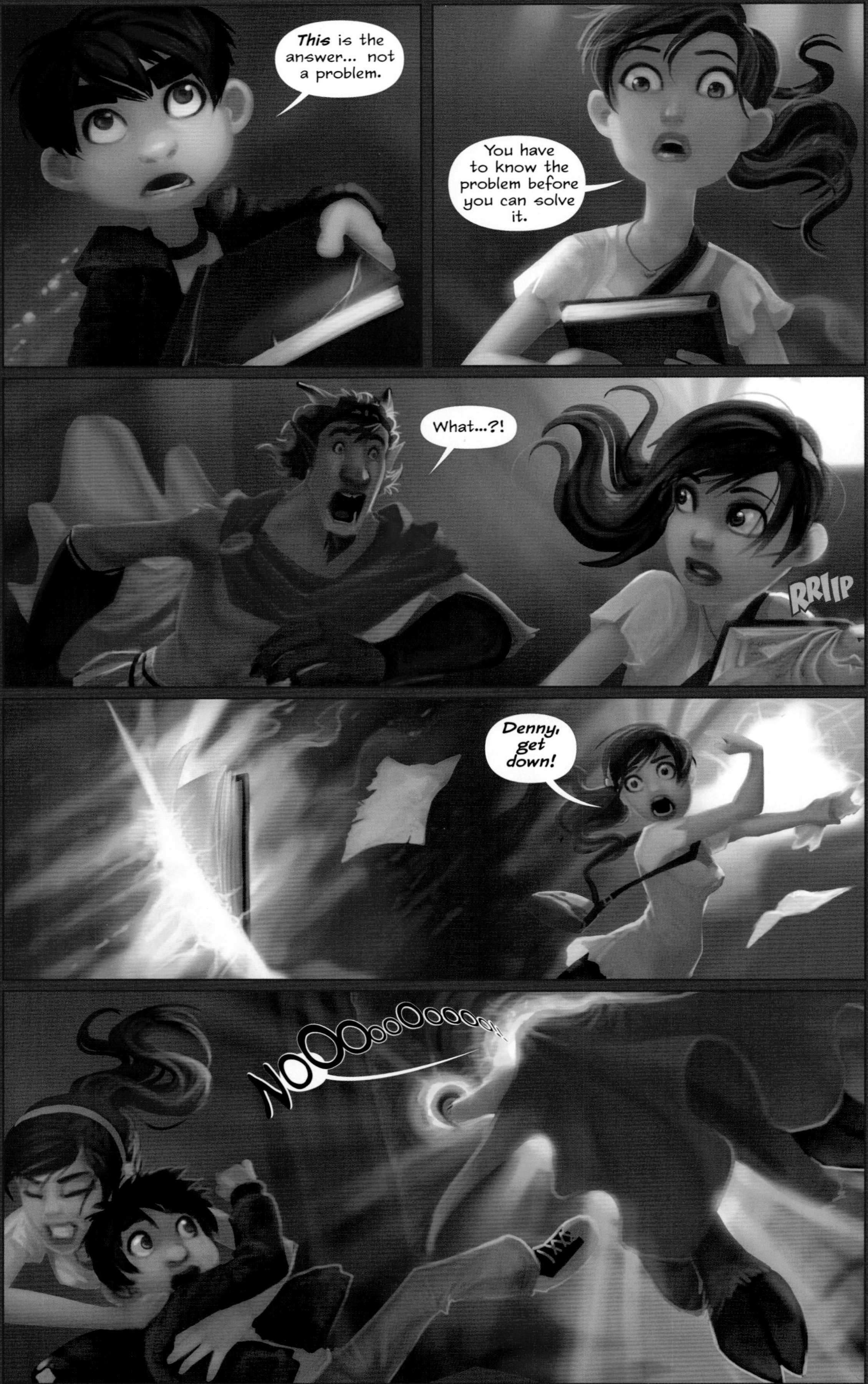
This is the answer... not a problem.
You have to know the problem before you can solve it.
What...?!
RRIIP
Denny, get down!
NOOooOoooo!

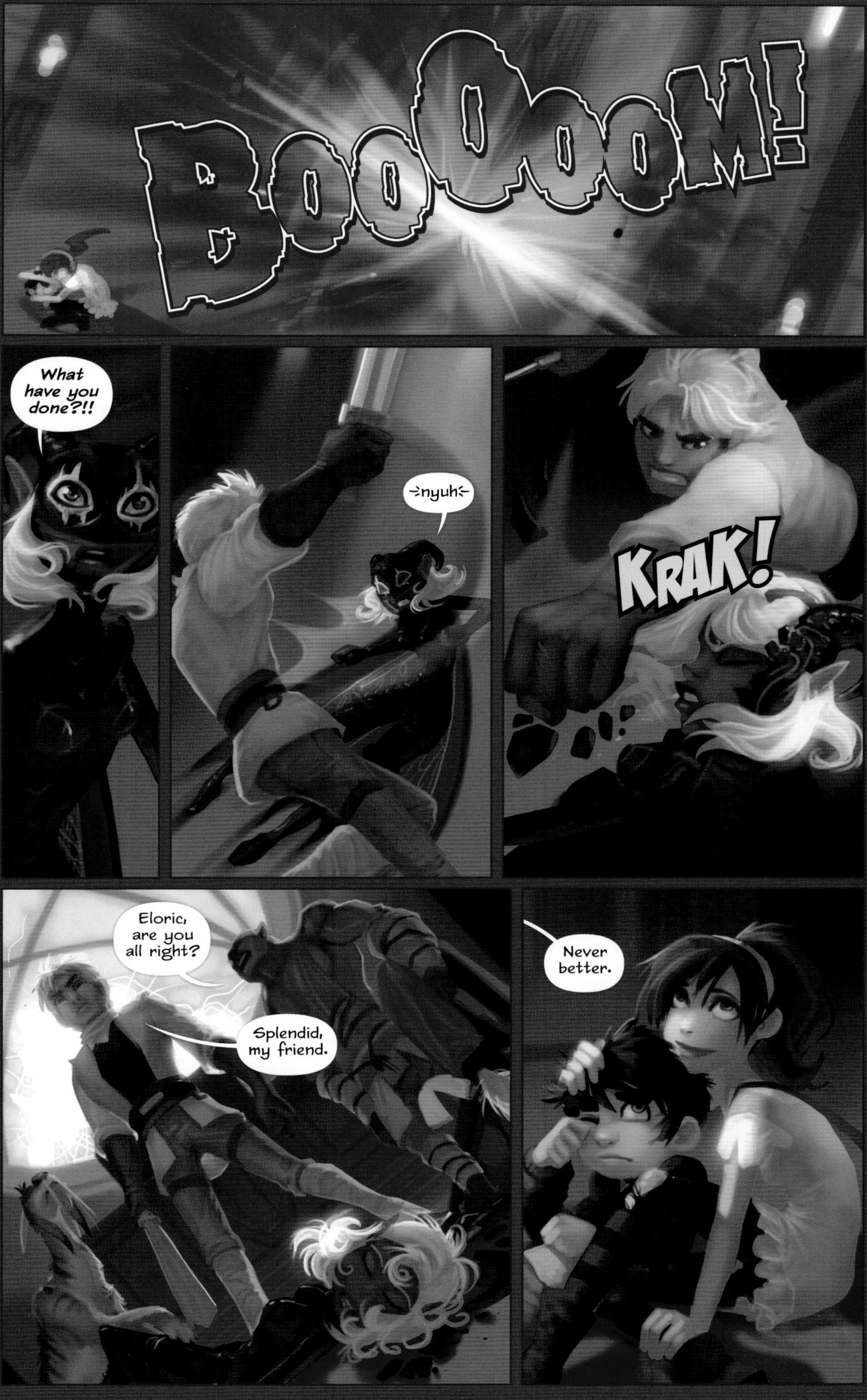
BOOOOOM!
What have you done?!!
nyuh
KRAK!
Eloric, are you all right?
Splendid, my friend.
Never better.

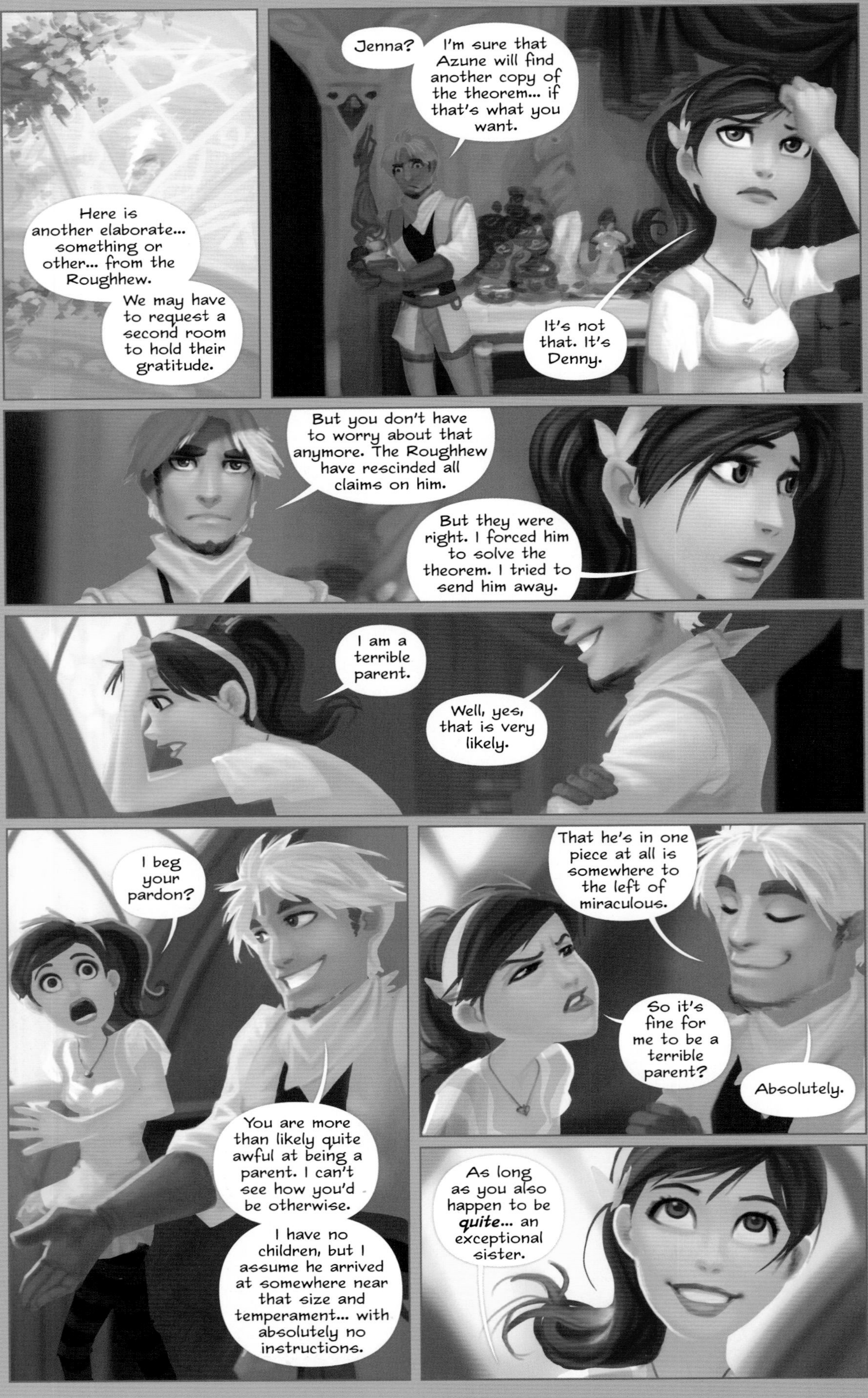

Here is another elaborate... something or other... from the Roughhew.
We may have to request a second room to hold their gratitude.
Jenna?
I'm sure that Azune will find another copy of the theorem... if that's what you want.
It's not that. It's Denny.
But you don't have to worry about that anymore. The Roughhew have rescinded all claims on him.
But they were right. I forced him to solve the theorem. I tried to send him away.
I am a terrible parent.
Well, yes, that is very likely.
I beg your pardon?
You are more than likely quite awful at being a parent. I can't see how you'd be otherwise.
I have no children, but I assume he arrived at somewhere near that size and temperament... with absolutely no instructions.
That he's in one piece at all is somewhere to the left of miraculous.
So it's fine for me to be a terrible parent?
Absolutely.
As long as you also happen to be *quite*... an exceptional sister.

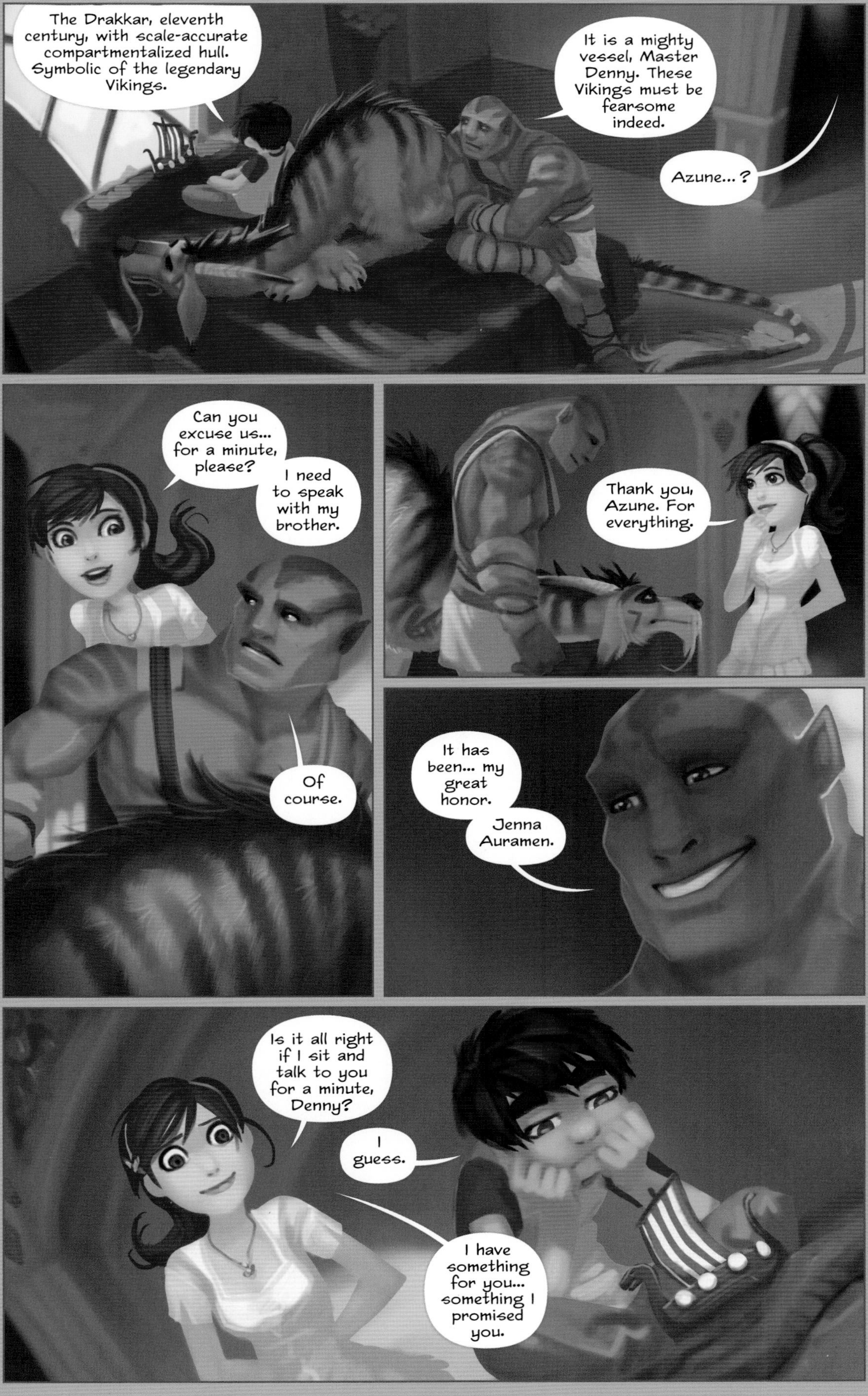

The Drakkar, eleventh century, with scale-accurate compartmentalized hull. Symbolic of the legendary Vikings.
It is a mighty vessel, Master Denny. These Vikings must be fearsome indeed.
Azune...?
Can you excuse us... for a minute, please?
I need to speak with my brother.
Of course.
Thank you, Azune. For everything.
It has been... my great honor.
Jenna Auramen.
Is it all right if I sit and talk to you for a minute, Denny?
I guess.
I have something for you... something I promised you.

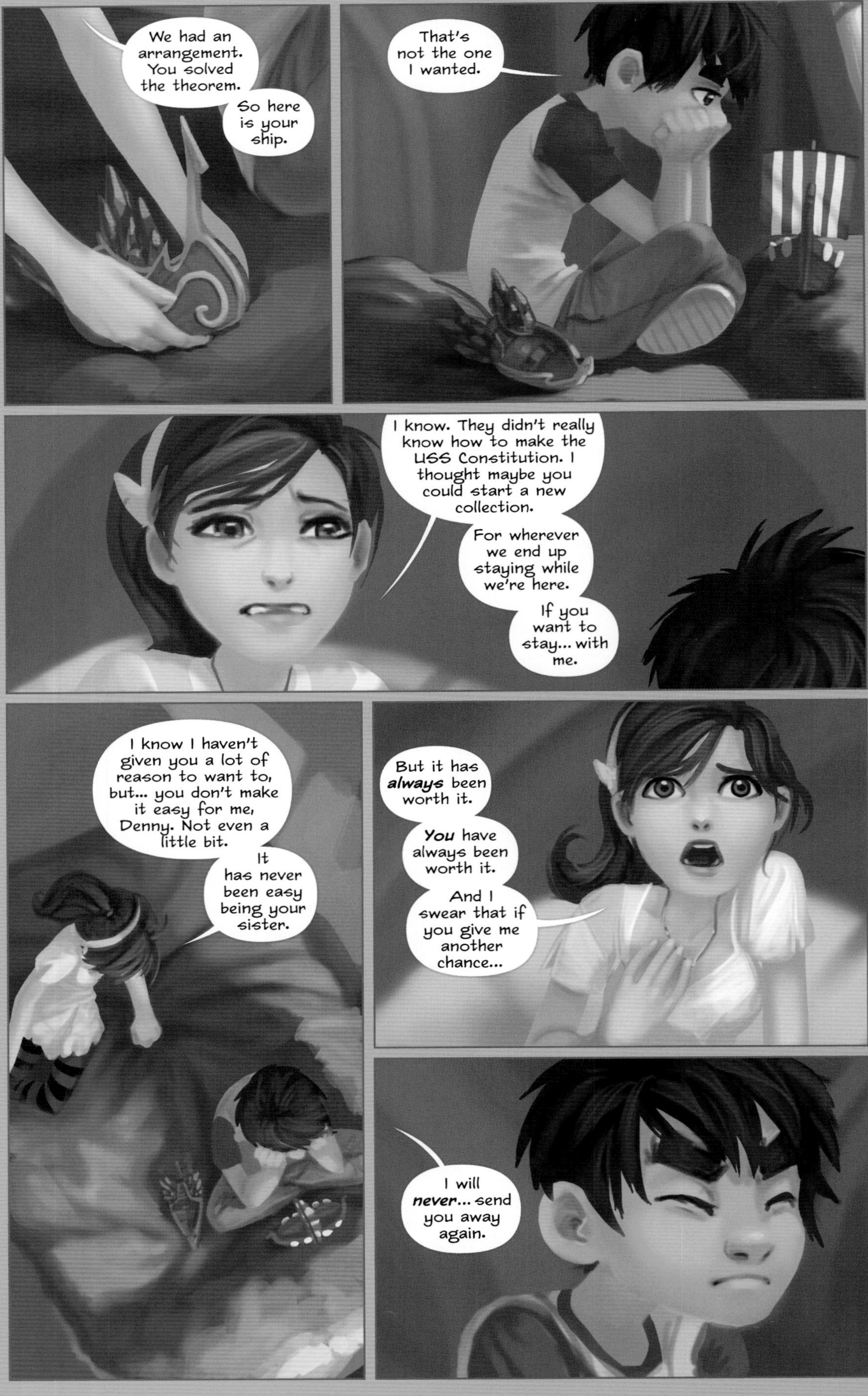
We had an arrangement. You solved the theorem.
So here is your ship.
That's not the one I wanted.
I know. They didn't really know how to make the USS Constitution. I thought maybe you could start a new collection.
For wherever we end up staying while we're here.
If you want to stay... with me.
I know I haven't given you a lot of reason to want to, but... you don't make it easy for me, Denny. Not even a little bit.
It has never been easy being your sister.
But it has *always* been worth it.
You have always been worth it.
And I swear that if you give me another chance...
I will *never*... send you away again.

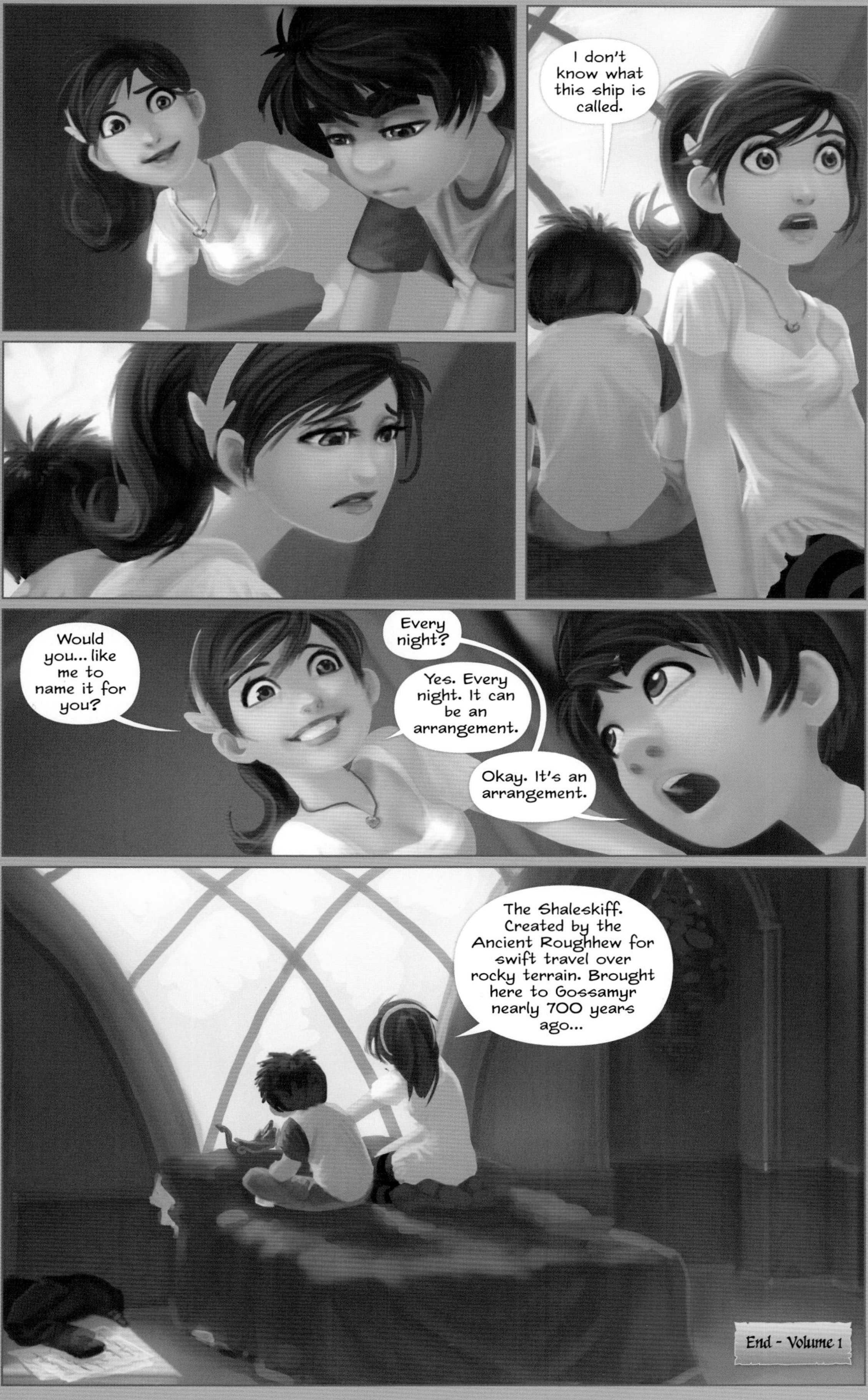
I don't know what this ship is called.
Would you... like me to name it for you?
Every night?
Yes. Every night. It can be an arrangement.
Okay. It's an arrangement.
The Shaleskiff. Created by the Ancient Roughhew for swift travel over rocky terrain. Brought here to Gossamyr nearly 700 years ago...
End - Volume 1

Cover Gallery

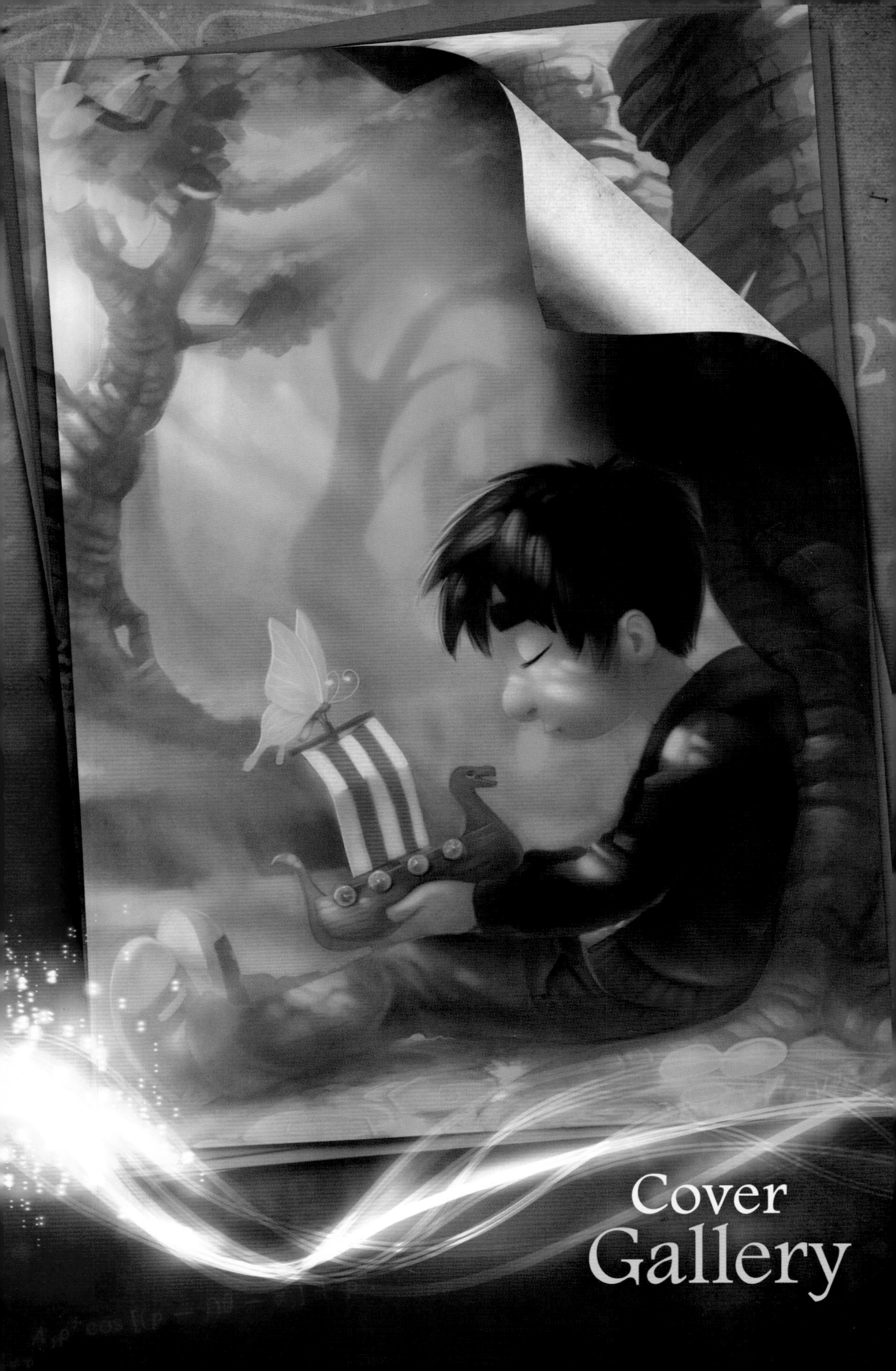

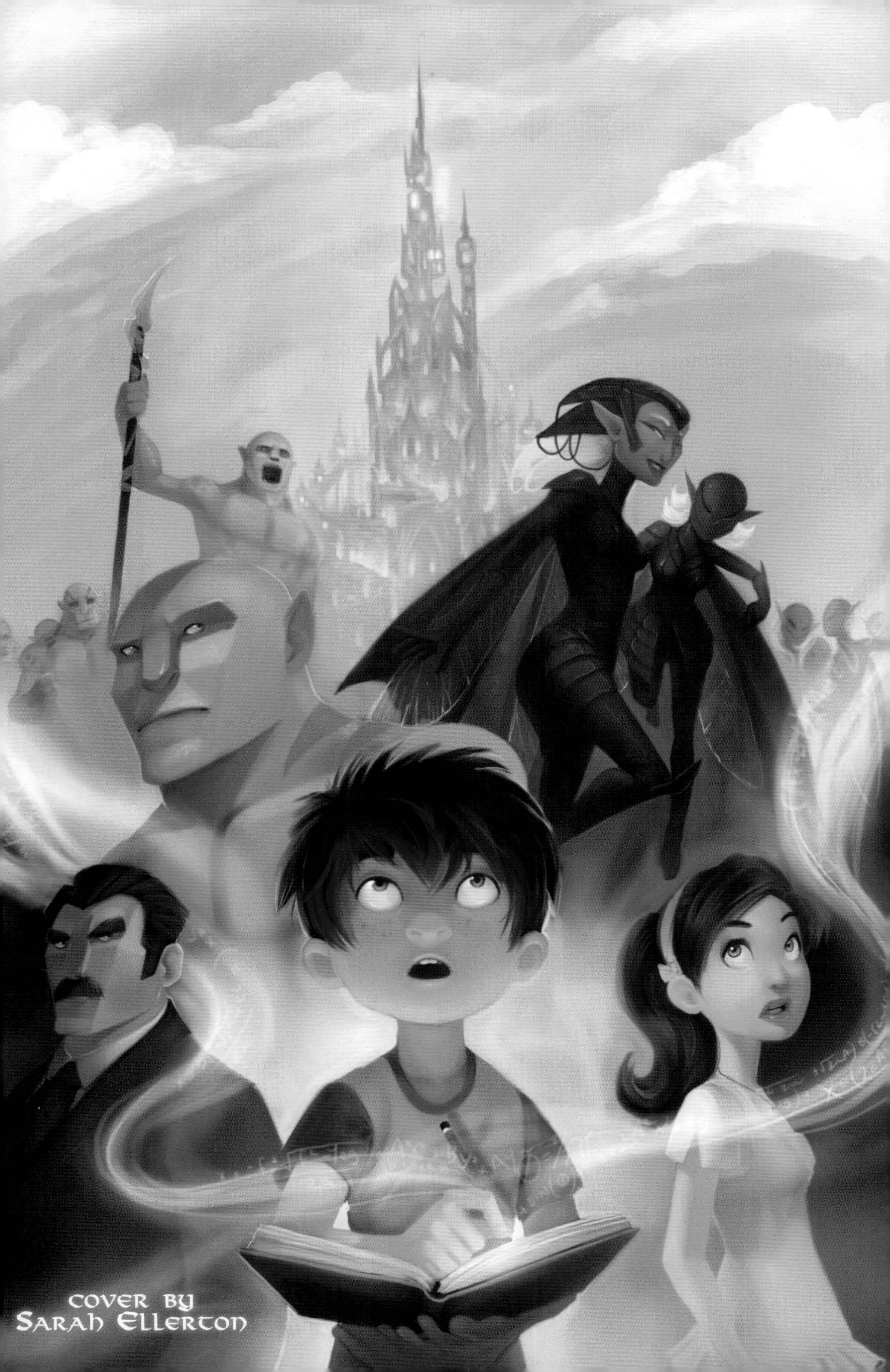
COVER BY
SARAH ELLERTON

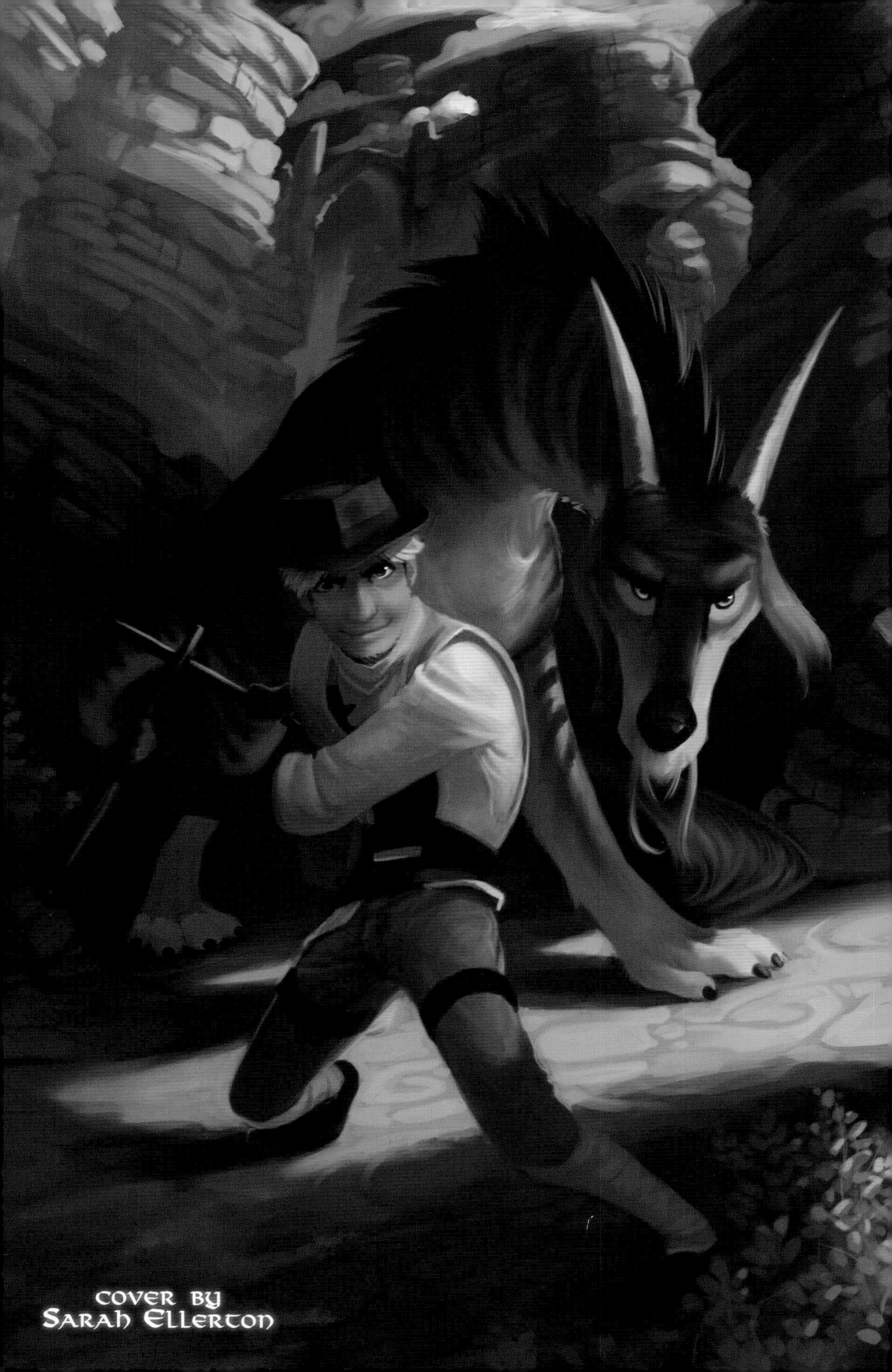
COVER BY
SARAH ELLERTON

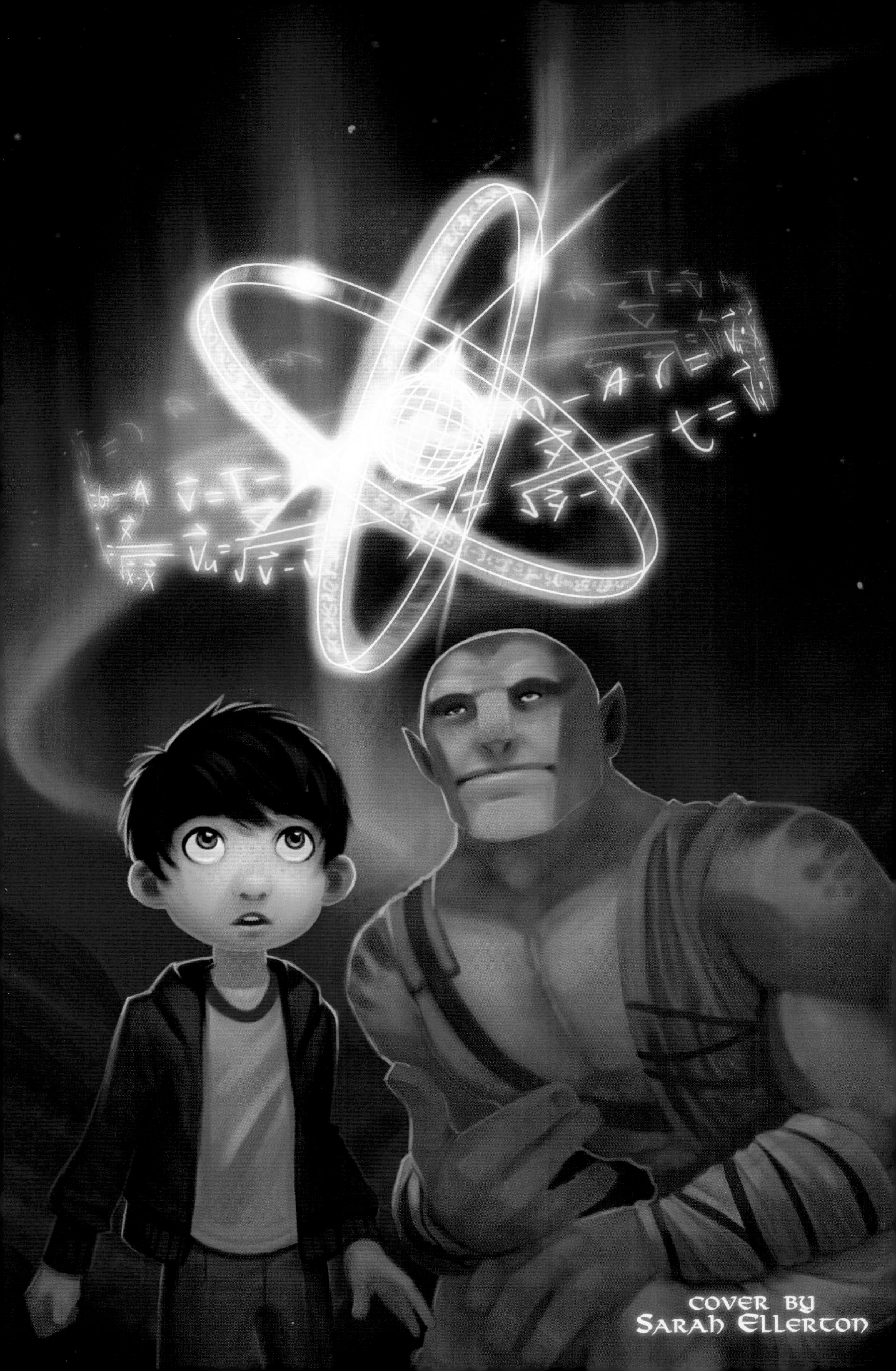
COVER BY
SARAH ELLERTON

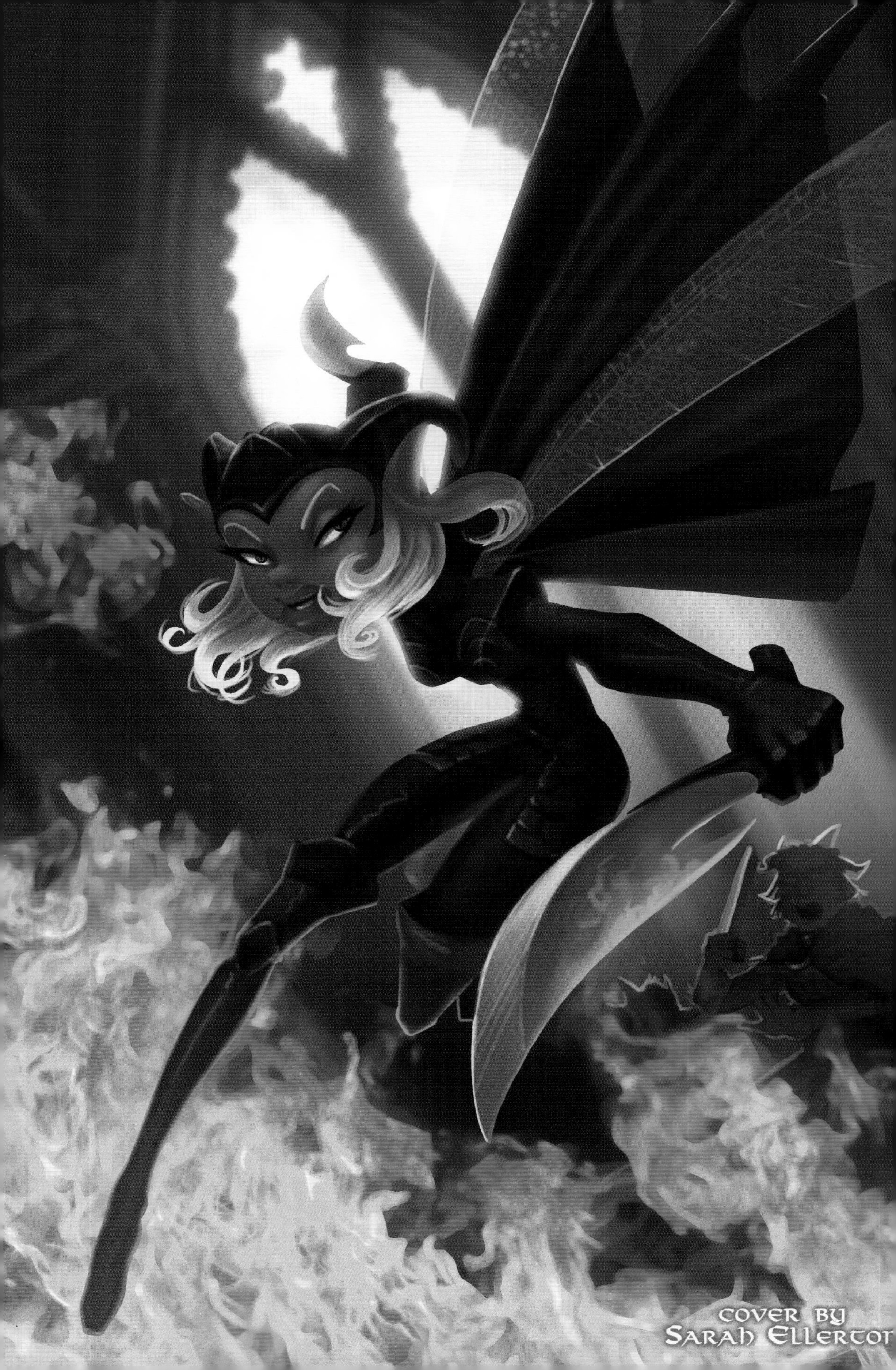
COVER BY
SARAH ELLERTON

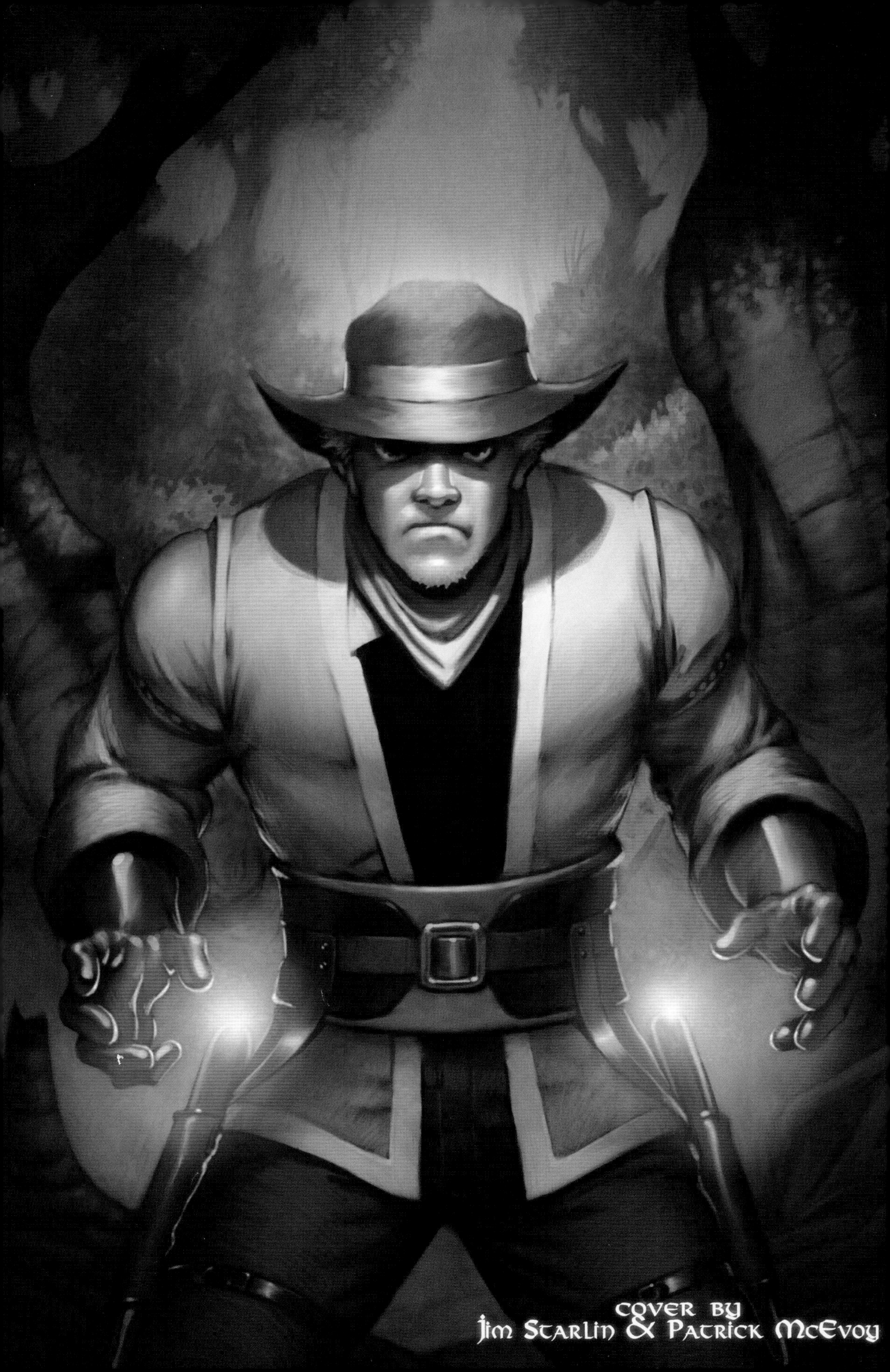
COVER BY
Jim Starlin & Patrick McEvoy

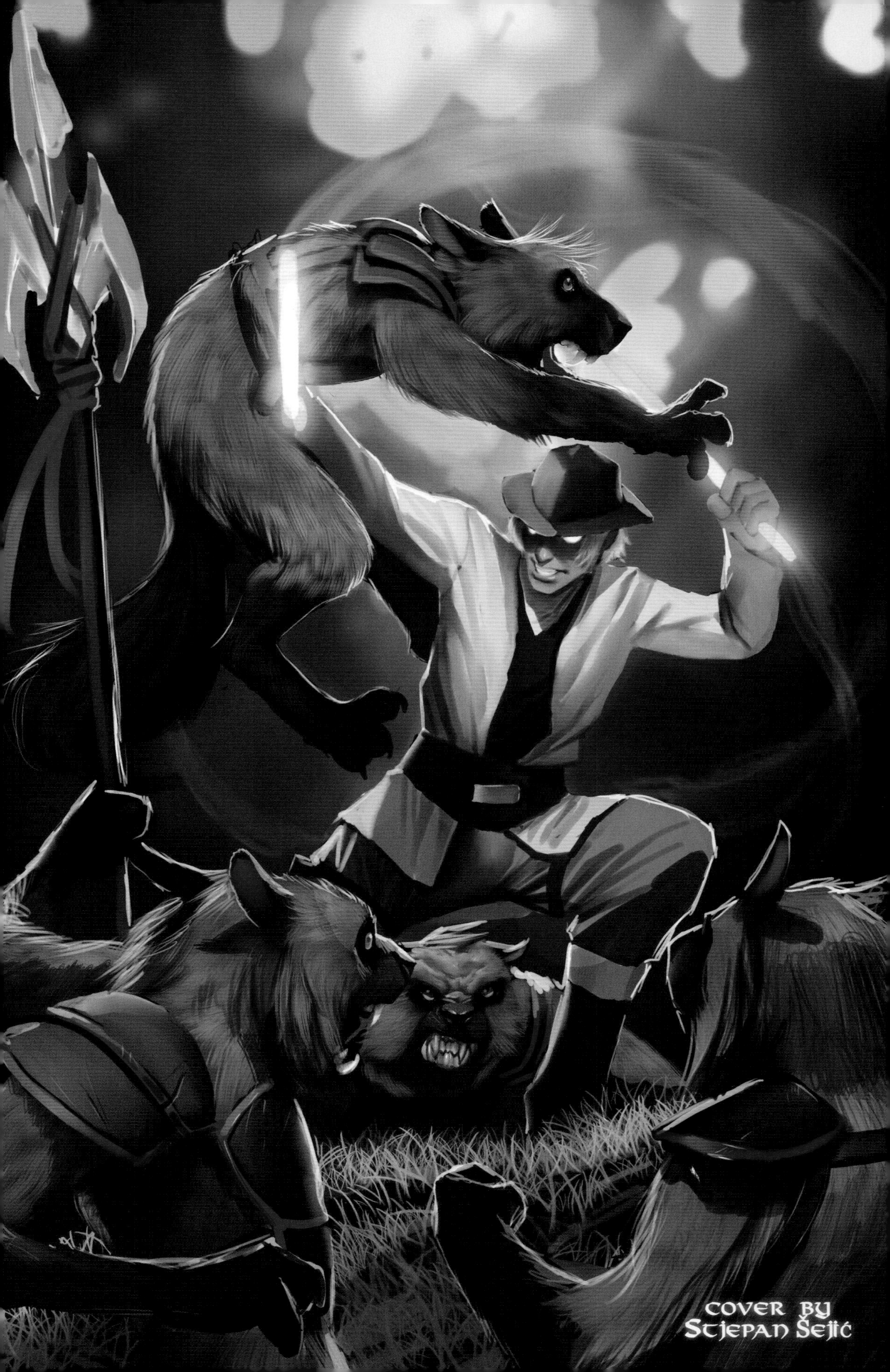
COVER BY
STJEPAN ŠEJIĆ

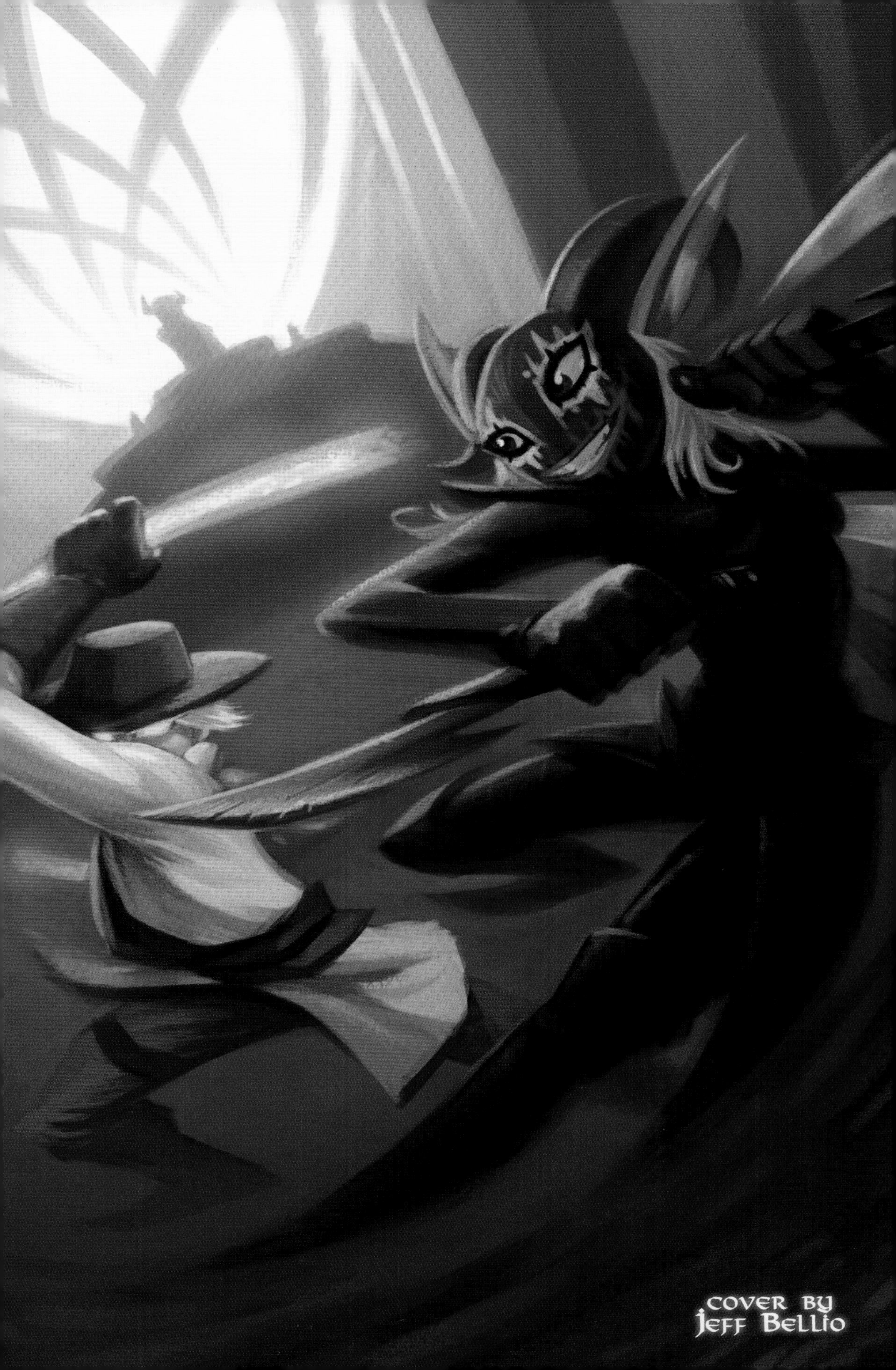
COVER BY
JEFF BELLIO

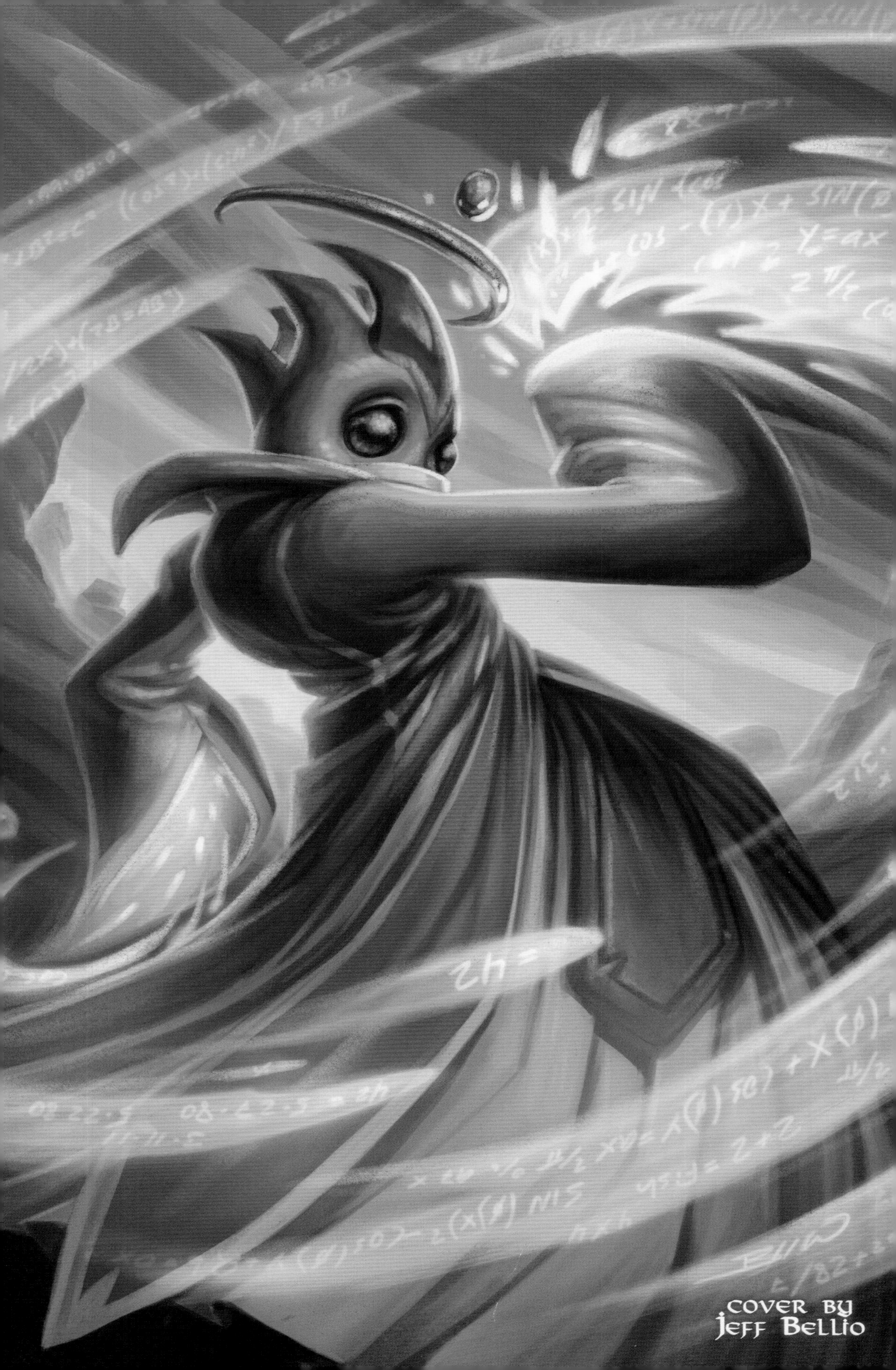
COVER BY
JEFF BELLIO

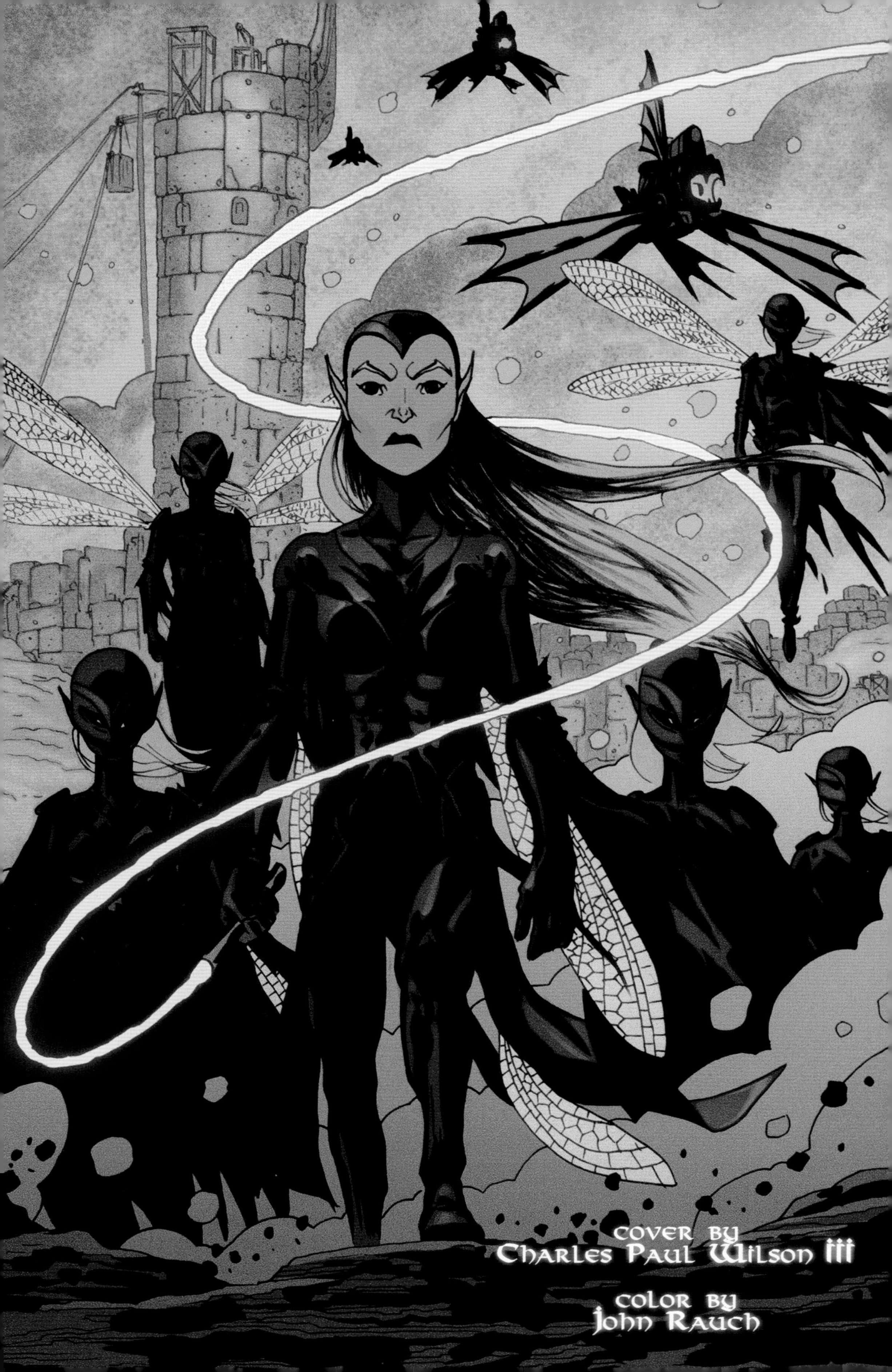

COVER BY
Charles Paul Wilson III

COLOR BY
John Rauch

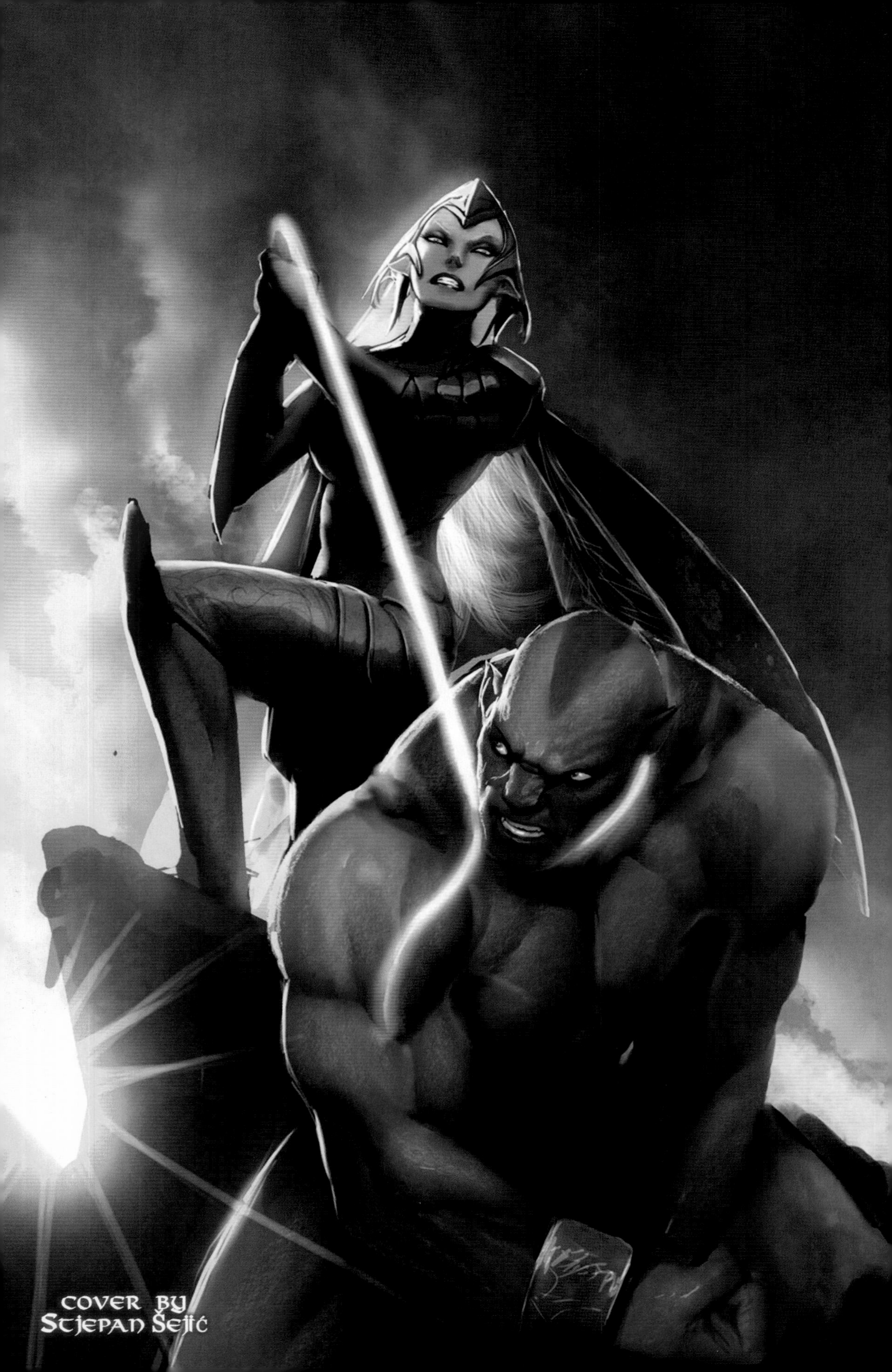

COVER BY
Stjepan Šejić

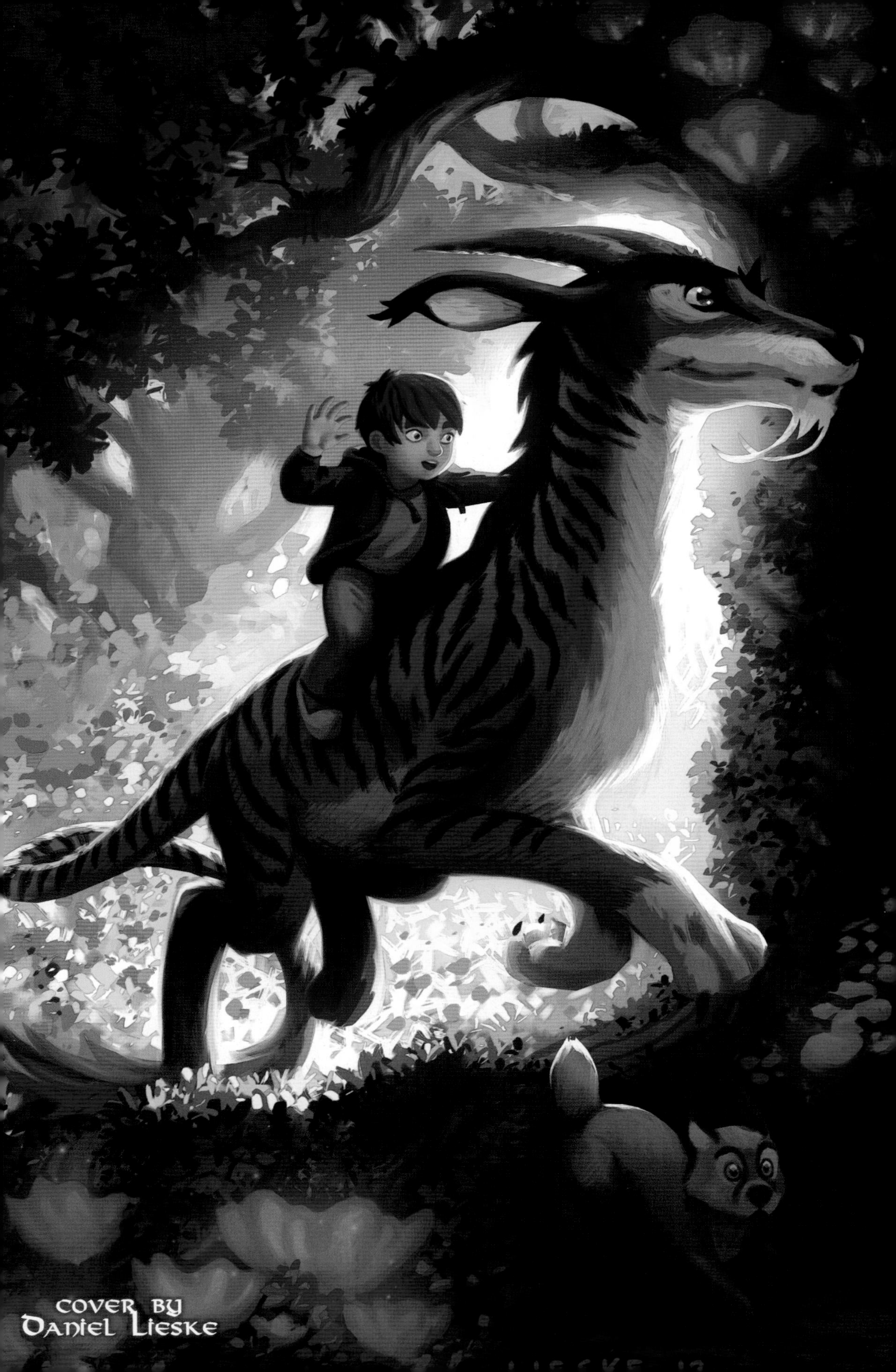
COVER BY
Daniel Lieske

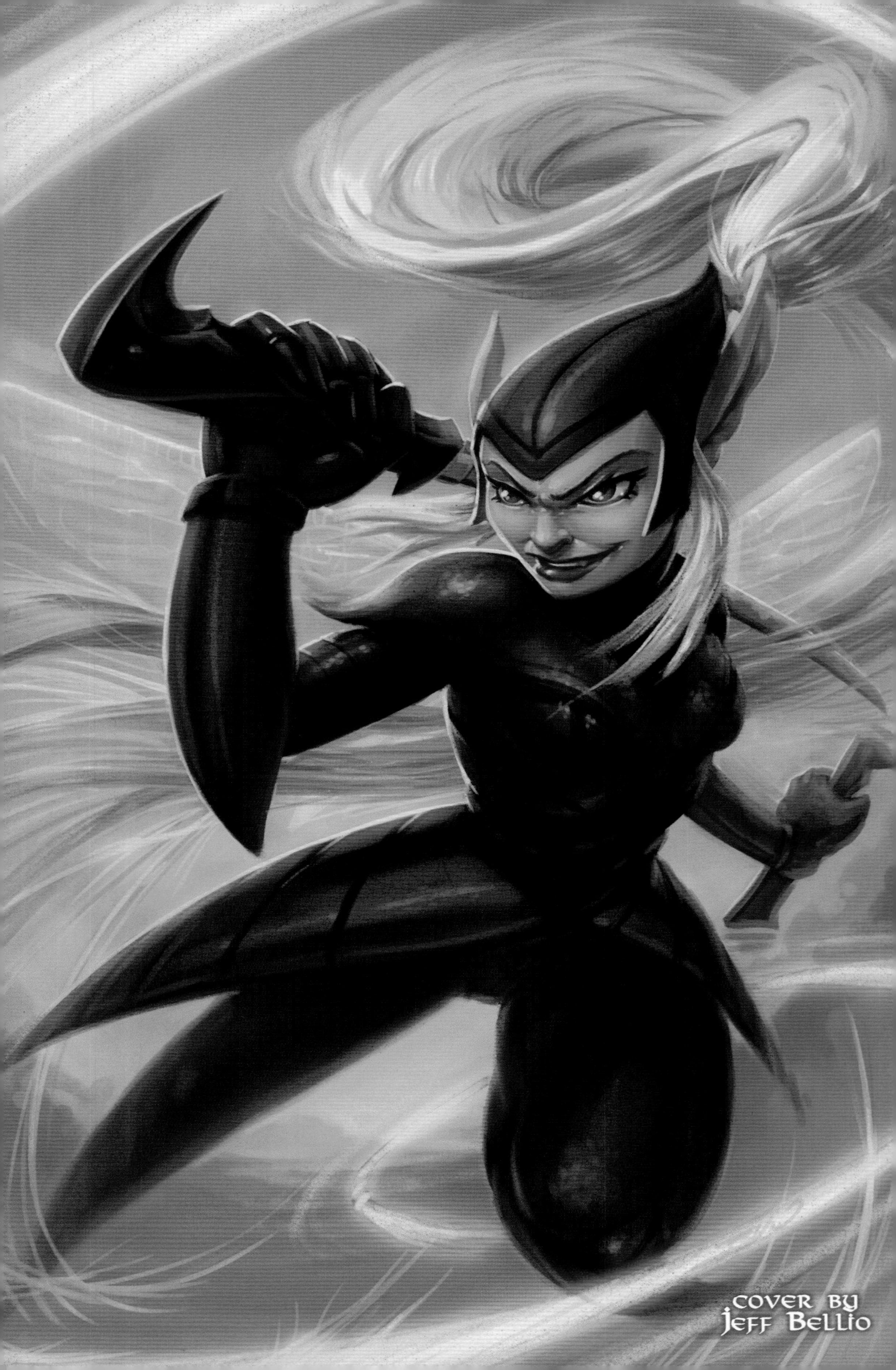
COVER BY
JEFF BELLIO

THE LORELARK CODEX

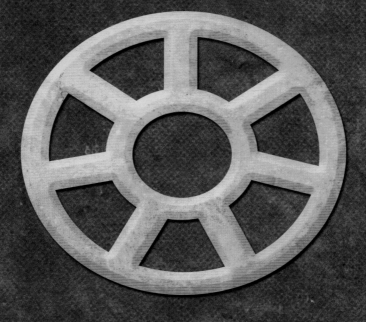

> "This place you have found... is both great
> and terrible... and like no other in creation."
> — *Azune D'tal, Peacemarshal of Lillienthal*

CHAPTER ONE

Gather closer, children. Oh, you have nothing to fear. It is only a hood and cloak woven of feathers. See when I pull it back? The Lorelark is just our uniform. Like a costume! When one sees *this* cloak of feathers, they know that they can come to us to hear the tales of our rich and wonderful world.

Why, of course I will tell you a story, child. Nothing would please me more. Sit close and sit quiet, and I will share with you the very *first* story of this grand place we all share — this place that we call Gossamyr.

Now, we are all travellers or descended from travellers. Our mothers and our mothers' mothers came from one of the Seven Worlds and somehow found their way here to Gossamyr — where our lives are long beyond reason and where knowledge can shape reality. Because, unlike the worlds we came from, Gossamyr is *synchronistic*. It is a world forged of will and magic... imagined and constructed by a group of powerful beings we all know as the Preservers.

No, child, the Preservers are not gods. But, you know, they aren't quite mortal either. They don't age and they are amazingly powerful, but they CAN be touched. And they can be... hurt... just like any one of us. But unlike you and me, the Preservers were never, ever children. That's right. They never had to do chores. They never frolicked outside. They were never tucked into bed at night with a story. In fact, they never even had parents because they weren't BORN. One moment they didn't exist... and then the next moment, they did!

Yes, I know it is a bit strange, but if you listen carefully, you will begin to understand. Gossamyr exists in "*the between*", which is what we call the space that divides the Seven Worlds. But long, long ago, before there was even an *idea* of a place like Gossamyr in "*the between*", there was nothing.

There was no light. No time. There was no before and there was no after... there simply *wasn't.* And because there was no time, it was like that for what seemed like an eternity and an instant. But then... something strange and WONDERFUL happened.

Somewhere, on one of the Seven Worlds, a person of impressive reason looked at this nothing, realized what it actually was and then did something incredible. They gave it... a NAME. Now, this might seem simple to you and me, but such a leap of reason had never before been attempted. And, my children, actions of this magnitude always have consequences.

Because as soon as someone named it for what it was... it became *more* than just *nothing.* It became "Nothing." Can you hear the difference? They turned ^ into a concept, which made it *something.* And how can nothing also be something at the same time? It created a great contradiction in the universe. The "Nothing that was Something" was a paradox of logic that *demanded* reconciliation, and it became something fearsome indeed... something we call chaos.

It was a battle of logic in the fundamental laws of reality! And the force of that struggle was a great cataclysm. But out of that cataclysm, a symbol of great power was forged.

$$0$$

Just a number? Oh, my dear child, you have to understand that *0* was never just a number! It is an idea that altered reality and the basis of all civilization forever. That is why only *0* was powerful enough to contain the impossibility that was the "Nothing that was Something." *0* forced order on the chaos, trapping it within its body.

Now, chaos is a vicious and determined thing. It fought and chafed at its prison of reason, but eventually order prevailed and the swirl of chaos became one with *0*... which made it more than just a concept. It made it perfect and unassailable.

And in that instant, perfection became TRUE awareness. Thirteen individuals made of pure mathematics came to life with the freedom to choose their own destinies and recreate a world in their images. And *that,* my sweet children, is how the Preservers came to be.

Yes, I know there are only twelve Preservers now, but there is a reason for that too. It's not a very glad tale, children, but it *is* a brave tale. And sometimes that is nearly as important.

CHAPTER TWO

The Preservers were a curious but detached group. They used their mastery over time and space to build dazzling constructs that allowed them to visit and document the Seven Worlds. And for a time, that was more than enough for them. But after a while, they began to feel that their existence was meant to serve a higher purpose.

Intelligent beyond comprehension they might be, but emotionally, the Preservers were really no older or wiser than any of you young ones here. And what they didn't realize is that their indirect interactions with these other worlds were changing them. They began to develop a deep appreciation for beauty and symmetry, and they wished to preserve that knowledge for all eternity.

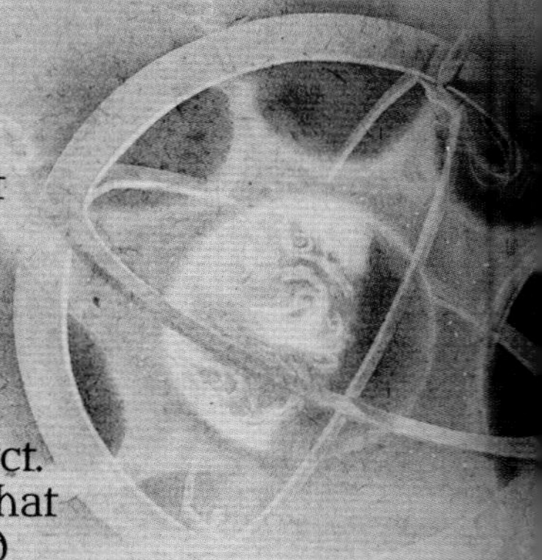

And this, children, is when the Preservers began constructing the *Synchronistic World* that we call Gossamyr. This would be the ultimate expression of what they had learned so far. It would be a land built on a foundation of pure mathematics that would exist within the heart of the Between and be safe from chaos.

The Preservers began their work in earnest, developing an engineering marvel called the Construct. There was a central ring with two additional rings that spun around it to create an artificial atmosphere and establish the fundamental laws of nature.

Then the Preservers drew in stray matter from the Seven Worlds to use as the building blocks of Gossamyr. They began to shape mountains, rivers, oceans, forests and weather patterns. They brought in new genetic material from the worlds they visited and created a perfectly balanced ecosystem of plant and animal life.

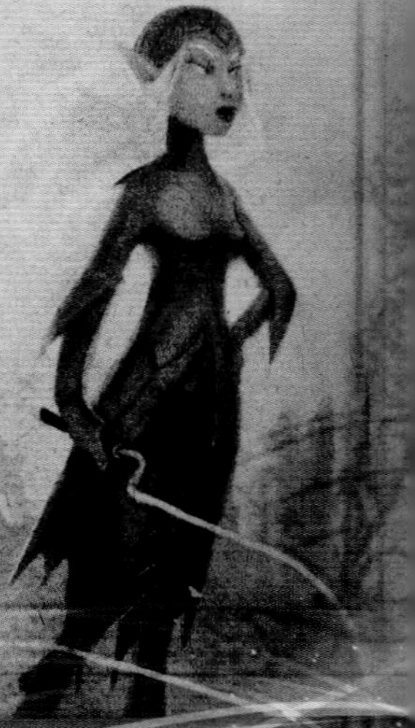

Once the Preservers had living things on their world, they quickly discovered an unexpected result of their endeavor. All living things on Gossamyr were extremely resistant to the effects of entropy! Which to you and me means that plants and animals here lived far longer than they did on other worlds, which was both wonderful and curious. And the Preservers, being so very curious, wished to test this phenomenon on something a bit more advanced than plants and animals. So they chose to go in search of higher life forms on a world called Nilus. And on Nilus, my sweet children, the Preservers would find both their greatest achievement and greatest failure.

Nilus was a world of rage and chaos; an entire world under the thrall of the brutal Skaythe Imperium. Shhh... it's okay, child. They can't hurt you here. But yes, they are terrifying. The black fairies of chaos used the energy generated by decay to perform acts of great power and violence. But even in a world of such despair, there is still a glimmer of hope and beauty. And on Nilus, that was found in the Skaythe's most impressive creation: the race of slaves they called the T'yalli.

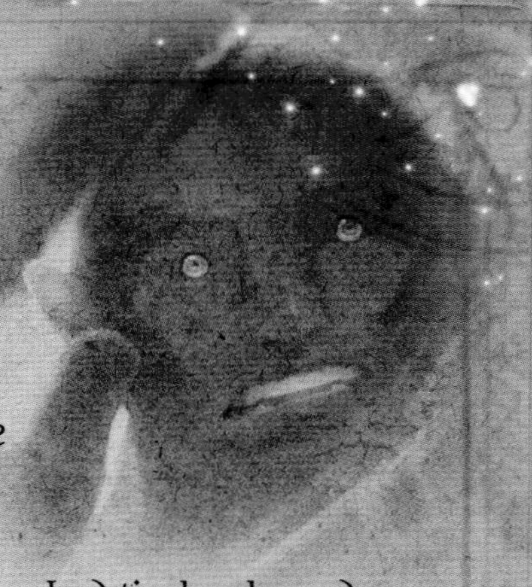

The T'yalli were a sturdy and quiet race who worked tirelessly under the lashes of the *Skaythe* and lived or died at the whims of their masters. When they became too weak to work, the T'yalli were slowly tortured and their bodies desiccated over time to create a vile ichor called *roil* that the *Skaythe* used to power their dark magic. The Preservers had long ago developed certain emotions as they pertained to beauty and creation, but when they witnessed this living antithesis of all they held sacred, they discovered what it meant... to hate. And for the first time since they had come into existence, the Preservers acted out of emotion and feeling instead of calculated judgment.

They used their considerable power over chaos to free the T'yalli from their bondage, but in doing so they drew the wrath of the *Skaythe* . The Preservers had never participated in violence and did not have a full understanding of danger... and they were unprepared for the onslaught of rage and aggression directed at them. And to make matters worse, the *Skaythe* themselves were *chaos-born*. Their natural state is one of contradiction and, as such, they were incredibly resistant to the Preservers' magic.

They could not stand against the fury of the Skaythe and so were forced to flee the world of Nilus. The Preservers and the T'yalli managed to make it back to the door and escape, but at a terrible cost. The eldest of the original thirteen Preservers ensured that his brothers and the T'yalli could escape, and then he kept them safe by sealing the door behind him with a complex theorem of order called the Disjunction Paradigm. The amount of power this required wreaked havoc on Gossamyr, creating a vast wasteland that scars our world to this day. But since the Skaythe were born from chaos they would never be able to solve this theorem, and they would be effectively trapped on Nilus forever.

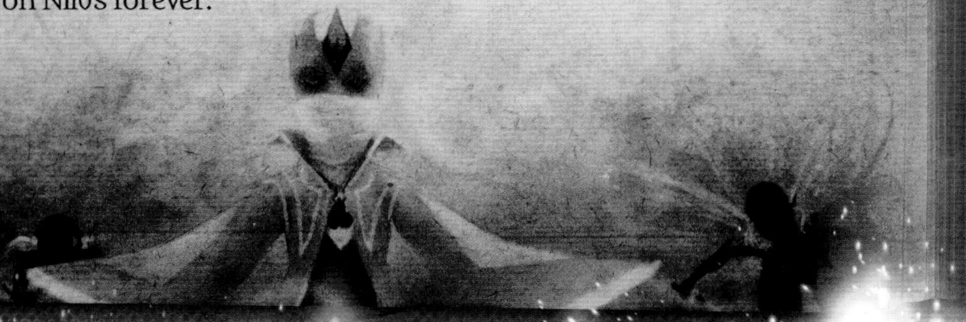

The T'yalli were grateful and beholden to the Preservers, and it was they who named them "Preservers of life and order." In return, the Preservers granted their Synchronistic World to the unhomed T'yalli, which they named "Gossamyr" after the delicate threads of power that bound it to the Seven Worlds. The T'yalli embraced this new world as their own, exploring and giving name to all they discovered and becoming the first of Gossamyr's settlers.

But the Preservers had been damaged to their very core and would never intervene in such a way again. They refused to repair the damage to Gossamyr caused by creating the Disjunction Paradigm. Instead, they left the desert as a permanent reminder of their hubris, and in their sympathy, the T'yalli called this place the Sandgrieve.

The Preservers retreated to the great keep called Lillienthal, where it is said that they continue to document and catalog all they observe on the Seven Worlds. And as time passed, the threads of the webwheel would line up perfectly with one of the six worlds, and travelers would make a pilgrimage here in search of the promise of long life and make their home in this brave new world.

Some were peaceful, but others were more self-serving and threatened to disrupt the harmony of Gossamyr. The T'yalli saw that if their new home was to flourish, someone would have to establish order. Although the Preservers had long ago decided never to interfere directly again, they would not allow their creation to be completely unprotected.

The Preservers chose a select group of the most trusted T'yalli to become Peacemarshals of Gossamyr. The Peacemarshals were charged with establishing peace and order. They would adjudicate law, mediate conflict and defend from danger. And over the millennia, their capacity to be just and even became as sure as stone, and all would abide by their decrees.

But they are not Gossamyr's only protectors, children. All over this wonderful world, our people choose, each in their own way, to honor the sacrifices of those that have come before us. They choose to preserve order and stand against the chaos that now threatens our world. They choose hope and refuse to surrender to despair. Where such ideas stand together, children, is where Gossamyr begins. And in that place there is never defeat. Not truly.

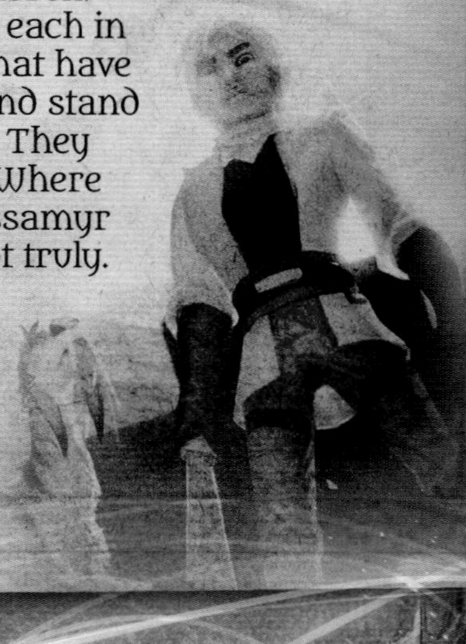

So smile for me, even when you are afraid. Not because it is a glad tale, but because it is a brave tale. And now it belongs to you.

GLOSSARY

PEOPLE

Addamos (AH-dom-os) [adəmos] - Head Artisan of the Roughhew, Addamos is a skilled and ambitious Psychomancer who chafes under what he perceives as the disregard of the Preservers. He makes a deal with the Skaythe to deliver them the Disjunction Paradigm and Denny in exchange for a position of power under the new regime.

Azune D'Tal (AH-zoon di-tahl) [azun dətal] - A former slave from the world of Nilus, he was liberated by the Preservers and was the first to pledge his loyalty, earning him the title "First Son of Gossamyr." He is one of the most trusted and respected of all the T'yalli and has served as Peacemarshal for over 500 years.

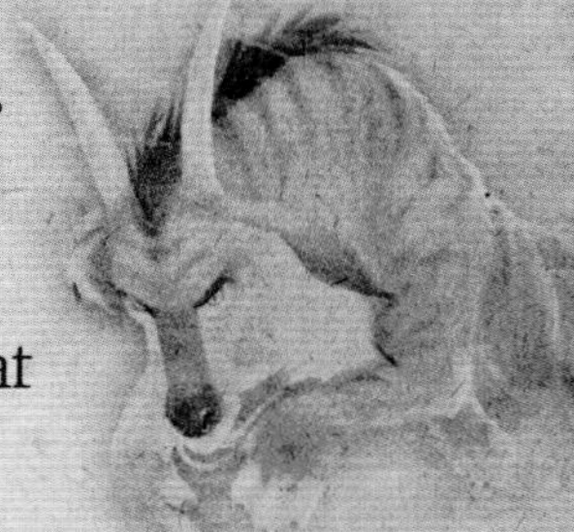

Barnabus (BAR-na-bus) [bɑɹnəbʌs] - Eloric's pet and best friend since they both were young. The oxlion's loyalty is without question. He is fierce and protective of his master, and their unique bond allows him to perform feats of strength and endurance that surpass the abilities of any normal oxlion. Barnabus has recently adopted Jenna and Denny as members of his extended pack.

Cassian (KASH-en) [kæʃən] - A scout of the Shalin who arrived in search of Eloric with Tarn and Azune. Like Tarn, he was impressed with Jenna's skill and courage.

Desecrator, The (des-i-krey-ter) [dɛsɪkretɚ] - Eternal and unquestioned ruler over the entirety of the Skaythe Imperium. She crafted the dark and ancient magics from the energies of chaos, and it was her power that brought the T'yalli into existence.

Donald Hamilton (DAHN-ald HAM-ul-tun) [dɔnəld hæməltʌn] - A noted and esteemed doctor of mathematics, he has dedicated his life to the study and advancement of rare theorems to increase the prestige of his academy and, by extension, himself, with little consideration of how it affects others. When he was unable to complete Denny's unfinished work, he manipulated the child into solving the Disjunction Paradigm.

Drake Daniel Auramen (drayk DAN-yel awr-uh-men) [dɹeik dæɲl "dɛni" ɑɹʌmɛn] - A gifted and deliberate ten-year-old boy with an incalculable ability to solve any mathematical or spatial problem presented to him, including the "unsolvable" Disjunction Paradigm. His days must be highly structured in order for him to feel at ease. Also called Denny, The Cardinality and Prover of all Truths.

Eloric Boothe (EL-er-ik booth) [ɛlɔɹɪk buθ] - The young warrior from the Sandgrieve who befriends Jenna and Denny upon their arrival in Gossamyr. He dreams of becoming more than just a farmer. He takes great risks to prove his worth and earn his steel as a Bladeslinger, but he is noble and kindhearted.

PEOPLE

Jenna Auramen (JEN-ah awr-uh-men) [ʤɛnɑ ɑɹʌmɛn] - The twenty-year-old caretaker of her younger brother, Denny. She spent two years interning with a rescue animal hospital and has had training in emergency animal care. Her dreams of studying biology abroad were halted when she took on the responsibilities of guardianship.

Nerissa Abendroth (NUH-rih-sa ah-bin-droth) [nʌɹɪsɑ ɑbɪndɹɑθ] - The leader of the strike team into Gossamyr, Nerissa is a Harlequin, one the Desecrator's premier generals and assassins. She has been tasked with subverting the disenfranchised people of Gossamyr, who are unhappy with the rule of the Preservers, and creating a power base for the future invading army.

Tarn (tahrn) [tɑɹn] - A Bladeslinger of the Shalin and cousin to Eloric. He was in the rescue party that arrived in answer to Eloric's summons by use of the Sounding Staves. Originally suspicious of Jenna and her brother, he eventually was swayed by Eloric's obvious trust in them and swore his own allegiance.

PLACES

Between, The (bi-tween) [bɪtwin] - The Nothing space that divides the Seven Worlds and the location of the artificial world of Gossamyr.

Earth (urth) [əɹθ] - Home to Jenna and Denny Auramen, Earth is one of the Seven Worlds. Its residents believe all of their magic is called "science."

Gossamyr (gos-uh-mer) [gɑsəmɚ] - Gossamyr is an artificial world built by the Preservers on a foundation of pure mathematics and is a bridge between the Seven Worlds. It is resistant to the effects of entropy and exists in The Between, the space that divides the worlds.

Lillienthal (LIL-ee-an-thol) [lɪliɛnθɑl] - The city of Lillienthal is the capital of all of Gossamyr and sits at its geometric center. It is an island constructed around the Spiral Tower in a wheel-and-spoke pattern. There are causeways that cross the crystalline waters of the Stillglass River and connect Lillienthal to the mainland. The causeways are made from memory stone, which build and deconstruct themselves when necessary for ships or people to cross.

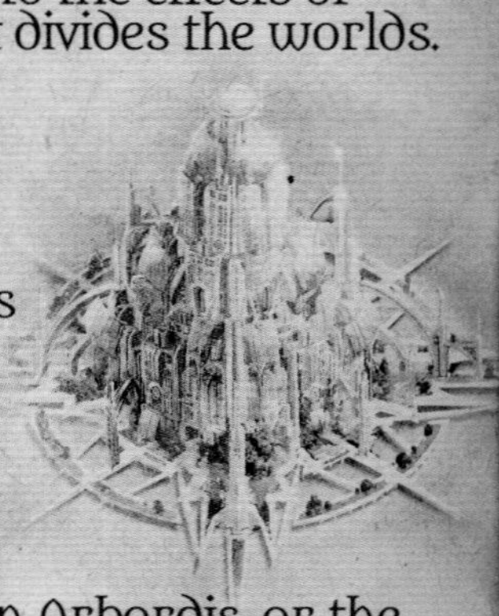

Lost Woods, The (lawst woodz) [lɔst wʊdz] - Avren Arbordis, or the Lost Woods, are a lush expanse of forest with towering bluebarked trees. The widespread branches of the treetops create a dense canopy, but scattered beams of sunlight break through to illuminate the leaves. It is so dense that it is easy for travelers to become lost, but some say there are other things hidden deep in the forest responsible for such things.

PLACES (continued)

Neksis (nek-suh s) [nɛksɪs] – The breathtaking capital city of the Roughhew is hidden high in the Redcloaked Mountains and is home to the Council of Artisans. It is where Jenna was forced to fight for custody of her brother.

Nilus (nahy-lus) [naɪlʌs] – One of the Seven Worlds and home to the Skaythe, this world is one forged of controlled chaos. The doors between Nilus and Gossamyr were sealed for thousands of years to keep the armies of chaos fairies from invading.

Redcloaked Mountains (red-klohk d moun-tns) [ɹɛd klokt maʊntənz] – The vast range of sharp and severe slopes is home to the enigmatic Roughhew. The heavy deposits of psinium ore give the mountains their reddish cast. The Roughhew mine this ore, using their unique gifts to shape earth with their bare hands and turn common rock into a sprawling city of paved stone with glittering ceilings of inset psinium.

Sandgrieve (sand-greev) [sænd griv] – The Sandgrieve is a vast desert that borders the edge of the continent. The Sandgrieve was originally a lush expanse of trees and plains that were later consumed when the Disjunction Paradigm was created. The portion closest to the inhabitable areas, called the Inner Ridge, has become a healthy desert that teems with its own life forms. The Outer Ridge of the Sandgrieve extends as far as the Blackice Sea and is unfit for most. It is now controlled by the adverse Bestials (Vulpine and Saurians).

Spiral Tower, The (spahy-ruh l toh-er) [spaiɹəl taʊɚ] – The repository of all knowledge from the Seven Worlds. The Preservers claim the highest chambers for themselves, but they have opened the doors of the Spiral Tower to share its learnings with all residents of Gossamyr. Also home to the Great School of Theurgy, where the finest Psychomancers come from far and wide to train in magic.

THINGS

Artisans (ahr-tuh-zuh ns) [ɑɹtəzənz] – The head craftsmen and governing body of the Roughhew, they are responsible for creating most items of wonder in Gossamyr, including fleshbind, shaleskiffs, the Peacemarshal spears and redpowder.

Bladeslinger (bleyd-sling-er) [bleidsliŋɚ] – Elite sword-warriors of the Shalin, the Bladeslingers are skilled with most weapons but are known for the distinct wheel tattoos on their palms and their uncanny ability to hurl their blades in a deadly spin and catch them safely on return. They grow even more dangerous when they tap into and channel chaos by using the Contradiction.

THINGS *(continued)*

Bloodwagon (bluhd-wag-uh n) [blʌdwægən] - Devastating Skaythe warcraft, powered by roil. They are light, swift-moving machines designed to be visually intimidating.

Burrowwyrm (buhr-oh-wurm) [bʌɹəʊwɜɪm] - Massive worms of the Sandgrieve able to quickly burrow through soil, sand and stone. They spend the days buried in the earth, taking sustenance from minerals, insects and other decaying materials. Shalin farmers use Burrowwyrms to till and aerate the coarse desert soil. Additionally, the worms' excretions are a potent fertilizer able to produce harvest in even the lifeless soil of the Sandgrieve.

Cardinality, The (kahr-dn-al-i-tee) [kaɪdɪnalɪti] - A title of honor given by the Roughhew to Denny Auramen, referring to his elevation above all other spell casters. They believe him to be the legendary "prover of all truths."

Contradiction, The (kon-truh-dik-shuh n) [kantrədɪkʃən] - The Bladeslinger ability that is triggered by reciting their Incantation. It allows them to create an impossible paradox in their minds and fuel their bodies with the ensuing chaos to make them inhumanly strong and fast. The "wheel" tattoos on their palms, which are stylized zeroes, allow them to safely contain this destructive energy.

> **The Bladeslinger Incantation**
> *All exists...and nothing exists.*
> *There is no virtue. And there is no evil.*
> *There is only absence.*
> *I gaze into the nothing...and give it name.*
> *I create the impossible.*
> *I embrace the contradiction...*
> *...and become the cataclysm.*

Disjunction Paradigm (dis-juhngk-shuh n par-uh-dahym) [dɪsdʒʌŋkʃən pærədaim] - The name for the nearly unsolvable theorem created by the Preservers to seal the doors between Nilus and Gossamyr that was recently solved by Denny Auramen of Earth.

Fleshbind (flesh-bahynd) [flɛʃbaind] - An adhesive bandage created by the Roughhew to put the power of healing into everyone's hands. It is imbued with magic that is able to instantly calculate and solve any minor to moderate damage to a life equation.

Harlequin (hahr-luh-kwin) [hɑɹlɪkwən] - A feared and dangerous rogue assassin of Nilus and the chosen of the Desecrator. Harlequins often lead the Skaythe into battle and are easily identified by their "death masks," painted faceplates marked up like murderous clowns that are lowered only when they intend to annihilate an enemy.

THINGS (continued)

Inverse (in-vurs) [ɪnvəɪs] - Someone whose life equation has become inverted due to malicious magic or exposure to chaos energy. They become gray and aggressive, and they have a powerful hunger to consume the "math" in other living beings.

Leaflynx (leef-lingks) [liflɪŋks] - A small forest creature with a long fluffy tail and oversized ears. Leaflynx are omnivorous and subsist on a diet of primarily fruit and nuts. They sleep in trees to avoid predators. They have dexterous paws with nonretractable claws that they use for climbing and manipulating objects.

Liegelash (leej-lash) [lidʒlæʃ] - A slave master of the Skaythe who uses a flexible metal whip to channel the power of roil.

Lorelarks (lohr-lahrk) [loɪlɑɪk] - A group of archivists and storytellers who reside in the floating cities of the Meridian and catalog and share the various myths and tales of the people of Gossamyr. They are easily identified by their vibrant feathered cloaks and birdlike hoods.

Lunablossom (loo-nuh-blos-uh m) [lunəblasəm] - Large-winged butterflies with long, graceful antennae that bloom from the Luna Bush. They form on the bush and, as they blossom, take wing. Lunablossoms rarely stray far from their bush, where they nest through autumn. When on the bush, their folded wings resemble fully bloomed flowers of many different colors.

Oxlion (oks-lahy-uh n) [ɑkslaiən] - Horned predatory cats with bluish fur and uncanny intelligence that have been domesticated by the rugged Shalin. In the wild, they are lone hunters that use their horns to gore their prey during short bursts of great speed.

Peacemarshal (pees-mahr-shuh l) [pismaɪʃəl] - Appointed by the Preservers to maintain order throughout Gossamyr, this group of T'yalli are charged with establishing peace and order. They adjudicate, mediate and defend, and they possess an ability to discern lies from truth. Over the millennia, their capacity to be just and even became as sure as stone.

Preservers (pri-zurv-ers) [pɹɪzəɪvəz] - The enigmatic creators of Gossamyr, these twelve beings are living and sentient math. Their mastery over the language of creation makes them immensely powerful, but the loss of their eldest member to the Skaythe and their inability to completely understand human emotion and consequences have caused them to retreat to the secluded towers of Lillienthal.

THINGS *(continued)*

Psinium (sin-ee-uhm) [sɪniəm] - A reddish stone with innate magical energy that forms part of the bedrock of Gossamyr. It is mined and smelted into pure metal to create weapons and armor, and it is pressed into red coins called "crimsons." When cut into gem form from pure state, it can be used to enhance natural magical ability.
Psychomancer (sahy-koh-man-sur) [saikomæns⊠] - A trained spell caster who is able to project mathematical equations into the air and solve them with a psychokinetic trigger to generate magical effects.

Roil (roil) [ɹɔɪəl]- An energy-rich fuel, used by the Skaythe to power their weapons and vehicles, that is created by the methodical and painful breakdown of still-living matter. The T'yalli were most often used in this process when they were still slaves on Nilus.

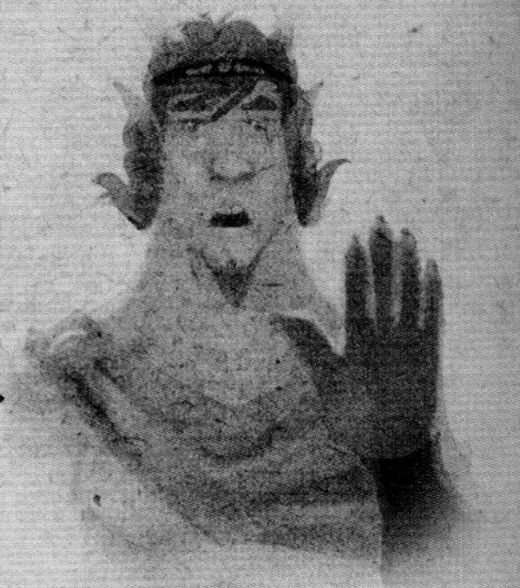

Roughhew (ruhf-hyoo) [ɹʌfhju] - The Roughhew are a slim and graceful people who move among the craggy vertical shelves of the Redcloaked Mountains as easily as most people walk on land. The Roughhew are known for being remarkable artisans and Psychomancers. Their natural gifts allow their Artisans to shape stone and metal with their bare hands and imbue them with powerful enchantments.

Seven Worlds (sev-uh n wurlds) [sɛvən wəɹldz] - The seven planes of reality that revolve around the other-dimensional space known as "The Between." They are connected to Gossamyr by the Webwheel.

Shaleskiff (sheyl-skif) [ʃeɪlskɪf] - A sleek ship crafted from stone by the Roughhew for swift travel over earth and rock. The shaleskiff skims through stone as easily as water, churning waves in its wake.

Shalin (shey-lin) [ʃeɪlɪn]- The Shalin are a hardy and fierce people with bronzed skin and hair bleached white from generations of living in the unforgiving desert of the Sandgrieve. They are farmers who can bring food from the dead soil with their mastery over Burrowyrms and warriors who stand against the threat of the Bestials, which stage raids from the Outer Ridge.

Skaythe, The (skeyth) [skeiθ] - The black fairies of Nilus are a militant and powerful race born of chaos and existing in a constant state of contradiction. They are savagely beautiful but cruel, and they live only to serve their Empress, the Desecrator. They have no lore or magic of their own, but they are able to harness the power of roil to perform terrible acts. They are peerless combatants who rely on their skill and natural resistance to magic to protect them. They have spent generations subjugating their world and have now set their sights on the prize of Gossamyr.

THINGS *(continued)*

Sounding Staves (soun-ding steyvz) [saʊndiŋ steɪvz] - Polished hardwood staves capable of producing a wide range of sounds and vibrations when struck together. Used by Shalin farmers to conduct and control the movements of Burrowyrms in the fields.

Spiral, The (spahy-ruh l) [spairəl] - The powerful theorem discovered by the Preservers that makes safe travel between the Seven Worlds possible. It is the backbone of the Webwheel, the Construct and Gossamyr itself.

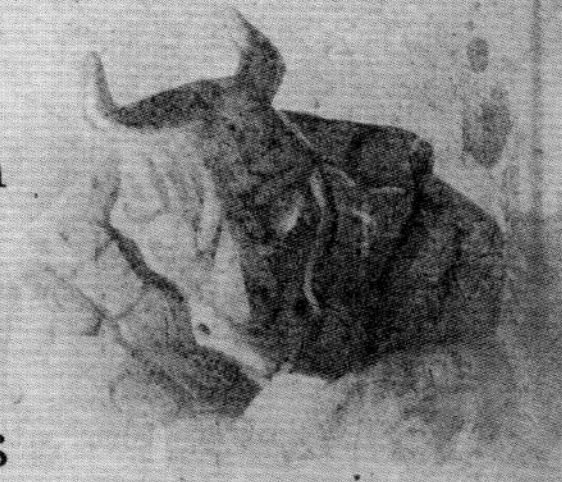

Stonewight (stohn-wahyt) [stonwait] - Massive, animated stone guardians infused with magical energy that protect the city of Neksis from intruders.

Theurgy (thee-ur-jee) [θi ɜr dʒi] - An alternate word for mastery of science and math that uses a psychokinetic trigger.

T'yalli (tah-yah-lee) [tajali] - The noble and serene first people of Gossamyr. The T'yalli were slaves on the world of Nilus whose name means "sub-servant." They were artificially created as a servitor race for the Skaythe. Bred for strength and endurance, they can accomplish seemingly superhuman feats of physical prowess by focusing their will. The T'yalli are very esteemed, and most of them serve as "Peacemarshals," acting as the voice and presence of the Preservers among the people of Gossamyr.

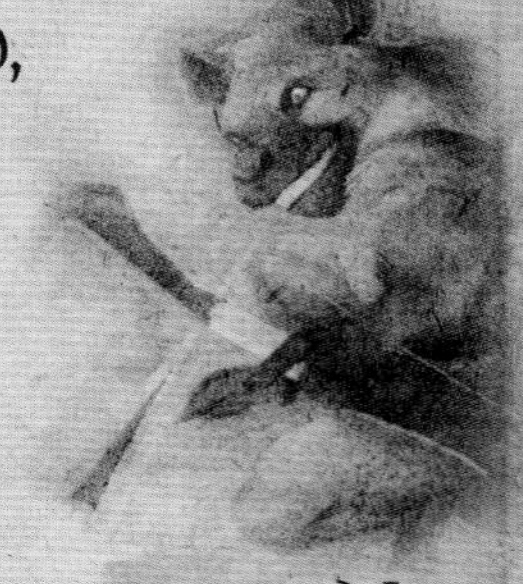

Vulpine (vuhl-pahyn) [vəlpin] - Wide-shouldered, foxlike creatures with powerful, back-bent legs that allow them to walk upright, though they can drop to all fours and use their long, powerful arms to lope at great speed. Their bodies are marked with complex tribal tattoos that indicate their status within the clan. Vulpine commonly use shortbows and wicked, jagged obsidian shortswords.

Webwheel (web-weel) [wɛbwil] - The Webwheel was created by the Preservers from delicate strands of magic to connect the Seven Worlds to The Between. It resembles a complex spider web with the world of Gossamyr at its center.

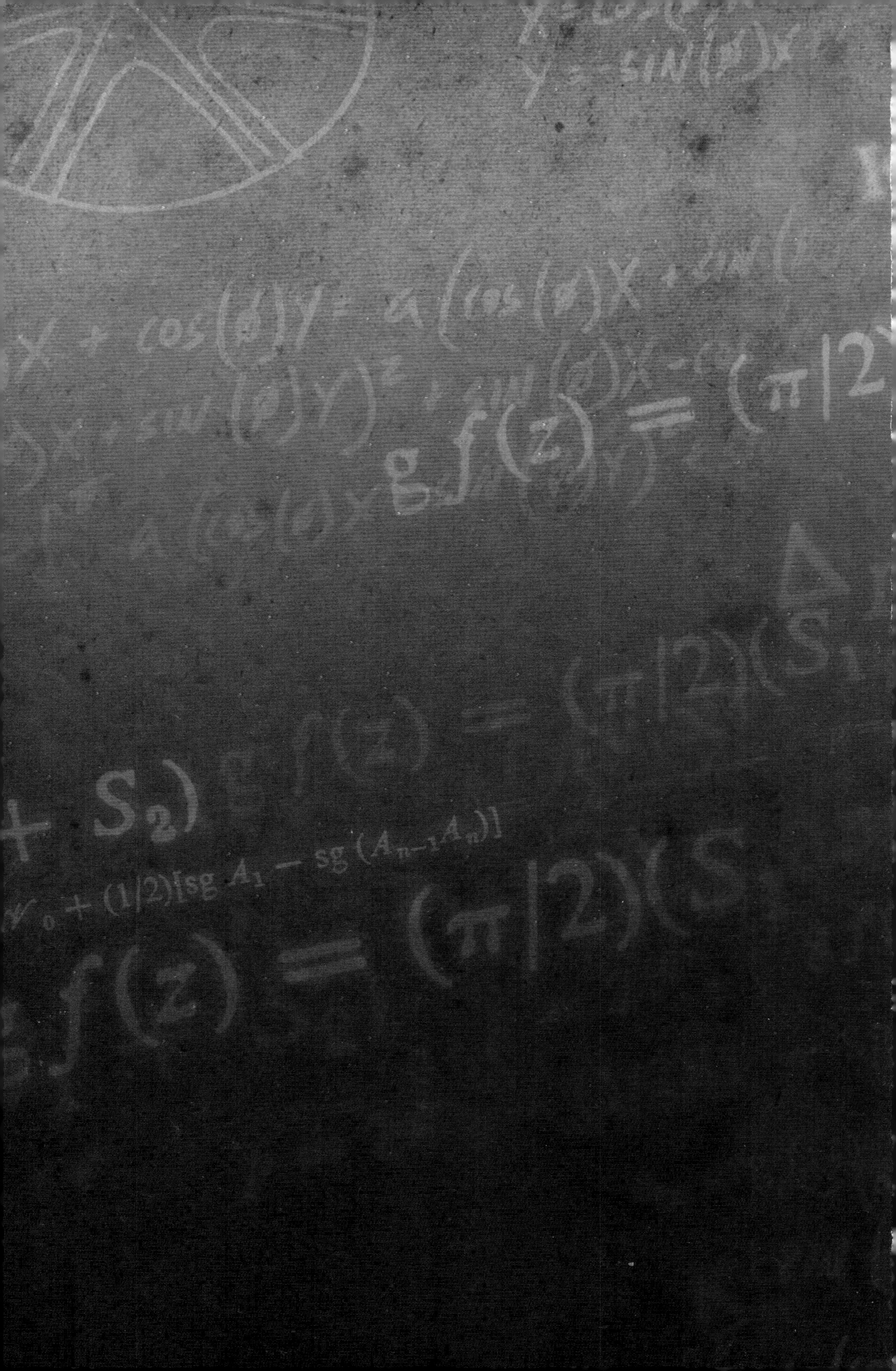

+ S₂)
(1/2)[sg A₁ − sg (Aₙ₋₁Aₙ)]
f(z) = (π|2)(S

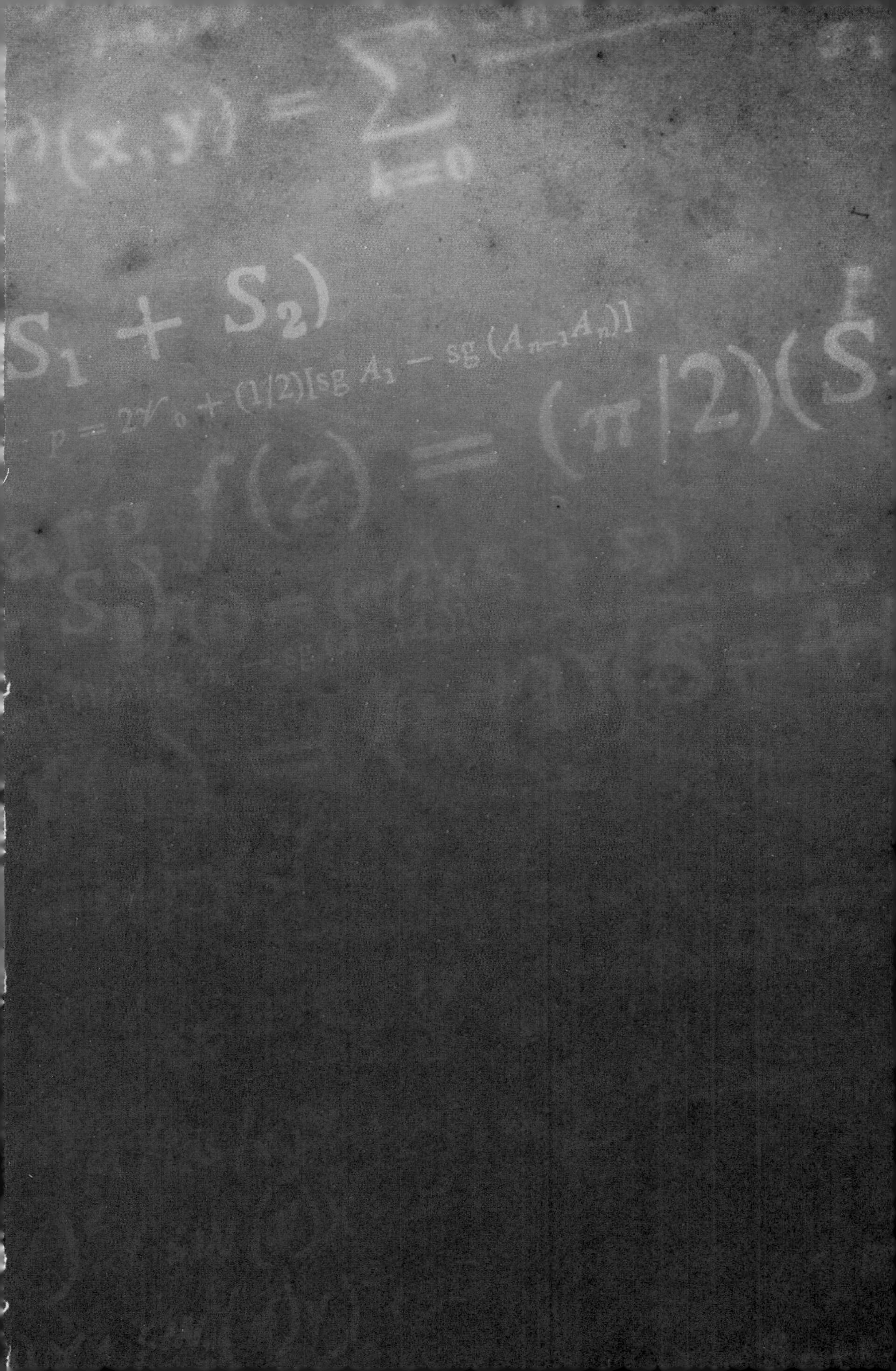

$(x, y) = \sum_{k=0}$
$S_1 + S_2)$
$p = 2V_0 + (1/2)[\mathrm{sg}\, A_1 - \mathrm{sg}\,(A_{n-1}A_n)]$
$f(z) = (\pi/2)(S$

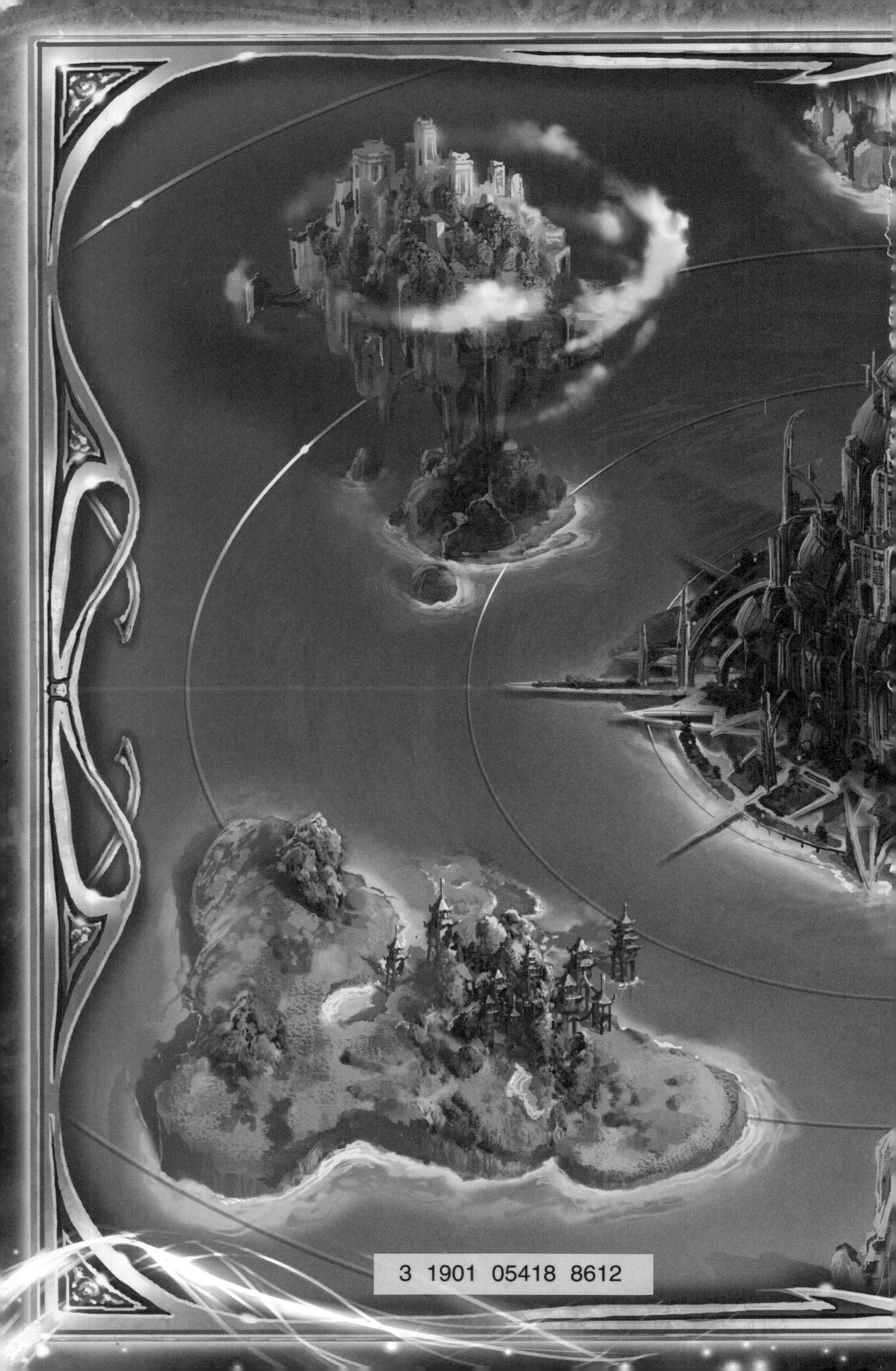